DRAGONLIGHT

What this dungeon needed, Matt decided, was light. He took a deep breath, extemporizing a spell, then began to recite.

There was a shattering roar, and light seared Matt's eyes. He fell back against the wall, while something huge and scaly rasped and grated against the wall.

"Who hath done zhish to me?" Light came again, a five-foot gout of flame, showing a mail-scaled snout with pointed teeth. "*Thou*! Dost think to hide from Shteo—from Shtegoman, worm of a man?"

Flame seared out again, and Matt leaped. The fire missed him as the dragon lurched to the side. The great eyes were bleary.

The fool beast was drunk!

And apparently he was the sort who grew mean in his cups. Now he was taking another blast-furnace breath, preparing to incinerate Matt to a cinder!

·HER·
MAJESTY'S
WIZARD

Christopher Stasheff

A Del Rey Book

BALLANTINE BOOKS • NEW YORK

A Del Rey Book
Published by Ballantine Books

Copyright © 1986 by Christopher Stasheff

All rights reserved under International and Pan-American Copyright Conventions. Published in the United States of America by Ballantine Books, a division of Random House, Inc., New York, and simultaneously in Canada by Random House of Canada Limited, Toronto.

Library of Congress Catalog Card Number: 86-90933

ISBN 0-345-27456-3

Manufactured in the United States of America

First Edition: October 1986
Seventh Printing: October 1989

Cover Art by Darrell K. Sweet

CHAPTER 1

Matthew Mantrell leaned forward across the little table in the campus coffee shop and tapped the sheet of rune-covered parchment before him. He tried to put some of the urgency he felt into his voice.

"I tell you, Paul, this is important!"

Paul just sighed and shook his head, reaching for the last of his coffee. He didn't even glance at the parchment.

Somehow, Matt never had been able to make others take him seriously. He was tall enough, he thought, over medium height, and fencing practice had kept him lean and wiry. But his eyes were an honest, warm brown——like his hair. His nose was out of Sherlock Holmes—but from Watson, not Holmes. He looked, unfortunately, good-natured, friendly, and kind.

Across the table, Paul put his cup down and cleared his throat. "As I remember it," he said, "you're supposed to be working on your doctorate. How long since you did any research on your dissertation?"

"Three months," Matt admitted.

Paul shook his head. "Then you'd better get on the stick, man. You don't have that much more time."

It was true. He had a month of the spring semester left, plus the summer. After that, it was out into the wilderness of two-year

1

college teaching, with little or no research time, probably never to emerge into the light of a Ph.D. and eventual professorship. He shuddered at the thought, but screwed up the remnants of determination and declared, "But *this* is important! I feel it in my bones!"

"So what are you going to tell your committee? That you dropped everything because—so you say—this piece of manuscript fell out of an old copy of the *Njaalsaga* while you were poking around in the library stacks?"

"It did!"

"So how come nobody else ever found it? They've been sifting that library for fifty years. How do we know it isn't a hoax?"

"It's in runes . . ."

"Which you—and who knows how many others—can write." Paul shook his head slowly. "One scrap of parchment, with runes spelling out words in a language that sounds like a mess of German, French, maybe Old Norse, and probably some Elvish and Barsoomian worked in."

"Yeah, but I feel it's a real tongue." Matt managed a tight smile. "The words just don't make sense—yet."

"So you've been trying to translate it from root words for three months—without a bit of luck." Paul sighed. "Give it up, man. June's next month. Your fellowship will be up, and none of your dissertation done. There you'll be, without a degree, and not much chance of getting one, either."

He looked at the clock and got to his feet, clapping Matt on the shoulder. "Gotta run. Good luck, man—and pull your head back to reality, huh? Or as close as we can ever get."

Matt watched him shoulder his way out of the coffee shop. Paul was right, from the hard-headed, practical point of view. But Matt *knew* he was, too. He just couldn't substantiate it. He sighed and pulled out his silver ballpoint pen to have another try at playing acrostics with the speech sounds in his manuscript.

He looked down at the parchment, and everything else dropped from his mind. He felt, illogically, that if he just stared at the black brush strokes, just repeated those alien phonemes again and again, they'd start making sense. Ridiculous, of course! He had to reason it out, starting with the root words and locating their place in the family of human languages.

He caught himself repeating the syllables again and stared at the blank notebook page beside him. Start with root words. *Lal-*

inga—the first word of all. Well, *lingua* was Latin for tongue or language, and *la* was the feminine article in the Romance languages. But the next words didn't seem to fit the pattern. *Lalinga wogreus marwold reigor* . . .

He leaned back, taking a very deep breath. He'd slipped into it again, chanting the meaningless symbols . . .

No, not meaningless! They *would* make sense! He was sure of it. If he could just find the key . . .

Dangerous, some remote, monitoring part of his mind gibed. *Very dangerous; that way lie dragons*. And insanity . . .

Matt buried his face in his hands, thumbs massaging his temple. Maybe Paul was right; he *had* been working this over too long. Maybe he *should* just drop it . . .

But not without one more try. He sat up straight again and took a firmer grip on the pen. Now, one more time.

> Lalinga wogreus marwold reigor
> Athelstrigen marx alupta
> Harleng krimorg barlow steigor . . .

Pull back, the remote part of his mind warned. *You're in too deep; you'll never get out* . . .

But Matt couldn't let go—underneath it all, somehow, the weird words were beginning to make sense. He head filled with roaring and beneath it, like a harmonic, the noise seemed to modulate into words:

> You, betrayed by time and space,
> Born without your proper grace . . .

The whole room seemed to be darkening, with only the scrap of parchment lighted; and even there, the runes were writhing, blurring, starting to run together . . .

> To a world befouled and base—
> Feel your proper form and case,
> Recognize your homeland's face.

The page darkened, left him enveloped in a formless, lightless limbo. He lurched to his feet, then sagged against the wall, squeezing the hard, cool cylinder of the silver pen like a talisman; but the words thundered on in his head:

> Cross the void of time and space!
> Seek and find your proper place!

Worlds whirled, suns swerved across limbo, wheeling him about like a dervish. Nausea struck as the floor swung out from under his feet. His knees tried to give; Matt clutched at a beam in the wall, holding himself up, trying to force his eyes open.

It passed; the spinning suns slowed, his feet touched hardness, then pressed up. Bit by bit, the churning universe ground down toward a halt...

Matt leaned against the wall, taking deep breaths, letting the dizziness pass and the nausea ebb. Paul was right; he *had* been working too hard...

A hand clasped his shoulder. "Here, countryman! Stand away!"

Matt looked up, irritated—at a florid, beefy face with a full beard, a puffy beret, and a fur-trimmed woolen robe over a linen tunic.

The hand shook his shoulder, almost knocking him down. "D'ye hear me? Stand away from my shop!"

Matt stared, unbelieving. The meaning was clear and familiar, but the words weren't English.

They were the language of the manuscript fragment...

He looked around, dazed. How had he gotten outside? Especially *this* outside—a narrow street, half-timbered houses with second stories sticking out over the cobblestones...

Where was he?

"Alms, goodman! Alms for the poor!"

Matt looked down into a grimy, grease-stained wooden bowl about a foot below his nose. There was a hand holding it—a filthy, scabby, dirt-crusted hand. The arm attached to it went with the hand perfectly, scab for scab and crust for crud. He followed it down to a motley collection of rags and a hideous, emaciated, grizzled old face, with a filthy woolen strip tied across the eyes.

The beggar gave the bowl an angry, impatient shake. "Alms, countryman! Give me alms! For charity's sweet sake, goodman— alms!"

The man went with the scene. The gutter was filled with garbage and sewage, a magnet for mangy dogs and scrofulous pigs.

While Matt watched, a rat shot out of a pile of garbage, and a mutt leaped on it with a happy yelp. Matt shuddered and looked away; a sudden wave of dizziness swept him, and he clutched at the wall again, leaning against it.

"He's ill!" The beggar sounded as if he were on the verge of panic; definitely overreacting, Matt thought dizzily.

"And he leans against my shop!" The beefy type didn't sound too solid, either. "Stand away, I say!"

Matt remembered something about medieval plagues and people accused of carrying them. He staggered upright, fishing in a pocket. "No, no, I'm all right." He pulled out a quarter and dropped it into the bowl. "Just a little dizziness; it was a hard trip, you understand..."

Why had he thought of *medieval* plagues?

The beggar's other hand closed on the quarter, scooping it out of the bowl with a satisfied hiss; but the tradesman spat an oath and snatched it out of the beggar's hand. He held it about two inches from his eyes, staring at it, his eyes bulging. Then he looked up at Matt, his eyes wide with a sort of horror, and maybe loathing. Matt suddenly realized he wasn't exactly dressed for the occasion. The others he saw all seemed to be wearing the same sort of basic outfit, with variations—a short tunic over hose, with some sort of cloak over it. It was the variations that gave Matt heartburn; they ran the gamut from about the seventh century to the fourteenth.

Most of them went barefoot. Some had cross-gartered sandals. Some wore shoes, but they were pointy at the toes. And the hats ran from a simple hood to the beefy individual's puffy beret.

"What manner of man is this?" a new voice growled. It belonged to a muscle-bound type in cross-gartered hose and a leather apron, with an interesting assortment of soot smudges and singed hairs in place of a shirt, and an even more interesting hammer—a squarish block of iron with an oaken handle. Now that Matt noticed it, there were two more members to the group, one with a quarterstaff and the other with an adz. And they all looked hostile.

"He's an outlander, isn't he?" Quarterstaff grunted.

"Mayhap," Puffyhat answered, "but he appeared in front of my shop when I had scarce glanced down at my counting-board. And look at his coin—have you ever seen such?"

The quarter passed from hand to hand, to the accompaniment of rumbles of amazement and suspicion.

"'Tis too polished," the blacksmith opined. "'Tis as if a king's statue could be shrunken down to the size of a coin."

"And such exactness, such precision!" Matt recognized a professional tone in Puffyhat's voice; he must be a silversmith. "'Tis in all ways wondrous. He who cast it must have been a wizard!"

"Wizard!" The knot of men fell totally silent, staring at Matt.

The ridiculousness of it hit Matt suddenly. He felt the tender glow of his own twisted humor and straightened slowly, fighting temptation. As usual, he lost.

He flung his arms straight up and started chanting in his most orotund tones, "Fourscore and seven years ago, our fathers set forth upon this continent a new nation . . ."

They backed off like kids in a dentist's office, arms up to protect their faces. Matt shut up, hands on his hips, grinning around at them, waiting to see what happened—which was nothing, of course.

Slowly, the townsmen lowered their arms and looked up, unbelieving. Then their faces reddened with anger, and their arms came down the rest of the way with fists on the ends. They moved in.

Matt stepped back and back again, till the stucco wall pricked his back. The mob started shouting, "Vile, impotent wizard!" . . . "We'll teach you to curse your betters!" . . . "Foul sorcerer!"

Sorcerer? Somehow, that had an ugly sound.

But "wizard" was another matter—and so was being used for a punching bag. Matt stabbed his forefingers at them, one after the other, right, left, right, chanting:

"To the top of the porch! To the top of the wall!
Now dash away, dash away, dash away all!"

There was a loud *pop*! Matt found himself facing an empty street, with a handful of gawkers on the far side.

He blinked and shook his head. It couldn't be. But where had Puffyhat and his friends gone? Matt looked around for a porch.

There wasn't any in the vicinity, but there was a low wall about fifty feet down to the right across the alley, with four huddled, moaning shapes on top of it.

One of them looked up—the blacksmith. He stared at Matt. Matt stared back.

Then anger wrenched the smith's face, and he jumped off the

wall with a howl, running straight for Matt, his hammer swinging up.

Puffyhat and the boys jumped down to follow him, bellowing gleefully.

So did everyone else on the street—letting the smith lead, of course.

There was no time to think. Matt stepped back, curling his left arm as if he were holding a book and thrusting up an imaginary torch with his right.

> "Give me your tired, your poor,
>   Your huddled masses, yearning to breathe free!"

They kept coming—a howling mob, charging the stranger who chanted in an arcane language.

> "The wretched refuse of your teeming shore!
>   Send these, the homeless, tempest-tossed to me!"

They were twenty feet away and still coming, but he had to catch a breath, because he was suddenly working uphill, pouring sweat, feeling as if he were trying to twist some huge, invisible field of forces that had suddenly enveloped him. He blurted out the last line:

> "I lift my lamp beside the golden door!"

Thunder split the alley, and men screamed. Matt squeezed his eyes shut.

When he opened them, the street was filled with bodies—the living kind, crawling with lice and festooned with rags. Every beggar in town must have been there all of a sudden—though Matt did wonder why there were so many Orientals in a medieval European burg. And weren't those Hindus, down on the right there?

The beggars straightened up slowly, mouths gaping open, staring around, gawking at each other. Then the screaming started again. But it was all under a tidal wave of excited babbling.

Matt came to his senses with a start. When you fill an inside straight, cash in. He leaped into the crowd, forcing his way through with elbows and boots. Hands groped at his belt every inch of the way, trying to find his purse. He thanked Heaven they didn't know about pockets and clapped a hand on his wallet as he twisted through the last rank into the clear. Then he took one deep breath and started off walking, fast.

There was a sudden, ominous silence behind him.

Matt kept on walking.

Then someone yelled, "There goes the sorcerer! Don't let him get away!"

The mob gave one huge, delighted howl, with the thunder of hundreds of running feet underneath it.

Matt wasn't about to try the wizard act again until he'd learned who wrote the script. He ran. The beggars gave a lusty bellow and charged, delighted to be on the chasing end for a change. Matt reminded himself he'd been a track star in high school and leaned into it. But high school had been a long time ago.

Matt didn't try to figure out where the beggars had come from; he was too busy panting. He dimly realized that he'd called for them—but just now they were calling for him, and he wasn't exactly eager to oblige them.

Fortunately, the beggars weren't in any great shape, either— Matt *had* specified something of the sort. He had about a two-block lead when he turned the corner—and ran smack into the gendarmes, mounted on war horses and wearing ring-on-leather iron mail.

The grizzled man in front leaned down to snag an arm as Matt went by. He had a very snug grip; it swung Matt around to land smack against the flank of the horse. "Here now," the man growled, "where d'ye think you're running?"

"*That* way!" Matt pointed the way he'd been going. "I'm trying to leave my past behind me!"

The front wave of beggars came pouring around the corner, howling. They saw the soldiers and stopped on a shilling. Then they went sprawling as the second wave hit. Those saw the soldiers and stopped dead in their turn. Just then the third wave hit, with the fourth coming up.

The sergeant, or whatever he was, just sat back in his saddle, watching and waiting, with the hint of a smile under his scowl. He kept a viselike hold on Matt's arm.

When the whole mob had gotten the message and more or less stopped, the sergeant cut across the muttering with a bull roar.

"Now, then! What happened here?" And to Matt he added, "Quite a past you have, fellow."

The mob got quiet then. A throat toward the back cleared itself, and Puffyhat came elbowing his way importantly toward the front. "This man is a sorcerer!"

"Is he, now?" the sergeant purred. "Well, that would explain his outlandish costume. What sorceries did he work?"

Puffyhat launched into a tale that would have done credit to Walpole, in which Matt figured largely and luridly. It seemed Matt had brought down a thunderstorm just outside Puffyhat's shop, changed base metal into silver, made the earth slip beneath the feet of four good citizens and true, tarnished the honor of the nation by conjuring up a horde of unskilled workers—who would doubtless compete with the locals for jobs—and changed an honest and worthy baker into a toad.

"That," Matt howled, "is slander! I never changed anyone into a toad!"

"But you did the rest?" He was a quick one, that sergeant. What could Matt say? "Uh . . . Well . . ."

"So I thought." The sergeant nodded, satisfied. "Well, then, Master Sorcerer—"

"Wizard." Matt figured he'd better set the record as straight as possible. "Not sorcerer. No traffic with the devil. None. Wizard."

The sergeant shrugged. "Wizard, then. Will ye now whisk yourself away from us in the blink of an eye? Or come with us to the guardhouse, that our captain may judge ye?"

"Uh . . ." Matt glanced at the crowd. Ever since Puffyhat's crack about imported labor, they'd been looking uglier and uglier; there was a vicious muttering passing among the townsmen which seemed to imply that Matt would look great with an apple in his mouth.

Matt made one of those impulse decisions. "Uh, I think I'll come along with you, Sergeant."

He had a little time to think it over on the way to the guardhouse, and it all came down to one simple question: What had happened?

Where was he? *When* was he? How did he get here? Where did all those beggars come from?

And what were soldiers doing patrolling a town? Why were they taking him to a captain, rather than a magistrate?

Martial law, obviously—which meant the town had been recently conquered. But by whom? The soldiers certainly spoke the same language as the civilians—with even the same accent, as far as Matt could tell. It must be civil war, then, which, in a medieval society, meant one of two things—a dynastic dispute, like the Wars of the Roses, or a usurpation.

Why wasn't the sergeant scared of a self-confessed wizard, though? Possibly he was a skeptic and knew any kind of magic was just so much hogwash. But, considering that even most of the best-educated among the medieval set believed wholly in magic, that didn't seem too likely. Which left the probability that he wasn't afraid because he knew he was backed by a more powerful wizard or sorcerer.

That shouldn't have bothered Matt at all, because magic *was* just so much hogwash.

But where had all those beggars come from?

The captain was the tall, dark, and handsome type, with some indefinable air of the aristocrat about him. Maybe it was the velvet robe over the gleaming chain mail.

"There is something of the outlander about you," he informed Matt.

Matt nodded. "I *am* an outlander."

The captain lifted his eyebrows. "Are you indeed? From what country?"

"Well, that all depends on where I am."

The captain frowned. "How could that be?"

"It's not easy, believe me. Where *am* I?"

The captain turned his head a little to the side, eyeing Matt warily. "How could you come here and not know where you've come?"

"The same way you don't know where you've come to when you're going to the place you're coming to, but you don't know how you're going or where you're coming to till you've come to the place you were going to, so by the time that you get there, you don't know whether you're coming or going."

The captain shook his head. "I don't."

"Neither do I. So where *am* I?"

"But . . ." The captain knit his brow, trying to figure it out. Then he sighed and gave up. "Very well. You're in the town Bordestang, capital of Merovence. Now, where do you come from?"

"I don't know."

"*What*?" The captain leaned forward over the rough planks of the table. "After all that? How could you not know where you've come from?"

"Well, I'd know where it was if I were in the right place, but I'm in the wrong place, so I don't know where it is. Or rather, I know where it is, but I don't know what it's called here. That is, if it's there."

The captain squeezed his eyes shut and gave his head a quick shake. "A moment, now. You mean to say you do not know our name for your homeland?"

"Well, I suppose you could say that."

"Easily answered." The captain sat back, looking relieved. Matt looked over his shoulder at the semicircle of soldiers surrounding him. The sergeant was watching him narrowly. Matt tried to hide a shiver as he turned back to the captain.

"Tell us where your homeland is," the captain urged, "and I'll tell you our name for it."

"Well, I suppose that's a fair deal." Matt nodded judiciously. "Only one trouble—I left my map at home. So I can't tell you which way my homeland is, till I know a little better where this country is."

The captain threw up his hands. "What must I do? Describe the whole of the continent to you?"

"Well, that would help, yes."

For a moment, Matt thought he'd pushed it too far; the captain's face turned awfully red. His brows came down, and his temples whitened. But he managed to absorb it; his face slowly eased back to its normal color, and he exhaled, long and slowly. Then he stood up and went to a set of shelves over against the undressed planks of the left-hand wall. The shelves were made of undressed planking, too; so was the whole place, for that matter. It had a very improvised air about it. Yes, definitely the war hadn't been over long.

"Here." The captain took down a huge parchment volume and came back to the table, leafing through the book. He laid it down open, turning it to face Matt. Matt stepped forward to look—and gulped.

He was staring at a map of Europe—with a few modifications. It looked like Napoleon's and Hitler's dream world—the English Channel was gone. There was a narrow neck of solid land between Calais and Dover. Denmark was joined to Sweden, and the pebble of Sicily was clinging to Italy's toe.

Something was definitely wrong here. Matt wondered how Australia and New Zealand were doing, or the Isthmus of Panama.

He looked up at a sudden thought. "What's the climate like, there?" He laid a finger on London. "Warmish in winter? Lots of rain? Heavy fogs?"

The captain gave him an extremely strange look. "Nay, certainly not. 'Tis a frozen waste in winter, and the snows pile up half again the height of a man."

That settled it. "Are there, uh, ice fields that never melt anywhere there?"

The captain perked up. "Aye, so they say—in the mountains of the north. Then you've been there?"

Glaciers in the Highlands! "No, but I've seen some pictures." No question about it, there was an Ice Age going on. Whether it was nature's clock that was off or history's didn't really matter; it still added up to just one thing.

Matt wasn't in his own universe.

The wind off those Scottish glaciers blew through Matt's soul, chilling him to the id. For a moment, he was very much lost and very, very alone, and the warmly lighted windows of a summer campus dusk were very far away.

"We are here." The captain laid a fingertip on a spot about a hundred miles east of the Pyrenees and fifty miles north of the Mediterranean. "Do you know where you are now?"

Matt shook off the mood. "No. I mean—for all intents and purposes. I think so."

"Ah, good." The captain nodded, satisfied. "Then where is your homeland?"

"Oh, somewhere along about—here." Matt stabbed a forefinger down, about two feet to the left of the map.

The captain stared, and his face darkened. "I have tried to aid you in every way I can, sirrah, and this is how you repay my courtesy!"

"No, no, I'm serious! There really *is* a land out there, about three thousand miles to the west! I was born there. Although," Matt added as an afterthought, "I expect it's changed a good deal since I've been gone. In fact, I think I'd scarcely recognize it."

"There have been rumors," the sergeant said darkly.

"Aye, of an ever-warm land where the wild grape grows, ruled by a saintly wizard and filled with fabulous monsters!" the captain snapped. "A land seen by dreamers, grown out of the dregs in their wine cups! Surely your are not foolish enough to believe in such!"

"Oh, the tale could stand to go on a diet, I'm sure." Matt smiled slightly, suddenly very calm. "But, even with the climate the way it is, they should still have warm winters in Louisiana; and wild Concord grapes are a bit tart, but really very good. They *do* grow wizards there—or they did, when I left. We didn't call them that, of course—but you would."

The room was suddenly very quiet, and Matt was sure that he had their fullest attention.

The captain licked his lips and swallowed. "And you are such a one."

"Who, me?" Matt looked up, startled. "Lord, no! I scarcely know what an atom *is*, let alone how to split one!"

The captain nodded. "Atoms I have heard of—'tis a sorcery of an ancient Greek alchemist."

Matt couldn't quite keep his lip from curling. "Democritus was scarcely an alchemist."

"He knows of such matters," the sergeant breathed.

"Knows them by name," the captain agreed.

Matt stared, aghast. "Hey, now! You can't think that *I*—"

"Do you know how to change lead into gold?" the captain rapped.

"Well, not really. Just the broad outline. It takes a cyclotron, you see, and..." Matt's voice trailed off as he looked around at all the flinty stares. He never *had* learned when to lie...

The captain turned away in a whirl of velvet. "Enough! We know he's a sorcerer; we need know no more!"

"Wizard!" Matt squawked. "Not a sorcerer!"

The captain shrugged impatiently. "Wizard, sorcerer—it adds to the same sum; 'tis greater than any authority I claim."

The sergeant raised an eyebrow, and the captain nodded. "Take him to the castle."

CHAPTER 2

They loaded him down with chains, at least one of which Matt was certain was silver, and heaved him into an oxcart for the trip uptown—literally; it was uphill all the way. They wound through curving alley-streets, constantly on the upgrade, through a mélange of domestic architecture ranging from about 600 to 1300 A.D. This wasn't out of the ordinary in a European town; what bothered Matt was that some of the seventh-century shops looked almost as new as the fourteenth-century ones. He gave up trying to make sense out of the historical periods; apparently every universe had its own sort of sequence.

Which reminded him that he was about as far from home as a man could get. What had that parchment fragment said? "Cross the void of time and space . . . ?" He had a sudden, vivid image of the chaos that would result as an infinite number of time tracks crossed and put the thought behind him with a shudder.

Enough. He was in a universe other than his own; let it stand at that. It was one where the Ice Age had stayed late, or humanity had come early, for starters—and how many snarls would that make, in history's long yarn? Starting with England still being connected to France, it could make quite a few. Sure, the Britons probably wouldn't have built a wall across that narrow neck of

land that connected Calais to Dover, but the Romans would have
done so; the Brito-Romans had probably built such a wall to keep
the Goths out, as Rome started to decline. If there had been a
Rome here.

Assume there had been; the language had some root words that
resembled Latin cognates. And the captain had mentioned ancient
Greece. The histories seemed to run a rough parallel; so there
probably had been a Mediterranean empire corresponding to Rome.

Okay. As Rome declined, the Brito-Romans probably would
have built the wall, and it probably would have been every bit as
effective as Hadrian's Wall—which is to say, in the long run, that
the analog-Goths simply ignored it. And the Danes had probably
come sailing in as merrily as in Matt's world.

So England would have had its familiar potpourri of peoples
and cultures, but with the pace possibly accelerated. Would that
also apply to the English doing the conquering?

It was possible. Henry II had made a fair bid for conquering
as much of France as he hadn't inherited or married. And Canute
was king of Norway, Denmark, and England all at the same time—
but he ruled from England. If an ambitious Englishman had started
moving in this universe, he might have taken the whole ball of
wax, since he didn't have to worry about naval supply lines.

That could explain the English-language influence in southern
France. Maybe Canute *had* done it. He was the one who'd commanded the sea *not* to roll in . . . For a giddy moment, Matt found
himself wondering if that might not be a better explanation of the
lower waterline than glaciation; after all, magic seemed to work,
in this universe . . .

He jerked himself out of the morass of mysticism; that way
lay dragons. Magic was just superstition and an interesting aca-
demic study; it didn't really work anywhere. There was a perfectly
logical explanation for the sudden appearance of so many beggars!
If he could just find it . . .

He gave his head a shake, forcing the flood of speculation into
the back of his mind, and found himself looking upward, along
a twisting hill road, at a square, forbidding granite castle. In spite
of the medievalisms he'd been seeing all morning, a cold-air movement coiled itself around his backbone. That castle looked so
damned military, so *real* . . .

The iron teeth of the portcullis seemed to bite down at him as
the guards rolled him over the drawbridge. With a sudden ache,

Matt wished with every ounce of his being that he were no place else than his own sloppy kitchen back in his off-campus, hole-in-the-wall apartment. *Home* . . .

They took him through a series of drafty corridors that seemed to grudge giving up an ounce of the winter's cold. Some had narrow, arrow-slit windows; some had an occasional torch; some had nothing. The stairways they marched him up were broad enough for an army, which was probably what they were designed for, but just as dark, and possibly colder.

The guards turned left suddenly and trundled him though a huge oaken door into a fifteen-by-twenty study with two large windows to let sunlight in through actual *glass*. How come no arrow slits? Matt took a peek and saw a courtyard—with soldiers drilling.

But the rest of the room was reassuring, though only by comparison. The two side walls were hung with huge tapestries, one showing the seige of a castle and the other showing a stag brought to bay; and most of the floor space was occupied by a brilliant purple-and-red Moorish carpet. So Spain *had* fallen to North Africa, which meant this universe had had its Mohammed, and probably also its Charles Martel and its Roland. In fact, that last hero might be more probable here than at home.

The furnishing was surprisingly sparse—a tall writing-desk and stool at the side, and a large, heavy table with an hourglass-shaped chair centered in front of the window.

The soldiers chained him to a wrought-iron torch sconce and left him there, with a certain fugitive haste that indicated the sergeant's casual attitude towards sorcerers was either rare or faked. Matt was alone for a few moments' thought. He looked around the study and decided he didn't like it. After the gloom of the castle halls, it was definitely too cheery. It was a setup.

A man slammed through the door. He was six feet tall and more, swaggering and swag-bellied, with small, close-set eyes in a pouchy face, a mouth two sizes too small, and a pig snout of a nose. He wore red, pointed shoes, bright yellow hose, a knee-length purple robe, and a crown.

Matt looked for some woodwork to fade into.

A slab of hand cracked across his chops. "Show respect, trickster! Look at your king when you're in his presence!"

Matt looked, though the view was a trifle blurry. Through the haze, he saw the door behind the king swing open and a half-dozen guards file in. Through pain and fear percolated the random thought that their presence might explain some of the king's blustering.

The king paced back and forth in front of Matt, strutting a little, sure he had Matt's full attention. "So this is the mighty sorcerer from the fabled Western world over the sea? Men must grow small and weak there. What magics could *this* work? Certainly nothing to fear."

The slab hand cracked out again, rocking Matt's head back against the stonework. "Answer, sorcerer!"

Matt blinked, trying to bring the room into focus. "Uhhhh . . . I . . . wasn't aware I'd been asked."

"You mock me," the king snarled, balling up a fist.

"No, no!" Matt cried in panic. "Nothing but respect intended, I assure—"

The fist slammed into his belly, and Matt folded, eyes bulging in agony. All he could manage was a gurgle.

"Why will you not answer?" The open hand slapped under his jaw. Matt rocked back again. "Damned impertinence!" the king grunted, and the slap exploded against Matt's temple. The room went dark, shot with pinpoints of light. Behind them, Matt heard the king's gargling laugh. "Is this the fearful sorcerer who conjured an army into the midst of the town? Where is his power now? Let him only come up against a real man with some meat on him! Then his spirit quails, and the cowardice that first made him seek sorcery comes to the fore once again. Bewitch me, churl! Do you dare, when you must face a strong man?" The king sneered, and the back of his hand smashed into Matt's face.

Through the darkness and the ringing, Matt felt blood seep from his nose, and fury broke. He called out:

"Then he swung aloft his war-club,
Shouted loud and long his war-cry,
Smote this gross and brutal kinglet
In the middle of his forehead!"

The king's head jerked back, yanking his body with it. He sailed backward five feet and slammed into the ranks of the guards. They bent to pick the king up off the floor, slapping his face lightly and calling for brandywine.

Matt stared. Vaguely, at the back of his mind, somebody was saying, "Oh, my. Did *I* do *that*?"

Somebody shoved a portable wineskin into the king's mouth. He gagged; his body jackknifed, and brandywine sprayed over the room. He spent a minute or so in diligent coughing; then he looked up, and his tiny, red-rimmed eyes fixed on Matt with a look that read like a death warrant.

Matt shrank back as the slob-king climbed to his feet with a slow, building potential for murder. He'd blown it, Matt realized; he should have pulled a follow-up spell while the king was out.

What was he thinking? He wasn't a sorcerer!

But that might be just the stall he needed—the unexpected. He summoned every iota of what little cold contempt he could manage. "Learn the lesson, royal Lord, and address me correctly as wizard! I'm not a sorcerer!"

"But I am," purred a velvet voice from the doorway.

It was highly instructive to watch the king backpedaling hastily. He looked up at the new arrival, startled, wary, and fearful. The arrogant bully suddenly turned into an intimidated pussycat who was trying to remember he was a warrior.

The self-proclaimed sorcerer glided into the room with a soft whispering of velvet, a tall, lean customer in a floor-length black robe and black conical hat, both embroidered with blood-red arcane symbols—pentagrams, runes, and others Matt didn't recognize. He was swarthy and handsome, with black eyebrows, moustache, jawline beard, and wavy black hair. With his mouth, he was smiling—polite, urbane, and as treacherous as California bedrock.

He looked the king up and down sadly, clucking his tongue. "A shame, Astaulf—it bit back! Will you never learn to leave things magical to those who can govern them?" He glanced at Matt. "You seem harmless enough—but 'tis well to be sure." His forefinger darted out, stabbing at Matt while he intoned a short, rhyming chant in an arcane tongue.

Matt doubled up shrieking as hot irons stabbed into his belly. He would have kept yelling, but his diaphragm tied a knot in itself, and he ran out of breath.

King Astaulf was pulling himself up by the nearest guard. "I can govern small sorcerers well enough, Malingo—they fear a strong man, even if he has not their Power. How was I to know that this stranger was not such a weakling?"

"You should always fear a sorcerer," Malingo chided, "till his powers are known. You ought to have left him to me, Astaulf."

Astaulf flushed, and Matt had a notion that he was missing something in the conversation; but he was missing his breath more. His belly was locked solid, refusing to inhale, and his vision was getting a trifle murky. Panic flowed, and he fought it back—this would be an asinine way to die, stranded in an alternate universe.

There had to be a simple, logical explanation for his sudden belly cramps. And there was: The sorcerer had hexed him.

"And what of the actions you should have taken?" the king blurted. "If a powerful new sorcerer has come amongst us, should you not have known of it?"

Malingo's face darkened.

Astaulf grinned and pressed his advantage. "You sent no warning—doubtless because the man was too weak for concern. Yet it appears he is not. How is this, Malingo? Has *your* magic failed you?"

An interesting point, Matt was sure—but just now, he was far more interested in getting the thumbscrews off his belly. *Logic, man*, he told himself. *You've been hexed; unhex yourself.*

He managed a bare whisper, reversing the first magic spell he could think of:

> Thrice from mine and thrice from thine,
> And thrice again to unmake nine.
> Peace! The charm's no more malign!

His breath hissed in as his belly muscles fell loose. Then his stomach bounced back, and the room seemed to swing about him as nausea percolated through him.

Malingo tossed his head impatiently. "Am I to notice every least and littlest happening in your kingdom? Why have you guards and spies?"

"Why have I a sorcerer?" Astaulf showed his teeth, enjoying himself. "I think you let too many things escape your notice."

Nausea was one thing, but when the floor seemed to want to join the ocean and started taking wave lessons, Matt had to do something fast.

"Explain yourself." Malingo was definitely a little white around the lips. "What things escape my notice?"

Astaulf's face darkened with wrath. "Rebellious nobles in the

West, for one thing, plotting to topple me from my new-won throne! And that idiot girl in the dungeons, who has still the gall to refuse my attentions!"

The floor was doing a really good wave action now, and Matt found himself beginning to wish it *could* rise and drown him. Anything to end this misery! He called on the old masters:

> Though related to a peer,
> I can hand, reef, and steer,
> And splice a selvagee.
> I'm never known to quail
> At the fury of the gale,
> And I'm never, never sick at sea!

It was a lie, but it worked; the floor flattened out with remarkable alacrity, and the nausea vanished.

"*That* is what escapes your notice!" Astaulf cried. "Not to mention a foreign sorcerer of unknown powers!"

"I agree; do not mention him," Malingo said between his teeth. "As for the wench, it may simply be that the crown does not dazzle her eyes when it rests on the head of one who's not a rightful king."

Astaulf froze, staring at the sorcerer, scandalized. Malingo smiled back urbanely.

Matt realized, dimly, that his appearance had triggered a hidden, building conflict into an open explosion.

Astaulf bellowed fury and yanked out a sword built on the scale of a snowplow. He swung it up above his head as Malingo's finger stabbed out, and the sorcerer rattled off a rhyme in the arcane tongue. The sword squirmed and writhed as Astaulf swung it down; then it looped its head back, jaws gaping wide for Astaulf's face. The king froze in horror, staring at the python; then he threw it at Malingo, swearing, "Take your snake, toad! To me, men!" He leaped at Malingo, cable-fingers clawing for his throat. "Aid me, foreigner! Bring down this foul sorcerer, and all his wealth and power shall be yours!" His fingers closed around Malingo's neck like the jaws of a pipe-cutter; he yanked the sorcerer off his feet and held him high, shaking him and tightening his grip. "Aid me now, I say! Black sorcerer though he is, he can't withstand the two of us! Counter his spells, and I will kill him!"

Matt's eyes flicked from one to the other, and he decided on the old Army rule: Never volunteer.

Malingo might have been getting red in the face, but his hands were weaving around Astaulf's arm in an intricate pattern, and he was mouthing silent syllables. Only Matt noticed that the python at the sorcerer's feet was stretching out and thickening, while three of the guards clustered around, trying to grasp the sorcerer's arms, to hold him still. Then a boa constrictor reared itself up, knocking Astaulf's guards aside as it flexed itself and threw a loop around the king's neck.

Astaulf's eyes bulged in horror; a choking groan leaped from his mouth. Malingo twisted in his hands and jumped free as the king clutched at the living hawser around his neck. Malingo's fingers darted out at the guards, his tongue rattling in the strange language—and their skin began to crack and peel, opening into running sores. They saw the flesh turn dark and gangrenous on their hands and screamed.

But Malingo didn't stay to look; he whirled back to the strangling king and stalked toward him with his fingers weaving, voice rising high and shrill. Then his hands yanked out stiffly as if snapping a thread taut—and the king was gone!

Malingo looked slowly down at the floor. So did Matt—and there, at the sorcerer's feet, sat a flabby and leprous toad, its mottled skin peeling.

It blinked, looking dazedly around—and saw the snake.

The boa's head swung slowly toward it—and froze, gaze riveted on the toad. Then, slowly, the head lifted, and the jaws gaped wide.

The toad gave a sort of groaning belch and turned, trying to hop away; but its hops were short and feeble. It was definitely not well.

The sorcerer's foot came down.

Not all the way—just enough to hold the toad in place. It squirmed under his foot, still trying to get away from the snake; but Malingo flung up a hand, and the snake's eyes flicked to him, wary and watchful. The sorcerer chanted a phrase and snapped his hand down, pointing at the snake. It never moved; its eyes and skin slowly dulled while its body seemed to flatten; and a giant's broadsword lay across the chamber floor, its blade curved, its pommel hooked.

A despairing, rattling groan sounded from the side of the chamber. Matt looked over against the wall, then yanked his eyes away again, the nausea rising in his throat. He'd seen a heap of rotting garbage among rags that once had been soldiers' liveries. Stench filled the chamber from what was left of the three guards who had been loyal to Astaulf. Matt swallowed heavily and mumbled his anti-nausea spell again.

The other guards were staring at the pile of carrion. It was very quiet, suddenly.

"Yes," Malingo said into the silence, "that is the fate of fools. And any man's a fool who gives his loyalty to princes when a sorcerer stands near. Remember, worthy guardsmen, and tell your mates; for your prudence saved your lives today—and may again."

He fell silent, his gaze holding level on them as, one by one, they wrenched their eyes away from the heap and up to meet the sorcerer's gaze—then quickly away again.

The sorcerer nodded slowly. "Enough. You've seen and will remember. Begone."

They turned to the door, managing to keep from running; but the last one out hesitated and looked back. "Lord Sorcerer—the King . . ."

"What said I of him who gives his loyalty to princes?" the sorcerer demanded; and the soldier shuddered. The latch clicked shut behind him.

Malingo stood, still and quiet, in the rays of afternoon sun that streamed in through the window, one hand half-raised, one foot still upon the toad.

Then slowly he lifted the foot away and stared down at the toad. "So, your Majesty." He made the title an insult. "Your pride had grown too large. Will this remind you of the true size of your soul?"

The toad blinked and stared up at him, terrified.

Malingo nodded slowly. "I think it will. But never, Astaulf, should you have dared to call me toad."

He straightened slowly and walked around the amphibian, gazing down his nose at it. It sat frozen, but its eyes followed his movements.

"No," the sorcerer said with infinite regret, "I must let you live."

The toad seemed to sink in upon itself with trembling relief.

Malingo nodded. "Aye; it was indeed a close escape, Astaulf. For a moment, hot blood nearly overcame cold sense; for a moment,

I almost let myself tread down. But it would be so tedious, seeking out another nobleman as foolish and covetous as yourself! And I, of course, must have a nobleman. Ah, the cursed set of these foolish aristocrats' minds that must needs see some trace of royal blood in him who sits upon the throne! As if none without relation to the reigning king could govern. Still and all, these noblemen must see such blood in him who'd claim the crown; for without it, they *all* would rise as rebels. Be thankful for your birth into a minor noble house—for it's all that saves you now."

Matt noticed that the sorcerer didn't say anything about his own birth. Obviously, he'd been born a commoner.

Malingo's teeth flashed in a grin. "Nor need I have concern that you'd seek my death again. Need I, Astaulf?" He waited, head cocked to the side. The toad shivered. Malingo laughed. "Nay, I thought not. For you know you could not hold your new-won throne against the Western barons without my power to aid you. Sorcery gained your throne, so only sorcery can hold it. Indeed, you only dared challenge me today because there's a new sorcerer here, and you thought he'd league against me. Foolish baron! You should have known no power in the land could equal mine!"

That rankled; Matt hadn't exactly thought of it as a matter of daring. Just common sense—don't choose sides until you have to.

Then he caught the baleful glare from the toad's eye and realized he'd had to.

So did Malingo. "No, you may not touch him, Astaulf! Not, at least, till I have done with him." He nodded judiciously. "Yes, I think you're schooled. I may restore you to your place; you'll not soon challenge me again." He stepped back, hands waving an unseen symbol in the air, chanting in the arcane tongue—a slow, rising chant that built to a peak as his hands flourished and snapped still.

The toad's form began to blur and waver; a cloud of vapor gathered around it, hiding it completely. The cloud grew and grew, like a gathering storm; then it began to sink in on itself, condensing, shrinking—and Astaulf stood rigid before the sorcerer. Then he sagged and staggered over to lean against the wall, eyes closed, face ashen and glistening with sweat, breathing in long, shuddering gasps.

Malingo stood back and nodded in approval. "Yes, you've

learned. Do not forget this, Astaulf. Next time I'll change you to the swine you are and dine upon your hams."

The king's eyes flickered open, then squeezed shut again.

The sorcerer's lips twitched into a sneer. "Ah, what a man he is! What commanding and kingly presence! But now, begone—I wish to have some words of my own with this new sorcerer. Begone, I say!" He stepped around behind the king, setting his palm between Astaulf's shoulder blades, and shoved. The king lurched toward the door, fumbling for the latch. He managed to get it open and stumbled out.

Malingo stood looking after him, shaking his head slowly, lip curling. Then he stilled and slowly turned toward Matt.

Matt fought the impulse to shrink back against the wall. He lifted his chin, but decided not to try to get to his feet.

The sorcerer nodded approvingly. "You showed wisdom, trickster. Or did you know you could not match me?"

"Uh—yeah."

Malingo raised an eyebrow. "I sense some hesitation. Could you believe you do have power to match my own?"

"Uh . . . well . . ."

The sorcerer snapped a forefinger out at him, chanting a quick, rhymed phrase.

Matt felt a sudden overpowering compulsion to lick the sorcerer's boots. His body started to bend forward of its own accord, even while every cell in his brain screamed outrage. His stomach knotted with sudden, hot anger, and he rapped out:

> "I cannot tell what you and other men
>   Think of this life; but, for my single self,
>   I had as lief not be, as live to be
>   In awe of such a thing as I myself."

It was blank verse, not rhymed, which may have been why it didn't work completely; but the compulsion dwindled. Matt shoved it to the back of his mind and straightened, even managing to give the sorcerer a defiant glare.

Malingo's eyebrows twitched upward. "Well, so! Ah, let's try sterner measures." He pulled a curving dagger from his sleeve and tossed it to the floor near Matt's knee, murmuring a rhyme. Total despair suddenly dragged at Matt, worse than any depression he'd ever felt—ten times worse. The room seemed to darken about him with a miasma of hopelessness. It was all a farce, this game of rhymes and gestures—this whole game of life, for that matter. Totally absurd, totally meaningless. Why bother even trying to fight back?

His eye fell on the dagger. His hand crept out toward it. To take it up, plunge it into his chest, be done with it all! Ah, the sweetness of nothingness!

Foul! shrieked the skeptic's voice at the back of his mind. *He's hexed you, fool!*

Matt paused, startled at the thought. Then his hand crept out toward the knife again of its own accord. He *was* hexed—and stubborn pride dug its heels in and balked, meaningless or not. Matt grabbed for Hamlet's lines:

> "For in that sleep of death, what dreams may come?
> Thus conscience doth make cowards of us all;
> And thus the native hue of resolution
> Is sicklied over with the pale cast of thought;
> And enterprises of great pith and moment,
> With this regard, their currents turn awry,
> And lose the name of action."

The depression remained—after all, Hamlet wasn't exactly exuberant till the end of the play, when he knew he was dying—but Matt's hand stopped, then began to move back to his side. It *would* be pretty senseless to kill himself, when the only thing he was sure of was that he existed.

Malingo's frown deepened. He made a circular motion, palm out, as if he were wiping a slate. Depression snapped away from Matt, almost rocking him with the reaction. He was just pulling his wits together when Malingo's finger stabbed out again, and his arcane drone buzzed.

Matt suddenly felt something was missing. Inside! That sinking feeling in his stomach could only be explained by his stomach sinking. Could his intestines have gone on vacation? No, surely not! This sorcerer couldn't have gone for the cheap joke, the literal interpretation of the standard adjective for cowards.

He had.

Matt had a vision of his stomach acids and by-products raining down unfiltered onto his kidneys. Whatever he was going to do, he'd better do it fast; peritonitis might not be possible without an

appendix to burst, but he was certainly going to have a close
equivalent.

Malingo watched him, grinning.

Dull anger burned—or was it stomach acid? Either way, Matt
set his jaw and dug back through twenty years of education for
an appropriate phrase. He could think of a few verses for pulling
intestines out, but it never seemed to have occurred to any poet
to celebrate the reverse. In desperation, he tried his own:

> "No law can pull apart
> Inherited entail.
> Heredity did start
> My very own entrail.
> Return to me, my own,
> By gene and chromosome!"

It was lousy doggerel, but it worked. Matt had a sudden sense of
fulfillment. He sighed with relief.

Malingo's face wiped clean of all expression.

Matt was suddenly alert. He had to move first, before the
sorcerer made another try. Well, he'd just been thinking of augury.
He declaimed,

> "What say the augurers?
> Plucking the entrails of an offering forth,
> They could not find a heart within the beast."

Malingo suddenly looked decidedly disconcerted. He clapped
a hand to his chest, swallowed heavily, muttered a quick incan-
tation, and traced a symbol over his breastbone, then relaxed with
a heavy sigh. Matt felt a surprising surge of relief, too—he'd
never really fancied himself a murderer.

Malingo's lips puckered in a frown. He stroked his beard, eying
Matt as if he were speculating on how many slices of fish bait he
could cut from his liver.

Matt lifted his chin and stared back stoutly. After all, there
wasn't much else he could do.

"You have some power," Malingo admitted. "Enough to be
useful to me. But, alas, that also means you've enough to be
troublesome. I ought to obliterate you here and now and would

do so without a thought—if it weren't for the possibility of your being more help than bother."

Matt pricked up his ears. What was this? A chance to join the local power structure?

Malingo turned away, strolling across the chamber with elaborate nonchalance. "You refused Astaulf's offer, and that could indicate any one of a number of desirable traits."

Sure, such as cowardice, greed, apathy, or a certain reluctance to attack while anyone was watching. Matt eyed the sorcerer's back speculatively—but of course, that was just what Malingo was expecting.

"We must, of course, test you further to discover which one it is."

Matt frowned. "Why bother? It's simple—I'm the cautious sort. I'm not about to choose a side before I know how the ground lies."

"How?" the sorcerer frowned, perplexed.

"I mean . . . Look. When the king jumped you, how was I supposed to know which one would win?"

"I see." Malingo nodded. "Well, at least you show some sense—though no great faith in sorcery. Still, there are worse values—and I can understand your uncertainty. Astaulf and I have been careful to appear on the best of terms when anyone was there to see. How could you know which was stronger, when you had no inkling of a quarrel?"

Apparently Malingo was forgetting that Matt was new in town. Or did he even know?

"I congratulate you on your prudence," the sorcerer said. "Such restraint and wisdom are rare in one new to the Power. You are wise to be sure which side can best advance you before you choose."

He strode back toward Matt and stopped, arms akimbo. "Well! You've seen it. The king cannot stand against me—but I can dispense with him, should I think it worth the trouble. League with me, and Astaulf cannot hurt you. My power still is rising, as yours will with it, if you swear fealty to me."

Matt just sat, staring up at the man, unbelieving. From football to ally in less than two minutes . . . ? No. From football to pawn!

Malingo frowned. "You hesitate? Perhaps I should not offer. What stays your mind?"

"Uh . . . well, I'm just naturally the cautious type, as I said."

Matt's mind raced. He had to make it sound good—but what would this trickster buy? "I'm really new in town, you see. I'd like a fuller idea of the lay of the land before I decide anything."

"But what more need you know? Astaulf is a fool, and I the power behind him. No other power in this land can stand against us, as we've proved within these last six months. What else?"

"Well, for starters—who's the power behind you?"

It was a dumb thing to say, and Matt knew it after three words, but it was a little late to stop. The sorcerer turned pale. Then, after a few seconds, he smiled slowly, and Matt dared breathe again. "You do not know? You truly do not know?"

"Well, I could guess."

"Do so." Malingo cocked his head to the side, interested, waiting.

Matt swallowed. "Well . . . Astaulf called you a sorcerer . . ."

Malingo nodded.

Matt took a deep breath. He didn't dare show the slightest sign of squeamishness. "Which means your power comes from Hell."

"There! You see?" Malingo spread his hands. "You knew it all along." He quirked one eyebrow. "You *are* a sorcerer, of course?"

Matt swallowed. "Well . . . that's a matter of definition."

"How?"

"High definition," Matt explained, "in which case it's a hot medium, and I gather a sorcerer is supposed to be a very hot medium indeed. Of course, at the other end of the scale, there's low definition, which makes a cool medium, and I like to think I keep my cool. Then, too, I'm pretty low on being definite."

He ran out of steam, and the sorcerer just stood, staring.

Then Malingo lifted his head. "Indeed. You seem to be somewhat confused. Are you truly ignorant of the distinction between a medium and a sorcerer? For if you are, you can't begin to know yourself."

"Yeah, that's it!" Matt leaped at the idea as though it were a life preserver. "The identity search, who-what-where am I. I'm very much in the middle of it! And never more than now . . ."

Malingo shook his head sadly. "You'll be no use to me until that's resolved, and you know what you are. Oh, I've heard of such cases before—young men discovering they've the Power, but not knowing what they would do with it, uncertain whether to work for Darkness or Light. Yes, I know your case—some of my best junior sorcerers were poised in such precarious state not long agone. They're greatly to be valued, I assure you—as you yourself may be, once you've resolved your doubts. No, we'll keep you yet awhile." He turned to the door and yanked it open. "Guards! Step now within!"

Two armored guards came in, pikes at the ready.

"Escort him to the dungeons." Malingo motioned toward Matt. "We'll give you, then, a while. I can afford it. You seem to have a spell or two I've not encountered. I must study this native power of yours more closely—when I have the time. For now, I have a cell to hold you, so think at length, deeply and carefully, on what you are and what you seek to be. Then, when you know you do seek sorcery, you'll swear allegiance to me." He flipped a hand to the guards. "Take him away."

They hauled Matt to his feet, but he turned back to the sorcerer. "Uh . . . I hate to ask foolish questions, but—what happens if I decide I'm, say, a wizard?"

The sorcerer bared his teeth in a sort of grin. "Why, then I've some particularly vile spells I've read about, but never tried. I'm quite curious as to how they'll work, actually. If you wish to side with Light, by all means, do—you'll still contribute to my power."

CHAPTER 3

For all the darkness and the ominous scurryings, the dungeon felt safe, though it was as chill and dank as any dungeon should be. How they could store food down here, Matt couldn't see; but he'd definitely noticed the smell of salt pork in the cell next door. And why else would those small, clawed paws be running around in the darkness? Actually, he had a notion he'd been filed between the salt meats and the extra arrows. If that was an indication of his importance here, Matt was willing to accept it. He felt as if he belonged.

It was really a relief to have a place of peaceful solitude where he could think things over. There was a lot that needed thinking! He let his head loll back against the slickness of the wall, closing his eyes and deliberately emptying his mind for a few minutes.

When he finally lifted his head, he felt better, though he still had to deal with the realities of the moment, if he could only find them.

Well, he wasn't in his own world any more; matter of fact, he probably wasn't even in his own universe. The parchment had done it, of course, with its line about "Cross the void of time and space." He had a momentary vision of thousands of universes, stretching away in a serried rank, each leaving its own bright

streak of elapsed time across the lightless, primordial void, each
with its own history, its own natural laws. He'd read once that it
was entirely possible that an alternate universe could have a completely different set of laws, and that what was superstition in his
own universe could be science there.

Well, magic *did* seem to work. But how about science?
Thoughtfully, Matt pulled out a matchbook, tore out a paper match,
and struck it by feel. It made a satisfactory rasp, but shed no light
on the subject. So . . . science *didn't* work.

But wait—the soldiers' swords had looked like steel, not plain
forged iron. So science did have to work here, after a fashion,
the way the medieval smiths had fashioned iron—or maybe the
pagan smiths; Matt seemed to remember that they'd been regarded
as specialized wizards who sang spells to the iron as they worked
it.

Matt fumbled out another match and struck it, intoning:

> "Fire, fire, burning bright
> In the jungles of the night,
> What mortal hand or earthly eye
> Could trace thy fearful symmetry?"

A twelve-inch flame roared up from the match-head with the
fury of William Blake. Matt dropped it in stark terror. Then he
saw the heap of damp straw it had fallen into and leaped to his
feet, stamping furiously. The light ebbed, faded—and was gone.

Matt breathed a sigh of relief and slumped down against the
wall again in the blessed darkness. So science would work, but
only by magic.

And there was something else.

He'd felt it before, been aware of it, in the street just before
the beggars appeared. Now that he looked back, it had been there
every time he'd worked a spell—that feeling of great forces gathering around him, modulating and fitting themselves to his words.
But it couldn't be very important, if he had barely noticed it when
he was under pressure.

What *was* important was figuring out some quick rules for the
maintenance and operation of magic. In spite of Malingo's poise,
Matt had sensed a definite undercurrent of anxiety; the sorcerer
wasn't quite as much in control of the situation as he wished to
appear. Which meant, since he was easily Astaulf's master, that

.

there were forces in the land opposing him. Malingo claimed to be an agent of Darkness, so his opposition would be agents of Light.

Matt had a notion he'd like to meet them.

Well, no man ever got anywhere by wishing. Though in this universe . . . No. Even here, he'd have to know how to wish properly. And he'd better learn fast; Malingo might get impatient.

How do you cast a spell?

So far, from all indications, it was done by poetry—or verse, anyway. And Malingo's gestures seemed to have a place in it, too. Would Matt's beggar summons have worked if he hadn't adopted a Statue of Liberty pose?

Matt took a deep breath. The next move was to experiment, validate the theory. Okay, he'd conjure up something—something safe, such as light. Only without a match at all, this time; he didn't need a bonfire.

Then a happy thought struck him; instead of fire, why not call for a fire-lighter? Or a lamplighter, at least . . . No, the way things worked here, he might wind up with a Victorian streetboy with a match on the end of a long pole. He wanted a local; might as well get some information, as well as company.

He felt the familiar gathering of force as he began to recite—but stronger now, much stronger.

> "It's light to which I do aspire;
> Send someone quick to light my fire!
> And long or short, by any name,
> So long as he's equipped with flame!"

There was a shattering roar, and light seared Matt's eyes. He fell back against the wall, covering his face, while something huge and scaly rasped and grated against the stone walls. *Fool!* Matt's monitor-mind gibbered. *When will you learn to be specific?*

The roaring slurred into words; heat seared Matt with syllables. *"Who?* Who hath done zhish to me? . . . *Thou!"*

Matt jerked his head up, staring. The light winked out, but the afterimage showed two burning eyes . . .

Light came again, a five-foot gout of glaring flame, showing a mail-scaled snout with flaring nostrils over pointed teeth and huge, scaly-ridged eyes. *"Thou!* Vile dung-heaped hunter of hatchlings! What! Dursht summon a grown dragon to ambush?

Temeritoush idiot! If thou dosht hope to drain Shtegoman's blood to shell to a shorsherer, thou'rt a fool, and will shoon be a dead one!"

A gout of flame seared out again. Matt yelped and leaped aside just in time. The dragon took a breath like a bellows and lurched against the wall with a clash. "Where art thou, worm of a man? Thinkesht thou to hide from Shteo . . . Shtegoman . . . in sho shmall a shpace? Thou'lt . . . thou'lt . . ."

The flame suddenly seared out again, and Matt leaped. But he needn't have worried; the fire missed him by five feet as the dragon lurched to the side. The great eyes were filmed and bleary in the firelight.

Then light snapped out like a strobe and, in the darkness, Matt realized, *The fool beast is drunk! And getting drunker.*

But apparently he was the unpleasant type of boozer, the kind that gets mean in its cups; and he was taking another blast-furnace breath.

"Hold it!" Matt snapped up a hand, palm out. "I'm innocent!"

"Indeed?" the behemoth sneered. "Then thou art the firsht man to be sho, shince Adam. Wherefore didsht thou shummon me here, if not to drain dragon'zh blood?" The glowing eyes seemed to wince slightly.

"Well . . . curiosity! I was just doing research!"

"Belike," Stegoman sneered. "And what wazh thish 'reshearch?' Didsht thou sheek to dishcover the limitsh of a dragon'zh enduranshe? How much pain I might withshtand? Nay!" The blowtorch spat again—but it wavered this time, inscribing a zigzag of soot on the wall; and in the light, Matt definitely saw the dragon wince again, eyes almost squeezing shut with pain.

Then it was dark once more, but Stegoman was inhaling. *Delay!* Matt thought frantically and called out, "What's the matter?"

There was a moment of silence; then the slurred voice asked suspiciously, "Matter? What dosht thou shpeak of?"

"Your pain!" It was an opening. *Get him talking! Keep his mouth too busy to use for a fire thrower!* "I saw you wince. Does it hurt much?"

"What conshern izh it of thine?"

"Well, gee . . . I just hate to see a fellow being in pain." Matt crossed his fingers in the dark and added, "I'm a doctor." *Well, not yet, and the wrong kind—but it's not too much of a lie.*

"Doctor?" The dragon fairly leaped at the idea, and Matt sighed with relief. "Mmm . . . indeed?" Now the beast was trying to sound casual. "And what conshern izh that of mine?"

"Well, I know pain when I see it and I *hate* seeing it. What's bothering you? Maybe I can do something about it."

The dragon rumbled deep in his belly, and his voice was surly. "I have a tooth in my jaw that cauzheth me pain, if thou musht know; but it will not keep me from roashting vile hunterzh who prey upon hatchlingzh!"

"Toothache, huh?" Matt commiserated. "Yeah, that can really get you down. But, if you don't mind my saying so, you seem a bit young to be having trouble with your teeth." Wild guess; all he'd seen so far was flashes of a huge, scaly head.

But Stegoman bought it. "A dragon is young for a century or two, ignorant mortal! The first hundred years are, I assure thee, quite long enough for teeth to begin to rot and to pain us."

"Really?" Matt forwned. "I should think you'd grow new ones every few decades."

"Thou art indeed ignorant of our ways," the dragon snorted. He seemed to be sobering up already, Matt noted. Strange, very strange. "We are born with the teeth we must keep all our lives; they are in our mouths when we hatch; they grow as we grow, like our skins."

"Your skins grow? I mean, you don't have to shed them once a year?"

The dragon gave a metallic rattle that might have been its equivalent of a superior chuckle. "Nay, certainly not! We are not snakes or lizards, man—though related to them, I doubt not, as thou are related to the kobolds and snow-apes. But dost thou scurry about in tunnels beneath the earth, or swing by long arms from a mountain peak?"

"Well, no—at least, not in most cases. Although I've heard of . . . Well, never mind. As you see, I don't know much about dragons."

"Thou art indeed a strange mortal," the dragon huffed. "What manner of man art thou, to be so ignorant of our race? Or dost thou not know our importance to thee?"

"Not really," Matt confessed. "A dragon's a pretty rare sight, where I come from."

"Scandalous!" The dragon snorted. "Are all men of thy land so unlearned?"

"You might say so. In fact, there are a lot of us who don't even believe in magic."

The dragon was silent, dumfounded; and Matt had that sinking feeling that, as usual, he'd said the wrong thing. "What manner of man *art* thou?" the dragon exploded.

Matt shrank back against the wall, but he managed to shrug his shoulders. "Well, the usual kind. You've seen me."

"Not well," the dragon rumbled. "Art thou afeared to show thyself?"

He had a nasty, suspicious tone to him. "Of course not!" Matt said quickly. "You want some light? I mean, something a little smaller and more constant than your house specialty?"

"That might be advisable."

"Oh, sure, sure! Right away." Matt yanked out his matchbook and tried to remember what spell he'd used.

"What dost thou wait for?" Stegoman growled.

"Uh, it takes a little time." Matt recited the skewed Blake quotation under his breath while he struck a match, remembering to hold it at arm's length. A twelve-inch flame gushed, and he ad-libbed quickly:

> "Let this light a candle kindle,
> So its light will last, not dwindle!
> Spearing dark and giving light,
> Letting us converse with sight!"

The matchstick seemed to slam against his fingers as it thickened abruptly, and Matt found himself holding a six-foot candle, two inches thick, with a foot-long flame like a spearhead on top. He'd overdone things a bit, but that was the hazard of improvisation.

The dragon's eyes were fixed on the point of light. "Most interesting," he murmured.

Matt stared back at him, seeing a thirty-foot Chinese-style dragon, with short, clawed legs, a slender, serpentine body, and a saw-toothed crest running along his backbone. There was an added European element, though— huge batwings were folded along his body. But the leathery skin hung from them in rags, with yard-long rents from edge to bone. The edges of the tears were heavy with scar tissue.

Stegoman turned his huge head toward Matt. Matt stood very still, aware that he was on trial.

Slowly, the dragon nodded. "Thou hast not the look of an evil man—though it is known that a fair face may hide a lying heart."

"Oh, I'm a lousy liar! Every time I try, I can't even fool myself!"

"That is somewhat necessary to effective lying, aye." The dragon nodded. "Still, mortals are not so forthright as dragons. If we dislike someone, or are angered by his conduct, we are quite quick and open in saying so."

"Mm." Matt pursed his lips. "I expect that leads to a lot of fights."

"Not so many, no. We each know our fellows are quick to anger; and we know their power as we know our own. There can never truly be a winner when two dragons fight; he who's left alive will be so sorely wounded that he'll need months to heal. Thus we respect even those we do not like."

"I see." Matt chewed at his lower lip. "There are ways of telling someone what you think of him without making it really an insult."

"Quite right." Stegoman looked faintly surprised. "Few mortals are so quick to see it."

Neither did Matt, really; but he'd had a smattering of anthropology in his undergraduate days and could recognize a highly individualistic society when he heard about one. The pride that underlay Stegoman's words, the outspokenness, coupled with relatively little fighting, meant a very stringent set of social conventions; without them, Stegoman's people would be at each other's throats constantly. They might be ornery, but these dragons must be painfully polite to one another.

Matt cleared his throat. "But doesn't that make it difficult to get any kind of united action going? I mean, discipline..."

"The discipline is within each dragon," Stegoman said tartly. "When we organize for battle, each dragon's honor is respected; he whom we choose to lead us knows we've chosen to follow his commands, so when he gives them, he's careful to avoid insult. We do as he directs, for we've chosen him for wisdom."

Their commanders must be diplomats as much as generals. Nice society to belong to—if you didn't mind the constant risk of getting killed in a duel. "One dragon to a hill, eh?"

"Mountain," Stegoman snapped. "Our homeland is the eastern

mountains—the range that divides this land of Merovence from the sink of sorcery called Allustria. Ever and anon, Allustria wars on Merovence or, less often, Merovence attacks Allustria; and to pass through our mountains, both attack the dragons. We are born and bred to war; each dragon will defend his mountain with his life, but all of us together must defend our land."

"I take it that when Allustria and Merovence attack you, they both lose?"

Stegoman nodded; dragons *could* look smug! "Since Hardishane first taught us order, we never have been conquered."

"Wait a second—who was Hardishane?"

Stegoman stared, scandalized. "Whence comest thou, ignorant mortal, that thou knowest not of Hardishane?"

Matt sidestepped. "It's a long story. Let's just say I haven't studied history. Who was he?"

"Why, the Emperor, thou unlearned one! The first Emperor—he who came, eight hundred years agone, to band together all these Christian lands against the force of evil! For that cause, he made alliance with us, and showed us the manner of fighting as an army—and thus, at last, we prevailed against the giants!"

Matt started to speak, then hesitated.

"Close thy mouth," the dragon growled, "and do not say, for I can see—thou knowest naught of giants."

Matt nodded weakly.

Stegoman sighed and curled his tail around his claws, settling down for a session. "The giants came nine hundred years agone, when great Reme fell. Reme, unlearned one, was the southern town that made an empire out of all the lands around the Middle Sea fifteen centuries agone, before the coming of the Christ."

So there *was* a Rome. But the name was Reme. Apparently, here, Remus rather than Romulus won the fight. Was that when this universe had split off from Matt's?

But still—the Christ; that Name was the same.

Why not? Athens was a going concern while Romulus and Remus were sucking wolf milk; Greek should be the same language in both universes, and Christ was a Greek word.

"So. Rome—uh, Reme—fell. But where did the giants come from?"

Stegoman shrugged impatiently. "Out of the earth, the rocks, or the mouth of Hell for all I know. They came; it is enough. They attacked us, and each dragon fought against them with fire, tooth, and claw. We died, till few of us were left. Great ugly brutes they were, tall as the highest pine but broad as any dwarf, covered with matted hair and filth. For an hundred years we fought to cleanse our mountains of them, sought to burn them out, and died.

"Then Hardishane came riding from the North, and with him came Moncaire, the mighty wizard. Moncaire waked up a hill into human form and gave it the name Colmain—a giant with the power of right behind him. He killed an evil giant, and we hailed him for a hero. Then Hardishane brought armies to garrison what few free mountains we had left; and he told us how all dragons could fight in unison, by one single plan, with no one dragon's head lower than the leader's. And he taught our elders tricks of battle.

"Thus, when the giants came, massed in a foul horde, shaking mountains with their bellows, they met an army fifty times their number, with an Emperor and a wizard at its head and a giant greater than the largest of them. Giant bodies walled our valleys. Then we hunted out the last behemoths left, burned them from their hidings, and drove them to Colmain. Thus we cleansed our mountains, and Hardishane passed through with all his army. Colmain strode out behind him, to aid him in the purging of Allustria. Thus they passed beyond our ken; but we never have forgot them."

Matt closed his eyes, gave his head a quick shake, and looked up at Stegoman. "An age of heroes . . ."

The dragon nodded. "We were born too late, thou and I, into a shrunken, latter world, with kingdoms in the place of empire, and barons where there once were giants."

"And from these heroes came your nation?"

The dragon nodded again. "Our nation and our law and lore; for only then did we begin to chant our history and our names, to hail our heroes and decry our weaklings, as a people."

He shuddered and looked away.

Matt's mental ears pricked up. Something painful, there. Now, if he had any sense, he'd leave it alone—but being himself, he had to pry. "So with your songs and sagas, you wrapped words around your customs and traditions and forged them into law."

"Aye." The dragon's gaze snapped back, eyes burning. "Our law, that says each dragon's pride is sacred, each dragon's life beyond the bounds of price—yet that both must stand within the shadow of the people."

"Ambiguous." Matt frowned. "Do you mean any one dragon has to be sacrificed if he endangers the society?"

Stegoman hunkered down, glowering. "You lay strange words against the thought—but, aye. A dragon's soul and person are inviolate—but so are every other dragon's. If he endangers another, then let them fight, or resolve it with sweet words, whiche'er they choose! But if a dragon, by his conduct or his mere existence, threatens three or more . . ."

His voice trailed off into a brooding silence. Matt had the picture. Stegoman had somehow turned out to be a menace to dragon society; so they'd clipped his wings and sent him into exile.

For what? Stegoman seemed a nice enough guy, allowing for a prickly disposition that probably went with being a member of a highly individualistic and very military culture. Matt somehow read him as the kind who'd never hurt another being, unless he were attacked. So what could he have done?

Gotten drunk.

It made sense. The dragon had appeared with a blast of fire; right after it, he'd been slightly tipsy. The more he'd breathed fire, the more drunken he'd become, till he was staggering and missing his aim. Then, when he'd quit breathing fire, he'd sobered up. The inference was that breathing fire made him drunk.

The thought made Matt a little giddy: all that dragon, cavorting around in the air, getting filled with the joy of flight till he just had to let it out—in a five-foot lance of flame. Then getting tipsy, which meant even more euphoric, which meant more fire, which meant a drunker dragon, and on and on.

If Matt was to judge by Stegoman, the dragons were a pretty realistic, practical sort; they must have been able to see that Stegoman was a menace to aerial navigation fairly quickly—or at least when he'd caused another dragon trouble the third time.

So he'd been grounded for drunk flying. And just to make sure it couldn't happen again, they'd put a few rips in his wings and exiled him.

Stegoman sighed heavily and resumed his tale. "For five hundred years, peace held; no man came against us, till Hardishane's Empire had dissolved. By then, we'd grown accustomed to our own army ordering, even though we lived in peace. It had proved too useful; we had built our dragon city and we'd done away with blood feuds. More dragons lived than e'er before, and the living was richer, safer. Then, when the Empire fell, the first men's army marched into our land."

"You chased them home, of course."

"Certes. But ever and anon, they try again—though it takes them near an hundred years to screw their daring up again."

"And you don't have any trouble with men in the intervals?"

"None dare attack—save vile hatchling hunters, seeking blood to sell to sorcerers." Stegoman shut his jaws with a snap, holding Matt with a fixed and glittering eye.

Matt swallowed. He thought he'd gotten Stegoman *off* that topic.

The dragon stretched and came to his feet with a rattling clatter. "Which brings to mind thyself. Art thou a hunter, a sorcerer—or both?"

"Neither," Matt said quickly. "I'm a wizard." He heard his own words and felt like a fool.

But Stegoman looked at him sidewise and slowly nodded. "Methinks there is some credit in that claim."

Matt heaved a sigh of relief that hollowed his backbone. "What convinced you? My native goodness glimmering through?"

"Nay, thine ignorance. Since thou knowest so little, thou hast only newly discovered thy Power and art still a wizard. Yet thou'lt surely find temptation yet! Be assured—I trust men to be treacherous."

"Comforting thought, I'm sure," Matt mused. "It *was* just research, you see—I was trying to find out if I really could work a spell, and the first thing I thought of conjuring up turned out to be you."

"And thus we are acquainted," Steogman said drily. "Tell me— whence comest thou, from what benighted land, that thou couldst know so little of our dragon lore?"

Matt started to give an honest answer, then caught himself. "Uh, I don't think you're going to believe this."

"Art thou so rare?" Stegoman demanded. "Tell thy tale; if there be truth in it, be sure that I've heard stranger."

"Okay, you asked for it." Matt took a deep breath. "I'm from out of this world. Not just this land—this world. Totally. I'm not even from this universe."

Stegoman lowered his snout onto his foreclaws, watching Matt with glittering eyes. "So thou art from another universe and world? How came this?"

"I couldn't rightly say," Matt admitted. "One minute I was reading an old scrap of parchment in my neighborhood coffee shop and the next I was standing in a street in downtown Bordestang."

"No doubt some magus here wished thy presence."

"You think so, too?" Matt leaped at it. "That's the only explanation I can think of. But who'd want me here? I scarcely know a soul."

"What soul knows thee? That's more in question." The dragon's tail-tip twitched. "Malingo, perchance—the King's vile sorcerer. Couldst thou serve him in any way?" He said it casually, but he was eying Matt as if Matt were a marshmallow ready for toasting.

"Well, no," Matt said carefully. "That is, I suppose I could be useful to him—but I don't think I'd want to be."

"Wherefore not? Malingo rides the wave's crest now; his tide still rises, carrying him up to glory. Thou couldst rise, too, to wealth and power."

"And the damnation of my soul." When in Rome, speak Latin. If they wanted to deal in medieval concepts, Matt pretty much had to, too. "Malingo strikes me as the kind of boss I couldn't trust. He might decide to put me down—six feet deep. Besides, I met the man already; he did some rather unpleasant things to me."

Stegoman frowned. "Thou dost not show it. Why did he mend the things he'd done to thee?"

"Oh, he didn't. But I couldn't walk around all day without my giblets, could I?"

Stegoman was very still suddenly, and Matt wondered, with a touch of panic, if he'd said the wrong thing. Then the dragon spoke and he almost sounded respectful. "Thou hast countered spells Malingo cast on thee?"

"Well, sure! I have this quirky thing about living—it's a nice pastime."

"Assuredly, it is," the dragon breathed. "Thou art, then, no weakling as a wizard, art thou?"

"Oh, now, wait a minute! Don't go making me out to be what I'm not! I'm sure Malingo wasn't really trying."

"Even so: thou dost live, and that doth show power. Too much—he should have made a servant of thee, or a corpse."

It was one of those very unfortunate situations where the only thing Matt could say that wouldn't get him into trouble was the truth—and even that was a little uncertain. He braced himself for the worst. "Well, I didn't exactly tell him no. I said I needed time to think it over."

"And hast thou thought?"

Matt took a deep breath. "Pretty much. I still need a few more facts."

"Such as?" there was a dangerous rumble under Stegoman's words.

Matt tried to ignore it. "Well, Malingo is rotten, and Astaulf's his patsy. But who's on the other side? And are they any better?"

The silence stretched out so long that Stegoman's glowing eyes seemed to be permanently burning themselves into Matt's retinas. At last the dragon spoke.

"Thou must, indeed, be new-come to this land, if thou knowest naught of those Astaulf opposes."

"Right. But I happened to be there when Malingo and Astaulf squared off, and—"

"Oh, did they?" Stegoman's eyes glinted. "A point of interest, I assure thee. And what didst thou glean from this confrontation?"

Matt took a deep breath and launched himself. "That Astaulf usurped the throne about six months ago, with Malingo's help. And the population isn't all that happy about it, or Astaulf wouldn't still have soldiers in the streets. And there's a bunch of loyalist barons fighting what amounts to a guerilla action, trying to bring Astaulf and Malingo down."

Stegoman nodded. "Thou hast caught the nubbin of it squarely. But who seek these loyal barons to place upon the throne?"

"Ah, there's the rub in the nubbin," Matt said with regret. "I didn't hear a word about the other side. Who are—I mean, were—they?"

"Thou hadst it more aright with 'are,'" the dragon mused, "but as for 'were,' 'twas the fourth King Kaprin. His wizard, full of years, had died; and ere he could seek out another, Malingo leaped, with Astaulf and his soldiers, upon this town of Bordestang. The fight was brief but bloody, and King Kaprin died."

"How about 'are'? That's the loyalist barons, I take it. Who do they have with them? A powerful wizard? If they do, he might be the one who pulled me here."

"Thine estimates are accurate." Stegoman eyed him warily. "Malingo cannot progress against the barons, nor can they gain an ell of land toward Bordestang. Thou riddlest well from tiny rhymes."

Matt almost blushed. "So the situation isn't a total conquest, it's a precarious balance. Astaulf and Malingo have the throne, but the barons have the people and a sizable chunk of the land. And I'd guess they're pretty evenly matched. So if you don't want that balance, introduce a random factor—me—to upset the apple cart."

"Aye," the dragon rumbled suspiciously, "but who would wish that most?"

"The barons," Matt said promptly. "Malingo has the upper hand, right now. For the barons, anything that breaks the stalemate is welcome, provided it doesn't come from Malingo."

"A fascinating theory." Stegoman nodded. "But it trips and stumbles on one point: the barons have no wizard."

"None?" Matt's eyebrows shot up.

Stegoman shrugged impatiently. "Oh, they have a few of minor power—holy men, monastery abbots and the like. But no great wizard."

"Hmm." Matt bit his lip. "You sure?"

"I am. Their strongest asset is the princess, and she's imprisoned."

"Princess?" Matt's head snapped up. "What princess?"

Stegoman sighed. "I forget how newly thou art come. Still, 'tis strange thou hast not heard of her."

"I've been a little busy. Who is she?"

"King Kaprin's daughter. Rightful heir to Merovence's crown."

"I'm surprised she's still alive."

"Be not. She is a lass of beauty. And Astaulf burns to have her."

"What's stopping him?"

"Malingo. He plans further ahead than Astaulf. To marry her would give the usurper legitimacy—but only if she comes unsullied to him, so that the marriage may be duly solemnized. And she'll not wed him."

"I don't blame her. And come to think of it, I did hear Astaulf say something about an idiot girl in the dungeons. I gather he's getting impatient."

"Quite," Stegoman said grimly. "Six months agone he moved her to the dungeons with the rats. Rumor says he speaks now of torture. But she will have none of his plan."

Matt nodded approval. "A girl with guts." He turned away, stroking his chin. "A real, live princess in durance vile!"

Stegoman regarded him with jaundiced eyes. "Thou hast a scheme in mind, man?"

"Matt," Matt said absently. "We ought to be on a first-name basis by now."

"Matt," the dragon conceded. "Thy scheme?"

Matt shrugged. "It's not really a scheme. I'm just wondering which is better—to wait here for Malingo to come and pull the plug on me, or to go looking for trouble when I have a good excuse."

Stegoman was quiet for a moment, chewing that one over. Then he sighed and rattled his spinal plates. "Thou hast the right of it, I fear; there's nothing to be looked for here. But how dost thou mean to leave this cell?"

"By going from bad to verse. Poetry got me into this fix; poetry should get me out."

He was silent, thinking for a moment. The dragon eyed him warily.

Then Matt began to recite:

> "There sits a prisoner in a cell of stone,
>   Whose eyes should weep, for she's alone.
>   Yet ill-becoming royalty are tears;
>   And she's a queen, though slight of years."

He took a breath to go on to the second verse—just in time for the dragon to blast out, "Hold!"

Matt leaped aside from the gout of flame, deciding Stegoman was a bit perturbed. "Yeek! Uh—was it something I said?"

"Nay, what thou wast about to say." Stegoman's eyes glowed in the candlelight. "Thou wast about to leave this cell!"

"Well, sure. I mean, we talked it over, didn't we? And decided—"

"That challenging blind fate would better suit thy taste than awaiting certain doom within this chamber. Aye, 'tis so! Yet didst thou think that dragons are more partial to such cramped and noisome quarters than are men?"

"Oh." Matt bit his cheek in consternation. "Sorry. I was in a little bit of a rush, wasn't I?"

"Aye, and thou wast near to making waste—of thee."

"I see your point." Matt eyed the dragon's cocked and loaded snout. "Well, suppose I get you out of here first? Any particular place you'd like to be?"

"Anywhere, so it be wide and free and open."

"The plains, then." Matt rolled up his sleeves. "How about next to a stream?"

"Stream, flood, or bog, I care not one whit! Only put me there!"

Matt nodded and began,

> "I know a bank whereon the wild thyme blows,
> Where oxlips and the nodding violet grows,
> Quite over-canopied with luscious woodbine,
> With sweet musk-roses, and with eglantine.
> And there you shall rest your enamell'd skin—
> Weed wide enough to wrap a fairy in."

Air imploded with a padded *thud*, and the cell was empty, except for Matt and the giant candle, flame streaming in the wind. He drew a long, shaky breath; he'd felt forces gathering around him again and was more certain than ever that they had been molding themselves to his words, somehow.

Idly, he wondered why there should be weed wide enough to wrap a fairy in, right after the line about enameled skin. It hadn't made that much more sense in the original, really—but Shakespeare had put it in, so who was he to turn it down?

Back to the matter of the moment—how had that prisoner verse gone again?

> "There sits a prisoner in a cell of stone
> Whose eyes should weep, for she's alone."

He felt it beginning again—a gathering of forces, like static electricity around a lightning rod, before the faint spark flew.

> "Yet ill-becoming royalty are tears;
> And she's a queen, though slight of years."

The feeling was much stronger now, with something slightly ominous about it. He wondered, fleetingly, what would happen if he built up a field as strong as this, then couldn't think of an imperative, a directing phrase, a route for the magic field's discharge.

Come to think of it, what was he going to use for an imperative to this verse? Umm.

> "Away, away, through walls I'll fly to her,
> And there about our fates we shall confer!"

A silent, invisible explosion blasted him; the floor seemed to slide sideways beneath his feet, and a huge hand squeezed him, then let him go. He looked up, panting, amazed to find himself dripping with sweat, and saw the princess.

CHAPTER 4

She was tall, about five feet ten, with long blond hair flowing down over her shoulders, curling out in smooth, full billows over high, firm breasts, then falling almost to her waist. She had an oval face, with clear, pale skin, arched, delicate eyebrows over large, long-lashed blue eyes, a straight nose with a hint of uptilt, full and very red lips, and high cheekbones. She was by far the most beautiful woman Matt had ever seen.

And that was without a bath—or a decent dress, for that matter. She was wearing muddy maroon rags that once might have been a long, tight-sleeved kirtle under a tight-laced, scoop-necked bliaut with wide, hanging sleeves.

At the moment, she was staring at him as if she were wondering whether he were an angel or a demon. Matt decided he'd better update her.

"Hi." He tried for a nonchalant grin. "I'm the new wizard in town. You must be the princess."

Her eyes caught fire, and she came up out of the low, hourglass-shaped chair like a lioness grabbing for a careless gazelle. "Wizard? You are truly such? You do not mock me, sir?"

"Uh—not the world's greatest wizard, mind you—but I do seem to be able to work a few tricks."

47

"Aye, most truly, if you can bring yourself into this cell! Why came you here?"

"Well, uh, I heard there was a lady around who could use a helping hand. Need anything?"

"Aye! I have great need, if you are truly for me." She straightened slowly, regaining her poise. "Whence come you, sir?"

Matt started to answer, then caught himself. "Uh—it's a little on the complicated side."

"I have no pressing engagements." She had more than looks; she had a sense of humor, too. "Pray tell me whence you come."

"From another world—another universe, really. I was there, and the next thing I knew, I was here. In Bordestang, I mean."

Her eyes widened. "You were witched into our world?"

"You could look at it that way, yes," Matt said judiciously. "Though I think 'witched' might be a little strong . . ."

"I do not." She was very sure of herself; Matt found it a little unnerving. "Was it a sorcerer brought you here?"

"No, I don't really think so. The only one I've met so far is Malingo, and he seemed a little surprised to see me."

"Good. Then belike you have it aright; no evil one brought you here. Therefore some good and saintly wizard must have transported you."

"Now, wait a minute," Matt objected. "I think you're making a questionable assumption, there—"

She cut him off. "I do not. How escaped you from Malingo?"

"Oh, I told him I wasn't quite ready to make up my mind about which side I was on, so he gave me some time to think it over."

Her eyebrows rose. "He must need your power, then; 'tis not like him to let a wizard live who is not subject to him. Did he wall you up?"

"Did he what? . . . Oh, you mean did he throw me into the dungeon! Yeah, right between the salt pork and the extra arrows."

"Aye, in a cell with a spell on it, to prevent your leaving. How did you escape from *that*?"

"A cell with a what?" Matt scowled. "Are you sure?"

"I heard the guards outside my door speak of it, when first they brought me here. The sorcerer charmed every cell within this keep in such a fashion."

Cogwheels ticked over in Matt's head. "So that's how come I felt so much more power build around me this time! I may have more of a lead than I thought!"

"You will have need of it," she said with full and total certainty. "Why came you to my cell?"

"Huh?" Matt stared, taken aback. Then he spread his hands. "Gee, I should think that would be obvious. Beautiful princess, durance vile, that sort of thing . . ."

"You have chosen, then, to side with me?" She looked directly into his eyes, a hard, searching gaze. "Be sure you're not mistaken. If you aid me in the slightest way, the sorcerer and his false king will slay you in an instant, if they have the chance."

Matt stood staring back at her while all the aspects of the situation reeled through his mind. But a certain solid determination moved in him, growing, evolving out of resentment into something akin to anger. Matt wondered if it were nascent self-respect. "There really isn't much to choose, your Highness. I've seen the other side."

Savage joy leaped in her eyes. "You are with me, then?"

Matt nodded slowly. "Yeah. At your service, Majesty."

"Highness; I am not yet crowned. I am the Princess Alisande, no more."

"Glad to meet you," Matt said drily. "I'm Matthew Mantrell."

"Well met, Wizard Matthew!" She latched onto his biceps with both hands. "And I implore you, take us out from here!"

Matt felt his chest puffing out a bit; this was the first time in his life he'd *really* had a chance to impress a girl!

Then he remembered what pride goeth before. "Uh—this isn't exactly a sure thing, you know. I'm kind of new to the wizard business. I've only been playing at it for a few hours."

Alisande's head reared back, appalled. "You are so new to the power as *that*?"

"Worse," Matt confided. "It's the first taste I've had of *any* kind of power." He was almost surprised to hear the words. Then he realized that he'd known it all his life and was only just now admitting it to himself. It a was a bitter pill to swallow. "So I'm not too sure of my abilities, you see. You could very easily wind up dead."

It rocked her, but she swung back quickly, frowning in thought for a moment. Then she lifted her chin and looked him squarely in the eyes. "No doubt I could; yet I know that I will not. You are the only chance I have, wizard, and the only one I'm like to have. I must stake my life and kingdom on you—and I know you will not fail me."

Her total, hundred per cent certainty was unnerving. Matt took a breath. "I hope you're right."

"I am." It was a simple statement of fact. "Take us out of this place."

Matt took a deep breath and clasped an arm about her. It was far more pleasant than it should have been, under the circumstances.

This time he chose a variation on the spell he'd used on the dragon:

> "I know a bank whereon the wild thyme blows,
> Where oxlips and the nodding violet grows,
> Quite over-canopied with luscious woodbine,
> With sweet musk-roses, and with eglantine."

The feeling was stronger than ever. There was tremendous power gathering around him, seeking a discharge route. It would take the first one it found, and if that happened to be right through him . . .

But the woman at his side stood proud and determined, if not completely unafraid, and he couldn't let her see him doubting himself.

> "There shall we fly, to tarry till the night,
> Lulled in these flowers with dances and delight!"

The universe swung around ninety degrees, and swung back. A small hurricane blasted Matt's face as light seared his eyes and a roaring filled his ears. The princess clung tightly to him, every flowing curve finding a corresponding niche in him. Unfortunately, Matt was in no shape to appreciate it. He just clung to her as something relatively solid in a crazy world, waiting for the earth to steady beneath his feet.

Slowly, things settled down; the earth solidified, and Matt's eyes adjusted to the sudden sunlight. He took a deep breath and looked about him.

He was in a forest, beside a small stream. A wide, sunlit meadow opened off to his right. The banks of the stream, on his left, were thick with flowers. He recognized wild thyme and violets. That must be eglantine, creeping over the low boughs, there, just above the dragon's head, and . . .

"Stegoman!"

The dragon fixed him with a glittering eye. "So—again. I thought that I had done with thee, most foolish of wizards."

Matt had an image to maintain, now. "Foolish? Hey! I got you free, didn't I?"

"To open plains, thou didst say," the dragon reminded him. "I find myself within a wood."

"Oh. Well, you can't expect perfection, can you?" Matt looked around. "I thought it was a nice place."

"So I would guess," the dragon rumbled, "since thou didst seek it after me. Or hast thou come to be so fond of my company?"

"Uh, little bit of both, actually." It was the first piece of scene-description verse that had come into Matt's head.

Alisande pushed herself away from him, albeit a little unsteadily. "How now, Sir Wizard! Have you brought me to your tame, enslaved familiar?"

"Enslaved!" Stegoman roared, torching two bushes and a stretch of underbrush in the process. "I, a shlave? What vile calumny and jackal'zh lie izh thish?"

Matt leaped to the side, yanking Alisande with him. "Watch it—he gets mean when he gets high. Back off, Stegoman! The lady was jumping to conclusions!"

The dragon paused on the intake, blinking blearily at Matt. "What shayesht thou?"

"A misunderstanding," Matt said quickly. "The lady could tell we'd met before. Can you blame her for thinking we were in cahoots?"

"Nay, truly! I see I was mistaken!" The princess cried. "You are, indeed, untamed and free, as all your people are!"

Stegoman cocked his head to the side, thinking that one over. While he was thinking, Matt slipped off his jacket and used it to beat out the brush fire Stegoman had accidentally touched off. He came back with his bargain-basement-best a bit charred, but with the fire out.

Alisande was cooing to an attentive Stegoman. ". . . nay, not one so strong and brave, with the power of giants and with naked beauty in the flow of polished scale o'er cabled muscles. You would not do so vile a thing as to attack an unarmed maiden!"

Her voice had a husky quality that touched off every ductless gland Matt owned. He pulled himself together and remembered his manners. "Your Highness, may I present Stegoman, a wanderer of the dragon people. Stegoman, her highness, the Princess Alisande."

The princess straightened, gathering dignity about her like an invisible robe, and inclined her head gravely. "Delighted am I with your acquaintance, Master Stegoman, though I could wish we'd met more formally."

Watching Stegoman, Matt preceived that royalty has its impact, even on a democrat. The dragon's eyes widened; then he bowed his head, plus at least three feet of neck. "Honored, Highness!" He turned to Matt. "So thou hast done it. Art thou more puissant than thou didst tell? Or hast thou but rash fool's luck?"

Matt was just opening his mouth to admit he'd been lucky, when Alisande gasped, "Oh!" He looked up at her, frowning; her hands were clasped at her throat, and her eyes were wide with wonder. "Air, and trees, and sky! Sunlight, blessed sunlight! And water!" she cried, runing forward to look down into the brook. "Running, open water!" She fell to her knees and caught a palmful to her lips, drinking deeply.

Matt watched in admiration. So slender, so lithe, so graceful . . . She fairly seemed to flow as she turned, rising to her feet again, and tossed her head, hair swirling back, finger stabbing out in imperious command. "Master Wizard, get you hence, I pray you; take your eyes away—and you also, good Master Stegoman! For I've not felt the blessed touch of water on my skin this half a year! If you please, I would bathe me!"

Matt bridled a little at the arrogance of her tone, but he couldn't very well refuse. "Uh—are you sure you'll be safe?"

"Come, come," Stegoman huffed, "let the lady be, good Wizard! We'll be close by; if trouble brews, we'll be within her call. Let the lady bathe! What monsters were her captors, to deprive her of the touch of water half a year!"

He waddled off toward the meadow. Matt could hardly be less of a gentleman than a lizard.

"Master Wizard!"

Matt looked back, startled. "Your Highness?"

"I loathe the thought of taking up again these rags!" The princess plucked at the remains of her dress. "Could you not conjure up some fitting raiment that hath not six months' filth about it?"

"Uh . . . yeah, sure." Matt bobbed his head, feeling extremely awkward. "Sure thing, your Highness."

"I'll thank you with each breath I breathe!" she cried and whirled away behind a thorn bush.

Matt reflected that the girl was somewhat given to hyperbole. Then he imagined how a shirt that had been worn, day and night for six months, would feel each time he breathed and decided that maybe she hadn't been exaggerating, after all.

"So! Thou art truly a wizard, it seems!"

Matt looked up, surprised. Was that a note of respect in Stegoman's voice? "Not really—no more than I was the last time you saw me. I haven't learned anything new, anyway."

"Then thou hadst more knowledge than thou didst know," the dragon stated. "How didst thou break Malingo's magic bond around the princess' prison? For that must have been the fiercest and most puissant spell he knew!"

Matt felt suddenly weak at the thought of having crossed spells with Malingo, even at second hand. "Well, I really didn't do anything much. I just recited a bit of poetry I happened to know, and here we are."

"Thou hadst no notion of the powers thou didst challenge?"

"Oh . . . I wouldn't say *that*." Matt remembered the heat, the feeling of being inside a dynamo. "But what else could I do?"

"Aye, I was quite confident thou wouldst play rash fool and take the risk." The dragon eyed him, brooding. "Yet thou art here; his spell is broken. I must think, then, thou didst work a spell unknown."

"Unknown to Malingo, you mean?" Matt pursed his lips, thinking it over. "Yeah, quite probably, now that you mention it. All the poetry I have in my head is old stuff, where I come from; but it would probably be brand new, here."

Stegoman seemed to shy away a little. "A new spell! 'Tis strange, and vastly dangerous!"

Matt stopped, rooted to the spot. *Now* Stegoman had his full attention. "Oh! Do tell!"

"I do indeed. Magic is elusive; it hath no principles, no rules of trade. It is an art, but one whose power shows in moments. Therefore good wizards cull old books for practiced but forgotten spells; all their world is a searching through of musty manuscripts. Their end-all and their be-all is in learning. 'Tis the search that they enjoy, the finding of old knowledge, new to them. They care little for its use."

"True scholars," Matt said thoughtfully. "They wouldn't happen to be on the scarce side, would they?"

"Extremely rare. But sorcerers sprout from every bush."

Matt looked up, frowning. "Sorcery is easier to learn?"

"Aye; ye've but to find a grimoire. And they never seem in short supply. I believe the powers of Darkness see to that."

Matt had a brief, dizzying vision of a rotary press churning furiously in the bowels of Hell. "That's all Malingo did? Just memorized a book?"

"One book, or two—it matters not. He will not take much time in seeking out new spells, unless he's challenged by a stronger; his time is fully occupied in gathering wealth and seeking out new enemies, before they garner power enough to challenge him. And ever and anon, he plucks some victim for the torture, to amuse his idle hours. But thus it is with sorcerers; they see their Power only as a means of gaining their desires. They will not take the time to seek new spells."

"And all the wizards do is research." Matt scowled, shaking his head. "It doesn't fit. Someone *has* to think up a new spell now and then—or there'd never be any change in the power structure!"

Stegoman regarded him quizzically. "A strange thought, that. Yet thou hast the way of it aright; each century or so, a man appears who doth work out a spell anew. Yet from all that I hear, the forging of new spells is like the walking on a knife's edge, o'er a pit of flames and vipers mixed."

"You use such picturesque similes." Matt swallowed thickly as he realized he'd been running just the risk Stegoman described every time he'd worked a spell—for, by local standards, all his spells were new. More to the point, he didn't know any of the old ones. Remembering the buildup of forces on his escape from Malingo's prison, he could easily believe what Stegoman had said; it wasn't hard to imagine that force shorting through him, leaving a charred and reeking husk . . . He shuddered and put the thought behind him. "If a guy let himself think about that, he'd very quickly lose his taste for magic."

"He would indeed," the dragon said. "Yet thou no longer hast the choice."

"What? Hey, hold on!" Matt's head snapped up. "I'm a free agent here—I'll do, or not do, as I please!"

"Assuredly," Stegoman agreed drily. "And I'm certain Malingo will respect thy freedom."

Matt dropped his eyes and shuddered. "Committed! The one thing I've been working to avoid most of my life!"

Then he froze, hearing the echo of his own words. *Did I say that?*

Why had he never known that before? More to the point—why could he suddenly admit it to himself?

Because now he *was* committed.

CHAPTER 5

Gibbering goblins crawled up Matt's spinal column and earnestly searched for a home in his brain. "Stegoman..."

"Aye?"

"I'm going to kill us all. I can't help it. There's no other way it can turn out. Any time I try to work magic, I'll drop us all down the chute—because *I don't really know what I'm doing!*"

"Take calm," the dragon told him. "Speak—art thou dead? And hast thou worked magic?"

"Yes. Thank you." Matt drew a deep, shuddering breath. "It's always helpful to be reminded of the realities." He swallowed hard and took a firm grip on his nerves. "Every time I've worked a spell, I've felt some kind of force gathering around me—magic force. It has to be a form of energy. So it should, presumably, function according to a definite set of principles, as gravity and electromagnetism do."

"Principles? What talk is this? Can there be rules to an art?"

Matt shrugged. "Personally, I think art *can* work by rules—but I know fields of energy definitely *do*. And if I can figure out those rules, I can manipulate those fields."

"What sayest thou?" the dragon rumbled. "Dost thou tell me thou canst frame rules for magic?"

"That's what I was getting at. Of course, I must admit that finding rules for this particular form of energy might be more the province of the poet and critic than of the scientist."

"I ken not what a scientist may be, yet this must needs be a poet's study in truth—for the greatest of wizards *are* poets."

"Which tells me where *I* rank. But it's pretty obvious—any magic here seems to be governed by verse—and any literary idiot can tell you the word is *not* the thing—it's just a *symbol* of the thing. A poet arranges sound-symbols in whatever way gets his meaning across most powerfully."

"Dost thou say the poet who's also a wizard doth the same to this magic force of thine?"

"Right." Matt nodded vigorously. "The words are just models; they give the poet-wizard something to focus his own energies on. The little bit of energy that the wizard puts in modulates the vastly bigger magic energy that's lying around all over the place, here."

"Modulates?"

"Changes. Reshapes. As he changes and shapes the sounds of the words to his meaning, he's also changing and forging the magic field into whatever shape he wants—and when he finishes the verse, lo and behold! The magic energy field does whatever he wants done!"

"It sounds well," Stegoman admitted doubtfully. "But hast thou the courage to test it?"

"Yes! If I don't wait more than a minute or so. Let's see..." Matt came to a halt, hands jammed into his pockets, looking about him. "What's a good spell to do?"

"Thou hast promised the princess new raiment," Stegoman reminded.

"Oh, yeah! Let's see, what will she need? Nothing too fancy, of course—I have a notion we're going to be doing some hard traveling. What's the standard riding outfit around here?"

"For a lady? 'Tis shift, kirtle, bliaut, boots—and a cloak with a cowl, for rain."

"We'll hold off on the last part until it gets cloudy." Matt took off his jacket and rolled up his sleeves. "Let's see, 'True Thomas,' now—there's a fine old ballad with some clothes in it, and it's even got magical overtones."

Stegoman backed off a few paces.

Matt raised his hands and began outlining the shapes of the garments—why, he didn't know; but it felt right.

> "She'll have a shift of finest silk
> And bliaut made of broadcloth green;
> Her kirtle shall be homespun cloth,
> With boots as fine as ever seen."

He was sweating during the last line; the field of force around him baked like a Juarez sun. But he finished the last line, snapping his hands apart as though tightening a knot. A patch of grass seemed to shimmer and sparkle as the air thickened above it, coalescing, gelling, and hardening...

And an ankle-length slip lay on the grass, next to a tight-sleeved underdress, a green overdress, and a pair of calf-length boots.

Stegoman sucked in a long, deep breath. Matt ducked out of sheer reflex.

"Yes-s-s-s-s-s," the dragon hissed. "Thou hast the Gift."

"Gift?" Every molecule in Matt stilled. "*What* gift?"

"Hast thou not come to see it?" The dragon stared at him as though he were an alien. "Thou dost not think *any* mere man can work magic, dost thou?"

"Well . . ."

"Disabuse thyself of such innocent's thought. This magical Gift is given to few, very few. Grimoires and old tomes notwithstanding, even the most learned of scholars cannot work a spell if he hath not the Gift."

"Oh." Matt's lips framed the letter carefully. "You mean, not everyone can sense the magic field gathering around him when he recites poetry, so he can't interact with it?"

"If that is what a wizard doth, aye. I would not know; I have not that Gift."

"Yes. Of course." Matt cleared his throat. "And these, uh, people who *do* have the Gift—does it do *them* any good, without training?"

"It may," Stegoman said judiciously, "though an untrained man, only newly aware of his gift, is far more likely to destroy himself and everyone near him. Why, I cannot say—but I've heard of many such cases."

"How *very* interesting! Do you realize I've been a walking

critical mass every time I've worked a spell? It's worth your *life* to be near me!"

"Nay," Stegoman said, with full certainty. "*Thou* art a learned man; *thy* spells are safe."

"Yeah, well..." Matt's eye fell on the riding habit. "I think the princess must be thoroughly clean by now." He had a brief flash of Alisande wading out of the stream and tried hard to suppress it; the euphoria wasn't worth the dizziness it caused him.

"Aye." Stegoman's head swooped down to the clothing. He mumbled something that Matt couldn't understand through the fabric and turned to scrabble back to the stream, leaving Matt sitting alone on the log, head in his hands, wishing very heartily that he was nowhere but in his own cluttered, messy apartment.

"Master Wizard."

"Unh?" Matt jerked his head up, dimly aware that he'd been lost in a fog of reminiscence.

Then he saw Alisande. If she'd been beautiful before, she was staggering now. The green gown set off the gold of her hair in a radiant halo, and her wide eyes were huge in the gaunt-cheeked face, almost enveloping...

She smiled roguishly and laughed, pirouetting. "You have excellent taste, sir. If you should ever wish to forsake magic, I doubt not you'd do famously as a couturier...Now!" She snapped to a halt, facing him, skirts swirling about her. "You have done so well by my clothing, I pray you—can you remedy near-starvation? I've had naught but a few mouthfuls a day for a fortnight!"

"Uh—sure," Matt mumbled, eyes glued to her. He squeezed his eyes shut, gave his head a quick shake, and didn't open them again till he'd turned away from the princess. Her laugh trilled about him, warm and melodious.

Food! If she had been on a starvation diet, she shouldn't eat much at once, and even that ought to be easy to digest. Soup!

> "Beautiful soup, so rich and green,
>   Awaiting in a hot tureen!
>   Who for such dainties would not stoop?
>   Appear before us, wondrous soup!"

And soup there was, complete with a hot tureen.

Alisande started, then stared at the tureen. Slowly, her brow furrowed.

Matt also frowned. "What's the matter? Prefer bouillon?"

"Nay, the dish is fine, sir, and so's that which is in it, but . . . Well, I had in mind your perchance hunting a hare."

Matt's lips thinned. "You shouldn't eat anything solid, if you're nearly starved. Maybe you'd like me to dig up a silver service, too!"

"Nay, nay!" She waved impatiently. "I fault not your efforts, Master Wizard. But, little though I know of magic, I *have* heard one should be chary of its use. It must not be tossed about at every whim or small desire. If it's not treated with respect, it may treat its user with contempt and cause much trouble."

"Isn't that a bit much?" Matt demanded. "It isn't a person, with emotions and a personality; magic's just a force, a kind of energy, impersonal and—"

A cloud of yellow smoke erupted with a *whoosh!* twenty feet away, in the meadow.

Matt swiveled to face it, his back hair standing on end. Then the first whiff of smoke hit. Sulfur! What was in that cloud, anyway?

It tattered in the breeze and blew away, revealing an ancient crone in a black, hooded robe, with a nose and chin that hooked to meet each other below yellowed, rheumy eyes. A few warts completed the effect.

"And what have we here?" she whined. "Surely it would be nothing less than another Bright Young Wizard! I said to myself, as soon as I felt two piddling spells in the half of an hour, 'Molestam, who else would be tossing magic about as if it were cracklings?' So I came for a look and, sure enough, there he is, fairly burning with ambition to oust poor old Molestam and have her lands for his own, to terrorize and bleed! If there's aught I despise, 'tis a pushy new magician!"

"Madam!" Matt straightened, trying to look the soul of offended righteousness. "I assure you, I have no—"

"As if there weren't enough competition in the magic business as it is!" Molestam wheezed. "Just when you think you're secure and can settle down to lord it over your own terrified peasants in peace, there's another cheeky young challenger to be put in his place. Not like the old days, it isn't, when a person could mind her own business and milk her own peasants, and no one to trouble her a bit about it. But now, a body can't do the first thing she wants in her own country, no she can't, especially not since that upstart Malingo started throwing his weight around. But not in my district! Let any young wonder-worker try his hand here and he'll not have a hand left—nor his life!" Her arms sliced down in an arc, fingers writhing into an intricate symbol while she shrieked,

"Murrain and jaundice now all betide ye,
    May Hell's devils and demons all leap a—"

"Nay!" Stegoman roared, leaping forward, and a ten-foot tongue of flame slashed out before him.

Molestam looked up, startled and horrified; then her eyes narrowed, and her symbol-hand darted out at Stegoman.

"By all the foul gargoyles that ever did plan it,
    Turn this fool monster to basalt and granite!"

Stegoman froze as if he'd been dropped into a block of quick-setting plastic. Slowly, his scales darkened into dull, black stone.

"Get down!" Matt shoved the princess into a dip in the ground and threw himself in after her. With that much carbon-based compound suddenly transmuted into silicon, there might be a hellish lot of loose radiation in the air, and he wasn't taking any chances. At least now they were out of the line of sight.

Above them he heard Molestam's voice screeching closer. "Ye'll not hide from me, audacious youth! I'll seek ye and find ye, and then woe betide ye!"

"Can you not stop her?" Alisande demanded.

"I'll try," Matt said grimly. He whirled a finger about as if he were spinning a top and chanted:

"Now the crone begins turning, just like a corkscrew,
    And her rash revolution I think she'll soon rue.
    For her conduct was such that she's long overdue
    To be drilled down to bedrock and vanish from view!"

With a startled screech, Molestam began to turn on her pointed toes. She howled with despair as she reached dervish speed. Her toes bit into the earth, and her whole body began to sink into the ground.

Then Matt began to regret the extremity of the fate he'd decreed. She was an evil witch, but he had no proof she deserved the death penalty. He set his jaw and added lines:

> "She is drilling through rock, but she'll come out alive,
> Where it's lightless and damp, down at full fathom five.
> She will spend her last days driving Pluto's pale kine,
> Where it's dark as a dungeon and deep as a mine!"

With one last tearing shriek of rage, the witch sank out of sight.

The princess sank against Matt with a sigh, limp with relief. He took hold of her elbows, holding her up. "All right. It's all right now. She's gone, and we're alive."

"Aye. We live." Alisande seemed to recollect her royalty. Her body moved a little from him. Matt was staring at what had been Stegoman, and she followed his gaze. "Oh, the dragon! The poor beast!"

Matt stepped toward the unwilling statue. "Well, he can't feel pain, at least. Let's see if we can do something about that. Uh, I mean . . ."

"Aye, I know." The princess caught up her skirts and came after him. "But what's to be done, Wizard?"

"I don't know," Matt admitted, coming to the statue. He laid a hand on the neck. "It's warm—but not hot. Look at the detail! If this were sculpture, I'd say it was the greatest piece of kitsch I ever saw!"

"'Tis your friend, not a statue," Alisande reminded him with a touch of apserity. "How will you thaw him?"

"Thaw? No, your Highness, I don't think it's so much a matter of thawing as of ontogeny recapitulating philogony."

"Of *what*?"

"The development of the individual summarizing the history of the species." Danger from new spells or not, the dragon was his friend, and he had to make an effort. "Some people claim all life began as chemicals leached out of rock by rain."

"What nonsense is this?" Alisande demanded. "All know God created life."

"Yes, but the accounts don't say much about how He went about it. Better get far away, your Highness. This might be dangerous."

The princess started to speak, then turned away, murmuring, "I prithee, take care. Your welfare concerns me."

"Me, too," Matt said absently, his mind on the problem. He decided that he'd need both vocal and physical symbols—rhymes and gestures. He should probably make allusions to evolution and God, and reinforce them by holding out a hand, totally stiff, then having it move a little and then more, like a statue coming to life.

He took a deep breath, stepped back, and began:

> "When at first the Lord all life was giving,
> Stone was leached to make a broth of living.
> Stone thus helped to turn the seas vermilion;
> Thing of stone, become once more reptilian!"

His hand undulated like a snake in a high breeze. He held his breath and hoped.

With a crackle like a thousand shards of ice breaking, Stegoman slowly turned his head. The dull gray eyes became milky; black pinpoints appeared in their centers and expanded into pupils and irises. The whole great length of body shivered, turning slowly to dark green. The dragon closed his eyes and stretched his jaw in a yawn. "What has happened, Wizard? Each separate muscle within me is leaden and sore."

Matt heaved a sigh of relief. "You were stoned, Stegoman. The real, authentic condition."

"Aye, I remember." The dragon smacked his jaws together. "The foul witch laid an enchantment upon me. Thou hast bested her, then?" He didn't sound particularly surprised about it. "Tell me the manner of it."

"Another time." Matt's knees began to tremble. He sat down abruptly on the grass, bowing his head between his legs.

"What ails thee?" Stegoman growled.

"Is he well?" It was Alisande's voice. "Oh! Pray nothing has happened to him! 'Twould be too unfair, after he strove so bravely against the witch and worked such wonders."

Matt shoved himself to his feet by grabbing a handhold on Stegoman. "No, it's—it's nothing. Just delayed reaction from this magic. It takes a lot out of a guy."

"Aye, but there's more of you left than was taken." She latched onto his arm, beaming up at him, eyes shining. "Assuredly, you are the bravest, most valiant of magi! Who else would attempt a new spell, risking destruction, to break a foul enchantment for a comrade? Surely you are the most worthy of wizards!"

That almost made it all worthwhile.

Stegoman looked startled. "How? Thou didst attempt a *new* spell to free me?"

"I had to." Matt shrugged. "I didn't happen to have any old ones."

"I am thy boon companion henceforth," Stegoman said firmly. "Thou shalt not taste of danger but I shall be with thee! How hast thou done this thing?"

"It's called novelty." Coming from a different culture definitely gave Matt a larger arsenal of spells than the average magician. "Something new always impresses people."

"Indeed!" Alisande affirmed. "What was this nonsense you told me of being a green and untried wizard? No venerable veteran could have done better!"

"Well, thanks. But there really wasn't much of an alternative."

"Would you have wished one?"

"As a matter of fact, I would. I'm not exactly the kind who likes a high profile, you know."

Dragon and maiden stood speechless. Scandalized, but speechless.

"It's Malingo," Matt explained. "You heard the old witch mention him, didn't you? That makes me wonder—did she bushwhack me on her own? Or did somebody put her up to it? I don't know how well-outfitted Malingo is with crystal balls and pools of ink, but I'd lay out very good odds he was watching us every minute."

"Ah." Alisande sobered. "He has a more stringent measure of you now."

"Just what I was thinking," Matt said glumly, "and I'm sure he's not done with the yardstick yet. What will he send after us next? A small demon?"

"'Tis no matter," Alisande said brightly. "You will defeat it." She sounded absolutely sure about it.

"Come, sir!" Alisande whirled away to scoop up a dead willow branch, then pirouetted to face Matt, holding the wand like a sceptre. "Approach me and kneel!"

Matt stared, dumfounded. Then he opened his mouth to protest, but Stegoman nudged into him, muttering, "Do as she doth direct, Wizard. Do not question royalty; she doth know her purpose and is sure of her deeds."

Matt shut his jaws and slogged forward, determined to do whatever Alisande asked, no matter how asinine—within reason, of course.

"Kneel," the princess commanded when he'd come about five feet away from her. Matt dropped to one knee, leaning his elbow on his kneecap—and was suddenly hit by the absurdity of his posture. Who was he—Sir Walter Raleigh? He hunched over and bowed his head, trying to hide a smirk.

"Matthew Mantrell," Alisande intoned, "you have this day proven your mettle and power, in battle against the powers of wickedness, in our service. Wherefore, this day, do we recognize your worth; and therefore will we accept from you oaths of loyalty and fealty, to bind you henceforth to the end of your days."

Matt fought to keep his head down and bit back an outraged squawk. Oaths! She'd accept them, would she? And what if he didn't want to give them?

Hold on, boy. Calm down. Remember where you are, what the rules are. You have to swear fealty to somebody, here. If you don't, you're an outlaw—or a king.

"Be not anxious; I'll speak the words; you've but to repeat them," Alisande whispered, for all the world as though they were in a cathedral, with a multitude listening. Matt's chuckle tried to burble its way up his throat again. He swallowed it sternly and looked up at the princess.

"Do you swear to serve us all the days of your life?" Alisande demanded.

"I do." What was this—a wedding?

"Will you, forever after this moment, answer our summons with all speed and haste, forsaking all other business and interests of the moment?"

A bit strong, maybe, but basically nothing more than a policeman or fireman had to do. "I swear that, whatever problem or pleasure occupies my attention, I shall cease to have interest in it when your Highness shall call." Might as well embroider it a little.

It was the right choice; Alisande looked pleased. "And will you, in defense of our honor and rightful claims, never spare of your labor and power, setting all fear and danger behind you?"

"I swear to work and to fight for your Highness's honor and rights, setting all weariness, fear, hesitation, and doubt far behind me, whenever your Highness shall call."

It was just a paraphrase of her own words, but Alisande beamed.

"And I, for my part, swear loyalty, justice, and mercy to you as my vassal, for now, and for all of my life; and, in thanks for your loyalty and in recognition of your worth, I do accord you honor, valor, strength of arm and of heart, and all knowledge and skill you shall need to traffic and fight for me with body and spirit— and a rightful place in my councils and among the peers of my realm. And I grant you the estates of Borvere, Angueleau, and Poilene, to you and the heirs of your body, till the end of your line."

She swirled the willow wand around in a flourish and planted its butt on the ground between them. "In recognition whereof, I set my hand to this staff. Do you so also?"

Matt reached out and grabbed the branch, a little dazed by the honors suddenly showered upon him, and very much amused. He had a place among the peers of her realm—if she won her realm back! And he had family estates—if he could ever kick out the present incumbents. Still, he had to admit it wasn't bad for a couple of fugitives in the middle of a meadow.

"Now are our hands joined to and by the wood of this land," Alisande said solemnly, "as it is joined to the land itself, from which it did spring. Earth, air, and water have made it; earth, air, and water now witness our oaths. You are my vassal, and I am your suzerain." She lifted the staff away. "Rise, Matthew Mantrell, Lord Wizard of Merovence!"

Matt rose slowly and, somehow, without the slightest inclination to giggle. She had called in, for witnesses, three of the four ancient Greek elements, the primal stuffs of which the universe was made. The land of Merovence was the seal and the bond between its royal house and a homeless vagabond. With a sudden, chilling prickle of memory, Matt remembered the power of words here and realized what the consequent power of an oath should be.

Alisande clapped her hands on his shoulders and leaned forward to kiss him on both cheeks. "Never have I been prouder to swear to a bond. You are mine own wizard now, Matthew Mantrell— wizard to the rightful queen, Lord Wizard!"

Then it hit Matt—he was a lord! The wildest dreams of his childhood fairy tales had come true! He was an aristocrat!

Dazed, with eyes glazed, he focused on her face. "Your Highness—your Majesty that should be—I'm not worthy..."

"Yet thou art," Stegoman rumbled behind him. "Thou art a good man, Matthew Mantrell, and a most puissant wizard."

"Yeah," Matt mumbled. He looked up at Alisande. "Uh, say, by the way—those estates you mentioned—who's the current holder?"

Alisande's eyes widened in surprise, "Why, the false Lord Wizard, of course—Malingo!"

Slowly, Matt pursed his lips. "Yes," he said, nodding. "How stupid of me. I should have realized, shouldn't I?"

"Pay no heed to it." Alisande's smile was full of gentle understanding as she took his arm. "When you have learned our ways, such things will come to you as quickly and lightly as breath."

"Yes, of course," Matt said, with a sardonic smile. "Till then, I suppose I'll just have to muddle through, won't I?"

He reflected that some things are the same in any culture— for instance, a setup.

CHAPTER 6

"Ho!" cried a distant voice.

Matt whirled about, startled.

And there he was—a real, authentic, plate-armor knight, way out there in the meadow, trotting toward them. The armor was black, and the horse was humongous. The knight held an oversized toothpick slanting up at an angle, waving the pennant at its tip.

Matt squeezed his eyes shut. "Oh, no. Tell me I didn't see it."

"Wherefore, Lord Wizard?" The princess knit her brows, puzzled. "Dost fear him?"

"Well, now that you mention it, yes—though that wasn't exactly what I had in mind. You'll pardon the cynicism, Princess, but as we stand now, I think we're better off assuming any stranger's an enemy, until he proves otherwise."

"But you need not fear a knight!" she protested. "They are all bound by honor, sir—even those who oppose us!"

"Even Malingo's knights?"

The princess reddened and lifted her chin a few notches. "They are foul, treacherous brutes who may lay no claim at all to the title of knight."

"Oh, definitely not. The fact that they ride Percherons, wear armor, and carry great big, sharp swords has nothing to do with it."

"Exactly." She beamed. "You learn our ways quickly, Lord Wizard."

It took Matt a minute to realize she was quite serious.

He turned back to the approaching rider, who was about fifty yards off now. "Yes, but how can we be sure this guy isn't one of Malingo's?"

"Why, because he wears black armor."

Matt dipped his head and came up looking at her. "Whoa, now! Isn't that supposed to mean he's an evil one, or something like that?"

"Why, no." Alisande seemed genuinely astonished. "In Heaven's name, Lord Matthew, what could let you think that? His armor means simply that he is a free lance, a knight unsworn to any lord—that is all."

Matt held her eyes for a long moment; then he spoke slowly. "Yes, of course—no economic security. He doesn't have the money or facilities to keep his armor polished. That it?"

"Precisely; and therefore doth he paint it black."

"Very practical." Matt turned back to the approaching rider. "But what's to keep one of Malingo's boys from painting *his* armor black?"

"Why, 'twould be dishonest, sir!"

Matt bit back the natural response.

The Black Knight pulled up his horse a little away from them and swung his lance upright in salute. "Hail, most fair lady! Hail, sir! Hail, you of the most free!"

"Well met, Sir Knight," Stegoman answered. Matt nodded acknowledgment; but Alisande said, "Well met indeed, Sir Knight! Your name and your arms?"

The knight laughed, amused, and hauled an empty, black-painted shield around to face them. "These are my arms, lady; any others I own, I may not reveal till an oath be fulfilled. As for my name, I am Sir Guy Losobal, for all men to know!"

Why not? Matt reflected sourly. "Losobal" was close enough to the French "Le Sable" for Matt to be pretty sure it was this universe's equivalent. In other words, Sir Guy the Black Knight. Very informative.

But he couldn't be outdone for courtesy, could he? "Well met, Sir Guy. I am Matthew Mantrell, liegeman to this lady."

"Ah, a liegeman!" From the tone, Sir Guy was licking his chops. "Come, then! Will you not break a lance with me?"

Matt goggled.

Recovering, he managed a feeble grin. "Gee, thanks for the invitation, Sir Guy, but I don't think I'm hard enough. It would just go right through me."

Sir Guy chuckled. "Most amusing, sir! But come—will you not ride against me, with a lance in your hand?"

"I'd love to oblige you," Matt hedged, "but I don't have a lance. Not to mention little things such as armor or a horse."

"Why, how is this?" Sir Guy's lance drooped. "A knight without armor or arms?"

"You labor under a misapprehension," Alisande informed him. "Lord Matthew is my liegeman, but is not a knight."

Sir Guy sat very still for a moment.

Inwardly, Matt groaned. Didn't this princess know never to give free information to the opposition? If he was a lord, and her liegeman, what was she?

Sir Guy turned toward Matt and asked in a rather cool tone, "How can you be lordly, without being knighted?" Then, before Matt could answer, he nodded. "Of course! You are a wizard!"

"Quick thinking," Matt approved. In fact, maybe too quick. "You'll understand, then, that I'm not exactly outfitted for a tournament."

"Nay, certes! One could not expect a wizard to fight with sword or lance!" Sir Guy's voice became velvet itself. "It would seem, then, that we must find weapons we both may use, with good conscience."

Matt shrugged. "Got any handy?"

"These." Sir Guy yanked off his gauntlets and held up his fists. "The peasant's weapons, that all men do own to."

Matt's smile vanished. Sure, he'd done the usual fist fighting when he was a boy and had even had a YMCA boxing class when he was a teenager—but that had been more than ten years ago. Still, a knight might be very well-trained with sword, spear, lance, mace, and battle-axe—but wrestling was for peasants, and Matt couldn't remember offhand any reference to boxing in medieval literature.

He nodded slowly. "Sounds good, Sir Guy. I'll try you a couple of rounds."

He walked past the Princess's shocked stare, shrugging off his sport coat. Sir Guy grinned, swung down from his horse, and got busy unbuckling his armor.

"Art thou mad?" Stegoman demanded, lumbering up near him. "This knight is trained in all forms of martial exercise!"

"*All* forms?" Matt raised a skeptical eyebrow. "I didn't think there was much training in fist fighting here."

"Indeed, 'tis mere brawling and could not be glorified with study of system and method; yet he is a warrior. And thou?"

"I," Matt said grimly, "have had *some* training in the use of my fists, including the system and method you sneer at—which *should* give me an edge, even in so lowly a sport."

"Sport? Nay, good Lord Matthew! Be assured, this knight will not fight in jest!"

"A point to consider," Matt said, nodding. "Even if this is more of a social bout than anything else, he'll still fight for keeps. Thanks for the reminder."

"Are you in readiness?" Sir Guy asked, stepping out into the meadow and holding up his fists. He'd stripped down to a loose linen shirt and trousers. Matt eyed the padding he'd tossed on top of his armor and decided the man might be ethical.

"Ready whenever you are, Sir Guy." He stepped forward, holding up his own fists.

He was right about having an edge. Sir Guy had the right crouch, but his fists were only chest-high, and at the same distance from his body. Which one did he think he was going to block with?

Good question—but Matt remembered Sir Guy holding his lance in his right hand. No, he wasn't a southpaw.

Matt started circling, warily. Sir Guy held his ground, rotating to follow him. Matt realized the knight was studying him closely, taking his measure, and returned the compliment. Sir Guy was on the short side, by Matt's standards—five eight or so. Of course, that was above average height here. But he was heavily muscled, with shoulders that would have done credit to an ox, and with an oiled smoothness to his movements that spoke of speed and precision. He had shiny black hair, cut straight across the forehead in front, ear-length at the temples, and halfway down his neck behind the ears. Very military—no hair to get in his eyes, but enough at the back to help protect his neck, in case chain mail and quilted padding didn't quite make it. He had a sleek black moustache that trailed down past the corners of his mouth, a square chin, large eyes set wide apart, and a nose that had been broken at least once. All in all, though, he looked friendly, cheerful—and wide open.

Suddenly Sir Guy moved, like a turnstile at rush hour—fast and abrupt, the right-hand side of his body slashing forward in a roundhorse lunge. Matt jumped, but a little too late—rock-hard knuckles jarred his cheekbone, and he staggered back through an instant of black shot with bright points of light. He kept on going back, though, shaking his head—Sir Guy wasn't the kind to allow recovery time.

His vision cleared, and he saw Sir Guy leaping forward, fist swinging down in an overhand chop. Matt shot up his left. Pain exploded in his forearm, and a small rock bit his skull, bringing black back as the grass slipped from under his feet and, a second later, struck his shoulders. *I've fallen*, he realized, surprised, and rolled, fast. But no feet kicked at him, and his vision cleared as he flipped up to his knees. Sir Guy stood waiting, smiling, amused.

Now, that was a predicament—being halfway up and having a set of muscles on two feet waiting for him to get up the rest of the way. Matt was sorely tempted to hold it right there.

Then he caught sight of Alisande, out of the corner of his eye.

She stood, straining forward, huge-eyed and pale, staring at Matt with pain etched in her face. Somehow, he just couldn't quit outright, with her watching like that.

He levered himself to his feet. Sir Guy was on him, right swinging around and up in a haymaker uppercut. Matt finally placed his style—broadsword.

He'd also placed Sir Guy's strength—phenomenal. No use trying to block that swing; Sir Guy would just drive on through, knocking Matt's arm back against him again. He leaned back, letting the haymaker slice past him, fanning his face, while he remembered a cutting man's weak spot—the lunge. Sir Guy was used to chopping, not stabbing.

So, while Sir Guy's fist was following through on its swing, Matt jabbed—hard.

Sir Guy saw it coming and flipped up his arm, throwing Matt's punch higher than he'd aimed; he caught the knight on the cheekbone—and nearly howled. The man was *hard*! But Sir Guy's head rocked, and he looked surprised.

Then the fist that had just finished the uppercut chopped down, backhanded.

Matt leaped back, not quite in time; knuckles sizzled across his chest. But he knocked the hand further aside and stepped in, throwing a right straight from the shoulder.

And Sir Guy's left snapped up, knocking Matt's arm toward the sky.

It threw Matt off balance; he lurched forward and slammed into Sir Guy's shoulder. The knight gave under him, then steadied. Matt snatched a quick glance at his face; Sir Guy smiled, eyebrows raised. "We become too familiar, Lord Wizard."

"No, I'm just getting to know you." Matt shoved against the knight's bulk and leaped backward, fists up. He should have realized Sir Guy would block well with his left—he was used to a shield.

The knight followed after him, slashing back and forth with his right. Matt backpedaled, waiting, and timed it; then he dropped low in a crouch and jabbed at Sir Guy's belly. Sure enough, the left dropped down to block—and Matt swung up for the chin, from the hips.

His fist smashed against Sir Guy's jaw, and the knight's head snapped back. Matt recovered, snapping his body back into a tight fetal crouch—but Sir Guy kept on leaning back until he toppled over.

Matt froze in the crouch, staring at the slack, unconscious body in disbelief.

Then, slowly, he straightened up, lowering his fists—carefully; he still expected Sir Guy to roll to his feet and start swinging. But the Black Knight was out cold, and Matt finally let himself begin to believe it.

There was a rustle of cloth, and he heard Alisande's voice, as dumfounded as he was: "You have beaten him, Wizard!"

Matt stared at the supine body. "Thank Heaven for small favors!"

"Nay, thank thy skill," rumbled Stegoman, beside him. "Thou hast beaten a full-belted knight, Matthew Mantrell, by force of thine arms and skill of thy body!"

Matt turned slowly, frowning. "Well, thanks—but I have a nasty suspicion I didn't."

"How so?" A trickle of smoke oozed from Stegoman's jaws.

"I think I won by a decision."

"Thou hast laid him low! What decision's in that?"

"His," Matt said sourly.

Alisande was kneeling over Sir Guy, patting his cheek, chafing his wrists, and murmuring soothing chants. The Black Knight blinked; then his eyes locked onto the princess, appalled. "'Zwounds! I have, then, been beaten?"

"Afraid so." Matt stepped up. "Just luck, though, Sir Knight. You definitely knew what you were doing; I didn't."

"Nay! That was no blow of fortune you felled me with; 'twas planned—and quite well!" Sir Guy rolled up to one knee. "I must kneel to you now, Lord Wizard; and, since you were the victor, yet spared me, I must in all honor swear fealty to you, to serve at your right hand, to make my body your shield and your enemies mine, till I've defeated the worst of them! And so do I swear, Matthew Mantrell, Lord Wizard!"

"Uh—well, I guess that's the best offer I've had since I came here," Matt said lamely. He sidled over to Alisande. "Can I turn him down?"

"You can, though 'twould be grievous insult," she murmured back.

"Went a little bit overboard, didn't he?"

"Somewhat," Alisande admitted. "An expression of honor and profound respect would have sufficed, by all rules of chivalry. Still, 'tis not unheard of."

That, Matt reflected, was the grinding part. If it was allowable under the unwritten rules of chivalry, it was almost obligatory for him to accept.

Sir Guy waited, watching him with a merry eye. *He knows* exactly *what he's done*, Matt realized, with slow, burning, resentment.

"You should accept him," the princess said, with sudden, total certainty.

That rocked Matt—not so much that she advocated accepting Sir Guy, but the sureness with which she said it. Did she see something in the Black Knight that he didn't see?

Sure—muscles. And, now that he thought about it, Sir Guy wasn't bad-looking—handsome, in fact.

"Are you sure?" he whispered. "Remember, if I say yes, he's an official part of our party, indefinitely!"

"I am mindful of it." The princess was giving the knight a long, speculative look. "And I mind me we're few and need every sword we can trust."

"Trust? We scarcely know his name! In fact, we don't—not all of it, anyway!"

"Naetheless, we can trust him. I'm sure of it."

She was, too—very sure. You could hear it in her voice. For a moment, jealousy flared; Matt couldn't help it. But he forced it to the back of his mind and turned back to Sir Guy. "I accept your proffer of loyalty, Sir Knight, and thank you from the depth of my heart."

Alisande was watching him, expectantly.

Matt sighed. He'd read enough about chivalry to know what she expected of him. "And I, in my turn, swear loyalty to thee, till this conflict be finished, or one of us dies."

Sir Guy's moustache hooked up around a grin. "Done!" And he leaped to his feet, clasping Matt's hand. "I am your sword and your shield till we die, or the worst of your enemies does! Where do we wander, Lord Wizard?"

Matt wished he could escape the feeling that he'd been conned. "Wherever her Highness says." Then he remembered his manners. "Uh, your Highness Princess Alisande—may I present Sir Guy Losobal."

Sir Guy's eyebrows shot up. "The Princess Alisande!"

"You know of me, then." Alisande extended her hand, and Sir Guy dropped to one knee to kiss it. The princess nodded, pleased with Sir Guy's courtliness, while Matt fumed. "And knowing who I am, Sir Guy—have you second thoughts as to joining our party?"

"But wherefore?" Sir Guy asked in surprise. "What I have sworn, I have sworn—and if I have enlisted in a noble cause, so much the better."

He said it so easily that Matt found himself sure Sir Guy hadn't bumped into them by accident—but the princess looked very pleased indeed. "Well, then, sirs!" she said, looking from Sir Guy to Matt and back. "What is your counsel? Whither should we march?"

"Away from your enemies," Sir Guy said, totally serious. "We are too few to encounter them successfully."

"Uh, toward your friends," Matt amplified. "I'm afraid we do need numbers."

"The greatest of my friends is the giant Colmain," the princess said judiciously. "He helped Deloman, the founder of my family, to win to his throne three centuries ago."

"Aye, he slew the foul giants that plundered our land," Stegoman added, "and locked the accursed titan Ballspear in combat, till the blessed wizard Moncaire could change him to stone."

"Accursed?" Matt propped up an eyebrow. "Ballspear? What was so bad about him?"

"What was not?" Stegoman snapped, spitting sparks. "He led the foul horde in their looting, caught fledglings in flight from the air for his food, and crushed mothers and hatchlings beneath his vast feet! A thousand foul tales we tell of him still." Flame licked and curled around his mouth as he finished.

Matt noted the emotion. "Yes, I see why the dragon folk would curse him. And if Colmain could beat him, or even hold him in a stalemate, I see why we should go looking for him."

"Yet Colmain himself is now stone," Sir Guy pointed out. " 'Twas the last, vindictive stroke of Dimethtus the sorcerer, when Deloman came against him, with Colmain and Conor the wizard, besting his troops and his powers of Evil."

"This I know as well as my name," Alisande answered, unruffled. "Yet also I know that a wizard accompanies me." She turned to Matt. "How say you, Lord Wizard? Can you turn a stone giant to flesh, even as you did with Master Stegoman?"

Matt remembered he was supposed to be a great wizard now. He spread his hands, shrugging. "What can I say, Highness? I'll give it my best shot."

"No more can I ask." She seemed far too satisfied.

"You might ask for an army," Sir Guy reminded her, "and you will find one in the West. Thence am I lately come—and they are strong, Highness, in all things but hope. Landless barons I saw, leading troops of knights whose suzerains had died, hiding in forest and glen, and riding out to harass the enemy. Yet most gather at monasteries, at houses of God, where the powers of Evil are weakened and confounded. Here gather peasants whose homes have been destroyed, masterless knights, landless barons, and all the good clergy who escaped Astaulf's sword. Strong in arms and in fighters they are, and armored with courage!"

"Yet you say they lack hope?" the princess demanded, frowning.

"Aye, Highness. Beneath their courage and faith, their foundations are crumbling—for who, they ask, can rise up to lead them? King Kaprin is dead, his daughter imprisoned. Who, then, shall win the throne from Astaulf? And how can they triumph, with no one to win? So they fight, determined that Evil shall fall along with them—but believing nothing shall rise."

"I must to them!" Alisande cried, her face flaming. "They must see me and know that their princess is free!"

"But they're in the West," Matt reminded her. "Where's Colmain?"

"Why, in the West also," Alisande cried. "He stands in the far western mountains, guarding our land in a long, silent vigil."

"Oh."

"Aye." Sir Guy nodded in sympathy. "There is no real choice. Bordestang lies in the East, with her enemies; Colmain stands in the West, with her friends. Where else could she go?"

"Unfortunately, I can't help thinking Malingo will figure that out, too," Matt pointed out. "You don't really think he's just going to let us ride peaceably along toward a welcoming army, do you?"

Sir Guy shrugged. "That lies at hazard, Lord Wizard. There is no war without risk; it must be borne."

"Maybe a slightly more devious route . . ."

"Nay." Alisande's voice rang like a bell. "If we deal in the devious, Lord Matthew, we lose—for Malingo is leagued with the powers of Evil, of prevarication and deviousness. If we wish to triumph against him, we must be open, honest, direct. We must travel west; I *know* this to be our best course!"

"With all due respect, your Highness, that might be good morality, but it's lousy strategy."

"What!" Sir Guy cried, scandalized. "You doubt the word of blood royal?"

Matt smiled thinly. "Titles don't mean quite so much where I come from, Sir Guy."

"Yet thou art not in thine homeland," Stegoman rumbled at his shoulder, "and art now bound by the rules of this world, not thine own."

Matt's smile soured as he turned to the dragon. "Here or at home, Stegoman, a title by itself means nothing."

"Yet blood royal does," Sir Guy declared. "A king or queen cannot be mistaken!"

"Oh, come off it!" Matt cried, exasperated. "There isn't a human being alive who never makes a mistake!"

"There do, an they be kings and queens," said Stegoman, "in matters politic, whether they be of the public weal, affairs of state, or the conduct of war."

"In these matters, royalty's infallibly right." Sir Guy spoke more gently, patiently. "There are those among men who are gifted,

Lord Wizard—you above all should know that for truth. And there are many sorts of Gifts, as there are types of people. He who is right in all matters public is made king, for the welfare of all—and those who inherit his blood inherit also his Gifts."

It did kind of make sense, in its own weird way. Matt couldn't deny, now, that magic worked here—he'd done it too often. And if he could have the Gift of magic, why couldn't Alisande have infallibility by Divine Right?

No reason, really. None he could think of.

He looked up at Alisande, a little sheepishly. "Uh—your Highness thinks we oughta go west?"

"I do," she said, very seriously. "'Tis our best chance."

Matt stood looking at her. Then he nodded. "Right."

He turned to Stegoman. "Care to come along? Seems like a shame to bust up the old gang now."

"Shame, indeed." Stegoman nodded. "'Twould shame me greatly, to abandon a princess in quest of her rightful crown."

"It's not exactly going to be guaranteed safe," Matt warned.

"Yet it will, at least, be of interest. Life can grow dull, Wizard."

I'd just love to be bored, Matt thought. Still, he could see Stegoman's point. With none of his own kind around, and not much chance of ever being with them again, there wasn't much to do but watch the antics of these quaint two-legged creatures. "Good to have you, Stegoman."

The dragon fixed him with a glittering eye. "How goodly?"

Matt halted, feeling a bargaining session coming on. "Uh, what did you have in mind?"

Stegoman glanced at Sir Guy and the princess. "Come aside with me; this is talk for dragon and wizard, and need not concern other folk."

"Uh—excuse me, your Highness. Sir Guy." Matt touched his forelock apologetically and followed Stegoman.

The dragon only moved about fifty feet off before he growled, out of the corner of his mouth, "There is . . . a certain matter in which . . . Well, if a wizard cannot manage it, none can . . . 'Tis one which doth touch me tenderly, a matter which . . . well, no doctor of physic could mend it, so . . ."

Matt suddenly recognized that Stegoman was trying to talk about something extremely embarrassing to him; the dragon couldn't quite bring himself to put it into words.

"A—a matter of appendages," Matt supplied. "Of certain members which are as vital to your people as hands are to mine?"

"One could say that, yes." The dragon growled it, but Matt caught a definite undertone of relief at not having to say it. "Canst thou mend where doctors of physic must fail?"

"I don't know . . . I certainly don't know any spell that would do what you want. Not offhand. But give me some time, and I might be able to work something out."

"Well enough." Stegoman shook his shoulders, as if he could already feel his wings healing. "I can ask no more, Wizard. Be assured I shall serve thee with each last ounce of strength and of skill I possess."

"Uh, wait! I can't *promise* anything, you know."

"What dost thou take me for?" The dragon glared down at him. "This is no bargain, mortal, but a bond of honor between us. I shall do as well as I may for thee and thine and will trust to thine honor to do thy best for me."

"I stand corrected." Somehow, Matt felt very much ashamed. "And I thank you deeply, Stegoman."

"Let us hope it is I who shall thank thee." The dragon turned back, lifting his head. "Shall we rejoin them?"

Matt slogged back to Sir Guy and the princess, watching the dragon out of the corner of his eye and feeling very glum. He'd just promised to do something that he hadn't the faintest idea how to manage; and on top of that, he knew there was no damn use trying to heal Stegoman's wings until he could cure his drunkenness. If he didn't, Stegoman would go home, get gloriously high off his own fumes, and take to the air as a menace to flying society. The other dragons would then just clip his wings again and send him back into exile. No, Matt definitely had to cure the drunkenness first.

But how? Matt didn't know anything about reptilian biochemistry, aside from their being cold-blooded—and he wasn't even sure about that, when it came to a fire-breathing dragon.

Whoa! Biochemistry might have nothing to do with it! Matt remembered Stegoman's diatribe against hatchling hunters, when Matt had first transported him to the dungeon. Why would *that* have occurred to the dragon, instead of sorcery, which was much more apparent? Evidence of a childhood trauma? Matt knew a little basic psychology and he had a good feel for people. The more he thought about it, the more it made sense—Steogman's drunkenness was psychosomatic!

But why would a trauma involving dragon hunters result in a propensity for getting stoned?

Wait a minute—Stegoman came from a military culture. He couldn't admit fear of anything, even to himself. The way that he'd charged at Molestam the witch bore that out—an overcompensation, rash boldness masking fear. Could his *real* problem be fear of flying?

But he couldn't admit that, even to himself—so instead, he got drunk when he breathed fire. Obviously, therefore, he couldn't be allowed to fly, which would take him out of the air, through no fault of his own.

But if Stegoman was getting what he really subconsciously wanted, he'd be murder to cure! And Matt knew he bore about as much resemblance to a psychiatrist as a photon does to the sun.

But he'd promised he'd try.

He hadn't set any definite time on his attempt, though. And they had time, all the way to the mountains. Maybe he'd think of something en route . . .

"Are you ready?" Alisande asked as they came up. Sir Guy was buckled into his armor again, his hand on the saddle.

"Ready as we'll ever be, I guess . . ."

"Come, sir! Be merry!" Sir Guy vaulted into his saddle. "We embark on a glorious quest! Pluck up your spirit; have joy in your heart!" He reached down to grip the princess's forearm. "Mount, and away!"

The princess leaped up, sitting sideways behind him with an arm round his waist. Sir Guy kicked his horse into a long, easy canter, and they set out toward the lowering sun.

"Come, Wizard; mount." Stegoman lowered his head to Matt's knee.

Matt eyed the great neck, a foot and a half thick, and the foot-high barbed fins along its top. "Uh—you sure?"

"Have no fear—thou'lt not fall, nor I falter. I can bear the load easily, if you bestride my shoulders."

"Well—if you say so." Matt swung astride the neck gingerly, right behind the head; then the ground swung away beneath his feet, and he clung for dear life. Stegoman turned his head back to his shoulder, and Matt changed seats, stepping delicately from one huge thorn-fin to another, settling himself between two wicked points. "Just don't pull any sudden stops, huh?"

"Fear not." The dragon started off in a waddle that seemed quite slow, but ate up the ground; then he gathered himself and sprang forward. Matt clung to a fin in sheer panic, bobbing back and forth, bracing his arms and trying frantically to avoid the great wicked point behind him.

Then he realized he was wasting effort; the great fin curved nicely, like the back of a bucket seat. Matt settled back as carefully as he could in the lurching ride, till his spine rested against the great horny curve, with the barb thrust out over his head. After a few minutes, he could even let himself relax a little. Not too bad, once you got used to it. "Stegoman?"

"What thorn pricketh thee now?"

Matt frowned, leaning out to the side to sight the dragon's head. "What makes you so surly, all of a sudden?"

"My tooth pains me again. What dost thou wish?"

"Mm." Matt leaned back, frowning. "We oughta take care of that for you at the next stop—pull it, you know."

"Pull?" There was an undertone of horror to the dragon's voice.

"Yeah—you know, take it out. Magic dentistry would be a little bit complicated."

"But—to part with a bit of my body, of my very being! 'Tis blasphemous, Wizard!"

"Blasphemous?" Then Matt remembered—some cultures that believed in magic were very careful about portions of the anatomy that had to be discarded, such as hair and nail clippings. If a witch got ahold of them, she could work evil magic on you. "Oh, don't worry—I'll do it up nicely, in a little leather bag to tie around your neck. You can still keep it with you."

"Even so, I like not the sound of it. I must consider this at some length."

Matt sighed. "All right, but don't let it go too long; it could poison your whole jaw." He exaggerated, but it was the easiest way to say it.

Stegoman shuddered. "Let us not talk of it further. What didst thou wish to speak of? Not of my pain, most surely—but of thine."

"'Pain?' Oh, yeah." Matt frowned, remembering his gripe. "Did you ever get the feeling you'd been set up for something?"

"Set up?"

"Yeah. You know—conned, railroaded. Somebody maneuvering you into position where you had to do what he wanted. Here I am, riding off to the West to help a girl get her throne back, when all I really wanted to do was to find a way home!"

"Am I mistaken," the dragon growled, "or didst thou not begin this whole coil thyself, when thou didst aid her to escape Astaulf's dungeon?"

"Oh, come on! I was maneuvered into that, wasn't I? I mean, as soon as I found out Malingo hadn't brought me here, it was only natural that I'd go looking for the opposing side, to get them to help me out! And I'm probably on the right track, after all. Whatever wizard brought me here probably *is* backing Alisande, but he won't let me go till she's back on her throne! Do I really have any choice but to help her?"

"Thou hast many," Stegoman snapped, "as thou knowest. Malingo hath already shown thee one, and thou hast refused it. Nay, even without allying with him, thou hast shown enough wizard-power to win thyself fortune and dominion over thy fellows. Indeed, thou mayest be a king, if thou wishest! Hast thou not thought of that?"

"Well, it had crossed my mind—but I'm the creative type. Administrative work is dead boring."

"Is it so? Then why dost thou not spend thy time seeking ways to send thyself home?"

Matt sat immobile, letting the initial terror of the thought wash over him, sink in, and ebb. "That would take a long time . . ."

"And this will not?"

"It could," Matt said slowly, "yes. But I can live with it, this way."

"Aye, because 'tis adventure to thee. Thou art bedazzled by dreams of great glory; thou dost feel thyself to be truly living— mayhap for the first time in thy life. Nay, seek not to gainsay me. Thou hast chosen this road for thyself; thou dost now what thou hast ever dreamed of. Admit this, at least to thyself, or be still!"

Matt was still.

These people didn't seem to believe in rest stops—at least, not when there were only four hours of daylight left. Matt climbed down off Stegoman as the sun was setting, feeling as if he would never be able to sit again. He could definitely see why saddles had been invented.

Sir Guy made it worse. He bustled about, setting up camp with a brisk good cheer that Matt found disgusting. Alisande wasn't sitting back on her title and relaxing, either—she was collecting brushwood for a fire.

Sore as he was, Matt felt shamed at not pitching in. He limped up to her and asked, "Can I help?"

She thrust the stack of brushwood at him, beaming. "Indeed, that you may. Lay and kindle the fire, if you would, and I'll see to your couches."

Then she whirled away toward a fir tree, whipping a knife out of her sash—a loan from Sir Guy, at a guess.

Matt tried to remember his Boy Scout lore and looked for a flat rock. Not finding one, he settled for a patch of bare ground and started breaking up the smallest twigs for tinder.

He just about had a good little teepee laid when Sir Guy came swinging up, two large hares spitted on his sword. "Ah, most excellent! We'll have fire, and right quickly a dinner!"

Matt pulled out his matchbook and tried to remember the "spell" he'd used, to get one to light.

Sir Guy's mailed hand came down over the matchbook. "Ah—thou dost not mean to use magic to kindle our fire?"

"Sure, why not?" Matt looked up, frowning. Then he remembered. "Oh . . . you mean that business about not using magic for everyday chores."

"Such as lighting a fire." Sir Guy nodded brightly, taking his hand away. "Even I do know that much, Lord Matthew. Power must be respected, or its use will surely corrupt the user." The Black Knight knelt down and pulled a small iron box from his belt. He opened it, taking out a wad of tow and a small rock. "Those with the Gift rarely begin by dedicating themselves to evil, Lord Wizard. Indeed, they firmly resolve to use their power only for the bettering of their fellows." He struck the stone against the steel box. Sparks flew; one landed in the tow, and Sir Guy breathed it carefully into a coal and tilted it into Matt's tinder teepee. "But they chance on a grimoire, soon or late, and work a few of its smallest spells. They use these spells more and more often; and, as time passes, they can scarce manage a small task without them."

"Dependent," Matt muttered, watching small tongues of flame curl around the sticks. "Hooked on magic."

"Even so. They become drunk with power; and the more power they gain, the more they desire. Then have they but two choices—

to devote all their lives to God and the Good, which may prove a lengthy duty, or simply to sign a blood oath with the Devil. The choice must be made—for how much power can a wizard gain without either Good or Evil to aid him?"

"That would depend on how good a magician he is," Matt answered. "If he could figure out the rules of magic, he might not need aid."

"Rules?" Sir Guy stared. "But magic has none!"

Matt rolled his eyes up. "Another informed layman! Have you tested the matter?"

Sir Guy seemed to consider. Then he shrugged. "As you will, Lord Wizard. Yet I bid you remember this: for a man with the Power, all temptations lead only to the same end—the Devil."

He held Matt's gaze for a moment. Then he swung to his feet, turned away, and strode toward Alisande.

Matt turned back to the fire. His eyes widened; the two rabbit carcasses lay skinned and gutted, waiting. Apparently Sir Guy had been working unobtrusively at dressing them while he'd been talking. He was the efficient type, Matt reflected as he selected a long stick to spit the carcasses—maybe a little too efficient. And what had he really been trying to say?

Matt selected two forked twigs and pushed them into the ground, then laid the spit across them. Sir Guy hadn't exactly expressed doubts that Matt had the moral strength of a wet noodle. But that had been the gist of the conversation, hadn't it?

CHAPTER 7

The campsite lay quiet, silvered by a gibbous moon, warmed by the glowing coals of the fire. Stegoman lay curled up under the trees, neck curled around his body, his tail overlapping his head. Sir Guy, Matt, and the princess lay under their cloaks around the fire, sound asleep.

Matt snapped awake, suddenly and totally. He stared through a gap in the trees at the plain that swept to the horizon. What had awakened him?

Then it came again—a long, drawn-out, despairing wail. A woman in trouble! Matt rolled to his feet and leaped around the fire to shake the Black Knight's shoulder. "Sir Guy, wake up! There's a damsel in distress!"

Sir Guy snored, then rolled over on the pine boughs. Matt shook him again, but the Black Knight didn't even snore back this time.

"Wake up!" Matt bellowed. "Fire! Earthquake! Ragnorak!"

There was no response.

"So much for chivalry!" Matt growled. He yanked a dagger from Sir Guy's possessions, wishing the knight weren't sleeping on his sword, and ran through the gap in the trees.

As he leaped out onto the plain, the scream came again—raw,

ragged, and much nearer. Matt swung toward the sound—and saw a girl running at an angle toward him, panting in terror.

Long, black hair streamed back from a finely chiseled ivory face. Full breasts stretched the fabric of her bodice taut, and her skirts whipped tightly about long, slender legs and the curve of her hips. Even in panic, there was something about her that promised impossible pleasure for the man lucky enough to possess her.

Matt kicked into a run.

She fled toward the horizon, angled his way, without even a backward glance, running for her life.

Hobbling and leaping over the plain on thick, stunted legs, giggling and drooling, came something eight feet tall and four wide. Four steel-cable tentacle arms flailed the air. Huge platters of eyes reflected the moonlight, and a foot-wide mouth revealed a set of sharklike teeth.

Troll, Matt's mind screamed at him. His body went into overdrive as he ran toward the girl. But he knew he wasn't fast enough.

The troll leaped, landing five feet behind her. She was hampered by her clothes—kirtle, bliaut, and cloak of rich fabric. A tentacle slashed out, snatching at the girl's cloak. She stumbled, her body slamming against the fabric, and it tore in a huge, jagged rent. She screamed, but staggered back into a run, the troll snickering behind her.

It slashed out again, catching her skirt. The kirtle tore. Two tentacles shot out, one catching the hem of her skirt, the other hooking into her collar. The girl spun about as the bliaut tore open in a long, jagged rent along its whole length. A third tentacle hooked the back of the neckline, and the bliaut snapped her arms up as it came away from her. For a moment, she stood poised, arms high in the moonlight, in only her shift.

Then a clawed tentacle slashed down at her, and she threw herself down backward to avoid it. The troll howled laughter and pounced, but she was too quick for him; she rolled to the side just in time and kept rolling.

She was free for a moment and was up and running. The troll howled and pounced. She threw herself to the side—straight against a thorn bush. She leaped away, but the shift caught in the thorns, ripping away in a jagged line just below her hips.

The troll caught her with a howl of glee, pinning her arms to her sides with tentacle loops, lifting her toward the gaping shark's mouth.

Then Matt reached the troll and leaped, striking home.

The dagger struck a tentacle and the troll howled, dropping the girl—and Matt suddenly realized what a fool he was to attack with only a dagger. He leaped away, chanting frantically,

> "Grow, blade of iron! Grow out and away
> Into three feet of steel, a razor-edged blade!
> Your needle-sharp point will protect this weak clay,
> Till at my feet this foul monster is laid."

The dagger surged in his hand like a living thing as the blade tripled its length. The edge glinted in the moonlight.

The troll was on him, with a howl like a steam whistle.

Its tentacles whipped out for him. Matt leaped to the side and slashed at its midriff. The blade struck a spark from its body and skidded. The beast was *hard*!

The troll twitched its tentacles out of the way and pushed its huge body toward him, giggling inanely. The huge trunk swung into the arc of the blade, and the sword clanged off its side in a shower of sparks. The jar shot pain up Matt's whole forearm. He leaped back, hanging onto the blade by sheer determination, while realization exploded in his mind. *Trolls were made out of stone!*

Steel was no use against stone. He needed something harder. Diamond!

He turned and ran, hearing the huge feet drumming the earth as the troll followed. Matt panted out a rhyme as he ran.

> "Sword blade of steel, become now for me
> A blade of black diamond, as hard as can be,
> But tough as forged iron, with a cross-section wedge,
> Honed down to a monofilament edge!"

The sword twitched in his hand, now black and gleaming.

Matt whirled about, swinging the sword with both hands. The blade scored deep into the monster's body, and it leaped back, its scream soaring to a height that pierced Matt's ears. Ichor welled out of the gaping slit in its belly.

Matt jumped in again, but the monster had realized it was in trouble; it bent forward, and sharklike teeth scored Matt's chest, while tentacles ripped at his arm, chest, and belly. He leaped away and swung the diamond blade at the place between head and shoulders, where a neck should have been.

The tentacles lashed out, dancing toward his face. But their tips were moving erratically; they weren't under full control, and the troll was staggering.

Matt leaped to the side and swung down in a full overhand chop. He caught the troll in the same place, and the sword bit in deep, cutting halfway through its head. Its whole body jerked in one mighty spasm. It fell, twitching and heaving, scrabbling about in the dirt. But the thing was already dead, its spinal cord cut.

The spasms slowed and stopped. Matt stared down at the huge, dead thing. The corpse looked shrunken somehow, lying still in the moonlight; it was only an oddly shaped boulder in the middle of the plain.

"You have slain it!" The girl stood just a few feet away now, with the moonlight behind her showing the shadow of her body against the thin cloth of her shift. Here and there, a long gash in the fabric revealed a smooth, creamy curve.

"You have saved me! Oh, you are my true knight!" She stepped closer, her body less than a foot from his. Then she gasped and flinched away. "But you are wounded!"

The cuts were still bleeding and had begun to sting sharply. But he shook his head. "Aw, they're just scratches."

"But they must be tended." She caught up the ragged hem of her shift to wipe at the blood on his chest, exposing more curves. "You must come home with me, where I may care for them."

"Milady!" A score of armed men suddenly came running up, drawn swords in their hands. "Milady Sayeesa! Are you . . ."

"Safe, little thanks to you." Her tone was severe. "But no matter. This brave knight has succored me. Now conduct us back to my home, that I may tend his wounds."

"Uh . . ." Matt shook his head, trying to dispel the haze in which he'd been since he first sighted the girl. "Thanks, but I'd better not. I've got friends back there, and they'll be worried."

"Then they shall be told and invited to share what comforts I can offer. Captain, see to it!"

The captain moved away to tell off a party of six men to head back to the campsite. Swords snapped into scabbards, and the rest of the men formed up for a march.

Matt found himself alone for the moment, holding the bare

sword in his hand, with no place to put it. He frowned, then recited,

"To carry this weapon, a sheath I do need,
Expressly designed for this wonderful blade,
Making easy the draw when the sword must be freed,
So here at my side let this scabbard be made."

A scabbard was suddenly at his hips, belted around his waist. The sword slipped easily into it, just as Sayeesa returned to his side. The captain's cape was about her shoulders now, but she seemed not to notice that it left an open strip down her front.

Her smile was compelling as she placed a hand on his arm. "Come, let us be off!"

With the girl at his side and her hip pressing against his, Matt forgot to notice in which direction they marched. Nor was he aware of how long the journey took.

Then the soldiers halted, and Matt jerked to a stop, staring.

Before him stood a palace. High walls glowed, and tall, slender towers glittered with fairy lights. The whole seemed to be made of jade. And from it came a procession of Sayeesa's servitors. There must have been a hundred of them, joyfully welcoming her. All were young and beautiful—except two. The pair of guards before the entrance were at least seven feet tall and half as broad, burly and ugly. Their skins were of a walnut shade.

"Does my home please you?" Sayeesa asked. At his enthralled nod, she waved her hand. "Then enter, that we may partake of its delights."

Inside, candles glowed everywhere. The air was filled with some heavy scent that seemed to go to Matt's head instantly. And the hallway was lined with statues, mostly of young men, though a few were of lovely girls. They seemed almost alive, each with a dazed but delighted expression.

"Marvelous!" Matt exclaimed. "What great sculptor shaped them?"

The girl hesitated, then admitted, "They are of my crafting."

"You? Lady, you're amazing!" He was standing very close to her, looking downward where the cape was open. "Almost unbelievable," he breathed.

She laughed and spun away with a coy glance at him. "You

regain your strength quickly, Sir Knight. But come hither, and I'll attend to—your wounds."

'Hither' turned out to be a Roman bath, tiled in sapphire, with a huge sunken pool. There she turned him over to a pair of female servants, making some excuse about more suitable garb. They seated him on a bench. One removed his jacket while the other stripped off his shoes and socks.

But when one started unbuckling his belt, Matt called a halt. "I'll do that myself."

The girl's face registered astonishment and a trace of what might have been fear. "But sir, 'tis our custom!"

"Not mine." Matt caught an arm around each girl's waist and ushered them toward the door. "Out!"

They went, but before the door closed fully, he caught a snatch of conversation.

"Fear not. Remember, the priest was like that."

"Aye, 'tis what troubles me."

Matt slipped out of his clothes and waded into the pool. From the edge, it went down in a series of foot-high steps. He stepped down twice, then seated himself and leaned back against the warm tiles behind him with a blissful sigh. Here the heady perfume seemed stronger. The warm, murky aroma seemed to fill his head, inducing visions.

Then he heard a silken rustle behind him. Sayeesa had slipped into something that seemed almost transparently blue and silken, low at the throat.

"Rest, Sir Knight," she crooned. Her hands crept to his shoulders, kneading and massaging. "My bath has wondrous minerals in it to heal your wounds."

Matt started to protest, but Sayeesa was now stroking a cool, scented cream over his shoulders and biceps, crooning a soft, restful song in some strange language. The feel of her hands spreading the salve over his wounds and her crooning, combined with the silken sounds of her movements, drove all other thoughts from his mind.

There was a rough knock, and the door flew open, to show the captain standing there.

Suddenly Sayeesa's voice was harsh. "You know better than to disturb me! Out!"

The captain seemed to cringe, but his voice was insistent. "The man and woman have arrived."

"You know where they go!" Sayeesa snapped.

"But . . . you have the keys!"

For a moment, Sayeesa stood irresolute. Then she nodded. "Very well. I'll come. Forgive me, Sir Knight. Matters of import call me. My servants will show you to your room."

She left; a moment later, the two serving girls were back. One held a supply of towels; the other laid a magnificent robe on the bench. They stared uncertainly, but left when he waved them away. By the time they returned, he was dried and attired in the robe.

They led him to two huge, gilded doors, which two other servants threw wide. Matt stepped into the bedroom of his less printable dreams. It was draped with tapestries, with a carpet which seemed to engulf his feet as he stepped on it. The bed was canopied, with curtains drawn back to show a gold-and-silver bedspread. It seemed that a squadron might sleep on its expanse.

"There is brandywine by the bedside and fruit in the bowl," one girl told him, while the other turned down the covers for him. "If you need aught else, you have but to call."

Matt stepped up to the bed, sat, and rolled onto his side. The pillow seemed to mold itself to his head, and his body was cushioned in total luxury. He yawned, and his eyes closed.

A touch on his shoulder brought him awake quickly, and he looked up to see Sayeesa in the sheerest of silken robes. She bent over him, and the robe parted. She slipped onto the bed and lifted the counterpane over her, stretching luxuriously. "You lack chivalry, Sir Knight," she purred, reaching out to caress his cheek. "Will you not show welcome to a lady?"

Matt was about to do so when a slow, seductive chant sounded, coming closer. Draperies across the room rippled and parted, and a blonde and a brunette stepped through. Each carried a sort of crystal vase with a thick-looking fluid in it.

Sayeesa sat up stiffly, and the look on her face made the two girls flinch back. The brunette gasped. "Milady, here are the oils. Do you not wish us to help . . ."

Their words wilted under her glare, they shrank away. Bowing low, they shuffled backward between the tapestries.

"How could I so lose control?" Sayeesa muttered to herself. "Is this one so much more that I cannot wait for each measure?"

"Beg pardon?"

"Why, naught." She turned to face him, her face smoothing

out into a lazy, inviting smile. "Or do you truly wish explanation, sir?"

"I hate explantions." Matt reached for her again. "I much prefer demonstrations."

He was about to begin when he felt her body stiffen. Her face turned dark with fury, and she sat up with an air of slow, building menace. "What do *you* here?"

One of the brawny, walnut skinned guards stood there, his arms full of ironware. Matt made out something like handcuffs and a pair of what seemed to be whips.

"Milady commanded me to bring them," the creature grated.

"I did not!" It was almost a shriek. "Wherefore should I wish for such vile instruments? Get you gone, or 'twill be the axe for you!"

The guard seemed to quiver with terror. He bowed stiffly and shuffled backwards, with a sound like sandpaper sandals.

Sayeesa slowly settled back, still frowning. Matt reached for her, but with a measure of uncertainty this time.

His doubts were justified. A great gong sounded, and she sat up abruptly.

The captain strode though the door, making no effort to be silent.

"What now troubles us?" Sayeesa demanded. "You had best have good reason for this incursion, captain!"

"Madam," he said, bowing to her, "there is a dragon at the gate, attempting to destroy all this palace. And he is demanding—"

"I can guess his demands," she interrupted. "Man the defenses. I shall take measures below."

She was gone in a rush, with the captain trailing her.

Matt lay back, wondering what madness afflicted this place. A dragon? But why should a dragon assault the lady's palace? He puzzled over it briefly, but his thoughts were hazy, and he began to slip back into a sort of fantasy in which Sayeesa did not go running off.

Then words seemed to burn in his brain.

Lord Matthew, I summon you by Earth, Air, and Water. Aid me now, for my peril is great!

It was the voice of Alisande!

Matt sprang up, staring in bewilderment at the garish surroundings in which he found himself. What devilish spell had be been under?

No time to think about it. He barreled through the door and along the hall to a cross corridor. Which way now? A bedlam of screaming came from both sides.

The ones to the right were louder. Matt kicked out in a run, just as a roar like an overfed steam boiler blasted out, and the screaming went wild. He skidded to a halt at the end of the corridor, where it reached the main hall. A line of soldiers barred his way, their backs to him. He lowered his head and charged, and they bowled forward like tenpins. He snatched up a battle-axe, to find himself facing the dragon, reared back on its hind legs, with its neck stretched out and fire in its mouth. Searing flame blasted out.

Matt leaped aside, and the flame struck the row of soldiers behind him.

"Stegoman!" he shouted. The gigantic head swiveled toward him, weaving, an ugly glint in its eyes. Matt had seen that look before. "Stegoman! I'm Matthew—Lord Wizard—your friend."

"Lord Wizh . . ." The dragon's eyes filled with confusion.

Matt leaped, bounced his foot off Stegoman's shoulder, and landed between two of the huge fins. "You came here seeking the princess, Sir Guy, and me—remember? Well, you've found me."

"Then let ush sheek out the otherzh!" Stegoman slammed down on all fours, searing a blowtorch arc across everything near him.

"You're wasting time, you loony lizard!" Matt had begun to put the clues he had together, now that his mind was clearing. "They must be in the dungeons—probably being tortured. We've got to find a way down . . ."

"Torture? I'll torch them! Vile hatchling hunterzh!" Stegoman reared back his head and blowtorched the floor. The marble cracked with a series of bursts and explosions. He let out another blast-furnace breath, and the floor gave way with a roar.

A huge shock jarred Matt's bones. He gasped and flung the battle-axe over his head, holding it broadside, like an umbrella. A few last shards of charred marble clanged off the improvised shield. Then things were relatively quiet.

Light from the huge hole overhead showed undressed stone walls and floor. They'd fallen at least thirty feet. "We're in the cellar," Matt said. "You all right?"

Before Stegoman could answer, a clamor of battle cries sounded from their right. Sayeesa's troops were probably gathering to protect the last stronghold.

Stegoman turned toward the noise, breathing torches. Fifty feet ahead, light gleamed off armor. The dragon jumped into a gallop, sending flame gouting twenty feet ahead. The lurid glow of his fire lighted tall, slender soldiers in golden armor. They shrieked, jamming into the second row behind them. In a moment, the hall was packed solid with struggling bodies.

Matt glanced at the ceiling, twenty feet overhead, and yelled, "Up and over, Steogman! Up and over!"

The dragon grunted and leaped. Matt pressed himself back against the fin, hearing howls of agony as the great claws tore at heads.

They burst into a huge room, lighted by a score of torches and a huge fire in a pit near the far wall. The place was cluttered with objects. Matt recognized a few: a tall coffin lined with spikes; the pallet and drum of a rack; and thumbscrews and whips lining the walls.

Alisande and Sir Guy were there, chained to the left wall, their arms manacled over their heads. Sir Guy was stripped to his shirt and hose, and Alisande to her shift. One of the huge guards was approaching with a six-foot branding iron, but they looked untouched, so far.

Sayeesa stood at the side, but she whirled as Matt and Stegoman burst in. Her eyes widened in terror, but she swung to seize the branding iron. "Now, Lady!" she screamed at Alisande. "Command them to stand fast, or you shall know the taste of hot iron!"

"I obey no foul minion of Evil," Alisande snapped.

The branding iron stabbed out. Matt bellowed, and Stegoman charged, roaring fire. Sayeesa dropped the iron and jumped as the flame seared the guards around her. Matt leaped down and ran toward the princess.

"Who movezh," Stegoman rumbled, "diezh!"

Sayeesa froze as Matt slid to a halt near Alisande, swinging his axe over his head.

"You come late, sir," the princess said. She moved her wrist along the wall, stretching out the six inches of chain.

Matt took a deep breath and chopped. The chain parted with a snap, and he circled to the opposite side. He chopped the second chain off. "Yeah, sorry I couldn't come sooner. I had a pressing engagement."

"And I know well what you were pressing," Alisande said between her teeth.

Sayeesa was screaming at her troops as Matt turned to free Sir Guy, and they were forming up again. Matt wasted no time in chopping through the chains that held the Black Knight.

"Late come—but well come," Sir Guy said. He turned to Sayeesa. "And now, what of the witch?"

"Witch?"

"Aye. What else could you think her?" Alisande had picked up the branding iron and was swinging it tentatively. "A foul lust-witch, who inflames men with desire—to their ruin. Already she has ended the lives of half a hundred, draining them of all energy." She glared at Sayeesa.

Sayeesa returned the glare with bitterness. Her voice rose. "Guards! Out upon them!"

The guards started forward, while Sir Guy snatched a poker from the fire. But Stegoman thundered, "Hold!" He scored the stone floor with fire in front of the ranks.

"Go! Upon them!" Sayeesa screamed. "Will you let them ruin all?"

Matt began chanting.

"Metal rods in the hands of the pure,
     Change to swords, both sharp and sure,
     With edges honed, keen as Saladin's blade—
     Damascened swords, by wizard-smiths made."

The irons twisted, growing and flattening into slender swords. Sir Guy grinned and cut at the air. Alisande threw a glance at Matt and turned to Sayeesa.

The witch shrank back. "Kill them now! Attack or I'll return you to nothingness!"

Despair washed over the faces of the soldiers, to be replaced by hopeless determination.

Stegoman let out a blast, sweeping the lines. But when his fire winked out as he paused for breath, they charged forward, pikes and swords slashing. Alisande and Sir Guy met them back to back, threshing death all about them.

But Sayeesa's threat to return the men to nothingness touched a response in Matt's memory. He chopped a guard aside and sprang to join the princess and the knight, laying about with the axe and crying, "They're only illusions. They seem solid, but they're made from nothing!"

"Then this illusion will have your head," a soldier howled. "Make me vanish, if you can!"

"Nothing easier," Matt shouted, blocking the blow.

> "Your revels now are ended! These your actors,
> As I foretold you, were all spirits, and
> Are melted into air, into thin air;
> And, like the baseless fabric of this vision,
> The cloud-capped towers, the gorgeous palaces,
> The solemn temples, the great globe itself,
> Yea, all which it inherit, shall dissolve;
> And, like this insubstantial pageant faded,
> Leave not a wrack behind!"

Sayeesa gave a long-drawn-out wail of heartbreak, and other voices caught it up, keening in unison, as everything about them began to waver and ripple. Colors faded; shapes flowed and merged into the rippling. The rippling itself faded, until it was a cloud of mist that thinned and disappeared, leaving only a heat haze.

Even that faded and was gone.

Matt's axe fell from numbed fingers. He stood in an empty crater with a causeway thrust in from the edge. At the lip of the crater, a double line of youths and occasional girls stood shivering, looking about them uncertainly. A few still forms lay among them— very still. Around the crater stretched a blasted heath. And in the center, Sayeesa knelt in a plain tunic and cloak, doubled over with grief, sobbing her heart out.

Suddenly she screamed and yanked a knife from her robe. She swung it high, then slashed it down toward her heart.

Matt leaped and caught her wrist, just as the knife grazed her flesh. Sir Guy grabbed her from behind in a bear hug and pinioned her arms, and Matt twisted the knife free.

Sayeesa loosed one last ear-piercing scream and collapsed, slumped in Sir Guy's arms and sobbing. "Let me die! I am damned beyond saving. My sins are too terrible ever to be shriven. Let me die!"

"Nay. You still have a part to play." Alisande strode up grimly. "For your sins you must atone." She yanked Matt's sash loose. He gave a startled squawk, holding his robe shut.

"Oh, try me not with your mockery of modesty!" she snapped. "Bind her hands." Sir Guy held Sayeesa's arms, and Matt began pinning her wrists together behind her back. The princess cut a ragged strip from Sayeesa's homespun gown and bound the witch's feet. Sir Guy let the girl down gently upon the scorched earth.

Alisande was gazing at the muddle of young people near the causeway. Matt followed her gaze. "Where did they come from?"

"Her victims. Lured to her and bedazzled by pleasures untold. Tales are recounted of the vile degradations she heaped upon them, till they were drained and could no longer please her. Then she turned them to stone statues—monuments to what she no doubt thought of as her 'power of womanhood'." The princess's mouth was tight.

"And now they've come alive again—most of them." Matt frowned at the milling group. "It seems impossible that I could have broken so many spells with only one verse."

"Ah, but you broke the master-spell on her," Sir Guy explained.

"A spell *on* her?" Matt's eyebrows raised.

"Aye, or so rumor has it." Alisande stood glaring at the sobbing woman. "She was naught but a simple peasant wench once, though of much beauty and charm—and far too much sensuality."

Sir Guy nodded. "She was a lass for all men, though 'tis said she was goodhearted withal. She was a lass for all men, seeking always to give more, until she ceased to have self."

"You don't mean that promiscuity destroyed her identity, do you?" Matt asked. "Maybe that *was* her identity."

"The identity goatish men wished for her!" Alisande glared at him. "She tried to be what they wanted, thereby losing what she was. Her sinning gave Evil power over her, so that an ancient, depraved sorcerer could cast a spell to transform her into the lust-witch you met—for his own pleasure, no doubt. He died in flames shortly after, but she still had power over men, and the power to cast the glamours that arise out of desire."

"Then all these illusions and powers—her fairy palace and her servants—were only outgrowths of the sorcerer's spell?"

Sir Guy nodded.

"What about her door guards?"

"Mandrake plants," Alisande said, with a trace of contempt. "Did you not recognize them, *Wizard*?"

"No, never saw one before." Matt considered carefully. "Then she's no longer a lust-witch—just an ordinary girl again."

"Aye." Alisande speared him with another glare. "But beware, Wizard. She still has the power she was born with—which has proved sufficient to ruin the strongest of men."

Sayeesa lifted her head from the dirt. "Give me the knife, loose my hands, and let me die! For I am too foul to live!"

"You are not, if you still can think so." Alisande stared at the girl, her look almost sympathetic. Then her face hardened as she turned to Matt. "Thus have men done to her!"

"Well, it wasn't my spell that did it!" Matt didn't know what was bothering the princess, but he was getting tired of her attitude. "Control your tone, Lady!"

Sir Guy's eyes widened, and Alisande froze, paling. Then she spoke in a low tone, quivering with anger. "We will speak of that anon, sir, when your duties here are done."

"Duties? I didn't hear anyone blow assembly."

"Did you not?" Alisande's finger stabbed out, pointing to the naked, bewildered young folks. "There stand those poor victims, stripped to their skins in the cold night air. If you claim to any morality, Wizard, you must clothe them. I, too, am lacking, and Sir Guy is without armor."

"Nay. After they bound us in our ensorcelled sleep and brought us here, they took all from us." Sir Guy turned away. "But perchance I may find them here."

He strode off, while Matt stood with his eyes locked on Alisande's. Then he sighed. "All right, I'll try. But don't expect miracles, Lady. I'm beat."

He thought for a moment, but memory was no help. This would have to be something original, good or not.

> "The wind is too cold at this time of year,
> And overexposure may bring on the flu.
> Let whatever each wore when entering here
> Reclothe now the wearer, without more ado."

There was a rustle, and the feeling of cloth against his skin. He looked down to see his clothes back on him under the robe. Alisande was again wearing the garments he'd first given her. And now Sir Guy was coming back, again clad in his black armor. He looked up, and the youths were all dressed.

'Reclothed,' eh? His spell hadn't just supplied the garments— it had dressed everyone with them instantly.

"Satisfied?" he demanded of Alisande.

She made no answer. Stepping forward to the edge of the crater, she held up her arms and called, "Hearken! Attend me!"

The youngsters quit "oohing" over their clothes and looked down at her, startled. They obviously hadn't realized she was there.

"I am Princess Alisande," she called out, proud and grave in the moonlight. She had the dignity and authority that could only come from being raised to it, from an impregnable sense of self. "I and my liegemen have saved you. We have broken the spell that chained you. You are clothed, and most of you live. Thank your God for that! Now stay not to marvel or doubt. Find a church to be shriven, to be granted new hope of salvation. Then return to your homes. Now depart!"

As he watched the youths begin to leave, bearing their dead with them, Matt felt a touch on his arm. He turned to see Sir Guy beside him, holding out his silver ballpoint pen. "I have never seen the like of this. Surely it must be yours. Perchance your magic wand?"

"My what?" Matt pocketed it automatically. "Uh—not exactly. Thanks, Sir Guy."

"And this?" Sir Guy held out the black sword in its scabbard. "A wondrous-seeming blade. Is it also yours?"

Matt nodded uncertainly. "Well, partly. I made it from your dagger. I suppose it's really yours."

"Nay, 'tis now yours." Sir Guy smiled. "Already I have two swords—mine own, and that which you magicked here for me."

Alisande had been watching the last of the youths depart, but now she came back, turning scornful eyes on Matt. "And now, Wizard, are you recovered from your night of revels?"

"What revels?" Matt demanded. "We'd hardly begun!"

"Begun the road to your death!" Alisande blazed. "But for your oath, you'd have been drained to a husk."

Matt stiffened. "Oath? What are you talking about?"

"The oath of fealty you swore when I created you Lord Wizard. Had it not been for that, I could not have broken the foul spell that bound you. Be assured, the words that you spoke gave me power over you."

"And me some power over you! I remember your saying a word or two."

"Aye, certes. My oath bound me to you, as did Sir Guy's—

to draw us into your danger. Or did you not realize, sirrah, that your lust led us all into peril?"

"Whoa! It didn't start with lust. There was a damsel in distress..."

"A comely damsel, no doubt, and one not overly clad."

"Oh, well. But you can't think I went off fighting trolls because I was hot for her body."

"Say, rather, you fought an illusion of hers under her total control," Alisande corrected him. "She was in no danger."

"But I couldn't know that." Still, it must have been true. And if he'd had no sword to fight with, she'd probably have brought up her guards in time to rescue him, then been all sympathy as she took him to heal his wounds.

"If there had been no sin in your soul, she could not have seduced you to her," Alisande said, with scathing scorn. "When free from sin, the minions of Evil have no power over you!"

"So what am I supposed to be? A saint?" Matt cried, exasperated. "And as for getting us into danger—why didn't you warn me that there was a lust-witch around?"

"Because, from the best we knew, her lair was a day's ride to the north," Sir Guy answered.

"It should not have mattered," Alisande declared. "And it would not, had you been a knight, not a slight country wizard!"

Matt bridled. "And just what could a knight have done that I didn't?"

"He could have known Evil when he saw it—and resisted it!"

Matt reared his head back, staring at her. "Sure, Lady! Knights never give in to temptation. Oh, never! I suppose Astaulf wasn't a knight before he usurped the throne!"

Alisande started to answer. Then she turned pale and snapped her jaw shut. She swung on her heel and stalked off into the night.

"What's the matter with her, anyway?" Matt asked Sir Guy. "Does she think I should be made out of marble?"

"She is, perchance, distressed to learn that you are not." Sir Guy pursed his lips, but there was a hint of amusement in his face. "If you can be tempted to sin by a woman's body, Lord Wizard, the princess's cause is imperiled."

Matt's brows drew down. "How do my lapses endanger the cause?"

"Because, Lord Wizard, you and I are her only true assets in the war for her throne; and of us two, you are the more vital."

"Seems to me wars really boil down to which side has the strongest fighters," Matt objected.

"Not so. For at root, this is a struggle between Good and Evil. And most potent for those forces are the wizards and sorcerers. Sorcerers must remain celibate—no human feelings must possess their attention. But even more must a wizard be virtuous, since the smallest sin weakens his power for the Good. Thus our Princess Alisande must have concern for your soul."

"Yes, I see," Matt admitted grudgingly. "But I also see that it is an invasion of privacy."

"Indeed. She most truly invaded your privacy when she summoned you by your oath, saving you from the witch." Sir Guy smiled in gentle mockery, then sobered. "Your oath was a bond, Sir Wizard, and protection against all but the most potent magics. No matter the charms the witch used on you, it would find a way to protect you against them—for a time, at least."

So that was why somebody had come bursting in on him and Sayeesa just when things started to get interesting. Then another thought occurred to him. "If I'm so important, could that have anything to do with Sayeesa's castle being suddenly so far south of where it's supposed to be? And could Malingo have anything to do with the sending of both witches against me?"

Sir Guy's brows knitted in thought. "'Tis not impossible. And that would mean more traps might be set for your soul. Were I you, Lord Wizard, I should spend much time in prayer! But come, the lady is ready to depart. Summon your friend Stegoman, and I will seek my good steed where he was left after bearing our bound bodies here."

CHAPTER 8

Matt rolled over on his bed of pine boughs, unable to sleep because of Sayeesa's heartbroken sobbing. She hadn't stopped crying since her dream castle had vanished.

They had come back to the campsite, with the witch trussed before him on a sobered-up Stegoman, while Alisande rode behind Sir Guy on his horse. Alisande had cut a new bed of pine boughs, and they had settled in to salvage what sleep they could. Now she and Sir Guy were deep in slumber.

It must be nice, Matt thought, to have a clear conscience, though hers seemed a little too clear.

He turned over, trying to shut out the sobbing and clear his mind of what kept gnawing at it. Again, he failed.

Was sin real, or wasn't it? Where he came from, it was probably only a delusion, safe to ignore. But he wasn't where he came from. He was in their world. Did that mean he had to play by their rules?

Not necessarily, he decided. He'd already figured out a few rules of magic, and everything he'd reasoned out about it had worked. None of his theories really required any mystical personality behind the power; they could all work nicely by regarding magic as an impersonal force.

He felt better when he thought of it that way. Reason and logic *did* work in this universe, which meant that the whole pile of nonsense about Good and Evil were merely human constructs, and sin and Hell were just superstitious folk tales, even here.

He'd simply let himself get shaken up by a new environment. All the fundamental things were really as they'd always been.

With that comforting thought, he opened his eyes to gaze at the warm, glowing coals of the campfire.

A small hole appeared in the ground between himself and the fire and widened like a yawn filled with flames. A leering devil hoisted himself out of the hole—a regulation, scarlet-skinned, horned devil, with a long, tapering face, a moustache and goatee, and a pitchfork in his hand.

"Let me congratulate you on your skepticism," the devil said. "Rationalists make such excellent kindling."

The pitchfork stabbed out, lancing into Matt's belly, knotting his diaphragm while it swung him up, arcing high, and sent him plunging down into the flames.

Matt screamed, and nerve ends shrieked all over his body with the raw, pure pain of the fire. It didn't stop, but kept building. The fire grew hotter. Matt screamed himself hoarse, but the pain grew worse and worse...

Then the pitchfork lanced down again, tossing him into a locker of dry ice that seared his flesh with absolute cold. He was in total darkness, burning with cold, and his nerve ends doubled their anguish. But they did not grow numb.

"Don't trouble to wonder. It doesn't get better."

Matt looked up in mid-shriek.

A sable, amorphous amoeba pulsed near him, shot with veins of fire. It spoke with the devil's voice. "Why, of course it is me," it chortled. "*Nothing* has real form or shape in this realm."

Hell, Matt realized.

"What did you expect from a devil? Oh, I know, it's not like your infantile conception of fire and brimstone. Don't you know what Hell is? The complete absence of ... the Source."

God, Matt thought numbly.

The blot flinched, shrinking in on itself, and away. "I'll thank you not to use that Name here. In fact, you'll find you can't, now; I've knotted the neuron that caused me such pain."

Matt tried to think of the Name, found he couldn't—and the craving, aching emptiness of isolation surged in. It wasn't just the loneliness he'd known when he'd been in a new town and broke. This was worse, a thousand times worse. And despair whetted the loneliness, because there was no way out, now—not even through death.

The cold of Kipling's wind between the worlds swept through him, chilling him to his ectoplasm. The numbing emptiness of absolute loneliness sank in. Nausea bit, trying to turn the soul inside out, to fold it up, to make it fade away, to escape from loneliness into oblivion. But it couldn't cease; it was caught, embedded in total despair that had no other side.

"Yes," the devil crooned, "Yes—forever. Forever."

Pinpoints of warm light winked in the distance. They swelled into discs, then into spheres. The nearest zoomed toward them, filling Matt's vision. A soul flailed there in anguish, mouth sphinctering in unheard screaming, as tongues of white fire enveloped it, and bright, glowing needles pierced through it.

"This is the hell of a hedonist," the devil crowed. "Hedonists claim the purpose of life is its pleasures. But mortals are quickly sated; the pleasures they're born to soon pall. They end by seeking sensation, any sensation, to remind them they exist; and what began as a search after pleasure ends, if they live long enough to find the extreme, in a searching for pain. They seek to come here, though they know it not. Here they gain the sensation they sought, for all time."

The hell veered off to the right, and Matt found himself staring at more of the glowing orange bubbles. They crowded above, they jostled below, they thronged all about.

"Yes, there are many," the devil crooned, "and there's room for a million times more. Hell is quite spacious. Each sinner's alone, in his own personal hell—for there's no companionship here. And we've no problem fitting a hell to a sinner, for each soul provides its own. You come here to the hell you've built for yourself all your life."

Another sphere swept toward them and filled Matt's view. The air about the soul within it was filled with bright points of light that swooped at it, while its head was tilted back, its mouth open, a steady stream of its substance being drawn out into space.

"No matter how much is pulled out, there'll always be more," the devil murmured. "The bright points of light are microscopic blades, each nicking its miniscule bit from the soul. This being claimed it wasn't guilty for the sins it committed—they were all predestined, or due to its upbringing, or to the socio-cultural matrix in which it was born. The end of it all is that the soul disclaimed responsibility for itself and sinned to its fullest, caring not a whit what damage it did to others—yet each sin was a breach of its integrity, its wholeness. So it lived, constantly losing itself; so it lives here—forever losing."

Another sphere hurtled up. The soul within was frozen in mid-step.

"It will stay forever frozen," the devil confided, "because it cannot decide. In life, it was a follower; when it knew not what was right, it asked its priest, or its minister—or it looked in a book, or asked its employer. It never thought for itself; it never decided. Here it stands, as it lived—but with no one about to dictate its movements. You have heard of 'the agony of indecision'? Behold it."

Matt felt a shuddering revulsion sweep through him.

The sphere swam away; another replaced it. The soul lay at the bottom, looking upward, contorted in horror, at a huge heap of foulness plunging down toward it.

"He knows that some day it will reach him," the devil explained. "We told him it would. Some day—tomorrow, or next year, or in a million years; no matter."

The whole heap plunged downward. The soul gasped, stiffening; but the heap halted an inch from its nose and withdrew. Matt wondered what could terrify it so.

"Its own words, its own thoughts. This is one who was sure he was better than his fellows—more righteous, or racially superior, or of a finer temperament. But each sneering thought, each word of insult, fell here and was stored for his coming. He waits to be buried beneath his own mental filth—and in terror, for he knows what it did to those at whom he sneered."

The sphere swerved upward and passed overhead. Inwardly, Matt flinched.

A new sphere swam up. The soul inside sat grinning frantically, sweat popping from its brow, clutching at a brightly-colored object in front of it. As its hands touched it, the colors faded, and the bauble evaporated. Another appeared to the side; he clutched at it, but it faded, too.

"This is a materialist," the devil cackled in glee. "He believed nothing was real save what he could see and feel. He sees it now, but can never touch it. Illusion—all he sees is illusion. Even should he touch his own body, he will find there no substance. He has lost his reality, you see. Still he'll go on, clutching at phantoms, in ever-failing hope that he'll find something real. Each creates his own," the devil went on, as the sphere swam away. "Each damns himself. All have chosen this; none are sent here who have not chosen it."

Matt realized, *Madness. They're all going mad—but they can never get there.*

"Of course," the devil gloated. "That's part of Hell."

The sphere disappeared, and a dark, empty one replaced it.

"Yes," the devil murmured, "this is yours. It is empty now, but 'twill soon be peopled. *You* will people it, with your own ungovernable fantasies; for you are, at the bottom, a solipsist—and your subconscious is out of control. Oh, by long and stern training, a man might gain mastery of it—but you have had no taste for such lasting, disciplined effort. Small wonder in that; all Hell is for such solipsists, of one form or another; but you have not chosen your form. These sinners you saw—there is something of each of them in you; but no one form of sinning has dominance in you. You are general, amorphous. All that may definitely be said is that you're convinced you're the center of the universe— you never *have* grown up, have you?—and that you're lost in your own illusions.

"Let them have you!"

The dark, empty sphere slammed up, and Matt plunged headlong against its surface. It gave beneath him, stretching, like a film of plastic; then it gave, and he broke through and in.

Suddenly, he could move again, of his own accord—and could speak! Screaming, he whirled about and dove at the invisible wall. It stretched beneath him, it gave—but it didn't break.

The devil throbbed and pulsed on the other side, howling with glee. "Oh yes, fight, struggle! But you'll never escape! Hell is forever!"

A last desperate hope touched Matt's mind. "But my hell is being the victim of my own uncontrolled illusions! If I can get them under control, it'll cease to be Hell!"

"Hell is Hell," the devil sneered.

"Is it?" Matt cried. "Or is it purgatory? That's supposed to be just like Hell—except that it ends! And if this might end, it might be Purgatory!"

"It might," the devil said thoughtfully.

"Yeah! So which is it?"

"Hell is not knowing," the devil murmured.

And it hit Matt, with the full weight of despair—the devil was correct in this. If you were in Purgatory, you knew it; you knew it would end. Not knowing, he knew this was Hell!

The devil was fairly bouncing with glee. "Despair! You do it so well! Ah, hope! It's so wonderful—when it's gone!"

Matt realized the devil had been deliberately baiting him, encouraging a last flare of hope only so that it could snatch it away. Anger kindled, plowing through the despair; Matt shot forward against the unseen wall, hands outstretched for the devil's theoretical throat.

"Rage!" The devil howled with delight. "Delightful to watch! I wish I could stay!"

Panic surged through Matt, burying anger. This devil was, at least, a sentient being. "No, please! Foul as you are, you're some bit of company! Don't leave me alone!"

"Alone," the devil mocked him. "That, at the bottom, is the nature of Hell. Farewell, penultimate skeptic! Farewe-e-e-e-e-lll!"

Its voice faded as it shrank down to a dot, receding, going, going...

Gone.

Matt was surrounded by darkness, total, impenetrable, without a single iota of light. Not even the pinpoints of distant, other hells were visible any longer. Despair plunged down on him, flattening the soul. He looked about frantically for a dagger, a razor, anything to end life!

Then he remembered—life *was* ended.

And the loneliness bit in through the despair, till Matt could have sworn there was nothing left of him but a consciousness that felt its isolation as a burning pain, worse than fire in each cubic millimeter. His whole being pleaded for madness.

A low growling sounded, swelling to fill the void.

Matt whirled about, panic clutching his throat.

It shot toward him—black, with curly fur and a blunted muzzle that opened to show long, pointed teeth, sharper than any dog ever had.

"No!" Matt shrieked, dropping into a crouch, arms up to hide his face. "No! I loved you! You were my *friend*!"

But the dog came on, its growl rising to rage, eyes reddening.

It was the pet dog from his boyhood, the dog who had died while he was at summer camp.

The growling modulated into words. "I died without you."

"It wasn't my fault, Malemute! I was a kid, I couldn't get back! They didn't tell me!" And his brain knew the truth of the words, but his subconscious didn't believe it.

So neither did Malemute. Knife-teeth flashed down. Matt screamed as they ripped furrows in his leg. He jackknifed over, clawing at the muzzle, trying to pry the jaws apart. But the dog bit down harder; teeth crunched on Matt's bone, and he shrieked. The dog chewed, ripping the leg into shreds.

"Give him to me!"

Jaws snapped open; the dog's head jerked up, looking back over its shoulder.

Long, golden hair, round face, huge, long-lashed eyes, impossibly full, ruby lips, long, tapering legs, swelling hips, and huge pillow-breasts—she advanced, smiling lazily.

But Matt didn't feel the slightest bit of sexual interest; he felt terror. He knew her; she'd filled his dreams, day and night, in earliest puberty. In his daydreams, she'd been very willing, extremely cooperative—after all, there hadn't been that much asked. But at night . . .

He plastered himself back against the yielding wall, sweat starting from his brow.

"Yes," she murmured sleepily, "this is a woman. Touching you *here* . . . touching you *here* . . ."

Matt's scream turned into a shuddering gasp. Her touch was like pliers drawing hot wire, drawing it out of the depths of his body. Fire lanced him from knees up to chest.

"The pain is the preacher's," she breathed, "but the lust is yours." Her face slipped up, and huge breasts descended, covering, enfolding his face, pressing down, cutting off sight and sound, isolating him, smothering. He fought for air, gasping, struggling; but nothing could move that huge, sodden weight . . .

"Stand aside! Let me through!"

Bolster-weight rolled off him. Matt jerked up, gasping for breath . . .

A knight in full armor advanced, broadsword in hand. He glanced at the fertility symbol, then averted his eyes. "Clothe yourself! Do you not know the law?"

"Law!" Matt grasped at the straw. "Here? What law?"

"The law of your mind," the knight intoned sternly. "The law buried there, in the depths, the prudish ethic—that nothing unclothed can be good."

A *friend*, Matt thought, with a surge of hope. "Yes! Show me some clothes!"

"I am they." The knight clanked up closer, three feet away. Matt realized, with a shock, that the slits in the visor showed blackness only. "I am clothes, or what you saw clothing to be— only armor, only a shield. You ever went clothed, for you feared other people."

Matt realized that the voice was echoing hollowly, and the fear of the nameless surged though him as the broadsword lifted. "Defense mechanism," the knight boomed. "So you thought clothes to be, thought them armor; but you forgot what accompanies armor and shields." His own shield swept up. Five razor-edged knife blades were welded to it, pointing at Matt. "Your defense gave offense. Those who sought to touch you, befriend you, you pushed away with your shield—and, in pushing, gave wounds." The shield slammed out, stabbing through Matt's chest and stomach in five places. He tried to scream, but only burbling came through the blood in his throat.

The scene reeled about him—dog, knight, and fertility symbol, clothed now in a high, pointed cap with a gossamer veil hanging down to the back of her velvet gown.

The sword! Matt tried to twist away, but the knife-points held him in place. His mouth stretched wide in a burbling shriek as he watched the guillotine-edge swooping down, biting into his neck. Pain shot through him; the scene jolted, then reeled crazily about him. He felt his head turning and falling. Then he bounced, rolled, and looked up at his own headless body, held up by the shield, neck fountaining blood.

The knight leaned into his field of view, sword dropping from his fingers, steel gauntlet reaching down at Matt's head. He felt himself lifted, saw the steel helmet zooming up as the left hand let go of the shield, letting the body crumple, to swing the visor up. "Look now at the truth of a soul that seeks to hide from all others," the voice boomed. And Matt felt himself jerked up to look down into the helmet. It was empty—hollow to the depths.

Matt's lips writhed back in a shriek, but no sound came.

How could a man of reason face the knowledge that all was

illusion—and the corollary that reason forced upon him: that he, himself, did not exist?

Then a thought wafted through his mind like a life preserver. There was an answer that had saved the sanity of countless others. And the answer was—faith!

At the thought, a pencil-thin ray of light lanced down through the void, striking his ear and filling his head with a pure, bell-like tone that became words: *Thou wast stolen here before thy true time was come. Hell cannot hold thee, if thou dost call upon God.*

"Cut off his lips!" the girl screamed as the beam of light winked out. The knight dropped his visor to catch up his sword.

But Matt's lips twitched into old Latin words:

De profundis clamo ad Te, Domine! Domine! Out of the depths I cry to thee, O Lord!

And breath came where there were no lungs, hissing the words. Hell had bound the name of God from his tongue, but it had not locked out the word "Lord". His voice croaked and swelled:

> "Audi vocem meam, Fiant aures Tuae intentae
> Ad vacem obse creationis meae . . ."

The woman screamed, and the knight howled; then their voices faded into distance, their owners sinking into vastness, receding, shrinking down to pinpoints . . .

And they were gone.

Matt was whole again, his head on his shoulders, skin intact and unblemished; but he shook, his whole body trembling. He shivered in the cold of the void. He stood, frozen and paralyzed. The hymn had banished illusions, but left him frozen forever in a lightless block, bereft of words.

But emotion was left; and his whole being surged up into one burning, silent, wordless plea, a pathetic, despairing cry for help. In the moment of extinction, the spirit wailed for its God.

And a pinpoint of infrared answered, a pinpoint growing into a dim, ruby glow of blessed light! Other small glows appeared near it. Their glowing grew, seeming too illuminate all of the darkness, to show him . . .

Ashes, charred stick ends, and the embers of a campfire.

Feeble, pale light breathed a cold benediction throughout the dome overhead. Looking up, Matt saw stars and realized he lay on his back.

Lowering his eyes slowly, he made out dim shapes in the darkness. A cloaked mound with a sword lying near a steel hand was Sir Guy. Beyond it, in a shroud of brown riding-cloak, lay Alisande. Stegoman's huge bulk blotted out stars across the fire from Matt. And the still, homespun mound at the left was Sayeesa, her sobs quieted now.

A howl of rage came from the ground, muted by miles of earth, screeching, fading—so faint that it might have been a tag end of dream. Fading. Gone.

He was home.

Matt breathed a long, trembling breath, and his whole body went limp as his soul surged up in an instant, huge blast of thanksgiving.

Then he stiffened, eyes opened wide. For a second, he could have sworn he'd felt an answer, like a benign, gentle hand cupping his soul for an instant, then gone.

He sat up, shaking his head, frowning. Illusion! It had to be.

No, it didn't. Not here.

But it could have been, all of it. It could all have been a nightmare. Did it matter?

He pulled his knees up, wrapping his arms around his shins and resting his chin on his kneecaps. No, it didn't really matter; because, even if it had been a nightmare, it had shown him what he really believed, at the bottom of his soul. Call it conditioning or brainwashing, if you wanted; it still came down to the same thing—in the depths of his being, he believed in sin and Hell.

And if he believed in sin and Hell, then he believed in virtue and Heaven, too.

Here, anyway. He wasn't quite willing to accept the jurisdiction of medieval Christianity over his rational home universe—but here, the theories of the medieval theologians took on weight and substance and became facts. He was in Sir Guy's world now and he had to live by the rules of chivalry.

He felt a sudden ache for someone to talk to and looked about him. He rose carefully, picking his way quietly around the campfire and over to Stegoman. He sat down by the huge head, frowning, wondering; then he shrugged and reached out to tweak the giant nose.

The great head snapped up with a snort; claws scrabbled at the ground.

"No, no, it's only me," Matt murmured.

The head swung around toward him, eyes dulled with a film of sleep. They cleared, and the dragon scowled down at him. "There is a burden on thy soul."

Matt looked at the ground, tugging at his ear. "I'm sorry to wake you, but—"

"Nay." The low, quiet voice cut him off. "Thou hast need. Speak."

Matt looked up at the great head, trying to marshal his thoughts. "It's all real here, isn't it?"

Stegoman frowned. Then his face relaxed, and he nodded. "Aye, all—you, I, the knight, the witch, and the princess."

"And Hell," Matt said softly.

Again Stegoman nodded.

"Yes." Matt nodded, too. "I had a dream tonight. It makes me think I have a moral responsibility I wouldn't acknowledge before." He looked up. "Do you understand that?"

"Better than thou dost think." There was a slight smile on the yard of lips. "'Moral' is a word that deals with more than vice and actions."

"Yeah. Sort of the condition of one's soul, I guess. If you don't accept your own morals, you're trying to split yourself in half, each half living by a different set of rules. So you're not whole, not integral. You've lost your integrity."

"Strange word for it," the dragon rumbled. "I would have said that a man who is not true to himself is not wholly himself. Right is good and Wrong is evil. He who seeks to straddle the two betrays Right and chooses Wrong."

"Umm. And here, it seems, Right and Wrong are real."

"Never doubt it," Stegoman assured him.

Matt thought that over for a minute. Then he sighed. "Another thing—in my dream, everybody wore clothes from this universe, not from my own world. My subconscious peopled my dream with medieval illusions. That seems to show that I want to be in this universe. I guess my secret self always wanted to be a wizard in a medieval world. And if this is the world I chose, then somehow it makes me responsible for what goes on in it."

"Thou hast said it," the dragon agreed. "Tell me, dost thou still think to return to thine other world?"

Matt's lips tightened. "The idea has never been far from my mind."

"Let it be," Stegoman advised him. "Abandon all homeward thoughts, Matthew Mantrell."

"Yes," Matt agreed, so softly he could hardly hear himself. One last surge of homesickness ached within him. His apartment, his friends, the life he had led . . . Then it faded to a dull ache. It would always be there; but most of the time, he'd be too busy to notice.

He shrugged it off and began describing his dream in rough outline to the dragon. "I never had a dream like that on my own, Stegoman. I could have sworn it was real. And I couldn't wake myself up—it never even occurred to me to try." He shook his head thoughtfully. "I think I had a little help on that dream."

"That most powerful wizard thou didst mention aforetime?"

"Yes. I think he sent me that dream to convince me that Evil really existed here."

"How couldst thou doubt it?" the dragon growled.

"Not hard. Not hard at all—at least, in my world."

"Then it may be that thou hast committed grievous sins. Thou must be freed of them, or thou dost imperil us all. Thou hast accepted the title of Lord Wizard from the princess. Be worthy of it!"

Matt sighed, coming to his feet. He leaned back, stretching. "I guess that means I'll have to get to confession—as soon as we come across a church."

"A priest will do," the dragon rumbled. "And do not wait for one to find thee. Seek thou him—and quickly!"

Matt nodded. "Thanks for listening. I think you've done me a lot of good."

"Thee, perhaps. Not thy soul." The hint of a smile touched the corners of Stegoman's lips. "I have done naught but listen, as any friend should do." He laid his head on his forelegs. "And now, good night."

"Good night, my friend," Matt answered softly. He stood a moment longer, watching as the dragon closed his eyes. Then he turned and made his way back to his pallet.

He lay down, tucking his robe about him for as much warmth as possible. Have to do something about that in the morning. Maybe a long, blue robe, embroidered with schematics . . . No, it would hamper his legs, and his life was likely to be pretty active for a while. He really needed clothing more suited to this world, though. Maybe just a doublet and hose, nothing elaborate, crimson and gold would do . . .

Vanity, said the monitor at the back of his mind, and Matt winced. Vanity was a vice, and he had to abstain from as many vices as possible, unpleasant as that might be.

And, of course, get to confession. Tomorrow. Or possibly next week . . .

But Stegoman wasn't quite so sympathetic when Matt tried to explain the delay the next day.

"Thou dost fear the priest," the dragon growled. "Is there so much vice left in thee still?"

"Now, hold on! Why should I be afraid of just listing my sins to a guy I can't even see? It's just not fair to *them!*" Matt waved a hand toward Alisande, fifty feet ahead, and Sir Guy, much closer. Sayeesa rode between them, bound to Sir Guy's saddle, hands tied to the pommel. But the saddle was on a small, shaggy mare, like the one the princess rode; Sir Guy rode his charger bareback.

Strange about those mares. Matt had been willing to magic up transportation, but Sir Guy had grinned and walked out into the open plain, whistling a weird sort of melody that seemed to slide around definite pitches, never quite hitting the orthodox ones. The two little mares had come trotting up out of a screen of bushes, their eyes rolling fearfully, but coming nonetheless, to tuck their noses under Sir Guy's palms and nuzzle at his armor. They'd seemed a bit skittish about having the girls on their backs; but Sir Guy had stroked their necks, murmuring to them the while, and they'd calmed. Matt had begun to suspect the Black Knight of some magical Gift of his own, till he'd remembered that Sir Guy was a knight, a *chevalier* in French; literally, a horseman. Even the word chivalry came from the French *cheval*, which meant "horse." Apparently there was a bond between horses and horsemen in this world; and the knights, being the best of the horsemen, had the most power over the horses. Which didn't explain why Matt was still riding a dragon—but he wasn't about to argue.

Unfortunately, Stegoman was.

"Look," Matt tried to sound reasonable. "To find a church, we'd have to leave the line of march. We could lose a whole day, maybe more. I can't expect the others to go out of their way that much, just because I want to natter with a priest."

"Scouring thy soul is something more than a nattering," the dragon growled, "and thy companions know its importance."

"Oh, come on! It can't be that important!"

"Canst *thou*?" the dragon snapped.

Matt frowned down at him. "What's eating you, anyway?"

"My tooth," Stegoman snapped. "And do not speak to me of tearing it out from my body. It may rot in my jaw; I'll not be parted from it."

"Okay, okay! It's your agony." Matt sighed, leaning back. "After all, who am I to talk? I feel the same way about confession."

He clamped his mouth shut, shocked at what it had said; but Stegoman turned his head back, fixing Matt with a beady eye for a moment. Then he turned away again, gazing forward. "Thou hast spoken the truth to thyself. Wilt thou not now speak to the princess?"

"About what?" Matt said, tight-lipped. "Calling off her war for a day, so I can find a box with a priest in it? Come on! I can't be that important!"

"The hypothetical wizard who sent thee thy nightmare thought thee so. Or the minions of Hell did, when they came to take thee."

Matt shook his head obstinately. "No. I can't buy that. It had to be a nightmare; a trip to Hell is a little too exorbitant. Why should I be important enough to rate such attention?"

"Thou *art* so important. What hast thou already done, *without* true dedication to the Good? Thou hast rescued the princess from prison and assembled protectors to aid her; thou hast buried a foul witch in the earth; and thou hast broken the spells of a lust-witch. Four times hast thou weakened Evil; three times hast thou strengthened Good. Both were balanced at loggerheads ere thy coming, a balance which thou hast already disrupted. In this coil come upon us, thou must needs be central."

A chill wind fanned Matt's back. "I definitely don't like the sound of that."

"Wherefore? Hath it too much of truth in it? Accept it, Wizard; for thou hast not overlong to accustom thyself. This coil's been eight hundred years in the making; it will not await thy convenience."

"Eight hundred years! What are you talking about? Malingo and Astaulf came into power less than a year ago!"

"That," the dragon said acidly, "is but the latest chapter in a rather long book. I have told thee how, eight hundred years agone, great Reme fell, and how chaos followed."

"And how Saint Moncaire eventually got sick of the mess and talked King Hardishane into taking over the continent, yes."

"Aye, because Hardishane had conquered the northern Isle of Doctors and Saints and was king by birth of a nation of Sea-Robbers; and was also, haply, heir to the greater part of Merovence, through his mother."

"Oh." Matt pursed his lips. "No, you left out those little details."

"Did I so? Well, 'tis no marvel; any hatchling would know it . . . For the taking of Merovence and her neighbors, Hardishane assembled a company of knights of greater glory than the world ever had seen, the Knights of the Mountain. They and the giant Colmain were his spearhead and Moncaire his fortress. Hardishane ruled from the far North, the Isles and the Sea-Robbers' lands, to the Central Sea's shore; and west to the coast of Ibile, east to the farther border of Allustria."

Matt sighed and rolled his eyes up. "So what does that have to do with the current world crisis?"

"That is my tale."

Matt looked up, startled, to see Sir Guy riding at his elbow. The Black Knight had dropped back to join the conversation.

"You're the resident expert on Hardishane's reign, huh?"

"And its sequel." Sir Guy nodded. "This tale concerns men more than dragons, Lord Wizard."

"Sequel?" Matt frowned. "All right—I'll bite. What was the end of Hardishane's story?"

"Why, he died." Sir Guy had his usual slight smile, but his eyes glittered. "He died, and Saint Moncaire entombed him in a cavern, hidden from all mortal knowledge; and as his knights, one by one, followed him into death, Saint Moncaire brought them there, also. The Saint himself died last, and none knows where his body went; for they laid it out in the church, to keep vigil over; but the knights who did guard it fell all at once into slumber. When they waked in the morning, the Saint's body was gone. Then the word ran 'mongst all the people, that Moncaire had gone to join Hardishane and his knights in their cave in the mountain."

"Let me guess." Matt held up a palm. "They're not really dead, nor really alive either, just sort of sleeping in a living death. Right?"

Sir Guy nodded. "Thou hast heard the tale?"

"Well, the plot, anyway. And when Merovence is *really* in trouble, up against an enemy it can't possibly beat, Hardishane and his knights will waken to save it. Right?"

"In a manner," Sir Guy said slowly. "Yet 'tis not Merovence alone; 'tis all of the Northern Lands; and the Emperor will not waken again till they must all succumb to Evil, or be joined again into Empire."

"Oh." Matt's eyebrows lifted. "That drastic, huh? It'll be either chaos or total system, anarchy or Empire? No middle ground?"

"None. We live now in the middle ground, Lord Wizard. Ibile, in the West, and Allustria, in the East, have fallen to sin and the rule of Evil; but Merovence stands in the gap not yet fallen; and I think it shall not fall in our time."

"Who're you? Chamberlain?"

Sir Guy looked up, startled, almost shocked, and Matt wondered what nerve he'd hit. But Sir Guy recovered, shaking his head. "I am what you see, am I not? A companion to your self and the princess, to restore her to the throne. And I think we shall win. The Emperor may sleep a while yet."

Matt let his eyes stray to Alisande, frowning, lips pursed. "What happened after Hardishane died?"

"Oh, his heirs governed wisely and well; and none sought to rebel against them, for the deathless giant, Colmain, stood there to aid Hardishane's line; nor was there ever a doubt as to who was the true Emperor, for Colmain knew it of a certainty and would kneel only to the eldest of Hardishane's line."

Better than a polygraph. "With a setup like that, how could the Empire fall?"

"For want of an heir. The blood grows weak in the deepness of time and, after five hundred years, the last of Hardishane's line fell to death—though there were rumors . . ."

"Of a child who grew up in a provincial knight's household?"

"Aye, an obscure and unknown knight; none could say who. The child was of the female line, descended from Hardishane's daughter, not from his son; but withal, of Hardishane's blood. And there were rumors, too, of a child reared by peasants. He was of the blood royal, and the male line, too, though of a cadet branch. Yet he was never found, and Colmain would obey no man, but roamed through the land, constantly seeking a man or woman of Hardishane's blood."

Matt had a vision of at least forty feet of blood and bone,

ploughing through fields and villages like an unprogrammed robot. "Would I be right in guessing that the country wasn't exactly in fine shape?"

"You would. 'Twas anarchy, in sum—every man's hand was turned against his neighbor. The barons ran riot through the land, each seeking to enlarge his own estates. Ibile and Allustria fell to rules of men that had no scruples and precious little good within them."

"And a fair amount of evil?"

"Aye, though neither was wholly a tool of Hell. But he who sought to conquer Merovence *was* such a tool. He was a sorcerer, one Dimethtus, who rose in the West. He bound up a corps of lesser sorcerers and one small army; and with these and much fell magic, he defeated baron after baron; and county by county, the land fell to his rule. Then at last Colmain discovered a king."

"How much time are we talking about?"

"Some fifteen years. The hidden child had grown to a youth on the verge of manhood, and his name was Kaprin. He was of the line of Hardishane's daughter. Colmain came upon him at a castle in the eastern mountains and knew him straight away. He knelt to the boy, and Kaprin knew all at once who he truly was and what was demanded of him. He commanded the giant to destroy the evil sorcerer. Then Colmain rose up and summoned the creatures who live by stone. Gnomes and dwarves obeyed his summons—yes, even trolls; and with this army and King Kaprin, he marched out against Dimethtus. Men of good heart rallied to King Kaprin's standard, and his army grew with every mile it marched. Then to him came another youth, a scholar from the Northern Isles, a doctor of the Arts, one Conor."

"A saint?" Matt inquired.

"Aye, as the fullness of time showed; but then they knew him only for a most powerful wizard."

"Yes," Matt said slowly, "there would have to be a wizard in there, if they were going up against a sorcerer."

Sir Guy nodded. "Heaven preserves the balance, Lord Wizard—always and ever."

A cold breath fanned Matt's spine and neck. "I do hope you're not trying to tell me I'm supposed to be playing Conor to Malingo's Dimethtus."

The amusement deepened briefly in Sir Guy's eyes; but he ignored the interruption. "The greater part of eastern Merovence quickly swore allegiance to King Kaprin; and he, with Conor's backing and Colmain's arm, marched west, to meet Dimethtus. They met with a clash of arms and howls of war; but Conor countered all Dimethtus's spells; and Kaprin, with the giant Colmain, sent the sorcerer's armies into flight. Thus did Dimethtus begin to believe the old maxim, which says that none can stand against a rightful king."

"He *began* to believe?"

"Oh, aye. None who hold strong opinions can be quickly swayed. He rallied up his forces and turned to battle Kaprin once again— and again, he lost and fled and rallied; he turned to battle and once more lost and fled and rallied. Thus it went, with Kaprin and his armies marching west, fighting for each mile of ground. At last the sorcerer was caught deep in the western mountains. There Dimethtus turned at bay, to wage a last death-or-victory battle 'gainst King Kaprin."

Sir Guy sighed, flinging his head back. "Great was that battle. Countless deeds of valor did King Kaprin and his knights enact. But in the hour of victory, Dimethtus's spell struck home past Conor's ward and changed the giant Colmain into stone. Yet in the doing, Dimethtus neglected to guard 'gainst Conor, and the wizard froze him in a timeless moment, while Kaprin led his armies raging through Dimethtus's host. At sunset, Kaprin held the field, with all his foemen slain or captured. Only then did Conor loose Dimethtus, and the sorcerer looked upon the field, knew his fate, and pleaded for salvation. Upon the word, demons thronged to claim his soul by his blood-contract. But Saint Conor held them all at bay, while a country priest hearkened to the long and foul tally of a sorcerer's sins. When he pronounced the words of absolution, the demons howled in despair and rage, retreating. Then Kaprin and his men could hang Dimethtus."

"You . . . don't say." Matt felt a little dazed. "A . . . very interesting story, Sir Guy, but . . . what's it got to do with us?"

"Why, our princess." Sir Guy's eyes glittered.

"You don't mean *she* . . . ?" Matt swallowed, turning to look at Alisande, then back to Sir Guy. "Well, well! King Kaprin's dynasty lasted a long time, eh?"

"Three hundred years, or nearly. Our princess's father was—"

"*Ho-o-o!*"

Their heads snapped around toward the princess' voice.

Alisande had reined in, one hand flung up to signal a halt. Then she beckoned to them, eyes still fixed straight ahead.

Sir Guy touched his heels to his horse's flanks, and the great beast leaped out in a gallop. Stegoman lumbered into a run.

They pulled up next to Alisande, who was pointing ahead, her mouth a thin, hard line. "Behold the fruit of evil kings!"

Matt looked—and saw charred ruins.

It might have been a village, once—maybe only last week. But now it was a jumble of charcoal timber ends, sticking up from ash heaps.

"It is even as she says," Sir Guy said softly. "This is the result of Astaulf's rule. The King is the symbol of the nation; he stands for all the people."

Matt knew the power of symbols in this universe. He nodded. "So whatever the King does, the people do."

Alisande nodded, thunder in her face. "He gained this land by theft; now many of my people live by theft."

"There has been much brigandage this last year," Sir Guy explained, as Matt stared at a blackened roof beam standing out from the rubble. "Troops of bandits roam the land. If the village will not pay tribute in food, gold, and virgins, the bandits howl through the houses like an evil wind, ripping plank from timber, stone from stone, and burning all to ashes."

Matt tried not to look directly at the low, charred, twisted mounds that lay here and there among the embers. It didn't help; he knew they were corpses.

Then something caught the corner of Matt's eye. "Stegoman— off to the left, there . . . Let's see it a little closer."

"Wherefore?" the dragon growled; but he waddled forward.

Alisande and Sir Guy looked up, startled. Then they nudged their horses to a walk, following, towing Sayeesa along behind. "What do you seek, Wizard?" the princess demanded.

Matt pointed for an answer.

It poked up out of the rubble—a burned and broken building, but still standing, twice the size of a peasant's hut.

"The church," Sir Guy murmured.

"How come it's still there?"

"The power it served protected it somewhat, Lord Wizard. This was consecrated ground."

Somewhat was right. The walls still stood, but they bore an

outer layer of char, and half the roof was gone. The empty windows stared in reproach.

But, desolate as it was, it waked Matt's conscience to uneasy pricking. He *had* resolved to confess his sins at the first church he found, or to the first priest. Okay, here was the church—but the priest was gone, if he was lucky; crisped, if he wasn't. Of course, if the bandits hadn't hit . . .

Matt stiffened, eyes widening. "How long ago would you say the raiders hit?"

The knight pursed his lips. "There's still some warmth . . . A day or two, or more. Wherefore?"

"Could it be . . ." Matt felt his stomach sink. "You don't suppose they could have done this to celebrate our arrival, do you? Or mine, I should say. If Malingo peeked into the future right after we escaped, he could have seen that I just might be passing this way—if I got this far, that is—and that I might be looking for a priest . . ."

Sir Guy's breath hissed in between his teeth, and Alisande grated, "Aye, most certainly. You have the right of it, Lord Wizard. This is the sorcerer's work."

Matt glowered at the building, feeling the anger and resentment grow. Okay, they'd headed him off—but he could still make the gesture of defiance! He swung his leg over Stegoman's neck and jumped down.

"What dost thou intend?" But from the tone of her voice, Alisande had guessed. "There can be naught within! And the roof could fall, the floorboards crumble! I prithee, Lord Wizard— abandon this folly!"

"Aye, abandon it!" Sayeesa sounded downright scared. "I feel strange forces lowering near that I like not!"

Matt could feel it, too, now that she mentioned it—just barely tingling. It felt like a snowbank ready to fall, a dragnet ready to tighten, just needing a pull on the string. But something tugged at him from the church, and suddenly he was certain that going in was right. "Just a quick look." He started walking.

"Thou hast no need!" Alisande cried.

But Sir Guy held up a gauntlet. "Let be, your Highness. What he must do, let him do."

Matt stepped up to the church, kicking chunks of burned timber out of the way. He set a foot on the rough-hewn charcoal that had been a doorstep and leaned his weight on it tentatively, then all the way. It held, and he stepped through the broken bits of door that still hung twisted on the frame and set foot on the church floor—carefully, until he realized it wasn't burned.

Nothing was, inside. The interior of the church was in amazingly good shape, though the roof over the sanctuary was gone. The sunlight streaming in over the altar lent an air of sanctity to the whitewashed walls and rough-hewn pews. Even the confessional stood intact—scarcely more than a wide, upright box with a partition down the middle, its near side curtained; but the homespun curtains weren't even crisped.

Matt looked about him, skin crawling at the nape of his neck. There wasn't a bit of char or fleck of ash to be seen anywhere—and the feel of magic forces was growing stronger, tingling along the strings of his neurons. His muscles tightened, readying for trouble. This wasn't just amazing—it was impossible.

"What seek ye, goodman?"

Matt whirled about, grabbing at his sword hilt.

A friar stood before him, old and bent, in a brown, cowled robe with a white rope for a belt. His hair and close-trimmed beard were white, and he'd once been tall. But he still looked solid, even stocky, and his complexion was ruddy. His eyes were bright, and his voice was deep and resonant. "'Tis not the custom to bring arms within a church, Sir Knight."

"Yeah, well, I'm not a knight." But most of Matt's brain was trying to add up oddball factors. The old man looked normal enough, but there was something about him . . . His habit was totally clean, and he looked remarkably cheerful for a priest whose parish had just been wiped out. But there was something else . . .

"What seek you in this church?" the friar inquired gently.

Go, something within him urged. *Here lies danger.*

Matt steeled himself against it. He saw no evil here, only great serenity. And there might be something strange about this strong ancient, but Matt was somehow sure he was a priest and a good man. "My soul is heavy, Father. I must confess."

"Ah." The friar raised his head—that explained everything. He turned away to his confessional, nodding. "Come, then. Speak your sins, and I will hear."

He disappeared behind the homespun curtain at the left-hand side, and Matt's stomach churned as every gland within him urged, *Away*! He tightened his jaw and stepped firmly into the confessional.

He knelt and slowly, very slowly, made the Sign of the Cross. "Bless me, Father, for I have sinned. It has been..."

His mouth dried up, tongue cleaving to his hard palate. The words wouldn't come.

"Yes?" the firm old voice urged gently, from the other side of the lattice. "How long since you've been here, my son?"

The question loosed Matt's tongue. "Four years." He swallowed, bending his head, and shifted into overdrive. "I've missed my Easter duty four times, skipped Mass 208 times, mocked my father six times..."

He worked his way through the Commandments, going so fast he could hardly make sense of it himself. Somehow, the sins kept coming to his mind, with a relentlessness that dumfounded him. It almost seemed that something was surrounding him, pushing the tale of his minor iniquities out of his soul like paste from a tube. He couldn't stop until, at last, he found that he'd run dry.

"FortheseandallthesinsthatIcannotremember, Iamverysorry!" he blurted, and collapsed over his white-knuckled hands with a sigh of relief.

"And there is nothing more?" the friar prodded.

Matt went rigid. He'd forgotten about Sayeesa! "Uhhh... Well, you see, Father, it was this way..."

He went on, running through the whole story, until he finally finished with the collapse of the palace. He sagged against the woodwork, breathing deeply.

"And?"

Matt stiffened. Was the old priest a mind reader? He sighed and leaned forward, elbows on the ledge. "All right, Father. After that, the princess and I got into a bit of an argument, and the end of it was that I got up on my high horse and denied the existence of Good, Evil, God, Satan, and sin. And that's it."

"What then changed your mind, that you came here?"

Oh, this guy was good.

He was really good. Matt took a deep breath. "Okay, Father. Let me tell you about this dream I had..."

He gave the friar a shortened version, emphasizing the despair, which was a sin, and his illusions, which couldn't exactly be said to be wholesome. When he finished, he waited in apprehension.

But the old friar murmured, "You were fortunate indeed to have a sponsor from the host of Good."

Matt nodded. "Yeah. I've heard that dreams can kill."

"You were dead already." The old man's tone sharpened. "Be sure! You *were* in Hell. Which was, most surely, penance..." The old man sighed. "But not earthly penance. For your sins, say five rosaries..."

It went on from there, and it went on for a while. Matt absorbed it all, amazed at the devaluation of sin since the Middle Ages.

"And ten Glorias," the old man finished.

"Thank you, Father." Matt started to get up.

"And one thing more."

Matt froze. Here came the goodie!

"For your latter sins," the friar mused, "I charge you with a mission."

"Uh, well, I'm kinda busy just now..."

"'Tis in your path, for your party must needs travel west. This witch, Sayeesa, must go to a certain place, there to atone for her multitude of sins. I charge you with safekeeping of this broken witch, till she comes to her destination."

Matt swallowed. "Anything you say, Father."

"Then go your way, and *try* to sin no more. *In Nomine Patri, et Filio...*"

Matt came out of the booth, shaken but resolute. He turned toward the door...

"A moment, my son."

Matt froze. *When* would he learn to move fast?

He turned slowly. "Uh, you had a postscript, Father?"

The old priest stood in front of the curtain, nodding. "Bring me the witch."

Matt stared.

Then he cleared his throat and said, "Uh, Father—are you sure? I mean, a witch..."

"Her power is broken, and you tell me her conscience now troubles her, so much so that she would destroy herself. She is in despair, one of the most insidious of sins. Bring her to me."

"I, uh, don't think she'll be exactly willing..."

"Did I ask if she was?" For a humble friar, he had a very commanding, penetrating stare. "Bring her to me."

Matt swallowed and turned away. "Well... okay. You know what you're doing... I guess."

Behind him, he heard the whisper of sandaled feet as the friar crossed to the center aisle and strode down toward the altar. In the doorway, Matt glanced back, doubtful, and saw the old man kneeling at the communion rail, head bowed, before the tabernacle. Sunlight struck down through the ruined roof, and a shimmering glow seemed to envelop him, a sort of aura...

Matt turned away, giving his head a quick shake. It must be his imagination. It had been overstimulated recently, no doubt about it.

Alisande stood by her horse, holding its improvised halter, looking worried. She saw Matt and quickly looked angry. "You were in the church overlong, Wizard."

"Sorry." Matt gave her a sickly grin. "Four years of sins take a little time."

"Four years...?" Sir Guy's eyebrows lifted. "Come, Lord Matthew! Do you mean to say there was a priest in there?"

"Still is." Matt took a deep breath, shaking his head. "Don't ask me how or why—but he's there, all right. And..." He nodded toward Sayeesa. "He wants her."

"Wants...?" Sayeesa stared, thunderstruck. "Come, sir—you jest! I, go near a priest? I, a witch? How would I dare?"

"What you would, or wouldn't, doesn't make any difference, apparently." Matt yanked a dagger from Sir Guy's belt and went to Sayeesa's horse. "Hold still, now—I'd rather not see blood for a while."

"But you cannot mean it! Why, I'd... Aieee!"

"I *told* you to hold still!" Matt sawed at the knot holding her hands to the saddle horn; the rope parted. He caught her wrists in one hand while he whittled at the rope binding her feet. "You still don't get the message. "You—are—going—to that priest!"

"You can't take me there against my will! What use is a churching, if it's forced? Nay! Leave me be!" She began to twist and thrash her arms. Matt hung onto her wrists for dear life. "Sir Guy! A little help, here!"

Frowning, the Black Knight came slowly over, caught Sayeesa's waist, and dragged her from her horse. She screamed, kicking and writhing. "Nay! You'll not hale me there! I *will* not!"

"Willing or not, you're going. There's something about this old friar that doesn't brook argument. Come on, lady!" Matt dropped the dagger and flung both arms around her.

"Stand away!" Alisande's face was dark with fury. "Take your hands from her, Lord Wizard. I command you!"

"Glad to comply," Matt ground out, "after she's inside. Let's go, Sir Guy!"

Sayeesa looked from Matt to Sir Guy as they hustled her toward the chapel. "But you are mad! You both have taken leave of your senses! I'll defile that church by my mere presence! Will you take a *witch* into a church? Bethink you of . . ." She broke off with a horrified gasp, staring at the inside of the church.

The old friar stood just inside the door, head bowed and shoulders hunched, staring gravely into her eyes.

Sayeesa screamed, and her whole body bucked in a frenzy of anger and terror. Her scream had words, but Matt preferred not to think about their meaning. He just hung on to the wildly whipping body for all he was worth and tried to ignore the feeling of unseen forces thundering in.

The friar's stern old face darkened, grave and somber. He drew a small, round, silver case from the breast of his robe. He opened it and held it up before Sayeesa's eyes.

It was the Host, the consecretated wafer of Communion.

Sayeesa went rigid, her breath rattling in, eyes bulging. Then she gave a hoarse and shrieking wail and went into convulsions.

Matt hung on grimly; so did Sir Guy. Matt felt two unseen wave fronts slam together, one straining towards the church, one away from it, crashing into one another at Sayeesa's body. She tossed and jerked wildly, whipped back and forth by colliding forces.

Matt became aware of another tone underneath her screaming, a strong and steady drone—the friar's voice, chanting Latin. It was beyond the liturgical Latin Matt had picked up at boyhood Masses, and it was taking on a strong and heavy beat. It grew louder and more rhythmic as Sayeesa'a screams weakened, and Matt realized her body had begun to twist in time to the old man's meter. The forces about them were tightening, but pressing against one another to a deadlock, without movement.

The friar's chant thundered to a peak as he thrust the Host up high, looking up toward it, toward Heaven—and Sayeesa screamed, a long, drawn-out shriek, agony from the depths of soul and body, both. Then her voice cut off, and she fell completely limp. The walls of force were gone.

Perspiring and trembling, the old friar slowly closed the viaticum, hiding the Host from sight, and slid it back inside his robe. He turned to Matt, nodding toward the interior of the church. "Bring her in."

Sir Guy swung Sayeesa's arm up over his shoulder and stepped forward; but the priest held up a hand. "Nay. The wizard only."

Sir Guy looked up, startled. Then, slowly, he stepped back, letting go of Sayeesa.

Matt caught the unconscious body, swung an arm under her knees, and hefted her up, staggering. He carried her into the church, slowly and carefully, wondering how such a slender woman could weigh so heavily.

"Lay her down," the friar commanded.

Slowly, Matt knelt, laying Sayeesa gently on the floor.

"Step back." The priest's voice was gentle again. Matt stood and stepped away. The old man knelt beside Sayeesa and began to pat her cheek, murmuring softly, in too low a tone for Matt to hear. The woman stirred, and her lashes fluttered. She looked up, frowning against pain. The friar laid his hand against her brow, still murmuring, and her face relaxed. Slowly, she sat up, looking about her, dazed.

"You are in a church, my daughter," the old man said gravely. "Come." He tucked an arm under her shoulder, turning her toward the confessional. Her eyes widened; then, slowly, she nodded and came to her feet, supported by his arm. The old friar conducted her into the right-hand side of the booth, then looked up at Matt as he lifted the curtain on his own side. "Await her coming. To pass the time—you might say your penance." And he disappeared into the confessional.

Matt had time for most of it—he had a long wait, with a constant, faltering, alto murmuring from the right-hand side of the confessional, occasionally interrupted by a basso from the left.

Finally, the right-hand side quit, and the left-hand started in. It went on for a while, too. Then, at last, both voices stilled, and Sayeesa stepped out, drawn, pale, and shaken—but resolute. She moved past Matt without a glance, hands clasped at her breast, lips a thin, straight thread, and turned down the central aisle, gliding with bowed head to kneel in front of the tabernacle. Matt stared, disconcerted. There was something about her, some sense of presence, dignity, that hadn't been there before.

"Guard her well."

Matt looked up, startled, at the old friar.

"Be mindful of your word, Sir Wizard," the old man reminded him. "Keep her safely till she comes to the place I have sent her. Beware of threats to her—and to yourself."

"Uh, thanks for your concern, Father . . . but I can't help thinking you're making a big deal out of a small one."

"Such thoughts trip the unwary, Wizard. You and she both have further parts in this fell pageant." The old man smiled quizzically. "Great deeds are due in this poor land, as Powers clash, and you and this former witch may do them. Your places are greater than you know."

That was not exactly a soothing thought. "Oh, I wouldn't say that, Father. My natural native modesty, no doubt, but—"

"Your native gift for seeing only what you wish, rather." The old man's smile was stern, but also amused. "Bear my words ever in your mind; and swear now to me that you'll guard her, till she's come to her own place."

Matt swore.

"Enough—and good." The priest nodded, smiling again. "And I'll trust you, for I believe you to be a man of honor, despite what you may think. Now here's your charge."

Matt looked up, startled, to see Sayeesa coming down the aisle. "Done with her penance? So soon?"

"Her words of prayer were but a prelude," the old man said sternly. "*She* must atone with her whole life. Escort her now, for she is weakened."

Matt stepped over beside the ex-witch, offering his arm. She glanced up at him, then away, and lifted her head, straightening her shouders. She looked so pale and shaken that Matt could have sworn she was ready to drop; but she made it out the church door and into the sunlight without taking his arm. Matt shook his head in wonder; he turned to thank the old priest . . .

And saw the interior of the church devastated, with charred and fallen roof beams slanting down to the floor, thrusting into a heap of ash and rubble.

He stared a moment, transfixed; then he let out a shout, and Sir Guy and Alisande were at his side. "What is it, what? What have you seen?"

Matt pointed, backing away from the church. The knight and princess looked in through the church door. Alisande went white as a coronation robe. Sir Guy stepped forward, setting one steel foot inside. The floor groaned and cracked beneath his weight, and he stepped back quickly, looking at either side, wide-eyed and pale. Neither said a word; they just went straight to their horses.

"Hey!" Matt called out. "Hold on!" He ran after them and caught hold of Sir Guy's bridle as the knight mounted his horse. "Come on! What's going on? Who *was* that man?"

"I think you'd best not ask." Sir Guy pulled on the reins, turning his horse's head to the west. "I shall not, for my part. But I think, friend Matthew, that we have a friend where we do need one most."

He turned away without a further word, riding slowly down the village street toward the west. Alisande and Sayeesa fell in behind him.

"Mount, Lord Wizard," Stegoman rumbled at his elbow. "Do you not wish to stay near your companions?"

"Huh . . . ? Oh, yeah!" Matt turned, setting a foot on Stegoman's knee, swinging the other up to the shoulder, then over between two great fins.

"Why dost thou seem so confounded?" the dragon rumbled as he waddled off after the horses. "Why question what has happened? Accept and be thankful."

"No," Matt said slowly, "I'm not built that way. I have to have an answer." He passed a feverish tongue over suddenly dry lips. "But I think I'm going to have to be content with the part of an answer I've got."

"What answer is that?"

"Somebody down here," Matt said, "likes us."

CHAPTER 9

The sun was sliding down the sky toward evening when they spotted the mob.

It was quite a distance away across the open plain, but Matt could make out flashes of green and yellow skirts on one of the women in the vanguard. "Uh, hold on, Stegoman. Your Highness! Sir Guy!"

"What troubles you?" Alisande demanded, reining in and turning around in her saddle.

"Uh, about those people approaching us . . ."

"Good peasant folk, no doubt. What of them?"

"With all respect, Highness," Sir Guy murmured, "no matter what the folk, we should approach with caution."

"Yeah," Matt agreed, "especially since I think I recognize one of the outfits I magicked onto one of the refugees from Sayeesa's joyhouse."

Sayeesa blanched, and Alisande's face turned grave.

Slowly, she turned back in her saddle, facing the oncoming crowd. "If that be so, let us await them here."

"*What!* Uh . . . if you don't mind a civilian's opinion, your Highness, it might behoove us more to find the quickest hole to bolt into."

"There's sense in his saying," Sir Guy said judiciously.

"But more in mine." Alisande sat stiff-backed and somehow gave the impression she'd just put down roots. "These are my people, sirs; I know them. They will not harm their princess."

It must be nice, Matt decided, to have such unswerving certainty. "Uh, let's try it the other way, your Highness. Let's say trouble starts—not that it will, you understand, but just in case it does—Sir Guy's got armor and a sword, not to mention a horse; and I'm riding a dragon and just happen to have a pretty mean blade myself."

"You have the blade," Alisande agreed, "but do you ken its use?"

"Well, my swordsmanship's not up to your kind of cuts, I'll admit. Still, I *do* have a sword—and the heaviest weapon they're liable to have is a scythe. Have you considered what kind of damage *they* might suffer?"

"None." Alisande sat back in her saddle, relaxed and certain. "Fear not, Lord Wizard; 'twill not come to blows."

Sir Guy looked relieved, and Matt's heart sank. That Divine Right clause again!

Then he remembered it was apt to prove true, and sat back himself. Maybe the princess *did* know what she was doing. After all, this wasn't exactly a personal matter.

But he kept his hand near his sword hilt, just in case.

The peasants came close enough to see armor and stopped, startled; they hadn't expected the nobility to be out joyriding. Then the girl in the yellow petticoat and green gown saw Sayeesa.

The ex-witch met her eyes, and fear was written on her face.

Hate curdled the peasant girl's face, and her forefinger jabbed out. "'Tis she, the witch who stole us all!"

The peasants stared; then a clamor of shouting broke out as they charged the companions. "'Tis she, the witch who corrupted my son!" "The sorceress who beguiled our children!" "Slay her!" *"Slay her!" "Slay!"*

They surged forward, a shouting bedlam, quilled with clubs and pitchforks, men and women shrieking for blood.

"Hold!" Alisande barked, like the best of drill sergeants; and the mob ground to a halt, poleaxed by the unexpected.

"I am she who freed your children," Alisande said severely, "and I tell you now: Hold your peace!"

"You did not save *my* child!" one woman wailed. "They brought him home, a corpse!"

And the clamor started again, not shouts, but scattered cries of outrage. It didn't seem inclined to boost any higher, though; Alisande sat her horse, staring coldly at them.

"They see me shorn of my power and come for vengeance." The fear was gone from Sayeesa's face, washed under by a look of resignation, almost determination. "And I cannot gainsay them; for I have taken youth after youth and drained them all." She bowed her head, squeezing her eyes shut. "Oh, dear Lord! If only . . ."

"Let us speak, instead, of how we'll meet this coil," Alisande said drily, "for I have no wish to harm them. They are good and worthy peasants, I doubt not, and their grievance is just. How shall we deal with them, Sir Guy?"

"Do you not see?" Sayeesa's head came up, wide-eyed in astonishment. "Surrender me to them! Let none more suffer for my sins!"

"Are you out of your mind?" Matt rounded on her. "They'll tear you to pieces! Sorry, lady—you don't buy free that easy. You've got some work left in this world, or the good Father wouldn't have put you in my charge."

"Charge?" Alisande swung about. "What geas is this?"

"Just a little matter of an oath," Matt explained. "The friar attached a rider to my penance, you see—I have to make sure Sayeesa gets safely to wherever he's sent her."

"And where is that?" There was a dangerous undertone to Alisande's voice.

Sayeesa turned to the princess. "I go to the convent of Saint Cynestria, there to spend my days in prayer and fasting."

Alisande's eyes held an approving glint. "Cynestria—the cloistered home of women who have sinned greatly, but now repent. You shall have high company there, wench."

Sayeesa nodded bitterly. "Aye, duchesses and ladies of high rank. Yet are there not many, too, of peasant blood? Is this not just?"

"Fitting, at least." Alisande turned back to look out over the mutinous, muttering peasants. Slowly, she nodded. "Yes, 'tis just—and may have some purpose in it, as Lord Matthew thinks." Her mouth tightened in chagrin. "I cannot deny it. You must needs journey there, Sayeesa. And we must see you come there safely."

Matt heaved a sigh of relief. "So what do we do, Highness? Lug out the swords? Tell Stegoman to whip up a bit of napalm?"

"I do not fear peasants, Lord Matthew. I protect them."

"Lady," cried a youth, "surely that is the dragon that aided in defeating the witch, and as surely you are the noble lady who commanded us to return to our homes. How, then, can you stand between us and the sorceress?"

"And why should I give her to you?" the princess countered.

"Why?" A portly man elbowed his way through the crowd to stand before Alisande's horse. "Why, because four of the children of this village went to the witch—and only three came home alive this day! She merits burning, Lady—'tis the punishment for witchcraft!"

"What punishment is her desert, God shall give," Alisande said sternly, "for she has repented and confessed her sins, and the priest has granted her absolution."

An outraged clamor broke, but Alisande glared stonily at the crowd, and they subsided to an ugly muttering.

"Absolution!" the spokesman squawled. "For a witch? For one who has sinned as deeply and widely as she?"

"Even so." The crack of the princess's voice cut off the muttering. "If there is a sin so great it cannot be forgiven, I know not of it. Is this not even as our Savior said?"

The spokesman hunched up his shoulders, glowering. "What penance could the priest require that could balance so many sins?"

"She goes to the convent of St. Cynestria, there to spend her life in prayer."

The mutter started up again, but now it had overtones of surprise and consternation.

"If this be so," the spokesman said slowly, "we have small claim upon her, for she is God's."

"*If* it be so," a crone shrilled.

"You doubt me?" Alisande asked it with the full weight of regal hauteur.

The crone blanched and ducked back into the crowd; but somebody in the back yelled, "The church!" Other voices took it up: "The church, the church!"

"Aye!" the spokesman cried. "If she is shriven, as you say, let her step within our church and take the Sacrament—for if she is a witch unshriven, she'll not be able to bear a holy place!"

"I tell you, she is shriven!" Alisande's anger kindled. "Who are you to doubt me!"

The spokesman shrank back from the lash of her voice, but answered stubbornly, "I do not doubt you, Lady—but even one of noble rank may be deceived."

Alisande started to answer, then caught herself, and glowered down at him in fury.

But Sir Guy was nodding, almost in approval. "A point well taken, goodman. Yet *we* have seen her shriven."

The peasant shook his head stubbornly. "It is even as I said, Sir Knight: noblemen may be deceived. There are mirages, weirds, glamours, and other foul dreams."

"True, true." Sir Guy chewed at his moustache, then cocked an eyebrow at Alisande.

Her lips tightened.

"Oh, come on!" Matt snapped. "Are we going to sit here all day, debating the nature of reality? They've cited a fair test, and I don't see any harm in it. I could do with Communion myself!"

The crowd gave a shout of triumph, and suddenly people were running, leaping in from every side, to surround Sayeesa's horse and drag her down. Matt saw a tatter of gray cloth go flying, and bellowed, grabbing at his sword. But a steel hand clamped down on his wrist, and he looked up to see Sir Guy shaking his head. Behind him, Alisande cried out, outraged, "Now I command you, *hold*!"

All movement gelled. Then heads lifted, startled, staring at the princess in disbelief. She glared back, eyes half hooded, grimly; and slowly the people began to step back, muttering angrily.

"Stand away and let the witch come forward!" Alisande demanded; reluctantly, the central knot of men parted. Sayeesa stepped forward, pulling the tattered robe about her, trying to hold the rips closed. She was pale and shaken, but the determined resignation was still there. She glared up at Alisande, and her voice was low, but clear. "Let them take me, let them rend me as they wish! I will not deny them, though I die; for it is just."

"*I* shall say what is and is not just and when you'll die or live!" the princess answered.

Matt looked at Alisande with a new respect. Here, royalty was more than just a word.

Alisande raised her head, gazing at the crowd thoughtfully. "There is some sense in this test of theirs, and 'twill not delay us long." She looked down at Sayeesa. "How say you, wench? Will you go to church?"

"Aye, and gladly! I have a lifetime's praying to begin and am eager for the Eucharist!"

The crowd stared, totally shocked. Then the outraged murmuring began.

"Be still!" Alisande barked over the rumbling. "'Tis even as you demanded! We shall go to the church!"

Sir Guy grinned and held a hand down to Sayeesa. She caught his arm and swung up on her own saddle. They turned to follow Alisande. The villagers crowded forward around Sayeesa's horse.

"Uh, Stegoman . . ."

"Aye, Wizard?"

"Not that I'm expecting anything, mind you—but maybe we oughta kinda ride close to Sayeesa, just in case."

"Fairly said." The dragon waddled up next to the peasants around the ex-witch.

One of the women spoke to her neighbor, not too far from Stegoman's side. "Do you not wonder that the priest failed to come, Joanna?"

"Aye," Joanna answered, "and more so since such a mission as this would be strengthened by a man o' the cloth. Why did he not come?"

"Oh, a deal of nonsense about leaving such affairs to the shire reeve and his men," the first said, with disgust. "'Mere peasants should not take justice in their hands,' quotha. As if there were doubt of her guilt!"

"Aye. He hides his true reason," Joanna said darkly. "Think, gossip—he left us for a week in fair May. Might he not ha' . . ." she glanced up and saw Matt was listening. "Hist!"

The first woman also looked up and saw Matt watching. She turned away, glaring at the ground in front of her.

It was only a couple of miles to the village, which was the usual ramshackle affair, a single street of thatched huts with a larger daub-and-wattle hut at the end—but this hut had a steeple. As the crowd marched up to the church steps, the big double doors slammed open before them, and a tonsured priest in a cassock stood on the threshold, fists on his hips. His hair was black and hadn't seen a comb for a day or two. His face was jowly, needing a shave, and his eyes were bloodshot. He was broad, muscular, and a little paunchy. He glared down at the crowd.

Finally, the spokesman stepped forward, clearing his throat.

The priest didn't give him a chance. "What means this, Arvide? How come you to march on my church in this fashion, like an outlaw band? You'll not pass this door till there's reverence in your hearts!"

"Reverence!" Arvide sneered. "Should *you* speak of reverence? You, who cannot bear the sound of the morning Mass bell, for that last night's wine still thuds in your head. You, with your whoring and brawling..."

"Mayhap," the priest growled, "but I've never come in to say Mass till I was sober and remorseful."

"Aye," jeered a voice from the back, "and how many mornings have we not had Mass?"

A chorus of catcalls supported him; but the priest stood, glaring them down, and they quieted. Then he called out, "Aye, there you have it! If I can't be reverent, I'll not come to the church—and I'll ask no less of you than I ask of myself!" His voice dropped to a dangerous growl. "And is there a man of you thinks he can march in here past me?"

A sheepish mutter ran through the crowd. The men shifted from foot to foot, but no one stepped forward.

"That's not what we've come for, Father!" Arvide protested.

The priest fought against a sneer. "What, then?"

"The witch!" Arvide shouted, and the whole crowd yammered behind him. The priest kept his scowl, but his eyes widened, and there was apprehension in his voice. "A witch? Among *my* flock?"

"Only as a wolf is brought in by the hunters, Father," Arvide said, preening himself. "Look upon her!"

The crowd parted, revealing Sayeesa.

The priest was braced for it, but his face showed a sudden softening—of recognition.

It passed quickly, but Sayeesa's eyes were wide, almost appalled. Then she seemed to relax; suddenly, without a line of her face changing, her eyes seemed to glow with an invitation. Matt found he was suddenly very conscious of the body hinted at by the drape of the rough homespun robe.

Then her shoulders straightened, her jaw tightened, and the aura of allure faded.

No one else seemed to have noticed, for Arvide was trumpeting triumph. "'Tis the vile witch Sayeesa, haled down from her throne of foul power, chastened and humble before you!"

The priest's eyes were riveted to Sayeesa. He muttered something under his breath, too softly to hear; but it might have been, "May the Lord forgive me."

He twisted his head, coming to himself with a start, and looked up at Arvide. "So. This is the witch?"

"She is, and I think that you know it," Arivde said somberly, eyes fixed on the priest. "Look to your soul, Father Brunel."

"I shall, be certain," the priest snapped. "Why do you bring her here?"

"I shall speak to that." Alisande rode forward, and the peasants cleared from her path.

Father Brunel looked up, frowning, then bobbed his head in salute. "Milady. Whom do I address?"

"A lady of high birth, and that is all you need know. As to the witch, she has repented and travels under my protection."

The priest stared, scandalized.

"She is shriven, Father," Alisande explained, "and travels to the convent of Saint Cynestria in the West."

Brunel's mouth tightened with some strong emotion; he swallowed heavily and turned pensive. "A fair tale, Milady—but hard to credit."

"So think your flock, and so have we come—to show that she may walk into God's church without shrinking, that she may gaze upon the blessed Sacrament, and that she may receive it in peace. Then will your villagers be content that she is indeed shriven and under God's wing again."

The priest lifted his head, unbelieving. Then he nodded slowly, turning away. "Come, then. The house of God is for those who seek Him: if she is in our Savior's favor, 'tis hers as much as any man's." He disappeared into the church, walking fast.

The peasants murmured to one another in surprise, almost outrage. Alisande turned to them, crying, "Come! This is what you wished, is it not?"

The crowd fell silent, staring up at her. Then Arvide spoke up reluctantly: "Aye. Bring the witch."

Dozens of hands reached for Sayeesa. She shrugged them off and walked into the church under no one's compulsion.

Alisande leaned down from her horse, caught the nearest peasant by the shoulder, and handed him her reins. "Tether this mare ere you enter." She dismounted and strode toward the church. Sir

Guy followed suit, and Matt muttered to Stegoman, "Be ready for trouble. We might have to leave town a little suddenly."

"Have no fear," the dragon rumbled, and Matt swung down to follow Sir Guy into the chapel. The peasants pressed in after him.

Sayeesa was pacing slowly toward the altar, head bowed over clasped hands. The crowd fell silent, holding its collective breath, as she reached the communion rail and knelt, gazing at the tabernacle. After a few minutes, she bowed her head in prayer.

The crowd began to murmur, scandalized; but it cut off as Father Brunel stepped out of the sacristy. He'd taken the time for a quick shave and wore his stole. He walked slowly and, somehow, with dignity; and he gazed at Sayeesa with a pensive frown before he turned to the tabernacle and genuflected. If there was any emotion in him, it was saddened sympathy.

He knelt before the tabernacle in prayer, and the peasants began to mutter again. Arvide demanded, "Come, Father! The Sacrament!"

Father Brunel turned his head, frowning back over his shoulder; then he sighed and came to his feet. He stepped up to the altar, unlocked the tabernacle, and lifted out a ciborium. He removed the cover and turned to face the crowd, holding up the cup.

The peasants dropped to their knees, suddenly becoming a congregation, totally silent, every eye glued to the tiny white wafer as he lifted it from the ciborium; and there was only a warmth, an imploring earnestness, in his eyes as he held the Host out to his flock, murmuring, *"Ecce Agnus Dei, ecce Qui tollis pecatta mundi."* Behold the Lamb of God, behold Him Who taketh away the sins of the world.

"Domine," the people answered in a murmuring whisper, *"non sum dignus ut intres sub tectum meam, sed tantum dic verbo, et sanabitur anima mea."* Lord, I am not worthy that Thou shouldst come under my roof, but only say the word, and my soul shall be healed.

"Domine, non sum dignus," Sayeesa repeated in a whisper, raising her head; and Matt saw with a shock that her cheeks sheened with tears. Lord, these people really took this rule-and-rote seriously!

Father Brunel's face was gentle, almost tender, as he stepped down, lowering the Host to place it on Sayeesa's tongue. Her mouth closed around it, and she bowed her head, shoulders trembling.

The peasants stared, wide-eyed, unbelieving.

Father Brunel closed his eyes, bowing his head over the ciborium for a minute. Then he turned, to place the cup back in the tabernacle—

And the peasants erupted.

"'Tis a trick!"

"The Host was not consecrated!"

"Nay, nor is this church!"

"Aye! Father Brunel has defiled our chapel with his sinning!"

Anger gathered on Brunel's face. "Who dares say this of me?" he bellowed, and the noise of the crowd slackened to an angry muttering.

Arvide called out, "Can you deny it, Father?"

"I can and do! I've never been guilty of sacrilege in this church, as God is my witness!"

The muttering became uncertain.

Father Brunel lowered his voice. The anger was gone, but steely conviction remained. "I have sinned, aye, mightily and often, God forgive me! I'm a man of weak will and strong cravings." His eyes flicked toward Sayeesa—then past her, seeking out individual faces in the throng. "But when I've sinned, I've not set foot in this church till I've walked barefoot to another priest and been shriven! I? Desecrate this church? Never!" His voice cracked like thunder over the heads of his parishioners, and many of them winced.

But Arvide stepped forward doggedly. "So you say, Father, so you say! But we cannot be sure; nor can we be sure this witch does not deserve death at the stake!"

"Nay, there may be truth in it!" One peasant woman thrust her way forward. "For often have I seen him trudge out of town barefoot, fear on his face, as though hell's outriders pursued him!"

"But he was often gone longer than confession requires," another cried. "Where was he, neighbors? And why would he not join us in hunting the witch?"

The crowd caught the direction of her thoughts, and a very ugly murmur started up.

"Aye!" Arvide's eyes lit. "He was one of her visitors!"

Brunel swallowed heavily, fighting for composure. "I'll not deny it. In truth, I sought the witch's castle—but directly after I'd left her, I sought out another priest and confessed it. He shrove me; I still say my penance."

"Yet how did you escape her power?" a granny shrieked, her arm outstretched and pointing at the priest. "Nay, speak truly! Are you not a witch also? Why else were you not turned to stone, like my son?"

"Why, because I had small enough power over him!" Sayeesa snapped. "This is a good man, beneath his weakness and lust—one who gives hurt to none and seeks to help all! He is dedicated to God—and therefore I could not hold him. Remorse overcame him, despite the strongest of spells!"

"Yet how could a man be a priest and still visit a witch of foul lust?" the granny shrieked. "Nay! He's defiled our church—and the test of this witch was no test!"

"Hold on!" Matt called out, before the crowd could react. "You admit he's always going to confession—so he couldn't have defiled the church!"

The crowd hooted derision, and the ugly mutter built up toward a roar.

"Nay, hold, good people!" Sir Guy shouted, and the crowd quieted, puzzled.

"How could he have defiled this church," Sir Guy asked reasonably, "if he was ever a-going to be shriven?"

The villagers turned to one another, murmuring uncertainly.

Matt felt the injustice of it burning his belly. He stepped over to Sir Guy. "Hey! You just said the same thing I did!"

"Aye, and I thank you for the words," Sir Guy said, *sotto voce*. "I'd never have thought of it, myself."

"But . . ." Matt fought down a surge of temper. "How come they didn't pay any attention when *I* said it?"

"Why, Lord Matthew," Sir Guy said, amazed, "you are not a knight!"

Matt turned away, fuming. If he ever found the guy who designed the rules for this universe, he decided, he'd send him back to his drawing board.

Father Brunel was nodding heavily with relief. "It is even as the knight says—you've yourselves admitted my remorse. Therefore your church is not defiled, and the test of the witch was a sound test! She has come to this House of God and received the consecrated Host under your eyes! I declare her no witch, but a woman of God, though a sinner—" His voice sank. "—like myself."

Then his head rose again. "And like everyone of you here! Aye, she's sinned far more heavily than most—but is there a one of you who can claim truthfully that he's not sinned every week of his life? Yet you're not damned for it, for you've confessed and been shriven, through the grace of our Lord! So has she!" He glared about him slowly, fairly daring them to contradict him.

There were some uneasy mutters and a lot of sidelong glances, but nobody spoke.

"Well enough, then!" Arvide glared, red-faced and furious. "She's shriven and in Grace again! But she caused many deaths and seduced many by foul enchantments! Should she not be punished for this?"

"Aye!" cried the granny. "Now burn her!"

"Aye, burn her!" The crowd took up the cry.

"Now I say *nay*!" Father Brunel roared. He glowered down at the congregation. "Death by burning is for witches and heretics. She is neither, now. If you wish the King's Law to judge her for what she has done, give her over to the king's men. But you shall not burn her for offenses of faith while I am priest here!"

"Aye, while you are priest!" Arvide shouted. "That can be changed, Father!"

"Aye!" a female voice cried from the back. "Burn them, burn them both! Let them die united by their sins, while the flames burn them clean!"

Father Brunel roared again. He tore off his stole, laid it on the altar, and charged into the midst of the crowd. They broke and fled from his path. He caught Sayeesa's arm as he passed, pulling her along behind him, and bulled his way through like a cannon ball, to the back of the church and out the door. The crowd stood a moment, galvanized; then, with a howl, they charged out the door after him.

Matt plunged into the back of the crowd. Sir Guy jumped in just ahead of him, ploughing his way through the mob by dint of steel elbows. Matt followed on his heels, with Alisande behind.

They broke through the front rank in time to see the priest turn at bay in the middle of the common, thrusting Sayeesa behind him. "Now," he bellowed, "we are out of the Lord's house! He who thinks he can take the witch, let him come and seize her!"

The mob jarred to a halt and milled about, yammering. Arvide glanced at the men to either side of him. They nodded, and he stepped grimly forward, with his two henchmen following a step behind.

Father Brunel seemed to set like concrete, waiting.

Matt tried to remember how the policemen on the cop shows sounded, and barked, "Awright, hold it right there!"

The trio jerked to a halt, staring up at him in amazement.

Matt strolled up toward them, his hand on his sword. "If you're coming in multiples, I'm stepping in on the priest's side."

"I, too!" Sir Guy stepped up brightly, his sword whisking out. "What's it to be? Our two swords 'gainst a mob? Well and good! An even fight, Lord Matthew, an even fight!"

Alisande had had enough. "Hold!" she strode into the center of the action. "Stand aside, Sir Guy! 'Tis not the office of a knight to strike peasants, but to defend them! And you!" She rounded on the mob. "The priest does naught but his office in protecting this woman—for she is a penitent and stands in God's grace again!"

Arvide's eyes widened. "Do *you* say this, too, Lady?"

"I do," Alisande answered, "and I am of noble blood. Here is my judgment in the matter: She is no longer a witch and goes free!"

Arvide, Matt thought, knew damn well that's what the lady thought; but it was a nice way out of the impasse, letting both sides back down without loss of face. Noble blood had said it; *de facto*, it was true. Maybe aristocracy had some uses, after all.

Arvide sighed, deflating. Then one of the villagers muttered something into his ear, nodding towards the princess, and Arvide's eyes widened to the size of dollars. He stared at Alisande as if he were seeing her for the first time. Slowly, he nodded, muttering, "Aye, she is! She is indeed!"

Matt fought down a surge of exasperation. There went security.

Arvide yanked off his cap and came forward, almost shyly, dropping to one knee in front of her. "My Lady and my . . ."

"'Milady' will do for the moment," Alisande said, with gentle firmness. She held out her hand.

Arvide kissed her ring and looked up at her, his face filled with devotion. He heaved himself to his feet, bowed, and turned away, striding back through the crowd. An avenue opened for him; then, one by one, the other villagers followed him, with reverent, almost frightened, glances back over their shoulders at the princess.

They filed on down the single village street; finally, the common ground in front of the church was empty. Matt turned slowly to Alisande. "I forget the kind of magic you can work in your own right, your Highness."

Alisande smiled, amused. "Be of good cheer, Lord Wizard; you shall yet learn our ways. Still, I find no fault in your conduct this day. I . . . must own, there are few men I would liefer have riding by my side in such broils."

Matt stared at her in shock. It seemed like an awfully abrupt turnaround. Then he realized it was a peace offering and he smiled back at her before he turned to Father Brunel. "Well, Father, the crisis is past."

"Aye, though he scarcely calmed them." Sayeesa turned on the friar. "I had small need of your aid. With any other priest, there'd not have been such a coil."

"True enough." The priest took it without flinching. "Yet 'twas not to protect you that I acted, but to protect my poor people from your armored knights."

"Aye, verily! You did it so well that you all but bred that very combat!"

"I did not ask the lords there to speak," Brunel growled. "If they'd stood by, I would have outfaced all my people."

"Well, it came out okay, didn't it?" Matt had to head them off, or they'd spend the entire day scrapping. "Sayeesa's unsinged, and your flock is safe."

"Aye." The priest frowned. "Though 'tis not done yet. While your Graces are here, there's no longer danger; yet there are hotheads amongst 'em who are swayed by the Devil and the vile forces unleashed in this kingdom. They will brood over not gaining their way in this matter. Then they'll start speaking aloud; and as the talk grows, so will their anger. By nightfall, they'll be worked up to rage, and they'll come to take her and burn her. None, even then, will move 'gainst your command, Lady, but 'twould be needless to see the coil bred. If you will take my good counsel——be on your way, and that quickly."

Alisande smiled sourly. "I assure you, Father, we had not meant to tarry even so long as this." She turned to the rest of the company. "Come, let us ride!"

She went toward her horse; so did Sir Guy and Sayeesa. But Matt reached out and caught Sir Guy's shoulder. The knight looked back, with raised eyebrows.

Matt turned to Father Brunel. "How about you, Father? If they're going to go witch hunting in the middle of the night and can't find a witch, they might take you as second choice."

The priest hesitated; then he nodded reluctantly. "There's truth in your words; they may seek to slay me. Yet if they do, there is justice in it."

Matt nearly blew his stack. Was *everybody* in this crazy country a walking death-wish? "You'll pardon me, Father, but you don't quite strike me as a hopeless case."

"Even so." Alisande had turned back. "Yet if penance you seek, we have a worthy endeavor that requires much hardship and sacrifice."

The priest frowned dubiously. "I have great need of such penance."

"Aye, even so," Sayeesa breathed. Brunel looked up at her, startled. For a moment, their eyes met, and the priest's face washed bleak with the naked craving of his hunger, while Sayeesa had suddenly become a magnet for male eyes.

Brunel tore his gaze away with a shudder. "Nay. If they come to hang or even burn me, 'tis for the best. I've shamed my cloth long enough."

"I will not hear of it," Alisande declared. "I think you to be a good man, in spite of your vices; and there are few such in this kingdom, in these dark days. You shall come with us."

The priest's face began to settle into obstinacy.

Alisande's tone warmed amazingly. "I will not leave a good man to a fate he warrants not."

Brunel caved in with a sigh. "I am not a good man, Majesty—"

"Highness, for this time," Alisande murmured.

Matt noticed how politely they both ignored the lack of a formal introduction.

"Highness," the priest amended. "And it is told that royal eyes always see clearly; so what you command cannot be in error. If you command it, I will come with you."

CHAPTER 10

"With all due respect, your Highness, you're out of your mind," Matt said.

They had been riding across the open plain for several hours.

"Out of my senses?" There was nothing he could pin down in her tone and expression, but somehow her horse seemed a few inches higher. "Indeed! Pray I am not, Lord Wizard, or we are all doomed to death."

"Princess, I'm sure Father Brunel is basically a very good man, and Sayeesa's a very sincere penitent—but haven't you noticed the way they look at each other? I mean, that's a built-in weakness in our party right there—just the kind of gap Malingo would love to have handy to inject a little trouble through."

"The sorcerer?" Alisande frowned. "What place has he here?"

Matt gazed at her for a moment. "Do you think those peasants back there came up with ideas about priest-burning all on their own? These are humble folk conditioned to obey a black robe, Lady! They'd have obeyed Father Brunel when he told them to let Sayeesa alone, if something wasn't egging them on! Or do your peasants usually go witch hunting all on their own?"

Alisande turned thoughtfully. "I *did* wonder at their marching out against even a broken witch, without priest or noble..."

Matt frowned. "Malingo keeps trying to get us, Princess. He tried to sabotage us with that witch Molestam; then he tried to get me with Sayeesa; now he tried to stir up trouble with a peasant mob. And you're willing to give him an opening by letting the priest stay along, in spite of the effect he and Sayeesa have on each other?"

"I am." The steel was back in her now. "Yet your advice is sound; we'll watch them closely."

Matt sighed. "Well, I suppose I should feel good about getting that much of a reaction, at least. But what *I* want to know is, why does Malingo keep trying these little penny-ante harassments? Why doesn't he just bring out an army and squash us?"

"Because, praise Heaven, I have loyal barons and abbots in the West who would sally out to reconquer the land, if Astaulf called even a small army away from them." Alisande sounded a little relieved at having the conversation back in her territory again. "Then, too, the sorcerer fears to risk a battle in the presence of the rightful queen of the land. Though I am yet uncrowned and hence unproven, he's reluctant to risk battle, so long as I have even a few loyal men about me."

Matt did a double take. "How could he be afraid to take on five of us with a thousand or so backing him up?"

"Because a rightfully crowned monarch cannot be beaten." Alisande smiled proudly. "When my forefather Kaprin fought for his crown, his forces lost only when he was not with them. So it has gone for all my line, down through the years. And while Malingo cannot be sure that power is mine, he hesitates to chance it."

"Divine Right again." Matt couldn't keep a trace of sarcasm out of his tone. "The crown automatically gives a monarch a sure instinct for tactics, eh?"

"Nay, 'tis the blood that can win a crown out of chaos—a power of sensing what will win or lose. When a king knows a battle impossible to win, he will find a way to avoid that battle. But if he *can* be brought to battle, be assured he will win, though he have but a handful of knights against a multitude."

Matt scratched thoughtfully behind his ear. "Where I grew up, we thought it only human to make mistakes."

"And you think I claim to be more than human," Alisande said drily. "Nay, Lord Wizard—I know myself to be quite mortal. In matters of my own life, I may make as many mistakes as other mortals. But on matters of the public good, if a monarch makes so many mistakes that her interest becomes opposed to that of the people, she should abjure all authority over the common weal."

"Yeah." Matt smiled tightly. "But I doubt that Astaulf is going to abdicate willingly."

"True. But having become corrupted, he no longer has claim upon kingly rights and can be brought down. Thus it came about in Ibile and Allustria. There kings came to power, but their descendants grew corrupt. Taxes crushed the peasants, and the barons ran riot. Then the kings were overthrown, to be succeeded by self-made ones who were equally corrupt. Their present kings have turned to sorcery and are sunk in debauchery. Thus has Merovence been a sole bulwark against sorcery, until the coming of Malingo."

"Is that the threat that kept your family clean?" Matt asked.

Alisande nodded. "We were reared knowing we might be beset by an army of foul sorcery at any time. I, like my ancestors, was schooled with sword and Book and the myriad ways our fathers have kept our land free. I was twelve when I followed my father's army against the sorcerer Bakwrog. At fifteen, he gave me command of a thousand foot and a hundred horse against the Baron of Carpaise.

"When my father died..." Alisande's voice faltered, but she blinked and went on, iron in her tone. "'Twas at table and sudden. I was too distraught to think to examine his food, but I now believe that he was poisoned. Then, by right, I was queen. But the land had never been ruled by a woman, and many barons were unwilling to obey. Even the Archbishop hesitated to crown me."

"And while he delayed, Astaulf and Malingo marched in?"

Alisande nodded, swallowing. "They roared through the land like a storm that levels all before it. Against the folk, they brought vampires, incubi, and succubi. Harpies struck from the sky to bring panic and chaos. Thus they came from the south in one week's time." She shut her eyes, bowing her head. "Thus fell my land."

Matt was silent, numbed, shaken—and scared. "So you *believe* you cannot be beaten in battle—but you can't *know*. And we're up against a vast army with amazing mobility, a fifth column of assorted monsters, and an air arm."

"Aye," Alisande admitted grimly. "What magic forces can you raise against them, Lord Wizard?"

"Um . . . That will require thought." Matt stalled. "I should be able come up with something. And I think we may have a support base to fall back on."

"Support base?" Alisande seemed puzzled. "Of what do you speak?"

"Well, I may have wanted to come here in my subconscious dreams—but I don't think I made it on my own."

She thought about that for a moment, then nodded her understanding. "You believe a more powerful wizard aided you. And you think he did it to support my cause?" She shook her head ruefully. "But I know of none such. Nay, you but speculate, and speculation gains us naught. We must depend on proven forces."

"And who are those?" Matt asked.

"The Western barons. For a hundred years, they and the dragons have guarded us from those who would have swarmed across the borders. And there are the soldier-monks."

"Soldier-monks?" Matt pricked up his ears, thinking of the Knights Templar of his own world. "I haven't heard of them."

"They are deacons and priests whose service to God is fighting the servants of evil by wielding shield and buckler. They are ever ready to defend the cause of Right. They are the Knights of Saint Moncaire and three lesser orders—the Liegemen of Conor, the Knights of the Hospice, and the Order of the Blue Cross. Their loyalty to the crown cannot be questioned, for it follows directly from their devotion to God."

"Who else can you count on?"

"Unfortunately, only Sir Guy and yourself. But if you can wake the giant Colmain, I shall need no more."

And that, Matt thought, would be quite a job, since Colmain had been spelled by a mighty sorcerer. It would probably be a lot more difficult than bringing back Stegoman from the witch's spell. Automatically, he reached for his silver ballpoint pen, touching it. It wasn't much, but it was somehow a connection with all he had known of his homeworld.

That was when he began to realize what a talisman was.

Late in the afternoon, they rode up from the plain onto an open moor. Matt felt almost daunted by the hugeness of the wasteland that rolled up toward the sky without a single tree or occasional shrub. Even the grass didn't grow very high here—probably because of low rainfall. The bleakness and loneliness made him feel swallowed by immensity.

Sayeesa felt it, too; she shuddered and wrapped her robe more tightly about herself. The rest of the party started looking very serious.

Still, it had to be crossed. By sunset, they were well out in the midst of the moor, surrounded by miles and miles of acres, and all of it scrubby.

Sir Guy pulled up his horse and smiled cheerily. "I suggest we go no further this day and I think we had best set up what defenses we can against those who prowl by night."

Somehow, Matt didn't think the knight was referring to the local wildlife.

He surveyed the emptiness with a singular lack of enthusiasm. "Where do we set up these defenses? I don't see a single good camping place between here and the horizon—any horizon."

Sir Guy shrugged. "The easier our decision, then. One place is as good as another. What says your Highness?"

"I have heard of these moors," Alisande said grimly. "By report, we will come to no decent defense for a day more at least. Aye, let us camp."

Matt dismounted, grumbling, and started looking for something that might serve as fuel for a fire.

"You are too delicate."

Matt looked up. Sayeesa knelt near him, lifting something from the scrub grass. "When you cannot find what you seek, you must needs use what you find—and here on the moor, Lord Wizard, our fuel is dried sheep dung."

Matt reminded himself that the American pioneers had burned buffalo chips. He sighed and started looking for sheep pellets. "Well, when in Rome—I mean, Reme . . ."

"Aye. We must do what we must," a deeper voice said.

Matt looked up. Father Brunel was kneeling near the ex-witch, gathering similar fuel. "Yet stand away," he told Sayeesa, "and leave the noisome task to me. A beautiful woman's hands were not meant for such." He looked up at her, and his gaze burned.

"Neither were yours," she answered curtly. "Are not those the hands that hold the Host?"

The priest smiled ruefully. "A poor parish priest must needs keep his own house and tend his own small garden, Sayeesa. There is dirt and filth aplenty in such tasks."

"You have used my name," she said somberly. "I had liefer you'd call me witch, as your peasants did."

"Why?" Brunel demanded, suddenly all priest again. "You should not wish the term, if you no longer are the thing. You should be mindful there is scant honesty in such a pose."

"And yours?" Sayeesa retorted. "What honesty is there in you, that you still wear the cloth?"

She rose, whirling away from him, to take her collection of fuel to Sir Guy, who had managed to cobble together a rough hearth out of stray boulders.

Matt watched her go, then turned to the priest. He wasn't too surprised to find the man's face darkened with rage. "Come on, Father—you can't deny you had it coming."

"In truth, I did. Yet 'tis none the easier to bear for that."

"Then don't give her the opportunity to score on you again. Just leave her alone."

"Aye, the wisest course." The priest climbed to his feet with a handful of sheep dung. "Yet know you what you ask of me?"

"Oh, I think I've got a pretty good idea. You're not the first man to be born with hot blood."

"Easily said." The priest gave him a dark glare. "Yet what am I to do, when such temptation's forced on me?"

"Pray." Matt's smile was bleak. "I know I will."

Dinner was, to say the least, a little on the tense side. Father Brunel kept trying to strike up a conversation with Sayeesa, who answered politely for about two sentences before she cut him off. Then, when she tried to be polite for a third sentence, she suddenly seemed to be communicating the kind of secret message that every man was born to decode. Her eyelids drooped, her mouth started to curve into a languid smile, and Matt found himself becoming uncomfortably aware of her body. Hope leaped and burned in Brunel's eyes; almost imperceptibly, he edged near her—and Sayeesa stiffened, her allure disappearing as if she'd slammed the lid on a box. Brunel's face flamed with anger.

Alisande stepped into the breach with alacrity, challenging the priest on a point of theology. Reminded of his office, Brunel sullenly turned away from Sayeesa to answer the princess.

From that point on, Alisande maintained a very energetic conversation with Brunel, while Sir Guy kept Sayeesa talking. Whenever Brunel tried to win the attention of Sayeesa, the princess and Sir Guy were always in his way. It was a dazzling display of mental footwork, but Matt found it singularly exhausting.

Finally he gave up. He gulped his last mouthful of roast moorhen, wiped his hands on a tuft of grass, and rose, turning away from the firelight.

"Lord Matthew!" Alisande's voice rang out like a challenge. "Where go you?"

"Out for a walk," Matt tossed back over his shoulder. "Don't worry. I won't do anything foolish, your Highness."

Her frown darkened. "'Ware, Lord Wizard. You yet lack knowledge of this world."

"Oh? Is there something especially dangerous about this particular stretch of moorland that you might want to tell me about?"

"Naught of which I know," Alisande said slowly. "Naetheless, be mindful—we are besieged, beset upon all sides. Not a step do we take that is not noted by our enemy. And should he catch one among us left alone, he will surely cut him out and cut him down."

"He can try," Matt said evenly, and immediately wondered at his own brass. "But I'm in a state of Grace now, your Highness— at last. And if I see anything but heather moving, I'll yell loud and quick."

"Yet may you be too far for us to reach you." Alisande glanced at Sayeesa and Father Brunel with an agonized look; then her mouth firmed with decision, and she pushed herself to her feet. "Lend me a sword, Sir Guy. If he must needs stroll about, indifferent to his danger, I'll pace beside him."

"Oh, f' cryin' out unprintably!" Matt burst out. "What do you think I am, a kid who doesn't know enough not to talk to strangers? ... All right, all right! If you don't trust me to take care of myself, I'll take a bodyguard. Stegoman! Whaddaya say?"

The dragon rose, grinning. He looked back at the princess. "I shall keep him safe. Though I bedoubt me an he will need it. Do not fash thyself, Highness."

"I shall," she said somberly, and Matt wondered at the sudden trace of hurt behind her flinty mask.

Then she turned away, closing her eyes, and Matt felt anger

seethe as he strode out across the moor. What did she expect of him, anyway? What was she trying to do to him? Or . . .

Was he doing something to her?

For a moment, hope leaped in his chest. *Illusion*, the monitor at the back of his mind schooled him sternly. *Never believe.*

It was true, and the taste of it was like bile in his throat. He reminded himself that he was a commoner born, and Alisande was royalty. True, he was technically a lord now, but it was the birth that mattered. Princesses didn't get seriously involved with anything short of dukes.

"What troubles thee?" Stegoman rumbled beside him. "I can return, if thou wouldst be alone."

"No! I'm glad of your company," Matt said quickly. "Stegoman, why were we created male and female? It only makes problems for us."

The dragon made a low, grating sound that resembled a chuckle. "Problems? Wait till thou hast mated and hast a nest of hatchlings."

Matt looked up, startled. *"You?* Ah—I mean . . ."

"Thou didst not see me as the family sort? Nay, thou hast the right of it." The dragon's eyes gleamed. "But as an eldest son, I have watched a parent's writhings and compared them with mine own. 'Tis a wretched life, unmated and wanting—or mated and responsible. In either case, wherein lies the sense?"

"Yeah. As they say in my world, you can't live without 'em and you can't live with 'em," Matt mused. "You never do control your own life. Ever since I came here, I've been slapped about, with no idea of where I'm going or why. Somebody grabs me and throws me to somebody else, who throws me to still another. Now I'm marching across a strange moor with a knight I don't know, a princess without a throne, a priest who shouldn't be, and an ex-witch. I'm getting a little tired of it all. It's time I got back in control."

Stegoman lifted an eyeridge. "Thou dost desire power?"

"Not to control anyone else's life—just mine. I mean, I scarcely know what I'm doing any more—or why. For all I know, I could help Alisande gain the throne, only to see her set up the kind of government I abhor."

"And what kind wouldst thou not abhor?"

"Oh—the greatest good for the greatest number, I suppose."

"Ah, thou dost speak of peasants. And what is their lot now under Astaulf?"

Matt remembered the burned village and shuddered. "Okay, you win that point. But would Alisande be any better?"

"Her blood is not corrupted," Stegoman said. "She will therefore rule like her father. I saw his reign the five years I have roamed this land, and always there was food and fuel. The barons knew their rights and duties. And each year, all had a little more than they needed. But now?" His back fins writhed in a shrug. "Hunger stalks, bandits ride, and few fields are planted. 'Twill be a long, hungry winter."

Matt sighed. "Yeah. So I guess I stick with the princess."

"Yet still thine assent lacks joy." The dragon eyed him doubtfully. "Mayhap thou must decide the why."

"Why?" Matt began an automatic answer, then stopped. His reason was no longer obvious. "You're right. Why *am* I doing it?" He mulled it over. "Maybe because..."

"Aye?"

"Well, I guess, back in my own world, I didn't amount to much at anything I tried; and I've tried lots of jobs. But here, things seem to work. Put the two-bit scholar, the so-so poet, the doubtful logician, and the indifferent swordsman together—and you've got a wizard. So now I have this feeling of achievement, and a chance to be a success. All the half-gifts I was born with add up to one big Gift, here."

"A talent must be trained, though," the dragon mused. "Did then thy studies provide such training in magic?"

"Well, no," Matt admitted. "Or, wait, maybe they did, in a way. I picked up some training in logic and the scientific method. With them, it's just a matter of figuring out the rules."

"Rules? But there are no rules of magic! As I have told thee."

"There must be laws and rules," Matt stated. "You just have to figure them out. Observe several events and find what they have in common; then you can see what proceeds from them. If you know how one proportion changes, you have a good guide to how the other does."

Stegoman's head performed a loop-the-loop. "I hear thy words, but thy meaning lies beyond me. Dost mean, if I have two gold pieces and wish ten, I've but to write 'two' on a parchment, then change it to 'ten', and I'll have ten pieces in my purse?"

"No, no! The symbol is *not* the thing. At least... not in my world..." Matt's voice trailed off, and his eyes lost focus. Here the symbol *was* the thing—or was at least closely enough connected with it. And words were spoken symbols. So it followed that the right spoken words might directly affect things. The problem was to use those word-symbols effectively.

Well, obviously poetry seemed to work. And apparently rhyme helped. Maybe the voice sounds, when reinforced, set up some kind of magical resonance. Umm, what had that professor kept repeating about poetry? Dense—that was it; good poetry had much greater density than prose. It was heavy in imagery that could have a lot of different referents, not just one.

So it should follow that better poetry would make better magic.

Probably it would work still better if it were sung—too bad he didn't have a better singing voice—especially if the pitches were chosen to resonate correctly with the meaning. The most effective combination of melody and words would be those that were written to reinforce each other and their referents.

It all seemed to fit together so well that Matt wondered why nobody here had been able to see the way magic worked.

Then a flash of insight supplied the answer. He'd been using linear thinking to analyze things. But thought in this world was not linear—it was gestalt. People didn't break things down into parts; they thought in total concepts and hunches. To them, magic was a thing, not a series of processes. Matt decided he'd have to do some heavy thinking about that, but it appeared that his linear approach should give him a big advantage here.

Then a nudge against his back reminded him that he was not alone, and he looked up, surprised at how far they had come while he was deep in thought. Behind him, Stegoman stood quietly, his head turned back toward the campsite in a listening position.

"Hearken!" the dragon urged softly. "Dost hear?"

Almost at once, Matt heard it—a scream, thin and distant.

"The princess!" Stegoman's head snapped up.

"Or Sayeesa." Matt ran to the dragon, leaped, and pulled himself up between two fin-plates. "What could be..."

Far away toward the camp, a wolf howled.

CHAPTER 11

Stegoman let out a thundering roar as he lumbered into the camp.

Sayeesa was crouched back against the boulder that had sheltered the campfire. Sir Guy stood in front of her with sword and shield, but obviously had found no time to don armor. Beside him, the princess stood with a sword to guard his back. There was no sign of Father Brunel.

In front of the knight danced a gaunt, gray wolf, snarling, snapping its jaws, and trying to leap at him from the side, but prevented by the two swords.

Suddenly, the wolf leaped high, attempting to jump over Sir Guy. The Black Knight's shield shot up, slamming against the wolf's chest, throwing the creature backward. Then his sword flashed downward, opening a long gash in the hairy side. Blood fountained out—but the flow slackened almost instantly, slowed to a trickle, and stopped. The wound began to close.

Matt's scalp prickled as his hair tried to stand on end. He'd done enough reading of horror stories to recognize a werewolf.

"I tell you, swords are of no avail," Sayeesa cried. "A silver crucifix, Sir Knight! Naught else will protect us!"

"We have none." For once, the Black Knight sounded less than amused.

The wolf gathered itself for another spring, and Stegoman let out a bellow. The wolf whirled. Then it sprang high into the air, straight for Matt's face.

Stegoman reared back his neck and let out a blast of fire. Flame enveloped the wolf. It screamed, a sound that was almost human. Then the blowtorch cut out as Stegoman hiccuped, and the wolf fell, a crisped and singed hulk, moaning and howling. Matt leaped to the ground.

"Stay clear of the fell beast!" Sayeesa cried, and Matt realized he'd landed only ten feet from the struggling hulk.

As he watched, the char fell from the wolf's body, leaving new, pink skin. Hair sprouted and grew. The moans turned into snarls. The wolf lifted its head. For a second, Matt stared directly into its eyes. They looked familiar...

The wolf floundered to its feet and leaped, slashing at him. Matt sprang back, and Stegoman's head swung down between him and the wolf, jaws gaping for another blast. The wolf sidled back and began to dance around them. Suddenly it whirled and leaped at Sayeesa.

Sir Guy moved to block its way. The wolf saw the sword stabbing and tried to abort its leap, but the sword laid open its side. It howled as it landed, and blood gushed again, to halt and begin healing at once. Then the wolf struggled to its feet and leaped for Matt's throat.

Matt twisted aside into a crouch and reached out to catch a paw as the wolf went past. He turned with it and yanked down, then let go. The wolf went flying, somersaulting for ten feet, to land on its back. Something cracked like a brittle branch, and the wolf screamed as it floundered about on the ground.

"Be not deceived," Sayeesa called. "His back will heal. Work your spell now or not at all!"

Matt nodded, closing his mind to the wolf's piteous yelps and howls. He reached for his silver ballpoint, taking a deep breath and scrounging mentally for a verse. Then he began chanting the spell.

> "Silver pen that wrote of life,
> Be a form inscribing death.
> Change yourself into a knife,
> Fit for stopping evil breath!"

The pen twitched and writhed in his hand, but Matt didn't dare look down at it, because the wolf had staggered to its feet and was stalking toward him, stiff-legged, snarling.

Matt flicked his hand; moonlight gleamed off the blade.

The wolf froze, staring.

Then a snarl of rage ripped from its throat as it leaped at Matt, death in its eyes.

Matt dropped to his knees, thrusting up with the dagger, scoring the wolf's belly. The wolf twisted in mid-air, snapping at Matt's hand, and fell on him. Matt covered his eyes with his forearm as the wolf's weight crashed down. An agonized howl filled his head; claws raked fire along his arm, and teeth stabbed into the hand that held the knife. Matt bellowed with pain and anger and jabbed. The teeth shot fire up his arm, but the wolf gave a choking cough and yanked its head back.

Then something slammed it aside, and Matt rolled to his knees in time to see Stegoman's huge snout swing like a wrecking ball, knocking the wolf another ten feet. "Wouldsht thou, then, trouble one o' my friendzh?" the dragon slurred, lurching after the wolf, inhaling.

The wolf scrabbled to its feet, saw the gaping jaws lining up on it, and leaped to the side with a howl as a gout of fire blasted the moor where it had been. It spun, snarling—and saw a silver blade hovering an inch before its eyes.

"Why do you stay?" Sayeesa cried. "Slay it ere it tears out your throat!"

But her words rang with despair, and Matt stayed his hand.

The wolf's head jerked up at the sound of Sayeesa's voice. It leaped to the side with a snarl; but Matt leaped with it, silver blade glinting, and the wolf howled in rage and frustration. It whirled about toward the open moor—and found Alisande blocking its path.

"Stand away!" Matt cried in panic. "You're not protected!"

The wolf sprang at her throat, and Matt leaped after it, stabbing. But Alisande fell back and away, to her knees, sword slashing out to open its belly as Matt's knife stabbed its hindquarters. The wolf howled in agony and sprang on past the princess, running out into the night on three legs.

Matt stood, staring after it.

"Well done, Lord Matthew!" Sir Guy's hand clasped his shoulder.

"Aye," Alisande admitted, climbing to her feet. "Though I could wish . . . what do ye?"

Matt didn't answer. He sprinted on past her, out into the night. He heard Stegoman bellow something slurry after him and a shout from Sir Guy, but he kept on running. Somehow, he was certain he didn't dare let the wolf get away.

It was a fine night for a chase, with a bright, full moon and wide-open country. There wasn't a bit of cover for the wolf to hide in, except for an occasional clump of boulders. Matt ran at a jogging lope, keeping the moving dot of the werewolf in sight.

The wolf was running on three feet, but it showed no sign of weakening. Werewolves were supposed to have amazing recuperative powers. The wound from silver would be slow to heal, but fatigue was no problem; it would recoup as quickly as it tired.

Matt wasn't so lucky. He was already tired.

He stopped to catch his breath. Then the idea hit. He'd projected those townmen fifty feet, right after he arrived. If he could do it to them, he could do it to himself. He thumbed through an imaginary rhyming dictionary in his head.

"The wolf is fast-moving, and so must be I,
    Till I'm far out in front, 'neath this bright midnight sky.
    He must be to me as the fish to the lure—
    At the front, have me waiting, far over the moor!"

Matt felt a slight jolt and was looking across a different section of the empty plain. As he turned, he could see a black dot limping along, far behind him.

Matt sighed. He'd overshot. Well, he hadn't exactly been specific. Maybe he could do better this time.

"The wolf is the reference to which I relate
    For position, direction, and also the rate;
    And since I need time to set adequate guards,
    I should be to his front by an even ten yards."

And he was. Thirty feet away, the wolf was suddenly slamming on brakes. It jarred to a stop six feet from him, snarling. Matt dropped to a crouch, knife out and ready.

With a snarl of fury, the wolf leaped in, feinting. It hopped to the side and leaped in at his face. Matt dodged to the left, swiping with the blade, but he missed the wolf by an inch. It landed and spun to face him, rage grating in its throat, stalking around him stiff-legged.

Now Matt was faced with a problem. He was pretty sure who the wolf really was, so he didn't want to kill it; but somehow he knew he didn't dare let it get away, either.

The wolf sprang, dodging out, then in again, in a series of dazzling leaps. Matt fell back, but teeth slashed his hand and claws raked his arm. The wolf danced about him, snarl rising to a high, manic pitch, never missing a chance to draw blood. And this with just three legs! Matt felt he'd underestimated the man under the fur. He swore, trying to keep the knife between himself and it; but as soon as he pointed the blade, the wolf was gone to the side.

It could keep this up all night. But Matt couldn't; his endurance was improving, but he was still mortal. He had to end it, and soon.

Out of the corner of his eye, he noticed a tall cluster of boulders, cutting a swathe of inky shadow across the moon-silvered turf. He dropped back, retreating a foot at a time. The wolf's growl rose exultantly, and it pressed the attack. In and out, in and out— and Matt fell back and back. He stepped into shadow and readied his verse. Then the wolf leaped in after him, out of the moonlight. He called out,

> "Be as thou wast wont to be,
>   See as thou hast wont to see!
>   Shadow, after moonlight's hour,
>   Hath such blessed force and power!"

The wolf howled in anguish as it fell, scrabbling in the dust. Its form blurred, seemed to lengthen, then to shrink in on itself— and a naked man lay writhing in the dust.

He saw the arm in front of his face and froze. Then he rolled up to his knees, staring up at Matt in horror and shame.

Matt scowled, feeling the fun go out of the night. "Good evening, Father."

The priest clapped his hands over his face, bowing his head. "Turn away! Do not look at me! I am a thing too foul for human sight!"

Matt's mouth hardened at the corners. He turned a little away,

so that he wasn't looking directly at the priest. Might as well spare
him as much embarrassment as he could.

> "Gird his loins and hide his shame!
> Let him seek and find his name!
> Spare his face and let him stand—
> Even now, this is a man!"

Father Brunel dropped his hands, eyes widening, startled. He
looked down at his midriff and saw a loincloth bound in place.
He looked up at Matt. "I thank you," he said slowly. "But it can
only cover my shame, not remove it."

Matt frowned, puzzled. "If it shames you, why didn't you guard
against its happening?"

The priest rose slowly, shaking his head. "It is not so easily
done, short of locking myself in my chamber when the moon
rises—and I could not do that tonight."

"No, I mean about going were at all. Or can't you do anything
to stop it?"

The priest managed a tight, ironic smile. "Aye—purge myself
totally of all lusty wishes. But if there's even the thread of such
a coveting left, I go were."

"And with Sayeesa nearby . . . ?"

"Aye." Brunel's voice was tight and bitter. "Yet the princess
commanded me to come."

"Okay, so you had to go were. But couldn't you have just run
out across the moor and chased rabbits all night?"

Brunel shook his head. "When I am wolf, there is nothing of
conscience, pity, or remorse left within me. All that's left are
appetites."

Matt pursed his lips, digesting that. "Under those circumstances, doesn't your . . . choice of vocation . . . seem a little . . ."

"False?" Brunel shook his head, with a sardonic smile. "I fled
to the Church for a purification, Lord Wizard. I sought to banish
this hidden nature—for look you, 'tis a thing of evil, to be such
a beast with no conscience; and evil must therefore begin it. So
I bethought me of purification—if I could keep my heart clean,
I would not turn wolf. What else could I do, not wishing to wreak
anguish? Suicide's a sin. Nay, when I found what I was, I fled to
the Church."

"'Found what you were?'" Matt looked up sharply. "You didn't grow up knowing it?"

The priest frowned, puzzled; then his brow cleared with a rueful smile. "Why, did you think I was born thus? Nay; or, if I was, it did not show in my childhood. I was a peasant's son, like any other, playing with my fellows and doing children's work. I did not fear the full moon's light till I began to be a man."

Matt pursed his lips. "About thirteen?"

"Twelve, for me. 'Twas then the sight of a neighbor lass quickened first my blood and shot heat through my loins. But I had been raised by chapel, bell, and Book; so when I caught myself at the bare beginning of wondering what lay beneath her bodice, I spurned the thought and turned it from me. Yet 'twas a struggle to do so, a struggle that became more difficult; and at last I yielded, staring, and lay awake that night to dream of answers and of actions."

"A night with a full moon?" Matt suggested.

Brunel nodded. "I wakened suddenly in the moonlight. The house seemed strange and fearsome. I bolted from my bed and leaped out through the window. I noticed that I had four feet and fur; yet it seemed not strange at all. I scarce had space to think of anything, save to seize the lass, to taste her flesh, to roll my tongue over that fair body, and . . . *no!*" He buried his face in his hands, fingers clenching in his hair.

"You're in the shadow." Matt clasped the priest's shoulder, shaking him. "You can't turn without moonlight, can you?"

Brunel swallowed thickly and shook his head. "And dawn transforms me back again. When the morning came and sunlight touched me with its blessed, healing wand, I became myself again, horrified at that which I had sought to do."

"Sought?" Matt seized on it. "No luck, eh?"

Brunel shook his head. "Her father, bless him, kept his house secure, the door and shutters barred. I crept back to my parents' house by day, knelt beside my bed, and wept with manhood's tears the whiles I vowed I never would become a fell and vile beast again."

Matt nodded thoughtfully. "So you went to the Church to purge the sin from your soul."

"For that, and more. I would devote my life to goodness and Godliness, to live within the shining mantle of God's Grace, so fixing all my thoughts on longings for eternal Heaven that, even in my most secret heart of hearts, I would never more seek sin."

Matt pursed his lips, turning the silver knife over and over in his hands, wondering if he could even have the heart to use it now. "I take it you got an 'A' for effort, but it didn't work."

"It succeeded fully," Brunel said sharply. "The monastery welcomed me. All there were strict and Godly men, devoting every minute of each day to piety and prayer, to body labor that would both feed them and tire the body, lessening its demands. I fasted and I prayed; I chanted hymns to God. I prospered in pursuit of Godliness and grew to my full manhood in His favor. Any sin of thought or wish I confessed at once, and never, ever, for ten years and five, did my heart betray me; never once did I turn wolf."

"Only fifteen years?" Matt looked up, surprised. "But that means . . . Wait a minute! How long ago was that?"

"Scarce five years." Brunel smiled bitterly. "I have aged quite quickly and harshly, though. I would have dwelt within the monastery all my life—and gladly; but our abbott died, and a new and younger one took his place. Hardly had he been elected then he summoned us to conclave, to tell us that the forces of Evil once more clustered thickly about the land. He said that there must now be one priest for every village, to guard each tiny flock with never-sleeping vigilance. Then we trembled, for we knew we must go out from safety to the world of sinners—priests among them."

He buried his face in his hands. "You cannot know the torment in my soul when the abbott commanded that I go out into the world, bereft of holy fellowship, to guide a flock. I shuddered in my heart of hearts, knowing the trial laid upon me."

Matt frowned. "Then why'd you go?"

The priest looked up, astonished. "Why, I had sworn obedience! And if it please the Lord my God to place me in temptation so much greater than any I had known, He must have done so as much for my own perfecting as for that of my fellows."

"Your faith does you credit." Matt tried to keep the sarcasm he felt out of his voice; he'd meant what he'd said—or his mind had.

"But my strength of will does not." The priest bowed his head. "Yet while the old king lived, I held my soul secure. I chanted psalms and prayers each moment that I spared from duty; I labored in my garden and among my flock. I worked and prayed and learned how to see only faces when I looked at women in my parish. And I stood fast! While the old king lived, my sins were small and not of fleshy lust! Even then, I quickly found a fellow priest, a village away, to hear my sins. For four long years, I never turned to wolf!"

"But the old king died," Matt said softly.

Brunel nodded, mouth hard and bitter. "And the usurper took the throne, the vile sorcerer Malingo climbing up behind him. We were weakened, and temptations grew ever more severe. The faces of the women in my parish seemed to dim, the contours of their bodies seemed to glow through their thick, homespun gowns. I strove; I fought, I say. But one lass flaunted herself ever before me, took each moment that she could to seek me out alone. I rebuked her; still she pressed herself upon me. At last, fearful of my own weakness, I fled the village, vowing that if I should sin, 'twould not be with one entrusted to my care. And . . ."

His voice hung in the air, eyes staring forward, glassy, lower lip protruding, moist.

Matt finished it for him. "You sought out the lust-witch."

Brunel squeezed his eyes shut, nodding, shoulders sagging. "Thus I fell from Grace—and I turned wolf. Time and again I sinned; time and again I ran to my brother priests, for shriving. And time and again, I became a wolf."

It had only been a year. How often could 'time and again' be? "How many times have you gone were?"

"Three times," the priest said bitterly, "and now 'tis four. I sinned in my heart; and the moon rides high tonight. I knew that I had sinned, but there was no priest nearby. I could not confess my sin, nor therefore purge it from me; so I became a wolf."

He turned slowly to Matt, face brittle, eyes empty. "Oh, friend, if you have within you any vestige of mortal, human kindness, take that silver knife and stab me through the heart! Stay my breath! Let me die, that never more may I profane the earth with evil! Kill me now, I beg you! For only one like you, a wizard with a silver knife, can end my sinful life!"

"And one like me won't do it," Matt grated.

Brunel grabbed Matt's collar with both fists and shook him like a rat. "Slay me, wizard! Or, if I turn wolf again, I'll seek you out and tear your throat!"

A furnace roared, and a huge form blocked out stars.

Brunel whipped about, to see a miniature mountain in reptilian form bearing down on him, jaws gaping wide to blast.

"No, Stegoman!" Matt shouted, leaping up. "He didn't mean it! He was exaggerating!"

Flame exploded from the dragon's jaws. Brunel howled and leaped back—into moonlight. He kept on howling.

Matt stood over the fluxing, changing form, silver knife in hand.

"Stab him!" Stegoman commanded. "Now, whilst thou canst! Do not doubt him, Wizard—he will slay thee, an he can. Slay him now!"

Growling fury answered him. A huge, shaggy shape rose up from the ground with eyes of fire.

"Strike!" the dragon bellowed.

"I can't," Matt grated. "He isn't shriven; he'd go to Hell."

The wolf howled exultantly and sprang.

Matt dived to the side and rolled, fast. Behind him, he heard a flame-blast and a long-drawn howl of anguish. He rolled to his feet, ran around the charred and churning thing on the ground, and leaped up Stegoman's shoulders.

"Aye," the dragon rumbled as Matt landed between two huge fin-plates. "Rest thee there, the whiles I purify this thing with fire."

"No!" Matt snapped. "This is a good man, in spite of his sins and weakness! Back off, dragon! He's a force for the good!"

The churning form gathered itself and rose up, charred no longer, blood in its eye and murder in its throat.

"What good could be in such a monster?" Stegoman demanded. "What ails thee, Wizard? Thou'lt help Evil, if thou dost let this monster live."

"No, I'll weaken it! Don't ask me to explain—I know I'm right!"

The wolf stalked forward stiff-legged, snarling.

Stegoman stretched his jaws.

"Turn and go!" Matt bellowed, slamming his heels into the dragon's throat.

Stegoman swallowed abruptly, jaws slamming shut. The wolf howled and leaped, landing on the dragon's muzzle with twenty claws. Stegoman bellowed in anger and high octane, and the wolf fell back screaming, curled around a burned-out belly.

"Now!" Matt bellowed in fury. "Go now, before you torture him any more!"

Stegoman drew back his head, startled by Matt's vehemence.

"Go!" Matt howled. Behind him, he could hear the burbling sobs of a wounded creature.

Stegoman muttered in mutiny, but he waddled into motion. His legs might have been short in relation to his body, but that was a lot of body, and the legs were still six feet long. He could move them quickly, too. Matt had no doubts about the dragon being able to outrun the wolf—if he could get Stegoman moving at top speed. "Go! We've got to get the party moving fast! They've only got horses; we've got to make sure they get a good lead on the wolf!"

Stegoman jolted into his fastest pace. Matt hung on for dear life as the landscape blurred by. When the wolf's howl of fury rang out over the moor again, it was far behind.

Matt pulled into camp with a bit of difficulty; stopping a dragon was almost as difficult as getting him moving.

Alisande and Sir Guy stood armed and ready, the Black Knight scarcely more than a glimmer of face and a sheen of sword in his midnight armor. Sayeesa knelt behind them, throwing earth on the coals of the campfire.

"You're armed and ready to ride?" Matt couldn't believe it.

"How could we not be, with the racketing across the moor?" Alisande nodded her head toward Matt's backtrail as a long, hungry howl echoed through the night again.

"I get it." Matt's lips thinned. "You thought you were gonna have to come pull my bacon out of the fire again. Your faith in me is touching."

"The dragon was sufficient, then." Alisande took her hand off the pommel of her sword.

"Definitely, though possibly not the way you're thinking. The bacon at stake right now, though, is Father Brunel's."

Sayeesa looked up, alarmed.

Matt noted it and tried to ignore it. "He's coming across the moor, hell-bent for leather, and I don't think he really cares whose hide he takes to the tanners. Mount and ride!"

"Flee?" Sir Guy frowned. "From one lone wolf-man? Nay! We have swords and a silver blade."

"You really want him killed?" Matt demanded.

The knight hesitated, but Sayeesa cried, "Nay! He has offended man and God, aye, but he must not die for all that!"

"She speaks truth," Alisande said with grim conviction. She

turned away to her horse. "Come, Sir Guy! We must ride out the night and this curse!"

Sir Guy pursed his lips and nodded, a gleam coming into his eye as he turned to his charger.

Matt looked as they pulled out of camp, with himself riding rearguard. A sleek, long-legged shape came loping over the rim of the moor as he watched.

They bent to the running, and Stegoman soon overhauled the horses and took the lead, in spite of Matt's protests. "No, no! We've got to stay back! I've got the only weapon that can do any good!"

"What good, when thou wilt not use it?" the dragon growled. He suddenly swerved to the side, just as a great white owl swooped low. The dragon's head snapped up, and he roared, "Harpies! Foul carrion females, preying on helpless fledglings!"

"No!" Matt wailed. "It's just an owl, Stego—"

The dragon blasted, and the owl shrieked, tumbling in flames toward the ground—and, tumbling, stretched, blurred, and hardened into the form of a man.

"Foul shorshererzh, who sheek dragon'zh blood," Stegoman growled.

Matt swallowed, hard.

The Sorcerer's form blurred again just before it landed. It shrank and hardened as it touched ground—and a dark-brown, three-foot iguana scuttled for cover.

"Lord Matthew," called Alisande, "what means this?"

"I get the feeling we're being watched," Matt called back. He had no doubt about whose orders the shape-changer had been following.

He also had a nagging suspicion that Sayeesa's presence wasn't the only reason Brunel had gone were.

CHAPTER 12

Ten miles later, Matt pulled up beside the Black Knight. "Sir Guy! Any idea where we are?"

"Far to the west of where we were," the knight told him. "Where else, matters little."

"We have tended much toward the north," Alisande added. "Saving that, we can say little."

Matt glanced behind; and, sure enough, there was the wolf, chugging along just this side of the horizon, loosing an occasional frustrated bay.

"'Ware!" Sir Guy cried, and Matt swiveled back, eyes front.

A long, dark line stretched across the forward horizon, sweeping away out of sight in either direction. It grew larger as they moved nearer; he began to make out masses of leaves and trunks gleaming silver in the moonlight. "A forest! Any idea where we are?"

"Aye," the princess said grimly. "'Tis the Forest Maugraime and it runs away a score of miles to either side of our path."

Matt nodded. "I take it there's no point in trying to go around."

"I would say not."

"Okay." Matt sighed, heaving himself up for the haul. "Any-

167

thing particular I should know about this place. Enchanted, or anything like that?"

"You have named it." Sir Guy's teeth flashed in the moonlight, and Matt almost shuddered. Bad things seemed to happen when the knight grinned. "'Tis a place of weird power, Lord Wizard— spells strung 'tween the branches of the trees. 'Tis old power here, but not always unfriendly."

Matt frowned. "Who runs it?"

Sir Guy shrugged. "Many, or none. This forest was spellbound before ever men came here, Lord Matthew; 'twill like as not hold enchantments when we are fled."

That Matt definitely didn't like. If the spirits that ruled here had been here before men, they were elementals, or close to them—embodiments of the forces of nature. Earth spirits and the like.

Then the companions were in among the branches, and it was too late to consider the matter.

Matt caught his breath in admiration. Silvered trunks surrounded him; festoons of long, black-and-silver leaves draped down, like Spanish moss. There was a hush to the wood, filled only with a faint, distant murmur of breezes ruffling leaves. They rode in close silence; the thuds of the horses' hooves seemed to strike right next to Matt's ear. The forest swallowed up sound.

Branches brushed by them; then, as they trotted further down the deer-trail, the branches stiffened, and the brushes became swats. *Not good*, Matt thought. It would definitely slow them down. A branch clutched at his sleeve; he brushed it away. The wolf, having a lower profile and pads instead of hooves, could make greater speed through the underbrush than they could.

Sayeesa screamed behind him. Matt tried to turn—and couldn't. Those clutching branches were *really* clutching. Something jerked hard on his arm, almost yanking him out of the saddle. Small twigs on the end of a branch had wrapped themselves around his arm; it felt like the clasp of a skeletal hand. Something yanked at his other arm. He looked and saw two more leafy hands clasping his other arm and thigh.

Alisande shouted in anger, and Sir Guy bellowed. Matt craned his neck around and saw the knight and the ladies clasped by a score or more of leafy hands. Sayeesa had been pulled up two feet off the back of her mare. She screamed, more in anger than in fear, lashing out with her feet at the nearest branch. A twig-hand caught her ankle and started pulling.

"Lord Wizard!" Alisande shouted. "Enchant a spell, I implore you! We cannot free our swords. If you cannot save us now, we will be bound up in bark!"

It was nice to be appreciated. "Stegoman! Light up!"

The dragon reared back its head and loosed a blast, raking the trees with flame, and Matt chanted:

> "We shall vanquished be, unless
> The Burnin' Wood to high Dunsinane hill
> Shall go from us!"

Then he added:

> "Anon, methought, the wood began to move!
> Within this three mile we may see it go—
> I say, a moving grove!"

Something tickled his eardrums— a high-pitched sound, almost too high to hear; but somehow, he knew it was screaming, filling the forest all about them. Stegoman swiveled his head around, blasting back high over Sir Guy's and the ladies' heads. Flamelets leaped up on branches, met, and grew, licking high along the limbs, running on back toward the trunks. Groaning filled the wood, echoing all about them, below the high-pitched screaming. The trees began to rock from side to side, as if a gale were blowing through the forest. Here and there, a great taproot yanked free of the earth—then another and another, until a tree actually pulled up its roots and began to walk backward. Another followed it, then three more, then a dozen, until the whole lane of trees was moving backward on its roots, like great, splayed feet, away from the dragon. Twiggy hands loosed their holds, dropping the humans. Sayeesa fell back on her horse; it jarred an imprecation out of her.

Overhead, branches whipped at other branches, trying to swat the flames out.

"Above you," Sir Guy warned softly.

Matt looked up. Tiny figures filled the branches, foot-high humanoids, wearing shaggy tunics of green and brown and cross-gartered biashosen, throwing shot-glass-sized buckets of water on the flames.

"Elves!" Matt cried. "There's intelligence here to reason with!"

"Dost'a wish to parley, then?"

Matt whipped around and found himself facing a slightly larger elf, poised atop the head of Sir Guy's horse. A circlet of gold bound his brow; he fixed Sir Guy with a glittering stare.

Sir Guy lifted his visor in respect. "You are the king?"

"Headman only," the elf said impatiently. "In your terms, perhaps a duke. I beg you, let not your beast inflame our trees again! If they die, we die! Call them back, the great Barked People! Let them not all flee us! Leave us these, our trees!"

"Yeah, sure," Matt murmured. Then louder, "Sure, anything, you say! If you call the trees off..."

But the duke didn't even seem to hear Matt. He dropped to one knee, pleading hands upraised to the Black Knight. "I beg you, Sir Knight! Let the flames depart! Call our trees to halt and set their roots again enduring!"

Sir Guy glanced at Matt, then back to the elf. "Assuredly, Lord Duke—if you rebuke your trees, instructing them not to harm us and to allow us passage."

"We will; 'tis done!" The elf leaped to his feet and shot straight into the air, landing on the nearest branch. "Old ones!" he shouted. "Ancient people! Speak you to your trees! Make clear to them that these mortals will leave off a-hurting them, if they hold fast, forebearing to molest the mortals!"

A murmur of talk, like the buzzing of a thousand bumblebees, filled the forest. The trees hesitated in their backward push.

"Douse the flames," Sir Guy said quietly to Matt, "and we'll have peace here."

"More hunterzh! I need more!" Stegoman growled, glowering about him. "Couldn't be these tiny ones; a dragon hunter towers high above a hatchling..."

"There aren't any dragon hunters here, old boy," Matt soothed. "Calm down; we're getting something resembling peace here, or at least a stalemate." Then he threw his head back, and called to the sky:

> "Rain, rain, come again,
> Now it is a time for rain!
> Let the trees start snoring,

Let the rain be pouring!
Let the flames all now be doused,
And the elves once more carouse!"

Fitting the symbol to the word, he uncapped his wine-skin
canteen and poured a few drops on the ground, then spat for good
measure. After all, if it worked for the Indians...

The forest was suddenly filled with the patter of raindrops,
pouring above, but gentled by the time it reached them. Steam
hissed as flamelets were doused, one by one.

Matt turned with a sigh of relief and saw Sir Guy. He frowned.
"You just paraphrased me, when you talked to the elf-duke; you
said the same thing I did! How come he listened to you?"

Sir Guy looked embarrassed, spreading his hands helplessly.
"'Tis the nature of this land, Lord Wizard. You are..."

"...Not a knight." Matt nodded, with irony. It was asinine,
but he was getting used to it.

The trees had quieted, though their branches still moved in a
slow susurrus. But one shuddered, giving off a groaning that
seemed to fill the glade. Matt frowned and looked up at the elf-
duke. "Hey! Your Grace! What's the matter with that one?"

"Can you not see?" the duke asked grimly. "Behold how greatly
that poor trunk doth bulge!"

Matt frowned. It did look like a case of advanced pregnancy
...His eyes widened as a memory tickled his brain. He took a
breath and recited, editing:

"He did confine thee,
In his most unmitigable rage,
Into a cloven oak, within which rift
Imprison'd, thou didst vent thy groans...
It was mine art,
When I arrived and heard thee, that made gape
The oak, and let thee out!"

The tree's groan rose into a growling, splitting crackle. A great
rift appeared in the trunk, lengthened to six feet, widened, and
rolled back. A nut-brown girl stepped from the trunk with a car-
oling cry of joy. She threw her arms up, back arching in a long,
luxurious stretch, and Matt's eyeballs bulged. Her figure was full
and voluptuous, and she moved with a grace that made her part

of the trees and the woods. Lush, tumbling hair of green cloaked her shoulders; and her brown skin was whorled, like the grain of knotty pine. She wore a tunic that fitted her like a coat of paint, leaves fastened together, edges forming fringes, revealing and accentuating every contour, though it covered her from the tips of her breasts to the tops of her thighs.

She lifted her face to Matt, eyes widening. They were huge and long-lashed. Then the lids drooped, and full, wide lips curved in a lazy smile. She undulated toward him, breathing, "A wizard! Surely, a wizard he must be, to free a dryad from a tree! My gratitude is deep, unbounded!" Her hand touched his foot, slid up along his leg, upward, coaxing, cajoling, urging him down. "I'll show you how deep, once you're . . ."

"What is this creature?" Alisande's voice was frigid.

Sayeesa answered. "A dryad, Princess—neither good nor evil, truly, but a nature-child. She does whatever Nature dictates. Avaunt thee, wench! For Nature may not rule us, here!"

The dryad looked up at her. "Be chary of your words; you stand within the forest! Who are you, to speak so to me?"

"One who yielded to the impulse, as you seek to, and knows the sorrow of it! Nay, beware—if you traffic with a mortal, you shall sin against that very Nature that does guide you!"

The dryad stepped back, eyes widening in horror.

"Back, away!" Alisande commanded sternly. "For all things natural must accord to mortal order, or they suffer! Your trees have lately learned this; would you, also?"

"Ladies, ladies!" Matt held up both hands. He swallowed with some difficulty and more regret before turning back to the dryad. "I'm complimented by your gratitude, Lady of the Wood; but I'm afraid our customs are a little different from yours. And besides, I'm afraid we're a little rushed just now—we're being chased by a werewolf."

Her eyes widened as her desire diminished. "Nay, I know that kind! Most foul beasts are they, that cross the mortal order with the natural!"

"As you sought, even now, to do," Sayeesa said dryly.

The dryad gave her a narrow look, and Matt hurried in to fill the breach. "So if you're really wanting to return a favor, Lady, find some way of slowing down that werewolf, will you? And get us through to the western edge of this forest before daylight, if you can."

The dryad looked up at him with lazy, questioning eyes, and Matt felt the attraction of her drawing him. He licked dry lips. "Please. It's a matter of survival."

The dryad sighed and turned away, shaking her head. "As you wish, then, Wizard. Ho! Duke of Elves!"

"What wish you, Lady?" The noble elf hopped over to her, doffing his golden circlet.

"Long has it been since I have seen you." Warm greetings were in the dryad's eyes; she smiled as she lifted the miniature duke on her hand. "Do you hear what these mortals have said?"

"Aye," the elf admitted, "and they have shown us some courtesy, which I fear we must repay."

"Then do repay it, I beseech you! Guide them through this dark, dense wood, to its western edge! And wing their heels; show them the fleetest of the ways—for they must be from this wood ere day!"

"'Fore the daylight should be hard." The elf almost seemed ashamed. "Yet still we shall endeavor the quickest footpath to discover. Mortals, come!" He leaped from her hand to the ground, and a host of Wee Folk leaped down with him. They trotted away into the night.

Matt nudged Stegoman, and the company started up behind him. He called back to the dryad, "Don't forget the werewolf!"

"I do not." Her back was turned to him; she frowned back over her shoulder, then turned to the nearest tree, murmuring in a language that sounded like the rustling of midnight leaves.

Matt tore his eyes away from her and focused on the golden circlet of the elf-duke, which had almost disappeared into the forest's gloom already. The trees seemed to pull back, leaving a clear way. They rode down it through the night.

"The word is sped."

Matt looked down, surprised to see the dryad trotting along beside him, apparently not even feeling the effort of keeping pace with a hurrying dragon. "I have spoken to the trees, and they will speak to the bushes and to thorns. The wolf shall find his progress slowed; for underbrush shall catch his coat, thorns shall prick and clutch at him and, ever and anon, a patch of wolfbane shall rear its leaves within his path, to fright him. His route shall be circuitous and long. Be certain, he'll not come upon you in this forest."

"I thank you, Lady." Matt was a little surprised at her efficiency. "Your communications seem to be quite efficient."

"All here are one." The dryad seemed pleased with the compliment. "We are bound together by the earth, from which we draw our substance, and to which the nourishment of our bodies returns when life is done. What one knows, all know."

A nice thumbnail summary of ecology, Matt decided. "How did a nice girl like you get into a place like that? The tree, I mean."

She sighed and turned away. "'Twas an evil sorcerer in this forest that bade me to his bed and pleasure. I did refuse, for he was ugly, and there was that about him that did reek of carrion death. Indeed, I mocked him for his pains. Yet on a sudden, half a year agone, comes he to me with a grin, and quotha, 'I have thee now, wood wench. Come thee to my bed, or suffer ever loss of liberty.' Yet how should I have known his power had grown? I laughed and mocked him, as ever I had. Then turned he upon me, crying fearful imprecations, and bade the tree to swallow me, with many a croaking cant in ancient tongues I did wot not of. And, foul amazement on me, his enchantment worked!"

"Yes," Matt said grimly, "the balance of power in the land had shifted. The old king had been slain, and a usurper had taken the throne, with the powerful sorcerer Malingo behind him to enforce his orders."

"Malingo?" Her eyes went wide. "Of him I've heard! A full fell thing is he, that does befoul the rivers with the caustic wastes of evil brews, and does fill the air with noxious fumes. A vile thing is he, that wrenches power from the land, returning only poisons! Is he behind this coil, then?"

"He is. And the sorcerer who enchanted you—is he still here, in the forest?"

"Nay," a nearby elf piped up. "He is fled, we know not where. A bramble heard him muttering, as he left, a curse upon the master who did command him hence."

Matt nodded. "Sounds like Malingo again. He called in all the minor sorcerers, to give him a sort of sorcery squadron." He turned to the dryad. "You see how it is, Lady—this wolf that's chasing us has the same gripe against Malingo that you have. In daily life, he's a priest."

The dryad stared, shocked. Then her lips formed the words: "But how is this Malingo's doing?"

"He took the throne, or took it for Astaulf, his pawn. That strengthened the forces of Evil in the land; and just as your local sorcerer grew stronger, Father Brunel grew weaker—morally, that is. It all stems from Malingo having stolen the king's throne. The man who rules the land is corrupt and wicked, and the people mimic their king."

"Aye, but 'tis deeper than that," the dryad said, brooding. "For look you, the king's the symbol of the land."

"Oh?" Matt looked up keenly; he was more sensitive to symbols these days. "Saying the king's the symbol of the *land* is going a bit far, don't you think? He's the symbol of the nation—the people who live in the land."

"Can you divorce the people from the land?" the dryad countered.

Matt started to answer and caught himself. These people still thought industry just meant good, hard work. To them, the whole earth, the wind, the trees, the streams, and all the elements were so inextricably intertwined with them that if the land's harmony was broken, so was theirs. "No," he said softly. "No, of course not. Here, the people aren't divorced from the land at all, are they? They're bone and fiber of it."

"They are," the dryad agreed, "and when they die, they return their bodies to it, as their forefathers have done for a thousand generations. The people *are* the land, or nearly; and if the king's the symbol of them, then he is the symbol of the land itself."

"Then," Matt said, frowning, "the whole land's befouled because a false king's on the throne."

"Yes." The dryad nodded, and cold fire flickered at the backs of her eyes. "Aye, that he is—an abomination and defilement upon the Royal Chair."

Matt stared, shaken by her vehemence.

The dryad looked up suddenly. "The dawn is lighting; sunlight stripes the land beyond the verge. And we are scarcely to mid-forest."

Matt looked up, startled. He gazed about him at the dark, deep gloom that shadowed all the trees. "How can you tell? It still looks like midnight in here."

"The topmost leaves do feel the sun's light; thus, so do we. Come quickly; we must find a quicker route." She hurried ahead, passing Alisande and Sir Guy to catch up with the elf-duke in the lead.

The princess dropped back beside Matt. "Well done, Lord Wizard. You have wrought mightily for me this night."

"Uh?" Matt looked up, startled. "How? I mean, Malingo's not all that apt to try to bring an army through this forest."

"True, but he'll march through the land. And 'tis even as this dryad says—all the forest is one. Yet further still, Lord Wizard, all the *land* is one; and the forest is tied to it, as thoroughly as its roots run out into the meadowland to mingle with the roots of grasses. What the forest knows, the moorland knows, and all the mountain pines. Nay, you have raised the forest for me and, in doing so, have raised up all the land. The very soil will mire Malingo's army for our cause."

The dryad was arguing with the elf-duke. A few words of vociferous debate filtered back to Matt; then it ceased, and he gathered the dryad had won her point.

They made very rapid progress after that. The dryad led, and it seemed as if the forest opened up to make a highway for them. The trees began to go backward past them, faster and faster, till they were almost a blur. They were making very good time, even though they were turning and twisting so many times that Matt began to wonder if they were following a snake with a twitch. Somehow, he suspected magic.

It was full dawn when they stepped out of the trees into the meadowland. Matt looked out over the long grass that blurred and faded into morning mist. The shadows of the great, gnarled trees stretched out ahead for a hundred feet. Beyond them was golden mist—but so thick that Matt couldn't see where shadow left off and sunrise began. All he could tell was that sunlight filled the meadow.

He turned back to the dryad. "I thank you, Lady of the Wood, and I wish I could have come more quickly, to free you from your bondage."

"Tush, sir!" The dryad turned coy. "Your advent was timely as it was. Yet when affairs cease to press you, I pray you, come this way again."

Matt felt his face heating and swallowed quickly. "Uh, thanks," he said, reaching down a hand. "It's already been a pleasure."

The dryad frowned prettily at his hand. "What novel custom's this?"

"Oh, just an idiosyncrasy of my people." Matt swallowed again. "Open hand, no weapon. It's our custom to clasp hands with friends."

"Oh . . . I most certainly wish to be your friend." Her clasp was firm, her hand dry and smooth, like polished wood. Her fingertips wriggled with a subtle pressure that sent heat coursing up his arm to his glands. "Do come again," she breathed.

Then she spun away toward the forest, leaving a laugh that merged with the whispering of the morning breeze in the leaves, as the shadows claimed her, and she was gone.

Matt took a deep breath, sitting upright on Stegoman, shaking his head to clear it. "Well! A most . . . interesting encounter."

"It was indeed," Alisande said, with an implied promise of incipient mayhem, "and I trust one was enough. Reflect on what was said, Wizard, on the crossing that's against all nature."

Matt gave her a reproachful look. "You still don't trust me. Should I be complimented?"

Alisande swung her horse about, face burning, and rode out into the meadow.

Sir Guy laughed softly behind him. "Come, Lord Wizard. Let us ride."

They cantered ahead. The mist turned deeper gold, thinning, showing them a swath of meadow. Matt saw a sheet of sunlight, laid out upon the waving grass, its near edge cut as sharply as a knife-edge by the shadow. He drew in suddenly, ten feet short of the shadow line.

"What troubles you?" Sir Guy frowned.

"I just remembered what this whole shenanigan was about." Matt swung down off the dragon. "You two ride ahead slowly with the ladies. And try to keep your neck hooked up, Stegoman, so no one can see I'm not with you."

"What hast thou in mind?" Stegoman blinked painfully against the sunlight.

"About what you'd expect. Try to make sure you keep in sight of the forest, and be ready to come a-runnin' if you hear a ruckus."

Stegoman turned his head slowly, doubtfully; but Sir Guy only asked, "What of yourself?"

"I'll stay here."

"A moment." The dragon blinked at him, frowning. "If the wolf should hap upon thee . . ."

Matt held up the silver dagger. "I'm ready—though I hope I won't have to use it."

Sir Guy frowned down at him a moment longer, then shrugged and turned away. "Come, Free Dragon! This is his fight, when all is done."

Stegoman went along, though he didn't look happy about it.

Matt stepped a few feet to the side and lay down in the long grass. The stems hid him from his companions, but also from the forest behind. He waited.

He didn't wait long.

A howl ripped from the verge of the forest.

Matt snapped his head up, looking backward, waiting.

A heavy, black form shot through the grass to his left, not five feet away. Matt leaped to his feet, just in time to see the great, gaunt wolf charge out of the shadow into sunlight.

It felt the warmth and howled, slamming on the brakes, leaning backward, clawing at the turf. It flailed about, wailing.

Hooves thudded as Sir Guy and the ladies came charging back toward it.

Then it rose up from the grass, already a grotesque and formless thing with half a face and half a muzzle, no longer a beast, not yet a man, struggling back toward the shadow line.

Matt ran forward, the silver knife out. The amorphous thing saw him coming and lunged forward desperately. But Matt leaped and landed on the terminator a half second before it.

It wailed miserably and rolled to the side, sheering off from the silver blade. It fell lengthwise, twitching, its whole form blurring, stretching out, elongating, paling—and Father Brunel scrabbled naked in the grass.

He rolled over onto his belly, face buried in his hands, sobbing in full despair.

Matt knelt, clapping his shoulder. "Calm down, Father. You're human again."

"Slay me!" The priest grabbed the front of Matt's tunic and yanked his head down. "I begged you before; I adjure you now! Slay me! End my shame!"

"No." Matt felt his face turn to flint again.

"Heed me!" The priest shook Matt like a rat, his face contorting with fury. "You would not heed me in the depth of night; look what has happed therefore! Take the silver blade and kill me!"

"Again I tell you, no!" Matt looked directly into the priest's eyes with a cold, hard stare. "I—will—not—send—your—soul—to—Hell."

He chopped down with his forearm against Father Brunel's elbow, knocking the priest's hands aside, and stood, glaring up at

Alisande, daring her to disagree. But the princess only nodded judiciously.

Surprised but relieved, Matt turned back to the priest again. "Your cure is penance, Father, not death."

The priest glowered up at him; then anger faded, and he squeezed his eyes shut, bowing his head.

"Come, sir!" Sir Guy said sternly. "Hope's not fully fled! Come, on your feet, and be a man again!"

"There's no help for it, Father," Matt said, more gently. "We're not going to let you out of it. Take up the burden of humanity once again."

The priest lay still a moment longer. Then he groaned and shoved himself to his feet again—or started to. He made it to his knees, then suddenly remembered his condition and sank back, shooting an appalled, appealing glance at Matt.

"Oh, good Heaven!" Sayeesa ripped a strip of cloth from her robe in disgust and tossed it to the priest. "Gird your loins, and have no fear—the princess and I shall turn our heads."

She turned her horse, and so did Alisande; but Father Brunel only knelt, staring down at the wide grey strip in his hands, and muttered, deep in his throat, "I should not touch your garment."

"'Tis not my garment more!" Sayeesa cried, exasperated. "'Tis separate from me now, as you shall ever be! Now gird yourself!"

Alisande stared at her in surprise, then turned away, brow furrowed in thought.

Matt looked up too, amazed. Then he sighed and turned back to Brunel.

The priest was on his feet, finishing tying the loincloth into place with a twist of skeined grasses. He looked up at Matt, face grave. "'Tis better thus. I am not fit to wear a cassock."

"Will you quit wallowing in self-pity!" Matt snapped. "Haul yourself out to the arid land of manhood! Or do you think a cassock would make you neuter?"

The priest glowered down at the ground. "I could wish that it did."

"Yeah, yeah! We could be such damn fine men, if we just didn't have to cope with women! They wouldn't even distract us, if we just didn't have glands for them to lead us by! We could win every time, if we just never had a challenge! Come off it, Father! Glory comes from keeping on trying when you're losing, not from giving up!"

Brunel's head snapped up in indignant anger—and, for a moment, he almost seemed to have a man's due pride again.

Then he lowered his head, eyes still on Matt. "Aye, there's truth in what you say: despair's illusion. I, a priest, should know that. No matter how I've sinned, there's always hope I will not sin again. 'Tis deeper shame that a layman must remind me of it."

Matt nodded slowly, almost with approval. "Then be a priest, Father, and thereby be a man."

The priest frowned at him a moment longer; then he turned away, planting his fists on his hips and staring at the ground. He looked up, nodding. "I thank you, Wizard. Now stand away from me I must be gone."

Matt lifted an eyebrow. "Quite an about-face. Where are you heading?"

"To the nearest church," Brunel answered. "Where should I go?"

"Why, with us, good Father," Sir Guy said cheerfully. "Let us find this church together."

"No." Brunel shook his head. "You must ride to the West, and quickly; and I would slow your party, as I've done already."

"Well, that's a matter of opinion." Matt looked back at the forest. "I'd say we made pretty good time, last night. About sixty miles."

"Yet you will concede, I did not aid you," the priest said, with a dark smile. "Nay, I'll go my ways. I would be liability to you, and—" He glanced up at Sayeesa, then away. "—and you to me."

Sayeesa's head swung around, eyes wide in hurt—but only for a split second; then her face was an impassive mask again.

Matt tugged at his lip, frowning. "There's some truth in that— but you're in this now, Father. You can't just sit back and watch the big guys fight it out."

"Can the people ever sit back thus?" Brunel asked drily. "You forget, Lord Wizard, that knights may lead the charge, but the greatest part of war is for the footmen. And the battlefield is farmers' trampled corn."

"Quite truly said." Alisande nudged her horse up to the priest, neck stiff, looking down at him. "What soldiers shall you bring to aid us?"

The priest looked up, taken aback. Then his brow furrowed.

"I had not thought of that. Yet what better army could you have in this fell war than a troop or two of monks?"

Slowly, the princess nodded. "What better force, indeed?"

"Uh . . ." Matt tugged at an earlobe. "Isn't there something a little bit paradoxical about that? I mean, men of God, out there with swords and pikes?"

Father Brunel turned to him with a wry smile. "It has been known before, Lord Matthew. Still, I had not such in mind. The weapons I would bid them bring are rosaries, scapulars, holy water, and the relics of the saints."

Matt caught the scoffing answer on his lips and shoved it into his cheek with his tongue. The weapons the priest had mentioned were all symbols, and very, very powerful ones. Given the rules of this universe, they were apt to do at least as much good as crossbows and a catapult or two.

Brunel straightened, squaring his shoulders. "Aye, this much I can do; and I see I must. Stand aside, Lord Wizard, let me by. I must find a church and robe, and every monastery that I can, while trooping westward." He turned back to Alisande, and something of the fighting man kindled in his glance. "Where shall I meet you, Highness?"

"In the western mountains." Battle-joy sparked in Alisande's eyes. "In the foothills north of Mount Monglore, hard by the Plain of Grellig."

"That's a ways to go, and you need to make good time." Matt looked up at Stegoman. "Mind splitting off from the main part? He needs rapid transport."

"There's some truth in that," the dragon said slowly, "yet would I misdoubt me of thy safety, Wizard."

"So would I, but I'd worry for Brunel's even more. He's got to have a companion he can't hurt, if he goes were—and who can keep him from hurting anybody else."

"Rest assured, I'll not turn wolf again," the priest said grimly.

Matt nodded in deference. "With all respect, Father, I've had some experience with good resolutions. Stegoman, I think I'll be a bit more effective if I don't have to worry about the good priest."

"Oh, as thou dost wish," the dragon grumbled, waddling over to the priest.

Brunel hesitated, glancing up at Alisande. She nodded slowly, and he sighed, turning to climb aboard the dragon. He settled between two great dorsal plates and looked back at the princess.

"At Grellig, then. I cannot pledge how many I will bring; but I think a good round hundred may take up your banner."

"I'll need each separate man, and a princess' thanks unto them. Your blessing, Father."

"You'll have it when I'm shriven," Brunel answered, with a rueful smile. "Come, good beast! Away!"

Stegoman turned his head and lumbered out into the meadow and the tatters of the morning mist, angling off toward the south. He turned back once to catch Matt's eye; the wizard waved; but Brunel kept his gaze riveted on the south. Stegoman turned back to the southwest trail and was swallowed in the mist.

"Pray God that he'll be safe," Sir Guy murmured, "for his sake, and ours."

"Be of good heart," the princess answered. "I do not think that he shall die till Grellig. Then, who knows?"

"Praise Heaven we are rid of him," Sayeesa said. "Now we are safe." But there was a lonely, haunted look about her as she gazed off toward the southwest.

Matt turned to Alisande. "The sorcerer doesn't make too much hay while the sun shines, does he?"

The princess puzzled over his meaning, then shook her head. "By daylight he must work through human beings, which lessens the danger to us. 'Tis night we must fear, when he can raise up foul embodiments of Evil."

Matt nodded. "Then we'd best be riding. There're at least fifty miles more of this moorland, but we've got some fourteen hours of daylight. We can cover a lot of miles."

"That we can *not*, Lord Wizard," Sir Guy said firmly. "Already our poor beasts have been ridden too long. I have spoken with the elfin duke. He tells me there is an outcropping of rocks and a spring, but six miles ahead. There we can rest in the shadow of the rocks while our mounts graze upon the dry grasses about."

"Okay," Matt said reluctantly. After all, the horses were not like the autos or motorcycles of his experience. "I guess we'll just have to find other shelter when we make later stops."

"Then mount and ride!" Sir Guy cried, swinging up onto his horse. Suddenly, as he looked down at Matt, his face showed embarrassment. "My apologies, Lord Wizard. I forgot."

Matt smiled up at him. "I do need something to ride on, don't I? Well, fortunately we have a good supply of sticks."

"Sticks?" Alisande frowned. "How will you ride sticks?"

Matt made no answer. He'd found what he was looking for—a six-foot stick with a sharp bend in the end, like a giant check mark. With twine twisted out of grass, he lashed on other sticks to form legs, shoving them into the ground to stand firm. With a bunch of dried grass tied on for a tail, Matt had a very rough semblance of a horse.

He stepped well back from it and chanted:

> "Mock horse made of sticks and straw,
> To your place your namesake draw!
> For my needs on mission royal
> Yield a stallion fierce and loyal."

In an area around the mockup, haze began to thicken. It turned impenetrable and began to boil upward, mounting far above Matt's head. An elephant would have been lost in it, and Matt frowned. But then it began to clear—and was suddenly gone. Where it had been stood a great chestnut stallion, its neck arched proudly. The horse turned its aristocratic head and looked at Matt.

But for Matt's needs, he saw that his enchantment was still incomplete. And two others in the party were riding bareback, which was hardly the ideal. He frowned and cobbled together another verse:

> "Let each wear, for riding fair,
> A bridle and a saddle ready,
> That the day finds us away
> Astride our steeds so strong and steady."

He blinked and saw that the horse stood bridled, with a western saddle on his back. Matt breathed a sigh of relief; at least he could ride in comfort for a change. And he saw that the other mounts now all had saddles, though not in the western style.

The chestnut walked up to Matt, nickering softly, and butted his head against Matt's chest.

"Yooo, big fellow!" Matt stroked the warm neck, feeling a strong affection for the beast. They'd get along together.

"With mine own eyes I saw it," Sir Guy breathed. He'd been staring speechlessly for the past few minutes. "Else could I never have given it credit."

"Just as well; I'm overdrawn." Matt swung into the saddle,

amused at the Black Knight. Sir Guy had seen him make a fairy castle vanish and cause trees to pull up their roots and walk, and the knight had scarcely lifted an eyebrow. But conjure up a horse, and he was awed. Nothing like professional interest . . .

They found the rocks and spring, as the elf-duke had said. And there Matt received a quick lesson from Sir Guy on caring for his horse, before taking the rations handed him and finding a shadowed place to eat them. He found he was missing Stegoman. The stallion was friendly and willing, of course. But the dragon could care for himself, and Matt needed his hard-headed realism to bounce his own ideas off.

"You may sleep now."

Matt looked up, surprised to see that Sayeesa had joined him. He shook his head. "Thanks, lady—but first guard shift is mine, and you'd better take your sleep while you can. You'll need it by the time it's your turn."

She shook her head. "I find I'm not inclined toward sleep. And 'tis folly for two to be waking. Take your rest."

"I appreciate the gesture, but I'm not sleepy yet, either," Matt told her. Silence fell awkwardly between them. To break the pause, he asked, "Am I wrong, or have you and Alisande grown more friendly?"

Sayeesa frowned, turning away. "Dislike is fading . . . I had thought she loathed me, but I see now I mistook. In some strange manner, she sees something of herself in me and thinks she has no right to even small contempt." She looked back at Matt. "Yet there can never be true friendship. She is, after all, a princess, and I a peasant's daughter."

"Class barriers!" Matt bit down on a surge of anger. "Why does that nonsense have to foul up a friendship?"

"You speak with more force than the matter warrants." Sayeesa smiled. "Do *you* wish to be friends with her?"

Matt swallowed. "Well, of course! We've got to fight together, so we should be on friendly terms, don't you think?"

"You scarcely seem enemies."

"I wouldn't exactly call us bosom buddies, either. You weren't there right after I got her out of jail. She was very warm toward me then—almost respected me, I think." He rolled his eyes up. "Why can't women take us as we are—human, with normal weaknesses?"

"When did her aspect change?"

"Right after—well . . ."

"Do not seek to spare me." Her voice was gentle. "When she saw you within my palace, was it not?"

"Yeah. What did she expect me to be—a plaster saint?"

"Nay." Sayeesa looked directly into Matt's eyes. "But was it your weakness that cooled her toward you then? Or my presence?"

Matt looked up, startled. Then he turned slowly away, his eyes losing focus as he gazed out over the plain. "That's pretty far-fetched, isn't it?"

"Why should it be?"

Matt's lips tightened in exasperation. "I'm not of noble blood. She can't let herself be interested in anyone who isn't potential royalty."

"Nay." Sayeesa smiled gently. "She might not allow an outcome of such interest—but the interest itself? No woman born can bar its rising."

Matt looked into her eyes for a long moment. Then he nodded slowly. "I see. When you put it that way, it almost makes her have to be cool to me, doesn't it?"

Sayeesa's smile broadened as she got up to leave him. "It may be that you're not completely a fool."

Matt brooded on the idea through his guard shift, then kept himself awake until Sir Guy's was finished and it was time for the princess to take over. After all, any hypothesis should be tested.

He approached her with more certainty than he felt. "I think I'm beginning to make some progress toward learning your ways, your Highness."

"Indeed?" Her voice was more brittle and aloof than it had been previously. But the others were asleep now, and he was effectively alone with Alisande. That, he decided, might account for her manner.

"That dryad wasn't exactly repulsive," he said. "But I thought I bore myself pretty well with her."

"Did you that?" Alisande turned on him. "Then tell me—how is it you understood the priest so well?"

CHAPTER 13

Sir Guy's armored hand shook Matt's shoulder, and he came awake. His eyelids felt gummy, and his mouth was dry. Every muscle seemed to ache as he forced himself up and went to join the others in a quick meal before beginning the journey again. A few sips of wine, he decided, were no substitute for coffee.

The afternoon sun was well down toward the horizon. The landscape stretched away before him, empty to the limit of his vision. Foreboding prickled his back. He turned to the knight. "I don't like the feel of what's ahead, Sir Guy."

The knight nodded grimly. "Nor do I. We must to horse and rise west with all speed, till we find some refuge."

They mounted and rode toward the west, alternating between walking and cantering, giving the horses enough rest to maintain their strength. The shadows of late afternoon stretched out toward them. Then the sun slipped below the horizon, fanning glory up into the clouds. As they rode, the sky darkened, and stars came out.

"What do we do if we don't find a convenient fortress?" Matt called to Sir Guy as they slackened to a walk again.

"Pray we shall not need one," the knight answered grimly.

Then, faint and dim, blowing on the night breeze at their backs, came a wild and ululating cry. It was a composite wail, many voices blended into one, a distant clamor that set Matt's teeth on edge and sent a thrill of fear driving up into his hindbrain.

"'Tis some evil, surely." Sir Guy turned to the ladies, swinging his arm forward. "Ride, for your souls' sakes!"

They kicked their horses into a gallop and fled across the plain. The knight was right, Matt knew. Whatever was making that noise wasn't exactly pursuing them with charitable thoughts.

They rode across the moor toward the west, the clamor growing clearer behind them.

"There has to be some kind of cover around here," Matt called to Sir Guy.

"We may have to fare without it," the knight called back. "Why not rein in, take what precautions we have time for, and meet this evilness in battle?"

"That doesn't sound like the best of tactics, Sir Knight."

"There's naught but grass for many leagues, Lord Wizard," the knight answered. "And our horses are too wearied to run throughout the night."

Matt shook his head doggedly. "I'm not in the mood for a confrontation."

"You may have it forced upon you," Alisande said acidly.

"We must stand and fight sometime this night, Lord Wizard," Sir Guy pointed out. "Why not here, while we're still somewhat fresh?"

"A point," Matt admitted, "but whatever's back there, I don't want to face it without some kind of fortification. Let's keep going on the off chance—we *might* run into a sizable clump of boulders."

"Or the Stone Ring," Sir Guy said thoughtfully.

"Stone Ring? Great big slabs of stone standing on end with lintels on top to connect them? And a smaller inner ring?"

"Quite, save that there's no inner ring." The knight looked up, interested. "Have you, then, been there?"

"No, but I've read about it." Matt wasn't too surprised to find a Stonehenge in this world; it seemed to go with the magic. "But what kind of feel does the place have, Sir Guy? Evil?"

"Therein should we pause." Sir Guy's brows knit. "'Tis a place of vasty powers; and as to good and evil, it is either both or neither. It was a temple once for men who worshiped the sun as the source of all good. Their sacrifices, so legend tells, were barley and wheat."

"Sounds as wholesome as home-baked bread. I assume they weren't the sole tenants."

"Nay. For that people faded from knowledge; and some centuries later, 'twas found and taken by a people said to worship the Dog Star as the source of all evil. Their sacrifices were human. Later came others..."

"I get the picture," Matt said grimly. "Anyone *know* how many cults have used it for a temple?"

"None have kept count; there are only legends. The place is *old*, Lord Wizard."

"So its tenants have alternated between devotion to good and devotion to evil?"

"Aye. Yet for some centuries, 'twas a place of great learning. Wizards came from the Isle of Doctors and Saints, so they say, when Hardishane's Empire was new. These good and wise men dwelt amidst the stones, teaching all who wished to come to them, and delving into all things, to discover more knowledge."

"Pure scholars." Matt nodded. "Teaching and pure research—knowledge for the fun of digging it out and learning something new."

"Aye. But their spirits do not rule there. 'Tis said the place is neither good nor evil of itself; it is what you make of it."

Alisande had dropped back beside them, listening gravely. "By all accounts, Lord Wizard, the place is quite treacherous; for there has been great fervor poured out by hundreds of thousands of people, as centuries rolled; and great and fell spells have been cast there."

"But great and good ones, too," Sir Guy reminded her.

"So this Ring is one great storehouse of power; but the kind of force a man's hit with depends on his own inclination?"

Sir Guy nodded. "The evil become more evil; the good become saintly."

Matt wondered what his own inclination really was and suddenly felt very wary of the Stone Ring. "Still, it sounds like our best bet."

"It is," Alisande said, with that full, unshakable certainty that meant she was discussing a public issue at the moment. "But how come you to know so much of this place, Sir Guy?"

The Black Knight only smiled. "I am not totally unlettered, your Highness. If we go there, we must bear a bit more toward the north." He clucked to his horse and moved ahead to take the lead.

Far behind them, the dim clamor united into one huge, hungry baying.

Alisande shuddered. "To the Stone Ring, Lord Matthew. It cannot be worse."

"I would not be sure of that."

Matt looked back over his shoulder toward the voice. Sayeesa rode behind him, hands clasped tight on the reins, eyes huge and haunted.

Broken teeth jutted up from the moor far ahead, seeming to glow in the moonlight.

"There it lies!" Alisande cried. "Ride for your souls!"

The clamor was louder behind them now, much louder; it had separated into growling and howling, baying and barking. Matt kicked his horse into a gallop.

The stone slabs loomed up before them, rising from silvered mist. Matt became aware of a tingling all about him; it was almost as if he could feel it on his skin. It seemed to sink inside him, stirring in his brain somewhere; something in the ancient stone pile resonated with the pitch and beat of his thoughts. He frowned, tasting the strange sensation, deciding he liked it as the feeling grew stronger with each stride of his horse.

He dropped back to Sayeesa. She was trembling. "Do not take me here, Wizard, I implore you! There was evil here once, and its aura still lingers. I know not what I may do here!"

"You are mistaken," Alisande said gently. She had dropped back, too, and her face was open and sympathetic. "There is good here, Sayeesa, great good! I feel it singing through my veins, like strong wine!"

"It fits." Matt eyed Sir Guy, who rode ahead, unperturbed. "We're picking up whatever we're inclined to."

"Please, pull away!" Sayeesa moaned, and there were tears in her eyes. "Stay away from this place! For here I might turn toward Evil!"

"But how could that be?" Alisande dropped the reins, spreading her arms. "I feel so great a good there that my heart longs toward it, as a dove toward its nest!"

"Ladies, please!" Matt slewed his horse into a turn and swung back to catch the bridle of Sayeesa's horse. "Whatever you do, don't stand here yammering! I hate to remind you, but there's a horde of monsters behind us!"

The hounds broke over the horizon, and their clamor rose to a frenzy. The pursuers doubled their pace, running flat out over the moorland—huge as small horses, long-legged and gaunt, with fox fire curling about their bodies and burning eyes. Steel teeth glinted in the moonlight.

"Ride!" Matt shouted. He yanked on the bridle, then slapped the rump of Sayeesa's horse as it sped past him. The pony leaped into a gallop and charged ahead into the Stone Ring with Sayeesa wailing in terror.

Alisande spurred her horse and charged in, her eyes glowing.

Sir Guy sat his horse by a sarcen, bowing the princess in. He looked up at Matt and beckoned.

Matt looked back at the tide of hellhounds, a hundred at least, closing the distance between themselves and the Stone Ring in a rush. He shuddered and turned away, kicking his horse into a gallop, and rode into the Stone Ring with Sir Guy right behind him.

Sayeesa clung to her horse, burying her face in its mane and weeping. But Alisande swung off her mount and spread her arms, twirling about. "Lord Wizard, this is a true holy place!"

"Uh, I know what you mean—I think." Matt jumped to the ground and stood tall, feeling the power of the Ring thrumming through him, so strongly that it made him light-headed and giddy.

"Lord Wizard." Sir Guy nodded toward the moor outside the Ring. "Our foes approach."

They did indeed; their clamor rang through the stones, driven by craving.

Dogs! What do you counter them with?

Cats, of course. Big ones.

Matt spread his hands, then stilled, eyes widening in surprise. He could feel power coursing through him, up from the ground through his body and into his fingertips. Euphoria swept him; what wonders *couldn't* he work here? He clapped his hands, then spread them again.

> "Wild is the moorland and empty,
> And dang'rous to men when alone.
> Lions who rule the vast wasteland
> Shall guard from the top of each stone."

"Be not so long with your spells." Sir Guy studied the outer darkness, worried.

Matt nodded upward. Sir Guy lifted his eyes to the top of the nearest sarcen. A mountain lion crouched on each stone slab, neck craned downward, watching the dogs approach. Pumas—well, Matt hadn't specified what type of lions; these would do well enough.

Sir Guy looked back at him with respect. "Well done, Lord Wizard! One beast for each monolith."

"Yeah, but there are only thirty or so sarcens." Matt frowned. He could have wished for a bigger Stonehenge. "These pumas will slow the hellhounds, but they won't stop the beasts."

The hounds were a hundred feet away, leaping toward the Ring. They broke into snarling howls of malicious triumph as they passed the fifty-foot distance. Then they screamed in shock as two mountain lions landed in front of them, claws and teeth slashing.

A ripping snarl seemed to fill the sky, leaping from stone to stone. Looking up, Matt saw the great cats leaping over the stones to the eastern blocks, then dropping, seeming to flow off the top of the Stone Ring in a tawny stream. They landed in the midst of a howling mêlée. Cats slashed throats and bit backs, breaking spines and tossing the hounds over their shoulders; but the hellhounds rallied, ganging up, three to each lion. Steel teeth flashed, tearing out throats and ripping stomachs.

"'Tis even as you said," Sir Guy admitted grimly. "'Twill slow but not stop them. And methinks the hounds mend as quickly as they are wounded. Small help, your lions, if you cannot heal them as quickly."

"Yeah," Matt said thoughtfully, "but I'd rather think up some way to keep the dogs from reaching us. This Stone Ring is basically a good design for a fortress."

"Aye, if some way could be found to close the gaps between the stones. But those are great, Lord Wizard."

Matt nodded. What he needed was something like a force-field—whatever that might be—to prevent ingress but permit egress. That was impossible, of course . . .

Wait a minute. Maxwell had proposed a hypothetical demon that could open a submicroscopic door to admit only fast-moving molecules of air. That, of course, was magic, not science. But here, magic worked.

"Long ago and far away,
Maxwell felt the need one day
For a Demon, scarce as high
As the atoms going by.
Over heat he gave it sway,
Making warmth go either way
From the vector Nature gave.
Maxwell's Demon, come and save."

"A *demon*?" Sir Guy cried. "Wizard, have you lost—"

A crack like a pistol shot split the night, and an infinitesimal point of light appeared, so bright he couldn't look directly at it. It hovered over the palm of his hand, and a singing hum filled the air.

"Who summons the Spirit of Perversity?"

"Wizard, you have fallen to Evil!" Sir Guy gasped, stumbling back away.

The humming voice snapped like a spark gap. "What dullards have we here? If there's not one who knows the difference between the perverse and the perverted, surely they are not worthy to be accounted among the living."

Matt felt the skin on his hands and face tingling with the need for caution. There was power here—and the spirit was possibly totally amoral. From the very name it gave itself, if Matt could not guess right, it would be completely unpredictable. "Please, spirit. It was I who summoned you—if you are indeed the one summoned."

The humming fell to a low, almost inaudible thrum. "Explain, if you have wit enough."

"I invoked the spirit who could do as Maxwell wished and violate all rules of common sense. Are you the one?"

The low thrumming continued. "You must tell me. Have I then that power granted, that I do what men deem impossible?"

"It would seem so." Matt relaxed somewhat. Out of the corner of his eye, he saw Sayeesa staring at the light point in fascination. He'd have to learn why, but the care of the Demon was the crucial point now. "It would be considered perverse."

The hum rose two steps in pitch, but the Demon was still being wary. "And what mean you by perversity?"

"Well . . ." Matt frowned. "Finagle stated it in his general law: The perversity of the universe tends toward maximum."

"Perhaps there is sense in that." The hum rose higher. "But any man can bandy words in such a fashion. Speak their meaning."

What did the spirit want, a kindergarten primer? "Well, a number of commentators have spelled out ramifications. There's Murphy's Law: If anything can go wrong, it will."

"Better, but somewhat lacking," the Demon hummed.

"Then there's Gunderson's Law: The least desirable possibility will always exert itself when the results will be most frustrating. Or, if anything can go wrong, it will—at the worst possible moment."

"There have been improvements in Adam's line since last I dealt with mortals," the Demon sang. "But speak on."

Matt eyed the light point askance. "Well, Freud wrote that living men were imbued with what he called a death-wish. And it has been said that those who most crave sainthood most often are driven toward Hell."

"Men have gained understanding. Yet be assured I have scant dealing with aught connected with the Hell-crew. They hate me, fearing I have some power over them."

Matt frowned. "How's that? Oh—because Hell seeks to defeat itself in ultimate goals. And that makes it perverted in itself, rather than perverse." He had remembered the first words of the Demon, and they should apply.

"You seem to understand. Yet I must think upon it." The spot of light snapped away from over Matt's hand.

Sayeesa followed its going with her eyes. Then she looked up at Matt. "What is this force you've loosed among us?"

"Nothing that wasn't there all along." Matt turned away, uneasy at the look on her face.

"A most learned discourse, Lord Wizard." Sir Guy was watching him doubtfully. "Still, what sense was in it? The universe cannot be perverse; it has no brain or thought."

"Aye! Speak to that, and quickly!" The Demon was back again, hovering beside Matt.

"Of course the universe can't really be perverse," Matt said, irked at having to point out the obvious. "Finagle spoke for people— from humanity's point of view. From where we stand, the universe *looks* perverse."

"Indeed. Why so?" the Demon demanded.

"Why?" Matt repeated testily. "Because human beings are inherently perverse. They'll project perversity into anything they look upon. The perversity's in our perceptions, not in the thing perceived—which is to say, it's in us."

"You have it!" The Demon leaped up a foot and was singing again. "Truly you understand the essense of my nature, which is to be and do what seems beyond your common sense. Your tasks I'll work gladly. Mortal, ask, and I shall do."

"No strings attached?"

"Nay, for I've sought long to find a guiding master. Without guidance, what is perversity? What would you have me do?"

Matt had heard the howls of triumph beyond the sarcens and now he looked up to see the hounds tearing at the last puma. "Then build me a Wall of Octroi between each two pillars, to join the Ring in an unseen shield."

"Your terms are strange, but your task belies common sense, and that shall I do." The spirit streaked off toward the space between the nearest pillars, paused a moment, then went on to the next.

"My apologies, Wizard," Sir Guy said. "You have not fallen. And indeed, I misjudged your scholarship, if it gave you power over yon Demon."

"Only influence," Matt corrected.

The dot of light was back. "The Wall's complete. Energies are bonded 'twixt each pair of stones, and none shall pass until you will it. What next do you wish?"

"Thanks," Matt said. "That does it for the night, I think."

"Naught more? You summoned me for so small a thing?"

If erecting three hundred feet of force-field was only a small thing to the Demon, what kind of power was Matt fooling with? He'd have banished the Demon there and then if he were sure he could. As it was, all he could do was grin and say, "Of course. Any other way would have been too much like common sense."

The Demon accepted that and retired to the far side of the Ring.

Matt mopped his brow and turned to Sir Guy. "Shall we take a look at the enemy?"

"By all means." Sir Guy clapped Matt on the shoulder, and they strolled to the nearest sarcen to observe the hellhounds.

Outside was foaming madness. The hounds ripped and clawed at the invisible barrier in their fury to get at the humans, but the Wall held them without a trace of its existence. Matt could just hear their howls of impotent fury. Strange, the sound should have come over the top of the Wall. With excitement, Matt realized that the shield curved up and over to form a dome.

The Demon, it seemed, had done a thorough job.

"They can not come in," Sir Guy observed, "but neither can we go out. What do we now?"

"Wait." Matt turned away, finding a convenient boulder to sit on. "Wait for sunrise."

Sir Guy nodded, raising his eyebrows and pursing his lips. "Fairly said. Indeed, we might sleep; 'tis the fairest chance we've had in some days."

He turned away and went over to his horse, to pull a heavy cloak from behind his saddle. He shook it out, spread it on the ground, and began to unbuckle his armor.

Matt shook his head in mute amazement. How could a man even think of sleep, with the exhilaration of this place singing through his veins?

Farther away, Sayeesa knelt beside her horse, head bowed over clasped hands, lips working silently in prayer, eyes squeezed shut. Sweat glistened on her forehead. The balanced forces in the Ring reinforced her inclinations towards good as well as her inclinations towards vice; in her case, it was a matter of which she chose to think about. So she was thinking holy thoughts, pitting prayer against vice—winning, too; even as he watched, the agony in her face was beginning to subside toward peace.

He shook his head in silent admiration and rose, turning away, to take a look at the princess.

Alisande stood in the center of the Ring, eyes wide in wonder and delight, lips parted.

It was so much unlike her usual demeanor that it frightened Matt. Was she okay? He went up to her quietly, almost diffidently. "Uh—is your Highness well?"

"Oh, very well!" Alisande breathed. "What a goodly place is this, Lord Wizard!"

"Well goodly isn't exactly the word I'd choose." Matt looked around him. "But I think I know how you feel; 'high' is what we called it back home."

"Nay, goodly! I feel as I have never felt this last twelvemonth, with calm, kind goodness filling all the air about me! 'Tis as if I curled again within my father's arm, as if—" Her eyes suddenly brimmed with tears. "—as if the good kind God himself looked down and smiled."

Whatever she had, it was contagious; as Matt looked about him again, he suddenly realized the Ring's resemblance to a great church. A cathedral hush enveloped them; the sarcens seemed like great Gothic columns; the occasional fallen slabs seemed like side altars. Moonlight filled the air and plated every slab with silver.

Alisande gave a little half laugh that caught in her throat. "Though I must own, if God has given shelter here this night, 'tis through yourself that he has given it! I had not known you could command a spirit of such vasty power. 'Twas most well done, Lord Matthew."

"Well, there was a lot at stake." Matt swallowed through a suddenly tightened throat.

"What man are you, who can command such forces?" Alisande breathed, stepping closer, face shining up at him.

Matt was tempted to launch into a lecture on science, out of sheer self-defense. He reminded himself he'd been wanting this. "I'm only a man, your Highness."

"Nay, more than that! The title I accorded you, you've earned a hundredfold this night!"

Matt could see nothing but her eyes. They seemed dark blue in the moonlight, long-lashed, huge, and deep . . .

He pulled himself back from the brink. "I've got to be honest, your Highness—I don't know if I could have controlled the Demon if it weren't for the power of this Ring. It's flowing through me, here; I'm just a channel for it."

Her face had softened, growing almost tender. "Aye, this Ring lends you its power—because you are, beneath all else, a very good and upright man."

Matt felt a thrill of danger course through him. This was getting out of hand. "Well . . . yes," he said slowly. "Aside from a few fleshly lapses . . ."

"Aye," she said, with a low, throaty laugh, "but you are safe from them in this place. I cannot believe that vice could touch you here, where every particle of earth and air cries out to me of goodness, order, and all things well done! Oh!" She pirouetted away from him. "I could sing, I could carol for joy! My body trills, in every bone and fiber, and craves good works to do!" She looked back at him. "Do you feel so, too, Lord Matthew?"

"Yes," he said, his eyes glued to her. "Right now, I do."

Her eyes flew wide in surprise; she inclined her head, looking up at him through lowered lashes, suddenly coy and roguish.

Then she turned away from him again, laughing with delight. "I have not known happiness this whole past year—and now I've that year's worth upon me in an instant!"

She leaped away, dancing in whirling turns and soaring leaps, laughing joyously. Matt followed her every movement, unable to pull his eyes away from the sweet, clean line of her body showing through her gown as it whipped about her.

At last she dropped to her knees, bowed over clasped hands for a moment, before she flung back her head, her closed eyes uplifted in prayer, bathed in moonlight, and Matt felt his excitement ebbing; the dance was done. Still he watched her, the peaceful rapture of her face framed in disordered golden hair.

Then she was coming toward him, almost on tiptoe, face flushed with exertion, gleaming with perspiration, eyes still alight, full lips parted in exhilaration. The breeze molded her gown to the contours of her body, and the full force of her voluptuous femininity hit Matt like a shock wave. His whole body sizzled with the sudden heat of passion, and he was striding toward her, reaching out.

Lust! the monitor mind yammered, and Matt realized that any vice let loose in here would feed back off the forces of evil lingering in the stones, fusing his mind into a mass of depravity. He slowed and stopped, sliding his reaching hand out to clasp hers, interlacing her fingers through his own. It sent a jolt up his arm into his chest, and he concentrated all his attention on the feel of her hand.

She'd lost her smile for a moment, but now it returned, with a greater warmth than friendship. "For a moment, you had frightened me, Lord Matthew!" She lowered her head, looking up at him through long lashes. "'Twas scarcely gallant."

Matt caught his breath, trying to ignore the thrumming along his nerves. "I rejoice to see you joyful, Highness."

"You've never seen me truly so." She looked up, suddenly grave. "You met me at a somber time; yet this wondrous Ring undoes my sorrow."

"Indeed it does," he breathed, and desire flamed in him again.

She saw it in his eyes and dropped his hand with a little gasp, stepping away and burying her hands behind her. "Lord Matthew . . . My most sincere regrets . . . I had not meant . . ."

"No," he said, managing to drown the desire under a flood of tenderness and smiling. "Of course not."

She turned away, confused. "A princess cannot think of love. She marries whom she must, for purposes of state. So, as I grew, I hardened my heart and learned to think of men and women alike, as people only. I disdained in any way to attract the male eye— until this night. For which, I repent."

"I don't." Matt drew a long breath. "Not for a moment, Princess. I'm still whole."

"You are," she said gravely; and, for a moment, there was almost awe in her eyes. "And I think I may begin to realize, Lord Matthew, what strength that required."

Matt stared, poleaxed by the compliment.

She turned to him, lifting her head and throwing her shoulders back, once again every inch a queen. She took his hand, but the warmth in her eyes was only friendship again. "I thank you for that strength, Lord Wizard; for I think you could have used my playfulness, this night, against me."

"Yes," he murmured, cursing his own gallantry. *Idiot! Chump! You blew your big chance!*

She leaned closer, her voice lowered, husky. "But I thank you more for letting me know, this night, the taste of my own womanhood, by your gallantry—for I'll flatter myself to think it was sincere."

"Oh, it was," Matt breathed. "Believe. It was."

She laughed, leaning away, coy for a moment again, then sobered with a sudden completeness that spoke of will power. "I do believe it, and I thank you deeply; but we must turn away from each other now, to our cold beds of turf. Yet if you were tempted here, be certain I was, also—and you cannot know how sorely."

"I might." Matt swallowed. "It will be a cold and lonely night."

"I think not." Her face lit with sudden warmth again. "I'll have dreams for company, warm and comforting—for I know I'm a woman now."

She leaned forward, reaching out almost shyly to touch his cheek. Then she was gone, gliding away over the turf toward her horse, to fetch her cloak and find some softer ground for sleeping.

Matt sighed and turned away, trying to summon the self-anger to regret his self-control—but found he couldn't. In fact, he felt a pleasant glow of self-esteem.

"What do you, Wizard?"

Matt looked down at the singing voice and saw the spot of brilliant light hovering near him. "Hiya, Max."

"Max?" The Demon sounded wary. "What has caused this foolishness?"

"Women," Matt said, grinning. "I'll never understand 'em."

"Why, how is this? They cannot differ greatly from you; they're of your species."

"Uh, that's a bit of a misconception." Matt pulled up a rock and sat down. "There's a certain contrariness to them, Max, and even more to our relationships with them."

"Indeed!" The Demon sounded extremely interested. "Explain this, Wizard!"

"As far as I can." Matt grinned. "Let's take Alisande, for example. She's a princess, see, and I'm a commoner—but an interesting one. You see . . ."

The Demon didn't, and Matt went on at some length, explaining the intricacies and ramifications of the situation, as far as he knew them.

After an hour, the Demon declared, "I chose aright. You truly comprehend perversity."

CHAPTER 14

"Awake."

Matt swatted at the steel hand and rolled over on his back, glaring up at Sir Guy. "It's too early."

The knight only pointed to the sky, and Matt realized Sir Guy was silhouetted against a brightening ceiling. Looking out, he saw the hellhounds still slavering and clawing at the force-field, without the slightest slackening of berserk ferocity.

"They will flee with sunrise," the knight explained, "but we must be ready to ride when they do, to make as many miles as we can by daylight."

Matt nodded. "So we have to start early." He clambered to his feet, sighing, and helped Sir Guy waken Alisande and Sayeesa. They breakfasted on journey bread, huddled in their cloaks and watched the dogs clawing at the eastern space between stone blocks.

The sky grew rosy as they watched. They finished breakfast and saddled up. The hounds went crazy as they mounted and rode to the center of the Ring, watching the east.

A sudden line of burning red bulged above the horizon. Scarlet rays stabbed out, flooding through the eastern portal.

The dogs screamed, wheeled about, and fled out over the moor.

But they'd overstayed; they seemed to grow thinner as they ran—translucent, and transparent, then . . .

"Gone." Matt exhaled a long, shaky breath.

"Back to whatever lightless place gave them being." Sir Guy nodded heavily. "Now let us ride."

They turned their horses, setting their backs to the sun, and rode out of the Stone Ring—quite reluctantly, with the possible exception of Sayeesa. She breathed a huge sigh of relief and slumped in her saddle as they passed between huge sarcens.

They rode west, alternating between walk and canter again. Alisande rode beside Sayeesa, chatting; and there was nothing particularly royal about her manner. She seemed only a young woman, wanting a good gossip. Sayeesa was wary at first, but she thawed quickly.

Matt kept trying to catch the princess's eye, but she always seemed to be looking the other way at just the wrong moment. After a while, he began to suspect it was more than coincidence. Finally, about midmorning, he managed to cut in between the two women during a canter and was next to Alisande when they slowed to a walk. "Good morrow, your Highness."

"Good morn." Her neck was ramrod stiff, and she didn't quite meet his gaze. "Lord Wizard, I must ask you to forget any words that passed between us yestere'en. You will understand that, due to the nature of the Stone Ring, I was not myself."

It hurt. It stabbed in and twisted, letting anger spurt out. "Of course—I should have expected remorse this morning. After all, you'd never felt like a woman before."

Her head snapped back as if she'd been slapped, and anger flared in her eyes—but beneath it, he could see the hurt. She inclined her head with cold courtesy. "I thank you for instruction, Lord Wizard. I assure you, I'm schooled—never to risk personal converse again."

She straightened in her saddle with the dignity of a glacier and rode away, turning her back to him.

Matt watched her go, cursing under his breath.

A spark hovered near him, visible even in sunlight, humming, "You may understand perversity, Wizard, yet you cannot prevent it."

"Oh, go make a hotbox," Matt growled.

By late afternoon, they were out of the plains, into a rolling, hill-and-gully land. Sir Guy was in excellent spirits. "We shall not lack for shelter this night, praise Heaven! We shall be well-housed indeed, at the monastery of Saint Moncaire!"

"Moncaire?" Matt frowned. "Hardishane's war wizard? What kind of monks live in *his* house?"

"A warrior order." Sir Guy gazed off into the distance with nostalgia. "Worthy men, sworn to holy orders as well as to arms, devoted to the protection of the helpless against the wicked. For years they maintained themselves in readiness, with fasting, drill, and marches, as if the time of their need should come on the morrow."

"And tomorrow's here." Matt chewed at his lower lip. "But isn't war a rather strange profession for a monk, Sir Guy?"

The knight shook his head. "'Tis a matter of whom the arms are borne against, Lord Wizard."

"Malingo." Matt nodded. "I keep forgetting that, in this universe, it really is possible to tell the good from the bad—and without much likelihood of rationalizing. Let's have a look at this monastery."

The monastery was there. So was an army!

It was a rather motley horde, falling into definite groupings by uniform color; but it surrounded the monastery on all four sides in a vast, sprawling circle.

Sir Guy drew in a long, whistling breath. "We have been anticipated."

"It is the army of evil," Alisande confirmed.

Matt frowned, brooding. "How far from the mountains are we?"

"Two days' ride," Alisande answered.

"What now is our order?" Sayeesa demanded. "Can we go around them?"

"We can," Sir Guy said judiciously. "But if we do, night will catch us far from any habitation."

"No." Matt shook his head sharply. "We might not find a convenient Stonehenge this time; and I somehow suspect Malingo hasn't run out of hellhounds."

"We go in, then." Alisande's sword hissed out of its sheath. "Come, gentles. We shall hew a way to those walls, or die with our swords reaping a harvest of evil about us."

"Very commendable." Matt touched a restraining hand to Alisande's hilt. "But personally, I'd prefer not to die. There's a better way. Max!"

"Aye, Wizard." The dot of arc light hovered in the air before him. Sir Guy and Alisande pulled back involuntarily, and the stallion shifted restlessly. Matt ignored them. "Does your power extend to time, Max?"

"Things move in time as in space. Thus there is energy spent; and where it is spent, I can hoard. 'Tis in my province."

Matt took a deep breath, sure of his words this time.

> "Tomorrow and tomorrow and tomorrow
> Creeps in this petty pace from day to day,
> To the last syllable of recorded time."

The dot of light winked out. Matt swallowed and settled in the saddle, motioning the others forward.

They rode down the hill at a trot and came to the rear of an army strangely stalled; all about them, soldiers and animals stood frozen in mid-movement.

"What has happened, Lord Wizard?" Alisande's voice was hushed. "Have you and this Demon of yours frozen this whole army in death?"

"No, Highness. They are not dead, but frozen in time, so that it might take a day for one to blink his eyes." Matt looked around him, trying to suppress a shudder. "But do not touch them. They move so slowly that each must seem as immovable as a whole mountain of granite."

They went through the army at a crawl, moving very carefully. It was slow going. Finding ways for the horses to move through the bunched soldiers was difficult, and they often had to backtrack and try another way. But they persevered and were almost to the wall when the men about them began to move again, very slowly, but getting faster.

"The spell's broken!" Matt bellowed. "Ride, and don't count the bumps!"

Horses lurched into a run as a midnight-blue figure thrust up above the crowd, its hands weaving an unseen pattern.

"Faster!" Matt called. "There's a sorcerer with a whammy back there!"

But the footmen were coming alive, with groans that rose to howls. Pikes thrust up at them from all sides. Sir Guy shouted and plowed ahead, bowling them out in a bow-wave; but the more adroit soldiers sprang back, then leaped in again, thrusting. Matt whipped out his sword and parried a pike, slicing its haft in the process. On the far side, Sir Guy dished out death, cut-and-parry.

The sorcerer's arm swung down in an arc, forefinger stabbing out at the company.

"Fight!" Alisande cried. "They are no longer helpless!"

Matt turned toward her, startled. Her voice had deepened, grown husky. Her body had thickened; laugh lines cupped her mouth. As he watched, crow's-feet sprouted, and silver salted her hair.

"You're aging!" Matt cried, and turned to Sir Guy. The knight was hewing and hacking, but more slowly now, and his hair was grizzled. Matt yanked his hand up in front of his eyes and felt his joints resist the movement. The hand was blue-veined and wrinkled. "He's hexed us! We're aging a year every second! *Max!*"

"Aye, Wizard?" The Demon danced before him.

"Make us younger, fast! Back to our natural ages! The sorcerer over there has speeded our time up!"

"Then I shall reverse it," the Demon chuckled. "What words will you give me?"

"Forward to yesterday! 'Turn back the hands of time!' 'I have a mandate from the people!' And while you're at it, drain that sorcerer's power!"

"I go, I go!" the Demon sang, and exploded into a sheet of flame, to clear some working space. Soldiers sprang back, screaming and beating their clothes. Matt felt his joints loosen and saw Sir Guy and Alisande quicken their movements as the wrinkles faded from their faces.

A despairing shriek rose over the battle; Matt yanked his head around in time to see the sorcerer collapse. Max had drained the magician's power—all of it.

A pike jabbed up at Matt's eyes. He flinched, pulling back, and it grazed his shoulder instead. Matt bellowed as pain seared him, and thrust with his sword. The pike head went flying, but two more jabbed in, and more soldiers were following from Matt's blind side. He swung his monofilament-edged sword like a scythe, reaping pike heads. "Your Highness! Get the gate open!"

"Aye; 'tis my task," Alisande cried, turning her horse. The Demon blasted some space for her as she rode to the fore, leaving Sayeesa sandwiched between Sir Guy and Matt.

Alisande cupped a hand around her mouth and called out, "Open to friends! Open the gate!"

Matt heard a shouted command above, and a torrent of cross-bow bolts plummeted down all around them. Soldiers screamed and fell back, and few seemed disposed to replace them. A knight swore in the background, swatting at his men with the flat of his sword; but they pressed back away from the company, for the crossbow bolts continued to fall in a drizzle.

"Who cries for entry?" a basso voice bawled above.

Alisande's mouth hardened. "Alisande, Princess of Merovence, commands you to open!"

The basso swore a startled, but very pious, oath, and the huge doors bowed outward on the instant, swinging wide. The besiegers howled and surged forward. But bolts hailed down, slowing them. Alisande galloped in through the gate with Sayeesa behind her, and Sir Guy turned his horse, facing outward, pulling in against Matt's side, retreating toward the gate while he hacked and slew about him. Matt admired his endurance; his own arm was ready to fall off.

They backed toward the gate. Within the archway, Sir Guy turned and galloped in. Matt slewed about, blocking the door. He clipped three pike heads with one last weary chop before he cried, "Max! Flambé!"

The Demon blasted a ten-foot half circle of charred earth clear around the gate. While the enemy was trying to rally, the rear ranks trying to shove through the huddle of moaning men in front, Matt pivoted and lurched into the monastery.

A moment later, the huge doors boomed shut behind him, and the foot-thick bar crashed home to hold them. Something huge and heavy slammed against them, rattling the bar; then howls of frustration filled the air outside the wall. Matt went limp in the saddle. Let them bring up a battering ram, now; his party was safe.

"Where's she that does claim to be Princess of Merovence?" the stern basso voice cried out above them. A tall, heavy figure in full plate armor clanked down the steps from the battlement, his breastplate embossed with a bright green cross. A cloak of the same green, with a gold border, snapped in the wind behind him.

"My Lord Abbot!" Sir Guy cried cheerily, saluting with his sword. "Well met in a dark hour!"

"Who speaks so?" The tall knight rumbled, lifting his visor to disclose a glowering face with a bush of moustache.

Sir Guy threw up his own visor, and the abbot's stern face broke to a slight smile, a warm glow in his eyes. "Sir Guy Losobal! It is long since I beheld your countenance. Have you come, to strive by our sides in our hour of need?"

"Nay, Lord Abbot—we have come to cry sanctuary from a house of God! And as to her whom we guard, look and see—can you hold doubt of her lineage?"

The abbot turned, frowning down at Alisande. His eyes widened slightly. "Nay—I cannot," he breathed. "Her parentage is written in her features."

Matt was amazed that so huge a man could move so quickly. He was at the bottom of the stairs in an instant, kneeling by Alisande's horse. "You honor our house, Highness, and have come to give heart to your most loyal liegemen in the darkest of hours! Forgive my rash doubts of your person!"

"Your caution was well-founded, Lord Abbot." Alisande sat straight in the saddle, royalty enfolding her like great, closing wings. "The thanks and praise of a princess, for all you and yours, who have held out 'gainst all hope."

"Thus we have ever done; thus we shall ever do," the abbot responded, rising. "Yet we fought with little heart, for we thought our cause doomed. But we know, now, that you live and are free! Nay, let them batter our gates! With their own swords, we shall dig them their graves!"

Alisande beamed, basking in the glow of his homage. "I am greatly blessed to have such vassals! Yet I err in etiquette. Lord Abbot, may I present my worthy companions." She indicated Sayeesa. "A penitent bound for the convent of Saint Cynestria."

The abbot bent an armored glance on Sayeesa. "Women are forbidden within these precincts; yet any attendant upon her Highness is welcome. Still must I bid you to the guest house in the eastern tower, milady."

"I cry grace for your courtesy." Sayeesa bowed her head. "Yet you have no need of such chivalry; I am lowborn."

"Your speech denies it," the abbot said, frowning. "Naetheless, you are welcome to such sanctuary as we can offer." He turned away, studying Matt. "And this, your Highness."

"This is Matthew, Lord Wizard of Merovence." Alisande's voice rang out.

The abbot stared, taken aback. "Lord Wizard! You dare to proclaim this, with the usurper's foul sorcerer claiming the title?"

"I do," Matt said grimly. "I have an ace up my sleeve."

"An ace?" The abbot turned to the princess with a frown. "What is this he speaks of?"

"I have not heard the term," she answered. "He is a rare scholar, Lord Abbot, and much that he speaks is quite strange. Yet I think that he speaks of the small bit of light which he terms—" She hesitated. "—a Demon."

"But be assured, Lord Abbot—he's not of the Hell-crew," Matt added quickly.

"How could that be?" the abbot growled. "A Demon, and not of Hell?"

"Well, that's just a label fastened on him from the outside— mostly, I think, because he wasn't human and produced heat."

"Nay, that cannot be!" the abbot said sternly. "None but God can create!"

"You're *right*! But you *can* take what heat is available and concentrate it in one place. That's really all you do when you boil water, isn't it?"

"Aye, in a manner of speaking." The abbot still frowned. "Is it thus your familiar does its work?"

"Not all that familiar," Matt said judiciously. "But yes, he does—and he sticks with me because I understand how men are basically self-defeating."

"Ah." The abbot nodded, his face clearing. "That the fault is not in Creation, but in man. Yes, I see—and if your spirit declares that, it could not be of the Hell-breed." He took a deep breath, his shoulders lifting. "Well, then—what would you say to hot meat and good wine?"

For the first fifteen minutes, they were rapt in total silence, broken only by the clink of knife on plate—the kind of silence which was the hungry man's highest tribute to good cooking.

After two pounds of beef, some scallions, and a glass of wine that out-burgundied Burgundy, the abbot heaved a satisfied sigh and set down his glass. "Tell me what you have seen as you rode from the East."

"Banditry and lawlessness," Alisande said darkly. "Poor folk striving still to be good, but with sad moral weakness come upon them." She looked up at the abbot. "Which should be little surprise to you—for I see many coats, other than those of your monks, here in your monastery, Lord Abbot."

It *was* a monastery, Matt had to admit—he'd found that out as they came through the inner gate. Suddenly it had been spread out before him—a collection of low-lying buildings, dormitories, cloisters, common hall, chapel, brewery, bakery, armory—all the buildings of a medieval monastery, with a few martial additions. Even an orchard, and a large truck garden. But the whole thing was enclosed by the great curtain-wall, turreted and battlemented. The House of Moncaire was a strange hybrid between monastery and fortress. It said a lot about its inhabitants.

"Aye, many liveries, Highness," the abbot answered. "The Duke of Tranorr is here, and the Duke of Lachaise. Earl Cormann has come, and Earl Lanell and Earl Morhaisse. Beneath them are Barons Purlaine, Margonne, Sorraie—the list is long, Highness."

"Tranorr, Mochaisse, Purlaine . . . those estates are near to Bordestang." The princess frowned.

The abbot nodded. "When the usurper's armies closed about them, they could choose only death or flight. They fled, that they might fight again for your cause. They came here, where the power of God strengthens the power of arms. Here, too, have come peasants made homeless by banditry, or by wars between barons— men who live now only to strike down the emissaries of Evil. We have footmen aplenty, and knights; those whose lords died in the war have come to us, masterless, seeking a suzerain, for they disdained to serve the usurper."

"Then your numbers are adequate?" Alisande inquired.

"They have been, till now." The abbot's face darkened. "Your presence here is a blessing, Highness—yet 'tis also cause for concern. Many of our men have fallen to wounds, and more than a few to vice. Our arrows and bolts are spent faster than our fletchers and smiths can renew our stock. We are weakened, in truth; for we've been here besieged nigh onto a twelvemonth. Till now, the usurper and his sorcerer have had to fight in many places at once; the troops before our walls are, therefore, a moiety of their force. Yet with your Highness here guesting, I doubt not they'll bring all their horses and men to this place and strike us with all their weight here this night."

"Do you say we are doomed?" Alisande demanded.

"Nay, surely not." The abbot smiled bleakly. "Yet I misdoubt our power to maintain our walls."

"I wouldn't worry too much, milord." Matt glanced down at the brilliant spark hovering in his cupped palm. "I think we'll manage."

The abbot's back stiffened as he turned ponderously toward Matt, inclining his head in a stiff, too-elaborate bow. "I thank you for your words of good hope, Lord Wizard; but while her Highness has paid tribute to your scholarship, I must ask: How sound is your knowledge of warfare?"

It was a good question, Matt admitted to the Demon—later. "How about it, Max? Can we hold out, you and I between us?"

"'Tis a fine question, Lord Wizard," the spark hummed. "I've not yet gauged the strength of your spells; that, you must judge for yourself, 'gainst what you know of their sorcerers."

"Yeah." Matt grinned. "You were able to counter that portable potion pusher very easily, though."

"Aye, easily, against one alone. Yet do not think me more than I am, Wizard. Had yesternight's stone circle been wider by two paces, I could not have closed the Wall of Octroi about it."

"Oh." Matt pursed his lips. "Limited range, huh?"

"Even so. Be mindful that mine is the power of concentrating or dissipating a force. I can do great works in small spaces—but only as you direct. I will not suggest."

The view from the battlements was less than encouraging. The army of sorcery lay all about the monastery like a human sea. Rivulets trickled into it from the hills—columns of footmen and knights trooping in.

"The abbot was right," Matt mused. "Malingo's gathering the troops." He was beginning to feel a bit chilly in the base of the stomach.

"I think we shall see the sun rise," Sir Guy said judiciously. "But 'twill be long till the dawn, Lord Wizard."

The twilight faded; night deepened over the valley, and stars pricked out. A vast, screaming howl rose from the besiegers, and arrows filled the sky, hailing down onto the battlements. The Knights of Moncaire crouched under shields with their allies, letting the hail of death roll off their backs with a long, rolling clangor. Here and there, a man shouted in agony, and brown-robed monks rushed out with shields strapped to their bent backs, braving the hail of arrows to drag the wounded man to cover.

"This is a covering fire," Matt called to Sir Guy. "What's it covering?"

"Yonder." the Black Knight pointed out toward the field. Matt looked down and saw the infantry charging all along the line, with scaling ladders angled like lances.

"Shoot not afar," the abbot commanded his men. "Hold till they're close; then pick your man and see him laid on the turf . . . Loose!"

Arrows leaped out over the wall to rain down on the infantry. The scaling ladders faltered, then halted, swaying—and swayed on down in slow, graceful arcs to slam into the sod. The infantry turned and fled, leaving windrows of dead and wounded.

"'Tis hard," the abbot said, glowering down at the casualties, "for most of these are constrained to be here. A year agone, I would have fought to save them, not to slay them. Yet now I must kill them in sheaves, or surrender my fortress—and with it, the hope of the land."

Matt pointed. "What's that?"

"Which?" The abbot sighted along Matt's arm. "'Tis the sorcerer who has command of this horde."

"And the two in dark gray there, with him?"

"His apprentices." The abbot stepped back, frowning. "What manner of wizard are you, that you know so little of sorcerers?"

"One who never had time for the formalities," Matt snapped. "What are they brewing?"

The three sorcerers stood hunched over a huge cauldron, the gray-clad men stirring the stew and occasionally tossing something in. Their chief bent low, making mystic passes over the pot and, presumably, chanting.

"Evil spells," the abbot said heavily. "Yet I do not too much fear them; for this is a holy place. We must trust to God and Saint Moncaire to protect us."

A sudden, faint sound caught at the back of Matt's brain. He looked up, frowning. "Milord Abbot! What's that?"

"Which?" the abbot demanded.

"That sound!"

"I hear naught."

"Under the sound of the battle—that buzzing! Hear it? It's getting louder!"

"Nay, I hear no such . . ." the abbot broke off, eyes widening.

Now they all heard it—a humming buzz, like a sixty-cycle square wave in quadrophonic sound, filling the sky.

Then the plague hit—like a plague of locusts, but worse: gnats, mosquitoes, bees, horseflies, swarming so thickly they blocked out the stars. The knights swore and leaped back from the wall, swatting at their armor—mosquitoes were small enough to get into the chinks. One knight howled and tore off his helmet—bees make unpleasant padding.

Matt looked up, startled, just as two three-inch sticks thudded against the battlements in front of him.

"Trespassers!" he bellowed. "Repel boarders! We're invaded!"

The knights forgot the insects and lugged out their swords; but footmen were streaming onto the battlements. Swords rang on shields; armor clashed; men screamed and died, flipping backward off the wall. Matt chopped through a shield, blessing his monofilament sword; but men were coming at him from all sides.

A voice behind him keened, "Wizard, to me! I'll clear space for your work!"

But the footmen heard the word "wizard" and fell on Matt like a screaming horde. He caught one sword on his shield, blocked another from his right with the flat of his sword, kicked the guy in the middle in the knee, turned his own blade and struck down, cleaving a head in half. Blood and brains started to spill, but he was already turning back to the man on the left—with his stomach starting to rise. He swallowed hard, clamping his jaws, as he swung up his shield to catch another blow, then turned to block another early chopper from his right. But he forgot to flatten the blade, and the soldier chopped at Matt's sword edge—and stared, horrified, at the stump of a sword he was left holding. He threw it at Matt and fled, howling. Matt ducked, but not enough; it clipped him on the side of the head, ringing a gong in his helmet and sprinkling stars across his vision; there wasn't much padding between steel and head. He turned, dazed, in time to see a sword chopping down at his nose. He rolled back, swinging his shield up. The sword ricocheted off the shield, and Matt thrust while the man's guard was down. The soldier screamed, arcing backward. Matt yanked his sword out and turned away before he could see the man fall. "Max, clear for me!"

"Aye," the Demon sang. Flame gouted over Matt's head to sweep an arc clear on the battlements. Matt ran till he slammed full against the inner rampart wall and leaned against it, shuddering, gulping breath. How did you get rid of a plague of insects?

You swallowcd thcm, of course.

> "Insectivores I do embrace;
> The chain of life sets forth the plan-o.
> Let swallows fall upon this place,
> On their way to Capistrano."

High-pitched cries filled the air, drowning out the buzzing. A horde of dark wings filled the battlements, swooping and diving. Knights and footmen alike shouted and hid their faces. The defenders came out of it first, realizing their advantage, and rushed the attackers with a shout while swallows dive-bombed bugs all about them.

When the sky cleared about ten minutes later, so had the battlements. Wounded men groaned on the stone, mixed in with dead bodies. Grim-faced knights stalked the length of the wall, dispatching wounded enemies with quick cuts or stabs.

"The birds were your work?" the abbot demanded, and Matt nodded. So did the abbot. "Where have they gone?"

"Back to fulfill their mission. Don't you take prisoners?"

The abbot turned to watch the slaughter, his face a stone. "'Tis hard. But we have no food to spare, nor medicine; and there is no way to say which one of them might turn against us."

Matt noticed each of the knights making the Sign of the Cross while his lips moved in prayer, before he stabbed his enemy. "What's this, Lord Abbot?"

"'Tis the words of conditional absolution they pronounce, Lord Wizard—if the men cannot speak repentance of their sins, they are forgiven."

Matt turned to watch brown-robed monks lifting wounded knights gently onto stretchers and carrying them away. "Where are they going?"

Sir Guy looked up. "To the chapel, Lord Matthew, there to be tended; they will heal more quickly there, and the sanctity of a church will protect them best in such a war as this."

"These guys really prefer to pray when they're wounded?"

"These are holy men. And, too, they know that each man praying in the chapel sends greater strength of grace to fortify us who maintain guard."

It was working, Matt realized—his body felt a little lighter, refreshed; magical power tingled in his limbs. Somehow, by the weird metaphysics of this world, prayer could translate into physical strength. The power of prayer was no empty phrase here.

"Ram!" a lookout bellowed.

Matt ran to the wall, craning his neck to get a view.

A wooden tunnel, thirty feet long, was approaching through the enemy forces, like a giant centipede.

"It has as many men as its length," the abbot growled by his shoulder, "and a great trunk of a tree within, I doubt not, hung from timbers. The armored roof protects the men from arrows, bolts, or aught else we might hurl down upon them. Well, let it come; of *that*, I have no fear."

"Malvoisin!" another lookout cried, and voices took it up, aghast. "Malvoisin! Malvoisin!"

The abbot's head snapped up. Matt followed his glance.

A fifty-foot-high scaffold was rolling toward them, three hundred feet away. It was a siege tower, a square, ugly, unfinished wooden structure, pulled by five teams of horses; but inside, there were steep stairways, and soldiers could run up them at amazing speed to come out the top door, and cross onto the battlements. The name meant "bad neighbor," which it certainly was.

"That," the abbot grated, "I fear."

He swung away. "Ho, archers! Slay me those horses! Have no regard for the tunnel; but put to death the horses that drag that foul scaffold hither!"

A heavy chant sprang up from the archers as they bent their bows and filled the air with volley after volley:

> "Saint Moncaire, our Order's name,
> Shrive my foe, and bless my aim!"

It seemed sacreligious, but Matt realized they meant it from the depths of their hearts. He didn't know enough theology to say whether the saint actually might bless an arrow aimed at another human being, even under these conditions; but it seemed to be working, whether magically or psychologically. In five seconds, the horses stumbled, fell in their traces, and rolled over, dead.

But the hail of steel points drew an answer—arrows rattled down onto the battlements, sticking in shields or clattering off them. An occasional one pierced armor, and a knight howled, falling. The brown-robes scrambled to pull him in, so the loss in firepower was almost balanced by the increase in spiritual power from the prayers of the wounded. Matt could feel a magic potential rising in him, singing; he felt like a capacitor waiting to be discharged. He wondered if he'd be able to *keep* from working magic.

Enemy footmen ran in to form a shield-wall around the horses. Hostlers ran in behind them, to unharness the dead beasts and put in replacements.

"Guard them!" the abbot called to the archers. "When you see an opening, loose!"

"The ram, Lord Abbot," Sir Guy reminded.

"What of it?" The abbot frowned down at the tunnel. It was only a few feet from the gate.

"Ought we not to fire upon them now?" Sir Guy demanded.

"Nay." The abbot grinned like a wolf. "Let them swing their ram."

The tunnel groaned on and connected with the gate, making a hollow boom. Its mouth nearly covered the great doors. A moment later, a huge thud shook the wall.

"Porters!" the abbot called. "Ready at the bar!" He began to count. "One . . . two . . ."

The porters yanked the great oaken beam loose, tossed it to the side.

"Five!" the abbot cried. "Prepare to open!"

The footmen set hands to the handles of the doors and braced their feet.

"Six!" the abbot shouted. "Pull!"

The porters heaved the gates wide open, and the butt end of a huge treetrunk shot through. It posed for a split second, then shot on in with a series of machine-gun snaps, broken ropes festooning it, soldiers tumbling in off-balance in its wake. Fiery swords flamed in their hands.

"Max!" Matt shouted. "Douse those blades!"

The flames slackened and guttered out as two barons, with five knights and twenty footmen, shouldered the attackers aside and charged out through the gate, laying about them with swords. The attackers, taken by surprise, roared and turned to attack the sally-party's rear; but the knights above upended a huge copper cauldron, and scalding water drenched the attackers. They screamed and pulled back into the courtyard.

"Archers! Loose!" the abbot cried, and the courtyard was sud-

denly filled with arrows. Matt turned away, sickened by the slaughter, looking out at the tunnel for an excuse. The sally-party was
doing very well; the tunnel roof was fallen, and the framework
halfway to kindling. While the laborers hacked at oak, the knights
and infantry hewed at soldiers. It was all over in ten minutes, and
the barons and their liege men pulled back to the sides just as the
few surviving attackers poured out through the gate. The barons
and their men chopped at them as they came; only a handful were
left to stagger back into the enemy line.

"In!" the abbot cried, for a regiment was finally pulling out of
the enemy line for a counterattack. The barons bawled orders;
knights and footmen alike leaped to catch up their wounded and
dead, then rushed back in through the gate. The huge doors boomed
shut behind them, and the great oak bar dropped into its brackets
as an exclamation point.

"Let them learn from this," the abbot growled; but there was
no joy in his eyes, for the talus slope outside the gate was filled
with dead and moaning bodies.

"Hold fire!" he bawled, as a small running party charged up
the slope from the enemy line. "Let them recover their wounded!"

They took care of their wounded, all right—with quick, sharp,
sword strokes.

The abbot shrugged. "Their comrades' swords or ours—what
matter?" But his face was long, and he made the Sign of the Cross
over the dead, muttering the Latin words of conditional absolution.

The inhumanity of the spectacle was clawing at Matt's brain,
trying to paralyze him, and he couldn't quite shake it off.

"Wizard," hummed the Demon by his ear, "I sense expending
of some force beneath us."

"Probably just the brown-robes, coming out to pick up the
dead," Matt muttered.

"Nay; I mean beneath the ground, within this mound of earth
beneath us."

"Down inside the motte itself?" Matt looked up, a surge of
adrenaline banishing the tendrils clinging to his brain. "Check for
miners, will you? Sappers, men trying to dig a tunnel under the
battlements and up into the courtyard. If you find them, bring the
roof down on them."

"And how shall I do that?" From its tone of voice, the Demon
knew quite well, but wanted to make sure Matt did, too.

"Weaken the bonds between molecules, of course!"

"There are few men within this world who'd know such things," the Demon chortled. "I go to search the underground."

It winked out. Matt stood scowling. The Demon was testing him, trying to find his limits. Why?

"Malvoisin!"

Matt looked up at the cry. The siege tower was rolling again—without horses. Faintly, he could hear a heavy work-chant. "They're pushing it from behind," he growled. "What can you do about that, Lord Abbot?"

"I can—*Ho!*"

Fog, sand, and a tidal wave of dust hit the battlements, churning so thickly that Matt could scarcely see the abbot, ten feet away. Men shouted, startled and frightened; then they began to cough all along the rampart, hacking and wheezing.

"Let fly at the malvoisin!" the abbot cried in despair, then broke off in a coughing fit. The archers began their chant, with many breaks for coughs and wheezes, loosing their arrows blindly into the dust.

This was a *real* emergency, Matt realized. The enemy could roll up their malvoisin under cover of the storm and send their men in, ready and equipped for dust.

"Use your power, Wizard," the abbot managed between coughs from somewhere near. "Banish this fell storm!"

Matt nodded, forcing his voice to be steady.

> "To remove this rain of dust,
>   Let there be a steady gust,
>   Blowing from the west with force
>   Toward the foeman's foot and horse!"

The western wind howled in. Men shouted; all about him, clanking spoke of knights clutching one another, to brace themselves against the blast . . . But the dust thinned with amazing speed and blew away. Matt turned, looking up, and saw a mammoth slab of whirling dust, its front as flat as if it had been planed, standing like a wall between the monastery and its enemies. That wasn't going to help much; it could still hide the malvoisin till it was too close to stop.

A knight howled as the wind hurled him before it, toward the outer edge. His comrades dived and caught his arms just in time. They hauled him back onto the parapet.

"Secure yourselves!" the abbot bellowed, then turned to Matt. "Wizard, this is your doing! Can you stop this wind?"

Matt shook his head. "If I do, the dust will come pouring back in. It's up to the enemy sorcerers to make the dust disappear; then I can stop the wind. What hour is it?"

"Midnight," the abbot shouted. "Five more hours till the dawn; and my men cannot hold against this wind!"

A roar, like a dozen subways homing in, filled the valley. Matt froze, startled. Then he ran to the wall, more blown than running, brought up sharply against the stone, hung on for dear life, and dared a peek out.

The roar was fading. A huge trench had opened in the field, arrowing from the wall straight back into the dust-wall. Dirt was still pouring in all along its length, along with an avalanche of enemy soldiers and knights from the bottom of the dust-wall.

"What means this, Wizard?" Sir Guy called.

"Sappers," Matt shouted back. "Miners. They were trying to dig their way under the wall."

"But how knew you..." The abbot's face froze; he shook his head sharply. "Do not say; I do not wish to know."

The dust began to thin.

"Ready your archers, Lord Abbot!" Matt called. "The enemy's realized he has to dump the dust! I can stop the wind in a minute or two!"

The abbot bawled orders as the dust dissipated; the last few tag ends disappeared. Matt heaved a sigh of relief, and called,

> "The dust is fled, our soldiers chilled;
> The howling wind our ears has filled.
> Let us have a bit of peace;
> Let the western wind now cease!"

The wind slackened and died—and fog rolled in, worse than London with a three-day calm. Thick, opaque fog settled over the battlements in a few seconds, hiding Sir Guy five feet away. Matt froze, alarm thrilling through him as he saw it hit. A freezing thought nudged his brain. Just before the fog wrapped around him, he took the deepest breath he could and hid his face in the crook of his arm. Around him, he heard men shout, then the clank and thud as bodies hit the stonework. Men choked and hacked as if they were trying to cough up their entrails. This fog wasn't just water vapor; it was a gas attack.

Matt spent all his breath in four lines:

> "Western wind, return to save us!
> Restore the breath you but now gave us!
> Blast this fog from off our wall!
> Rid us of this reeking pall!"

Then he clamped his jaws shut, trying not to breathe, as the Western wind howled in, hurling the fog out toward the enemy—and revealing the malvoisin, only a few yards from the wall. A knight stood in the doorway at the top. His knees buckled as a tag end of fog coiled into his helmet, then he fell forward, hurtling down. The enemy line filled with a single, roaring cough as the gas attack hit. But even as it struck, the fog thinned, faded, disappeared—and the malvoisin rolled forward the last few feet, almost touching the wall itself.

The boarding ramp fell down, and arrows began to plummet from the top. Swords rang, footmen fell, and the parapet ran red.

The defenders were forced onto the defensive, being driven back toward the stairway, though every inch was bought with blood.

Now, what would stop these enemy soldiers? Most of them were here only because they'd been forced to it. What could buy them off?

Gold, of course. Matt shaped his spell on that idea.

> "For our foemen, I am told,
> All that glitters now is gold.
> Oft a man his life hath sold
> One doubloon but to enfold.
> Monkish knights, of virtue bold,
> Swords and armor still may hold!"

The attackers shouted in horror as every bit of steel and iron about them turned to gold—pure gold. The Moncairean knights and soldiers shouted triumph as their steel cleaved through golden armor like hot knives through margarine. The attackers howled and turned, trying to jam back into the malvoisin *en masse*. But the ramp was narrow, and there were six feet of open space between malvoisin and wall, enough for ten or twenty men to plummet screaming to their deaths before the last footman could scramble back over the ramp. Footmen braced their pikes and heaved, pushing the malvoisin away from the wall; and knights stalked the battlements again, intoning conditional absolution and plunging their swords into the wounded.

The sounds of a howling, cursing brawl came from the malvoisin, like a congregation of fishwives. The whole structure trembled.

"What broil is that?" the abbot growled.

"The enemy." Sir Guy grinned. "They squabble over treasure. Yet 'ware; look down." He pointed. Matt and the abbot craned their necks, looking down over the wall, to see fresh troops running into the bottom door of the malvoisin.

"Max!" Matt bellowed, and the Demon hung before him in the air. "Aye, Wizard?"

"Upgrade the entropy on that firetrap." Matt pointed at the malvoisin.

"Aye," the Demon chortled, and winked out.

"What was that spell?" the abbot demanded.

"Watch." Matt's eyes glittered.

The malvoisin gave a long, preliminary groan; then, with a roar, the whole structure fell apart, beams crumbling into dust as they fell.

"Dry rot," Matt informed the abbot. "Accelerated."

A ten-foot heap of wood dust lay before the gate, filled with struggling, shouting troops.

"Scald!" the abbot called out, granite-faced. "Wash this dust away!"

Two knights upended a hundred-gallon kettle. Boiling water gouted down into the dust-heap. The enemy soldiers screamed, leaping out of sudden mud, landing running. But some of them only made about ten feet before they fell; and some never even got out of the dust pile.

"Archers!" the abbot bellowed, and arrows leaped down from the battlements to turn the fallen into pincushions, while the abbot recited the conditional absolution.

"A horrible end," he growled then, "but we could not have them there, upon our gate. Yet most shall live."

The last few golden-armored men staggered back into the enemy lines. They'd barely gotten there when knots of howling struggle erupted all along the line as footmen and knights alike fought over golden armor, swords, and pike heads.

"'Twill be some time ere they restore order." The abbot leaned back, lifting his helmet to wipe his brow. "We have some breathing space, I think. Brother Thomas! What's the hour?"

"The eighth of the night, milord," a brown-robe shouted back.

"An hour left till dawn." The abbot secured his helmet again. "Prepare yourselves, good knights! They'll not give us overlong to rest!"

But it was long—ten minutes went by, then fifteen.

Matt bit his lip. The enemy only had forty-five minutes left. What were they cooking up that took so long and could be worth the time when there was so little of it left?

His answer appeared, only a hundred feet away from the wall, diminished by distance—but her body glowed in the dark, and every detail was crystal-clear, the more so because she was nude.

All the defenders stared, transfixed.

Matt couldn't see her face too well, but her body was the most voluptuous he'd ever seen, fairly reeking of desire and secret, almost unbearable, pleasures. She stood turned three-quarters toward the monastery, long black hair flowing down over shoulder and breast, looking up at the wall sidelong.

Then most of the knights tore their eyes away, squeezing them shut, bowing their heads over clasped hands, and mouthing prayers as if they were racing to see who could finish the Rosary first.

"Lord above!" A black-bearded knight near Matt shuddered. "'Tis Anastaze—she whom I wronged, who slew herself, ere I came here repentant! Dear Lord, what have I done, to put her in the mouth of Hell?"

"'Tis not your lass!" the abbot boomed, clasping the man's shoulder. "'Tis a succubus from Hell! Or a foul glamour, made to look like one you knew! Up, away! Get you to the chapel! Pray! You cannot stand 'gainst *this* enemy!"

The knight rose and turned, stumbling past the abbot to the stairway.

"Mother of God!" a young knight at Matt's right breathed. "Lord above, save me!" His eyes fairly bulged.

"Why, then!" Sir Guy clapped him on the shoulder. "You came a virgin to this place? Nay, be proud! It lends you greater power, in such a war as this! Come, lad, shield your eyes and pray!

There's nothing nearer Heaven than a true, good woman; but there's nothing farther than yon succubus!"

Succubi, he should have said—for there were many of them now, sauntering past the wall in a languorous parade.

The young knight hid his eyes and began to pray.

"Hold firm!" The abbot clasped his shoulder. "Each temptation refused gives greater strength to withstand the next!"

Matt looked up; all along the battlements, odd knights were stumbling toward the stairways—more casualties than any other single attack had taken. But most of them watched without flinching, with chilled eyes. Each man's lips moved in silent syllables of prayer; they stood with arrows nocked, or swords half-drawn, charged with tension, waiting for an enemy to strike at.

But the auxiliaries were another matter.

"By Heaven!" a baron's knight gasped, "see you not yon damsel? Nay, I've never seen a wench so fair! Come, we must have at them!"

"Hold!" The nearest Moncairean clasped the knight's forearm in a grip of iron. "They are but fell illusions!"

"Then let me die in dreams," a footman cried. "Nay, brothers! See you not those lips, those hips, that tumbling hair? What beauty's there!"

"I must have one!" another gasped, and started toward the outer wall at a stumbling run. The Moncaireans turned to catch him. Hoarse shouts sounded all along the wall as a hundred others followed his lead. Shouting erupted, and the ringing of steel on steel.

"Nay, nay!" cried one lay knight, twisting and writhing in the monk-knights' grasp. "I must to them, must touch them! Nay, my manhood will mock me till my death, if I go not to them!"

"And your death will mock you to your manhood," the Moncairean growled. "You forget a hundred feet of empty space beyond that wall."

"Then let me die in ecstasy!"

"And fry in Hell," the other Moncairean grunted. "Yon's a succubus."

"Men!"

The single word cut through the clamor, flat and harsh, charged with woman's most stinging contempt. The fighters looked up, startled.

Sayeesa and Alisande stood at the base of the tower, bright in the moonlight. They sauntered toward the soldiers, looking at the knights and footmen with sneering contempt.

"How is it every man's a dog, when moonlight and a figure fair play upon his mind?" Sayeesa demanded.

"'Tis true," Alisande agreed. "Their tongues grow thick; they sweat and drool like feeble dolts."

"Aye. They withstand fire and steel, arrows, and the hail of bolts—but show them once a woman's form, and they'll crawl upon their bellies to be near her."

Were they out of their minds? They were fairly daring the soldiers to try rape!

Then Matt looked at the faces about him and saw them darkening with sullen anger—but looking at Sayeesa and Alisande, not the succubi. He looked at the women again. They were both beautiful in the torchlight; but the beauty was in their faces, for their bodies were draped and hidden. Somehow, neither looked the least bit sexually attractive at the moment. Even Sayeesa seemed to carry a frigid shield before her. Anger and scorn brightened her face, but the anger was cold, and all that radiated from her was chill. They were rousing anger, but also stilling lust. Matt found himself remembering that this was Sayeesa's area of power; but he hadn't known she could quench lust as well as she could raise it.

"Let them say what they will," one man-at-arms growled. "If I must choose 'twixt their like, and the ones without the walls, I'll go to those outside—or call them in!"

He scrambled to his feet and ran for the stairs. A dozen men shouted approval and ran after him. The rest snapped out of their dazes and made flying grabs at the renegades, who twisted aside and ran down the stairs, heading for the gate.

"Stop them!" the abbot bellowed. "Slay them as they fly, if you must! They must not near that gate!"

The porters sprang to readiness, whipping out their swords, and nearby brown-robes caught up staves.

"Max!" Matt bellowed. "Stop 'em!"

The Demon appeared between the two bodies, then exploded into a sheet of flame, filling the stairway just in front of the charging renegades.

The leader shrank back against the men behind him. They clambered back up the stairway as a party of Moncaireans clattered down to meet them, grappling their former fellows. There was a brief, chaotic clamor, shouting and the clash of steel; then it was stilled, as the Moncaireans dragged unconscious renegades off to a lockable room.

"The spell's not broken yet!"

Matt looked up, startled by the fury in Sayeesa's voice.

"See you not what happens there?" she demanded, pointing.

Matt looked out over the wall and saw some of the things the succubi were doing. He also heard the harsh, wet hiss of indrawn breath all along the wall.

"These men are goodly and strong," Sayeesa snapped, "yet they are only men, and many will not withstand that sight! Hide them, Wizard, ere your army's broken!"

"Uh—yeah." Matt pulled his eyeballs back into his head with an almost-audible snap and nodded, catching his breath. "You're right. Yeah. Sure.

> "Dust, that came at evil's call,
>   Return now here to hide our wall,
>   Churning high and thick and deep,
>   Hovering near to hide our keep."

It boiled in, filling the air just beyond the battlements, thick enough to hide the succubi from sight. The defenders shook themselves, seeming to come out of a trance.

"Nay! What hell-brought spell was that which almost sucked us to our doom?" one gasped.

"Cover your mouths," Matt called. "The wind might blow our way!" To Sayeesa, he asked, "How long till the sorcerers get the idea, do you think?"

"Not long," she replied. "They'll forego their spell, when they see there is no profit to it."

Double sticks thudded against the outer wall, and mail-clad men scrambled up over the battlements.

"Invaders!" Matt bellowed, and the cry ran along the wall as knights lugged out swords and footmen hefted their pikes, turning on the attackers with a roar of delight; they were charged with tension and needed an outlet. The parapet turned into churning chaos, filled with the clangor of swords and the bawling of soldiers. But attackers kept pouring in, and the garrison was weakened.

"We must die in this last hour!" The princess loomed up next to Matt, her sword a flickering death about her. "Can you not expel this army of sorcery?"

"I was thinking along that line." Matt wielded his sword, blocking blows, feeling the charge of spiritual power that had been building in him as more and more knights went to the chapel.

> "Let the dust die down and cease;
> Let us have a morning's peace!
> Where the dust no longer flies,
> Let a light to Heaven rise!
> May St. Elmo lend his presence
> With his spectral phosphorescence!"

As the dust dwindled and disappeared, the battlements began to glow with pale fire, brightening till it nearly hurt the eyes. All the soldiers froze in superstitious terror, with oaths and cries of fear.

"It's *cold* fire," Matt cried. "It will not hurt the godly!"

The Moncaireans came out of their trance with a shout. Discipline took over as the abbot bawled, "Attack!" The soldier-monks went to it with a roar. The attackers backed away in fear, until they realized their choice was between St. Elmo's fire and certain death from steel. Then they clambered back into the battle, but it was too late. The Moncaireans had gained momentum, and the enemy soldiers fought in fear. Bodies flew from the wall; men screamed and clutched the steel that bit them. From there on, it was a cross between a slaughter and a clean-up session.

Matt decided not to give the sorcerers a fighting chance. He took a breath, searching his memory and adapting:

> "Let our foes turn about and all look to the east,
> Ere the dawn shall emerge from the dark;
> For 'tis there will be found a most curious beast,
> Best known as the fabulous Snark.
> But, oh, beamish foeman, beware of the day,
> If your Snark be a Boojum! For then
> You will softly and suddenly vanish away,
> And never be met with again!"

Nothing seemed to happen, and Matt felt a stab of dismay.

Then he realized that this spell might take a few minutes to work.

Soldiers were pouring down the scaling ladders! The battlements were almost clear, except for the dead and wounded. The Moncai-reans began to push the scaling ladders over with bellows of joy, and the attackers were running back to their own battle line, while their captains bawled threats, trying to rally another charge. Troops being shoved forward met fleeing troops returning; they clashed and churned into swirls of shouting confusion.

Then a high, piercing shriek wafted dimly over the noise of battle—men in absolute terror. Matt's eyes snapped to the far side of the enemy army. Something had taken a nice, semicircular bite out of the back of the enemy line—no corpses were left, just empty grass where a hundred men had stood.

The Snark, it seemed, *was* a Boojum!

Howling shrieks of fear and confusion filled the field, and the whole attacking army turned into one vast mêlée, while the silent semicircle expanded and kept expanding.

Then the growth stopped. Somehow, the enemy sorcerers had managed to stop the Boojum without knowing exactly what they were fighting.

Matt tried another spell:

> "Let us have a western wind.
> Blowing toward the ones who've sinned.
> Let it carry o'er the field,
> Till our enemy does yield,
> A scent that they all will be rapt in—
> Pure skunk oil—butyl mercaptan!"

The wind sprang up, but even so, the stench rising to the battlements from the enemy army was disconcerting. Below, the whole field was a vast sea of coughing and choking.

"They are beaten, Wizard!" a spark hummed at Matt's shoulder.

"For a moment. And it's almost daylight. But I'd like to stack the deck a little . . . Know what metal fatigue is?"

"Metal crystalizing, hardening until it falls apart at the slightest blow."

"Right. Suppose you give every bit of enemy metal a case of such fatigue?" Matt suggested.

"'Tis done!" The Demon winked out.

That would destroy their weapons. Sorcerers could whip up new ones quickly. But there were other things they might not be able to counteract so easily, knowing nothing of microbiology. Matt considered that, then decided to add a bit of comfort for his side:

> "They'll breakfast when the sun has risen:
> At eventime they'll eat again.
> Salted through the meat and grain
> Pray let there be some botulism."

Then he added a second spell:

> "The wind has blown, the army's stilled;
> Now their taste for battle's killed.
> So let the wind die down to calm;
> Let us know the morning's balm."

The wind slackened and died; the odor of skunk reeked, but was only an inconvenience on the battlements. The enemy army still churned; it would be some time before they managed to restore order.

The sun's edge swelled above the horizon.

A shout of triumph rose from the monastery walls. Knights embraced; footmen danced jigs. The abbot stood, seeming to rise a little as relief filled him—relief and, Matt saw, something more, almost awe. And as the din of celebration slackened, he began to chant:

> "Praise God above, whose mighty mace
> Banished night by His stern Grace!
> God of Battles, praise we sing,
> Who has wrought this wondrous thing,
> Out of night, and reeking breath,
> Saving us from steel-clad Death!"

One by one, the Moncaireans took up the chant, and the auxiliaries after them, till the whole length of the battlements thundered:

"Joyful in the dawn, we thank Thee!
God immortal, Who did bring
Thy poor, undeserving servants
Through the dark night! Praise we sing!"

The hymn died, and the abbot removed his helmet, mopping his brow.

Matt turned to survey the enemy army, still disordered. "Congratulations, milord. We held out against the worst Malingo could throw at us."

"Worst?" The abbot looked up, startled. "You did not sense the slackening?"

"Slackening?" Matt's euphoria vanished. "No, I didn't."

"'Twas hard after midnight, Lord Wizard. The force of their attack failed to strengthen, as I'd thought it would, in the darkest hours of the night. There was not light enough to see, nor time enough to survey; but I'd wager forces trooped away into the hills!"

Matt stood very still, watching him.

"This attack, though worse than any we have had, was still far weaker than I'd feared," the abbot went on. "I had thought to face foul monsters, spells to chill our marrow, Hell-spawned nightmares. Nay, Lord Wizard—this was far less than Malingo's fullest force!"

Matt swallowed, heavily. "So. Just a good training session, huh?"

"Nay; far more," the abbot admitted. "There was more magic in this battle than ever I have faced. I am glad that you were here, Lord Wizard."

Matt just stood for a moment; then he bowed. "Thank you, Lord Abbot. I am pleased that I was some worth to you."

But he began to wonder. If this army had been depleted since midnight, what had Malingo done with the spare troops? And why? And what was it going to be like when Matt had to fight the whole mess of them?

As he started to dive-bomb toward depression, a sentry cried out, "Hold! Who comes?"

Matt looked up, startled.

Beyond the far side of the army, around the base of the hill, a great dark-green shape waddled, with a dot of black on its shoulders.

"Stegoman!" Matt grabbed the abbot's shoulder. "That's a friend of mine—and the guy on his back is one of your own kind! A little remiss, maybe, but yours nonetheless! If they try to get in here, we've got to get them through!"

"Enough, enough, Lord Wizard!" The abbot twisted free and clamped his helmet back on. "We'll see them in!"

The distance-dwarfed dragon paused; then it charged at the back of the swirling army, a great gout of fire clearing its way. Shrieks came dimly to Matt's ears, and a path opened before Stegoman. He bulldozed through, roaring; but a baron bawled orders, and a knot of soldiers began to form up against danger. Nearer the wall, a sorcerer rose up, arms weaving a spell.

"Max!" Matt snapped. "Drain that wizard!"

"Done!" the Demon sang, without even bothering to appear; and the sorcerer tumbled.

"Great!" Matt shouted. "Now clear a path for my friend!"

Soldiers and knights began to drop of sudden exhaustion, in a straight line that met the dragon's flaming breath.

Stegoman plowed on through, waving his head from side to side, cutting a great circle of flame, like a pie with a slice missing, about him. Pikes and swords rushed toward him, then rushed back as the heat wave hit.

"I believe he will come to us unharmed!" Alisande cried, gripping Matt's forearm.

"Well, there's a good chance, at least." Matt frowned, peering down. "What's happening there?"

A last rally of men had formed, splitting off from the army of sorcery to gather in a skirmish line between the dragon and the monastery gate, just out of bowshot.

Stegoman bulled his way through the last ranks and paused, glaring at the battle line.

A baron barked out a set of orders, and the archers bent their bows. But a spark of light danced among them, and the bows snapped, sending the archers staggering back. Soldiers propped pike butts against earth, pointing the spear blade tops at Stegoman's chest height; but Matt could see the bright metal browning with rust.

Stegoman bellowed and charged.

Pike points broke against his scaly hide; swords cracked and crumbled at the first stroke. The dragon blasted flame about him, and the soldiers ran screaming.

"He has triumphed!" the princess cried.

"Thanks, Max," Matt muttered.

"'Twas pleasure," the spark sang. "You have irony."

The dragon charged headlong at the gates, and the abbot cried, "Open! These are ours!"

The doors groaned wide, and the sorcerers' army howled, seeing their chance. A thousand footmen sprinted for the portal, pikes high, while sorcerers popped up behind them, hands weaving frantic spells.

"Stegoman! Torch 'em!" Matt yelled, and the dragon slewed to a stop in the gateway, skidding in a full turn. He roared, and a ten-foot bar of flame shot out toward the attackers.

"Give him a boost there, will you?" Matt said, aside, and Max sang, "Aye, Wizard!" and winked out.

Stegoman's flame shot out to thirty feet. The dragon's head whipped back in surprise, accidentally charring a careless sorcerer who'd thought he should lead, for a change. Then Stegoman recovered and depressed his aim, turning his head. Flame swept a clear arc around the gateway, and enemy footmen screamed; body armor conducted beautifully. They pulled back—or ran, more truthfully, the ones who were still ambulatory. Stegoman bit off his flame and shifted into reverse, backing up fast. Monks heaved, and the great doors boomed shut.

A shriek of frustration went up from the enemy lines, and the abbot turned to Matt with a hard smile. "Well done, Wizard. They'll not prevail 'gainst our gates."

"'Tis a priest, Lord Abbot," a knight called from below, "one near to exhaustion."

"We ha' known it," the abbot called down. "Bring him up to us."

"Must he come up?" Sayeesa objected. "Can he not speak from below?"

"I think it unlikely," the abbot said, frowning. "Did you not hear Sir Pedigraine? The man's nearly spent!"

Brunel appeared at the top of the steps, gasping, propped up by a knight and a novice. "God be . . . praised! I ha' ridden as though . . . a demon pursued me this night, in hope . . . I would find you!"

"Welcome, Father." But there was a dubious undertone to the abbot's greeting.

Matt tried to sound hearty. "Good to see you again, Father! Did you rouse any monks?"

Bruncl nodded, beginning to catch his breath. "The Knights of the Cross, and . . . the Order of Saint Conor. And, yestere'en, I rode toward the convent of Saint Cynestria."

"The convent?" Sayeesa cried. "What business had *you* there?"

"There are warriors among them," the priest said simply.

"Yes, and probably some beauties, too." Matt frowned. "I should think that wasn't too wise, Father—for you."

The abbot frowned, puzzled and angered; but Brunel smiled sourly. "Secure, I assure you. There may be beauty there, but a man who shows recognition of it might suffer—and harshly. With such knowledge in mind, there's scant chance of desire arising."

The abbot lifted his head, beginning to understand; and Matt hurried on before the knight could start catechizing. "You only said you rode *toward* the convent. Did you get there?"

"To the hill above the plain that surrounds it, aye. But there, in the dark of the moon, I saw an army of Evil gathering about its walls!"

Alisande gasped, hand covering her mouth, and the abbot swore, "By'r Lady!"

But Sayeesa gave a short, mocking laugh. "A fool's errand, that! If any could withstand a fell Hell-host, 'twould be the House of Saint Cynestria!"

"There is truth in that," the abbot said, frowning, "yet they, too, are only mortal . . ."

"It may be as you say." Brunel avoided looking at Sayeesa. "But there were foul beasts among them and fell things of most unholy sorcery. Still, their walls were unbreached when I turned, and this great dragon and I rode to find you."

"Siege," Matt mused. "About what hour did you come there?"

"The fifth, after midnight." The priest frowned. "Does that signify?"

"Aye!" The abbot's eyes lit. "'Twas midnight when their host round our walls did lessen!"

"You must go!" Father Brunel blurted. "Do not ask the why of me; still, I know it, and my bones know it, that 'tis yourselves must ride to their aid!"

"So we shall," Alisande said, with iron resolution. "You are right in this, Father—I am certain."

That decided the issue, Matt knew. Still . . . "Uh, with all due respect, your Highness—wouldn't an army do little more good?"

"What army?" The princess rounded on him. "Those gathered here? If they come out as slowly as an army must, there will be a great battle outside these walls—and, even though lessened, the warriors of Evil outnumber the Knights of Moncaire!"

"'Tis as her Highness says," the abbot agreed somberly. "A small party can travel quickly; with support from the walls, they might carve a path through this host. But an army could not; there are too many to travel quickly enough to avoid all the blows. Yet I am loathe that ye should depart; for Heaven knows we might have fallen this night past without the aid of this good wizard and his . . . spirit."

Still avoiding the word "Demon," Matt noted. "I wouldn't worry too much about that, milord. You see, Max did a number on their weapons and armor, and set a microorganism on their food supplies."

The abbot frowned. "What means this?"

"It means that, by nightfall, their metal will fall apart at the slightest blow," Matt grinned. "And right after dinner, the effects of breakfast and lunch should start showing—abdominal cramps, nausea, diarrhea, and fever. They won't have much stomach for fighting—those who survive."

The abbot stared, his mouth gaping open.

Then he grinned and clapped Matt on the shoulder. "Aye, we should live through the night, even without you! Go, then, with good heart! I would I could lead my hosts out behind you. Yet after your spell has done its work, by morning there should be but a remnant of their army still standing. Then may we sally out to cleanse our environs and, after, ride west to meet you at the convent."

"Great." Matt smiled. "And, uh—I don't want to sound unduly optimistic, but—if the army's gone from the convent when you get there, keep riding west, will you? Be nice if you could meet us in the mountains."

"Aye; we will have strong need of you there," Alisande agreed.

The abbot bowed to her. "We will, then, your Highness. At the convent, then, or the mountains."

"And we will ride to the convent—now." Alisande turned away, toward the stairs.

Matt could have pointed out a few unpleasant facts, such as

the unlikelihood of four people and a dragon being able to help much against an army that included a strong corps of sorcerers; but he knew what the answer would be. This was a public matter, so Alisande had to be right. He sighed and turned to follow her.

"'Tis my choice also," Sayeesa breathed, cutting ahead of him. "I cannot see Saint Cynestria's walls too soon!"

"I, too, shall come." Father Brunel started to limp after her.

Sayeesa spun about, rage flaring in her eyes; but the abbot pulled rank.

He put out a palm and caught Brunel in the breastbone. "Nay, Father. Methinks you will stay here amongst us; for you are wearied and not fit for travel."

Father Brunel started to stutter a refusal, but there was the gleam of combat in the abbot's eye, and he *did* rank a simple country priest. Brunel swallowed his objections and lowered his eyes. "Even as you say, of course, Lord Abbot."

"Of course," the abbot echoed grimly. "And when you have rested, good Father, I wish to have some converse with you."

Father Brunel looked up, alarmed. Then he swallowed heavily and looked away again.

CHAPTER 15

Stegoman shouldered up beside them as they waited behind the great gate.

Matt looked up, surprised. "You haven't had much sleep."

"Nor have I need of it," the dragon snorted. "I am easily fit for another twelve-hour chase. Do not seek to dissuade me, Wizard."

"Wouldn't dream of it," Matt murmured.

"'Tis well," the dragon said gruffly. "Mount, Wizard."

Matt climbed aboard, picking his way carefully between pointed fins. "I really appreciate this, Stego—"

"Loose!" the abbot yelled above.

A hundred arrows darkened the air, arching high to hail down on the enemy. Shields snapped up all around the gate; enemy soldiers cowered under their shells.

"Open the gate!" the abbot bellowed.

"Ride!" Alisande cried, and charged out as the gates cracked open.

"Don't let her lead!" Matt cried, and Stegoman shot ahead, past the princess's horse. She howled in anger as he cut in front of her, then saved her breath as the dragon's torch lit. He charged out like a flame thrower into Hell, carrying Matt, with Alisande, Sir Guy, and Sayeesa galloping behind.

Even then, the sorcerers almost got them. A geyser of fire erupted right under Stegoman's nose, and the dragon pulled back, almost starting a chain collison. Sir Guy and Alisande just barely pulled their horses up in time. Then the footmen charged in from the back with a howl, and the princess and the Black Knight turned to meet them with razor-edged steel. They bought just enough time for Max to douse the volcano and make it re-erupt right under the enclave of sorcerers. While they were busy screaming and running around swatting out flamelets on each others' coattails, Stegoman let loose a fire-blast with a Demon-assist and torched a path through the army. They rode out full tilt, and nobody seemed minded to dispute the right-of-way with them.

Sir Guy reined his horse back to a walk when the bulk of the western foothills hid the monastery from sight. He opened his visor and yanked off a gauntlet, so he could wipe his brow. "That was hot, heavy work, Lord Wizard."

"Shoulda shtayed aroun' 'n' burned 'em down t' the' groun'," Stegoman slurred.

Matt eyed his mount warily, but he seemed docile enough for the moment. The ride was a bit on the bumpy side, though. "Well, we got out with only a few scratches, and that's what matters, Sir Guy . . . We *are* heading west, aren't we?"

"Aye." The Black Knight grinned. "The dragon did not swerve *too* badly. We should arrive at Saint Cynestria's convent ere nightfall."

"Good." Matt pursed his lips thoughtfully. "I have a feeling that somehow, without us, they're in heavy trouble."

"Not unless the army besieging them is far more fell than that which we battled last night," Sayeesa said grimly.

"Which it is," Matt replied. "I'll lay you long odds on that one. I have a sneaking suspicion the whole situation is set up to guarantee that *we* have to be there, to give the Cynestrians a fighting chance. Why else would they attack this particular convent?"

"I think it has to do with our good Sayeesa," Alisande said thoughtfully. "She may have a greater part to play in this war than we ha' known."

"Yeah . . ." Matt chewed at the inside of his cheek. "The priest who heard our confessions in that country church said something of the sort."

"Nay, surely not!" Sayeesa frowned. "I am humble and a sinner! I could not have such great import!"

"Yet still 'twas said," Alisande pointed out. "And if 'tis so, the sorcerer has done all he may to prevent her coming to the convent..."

"Without much luck," Matt added.

"That *is* to your credit," Alisande admitted. "Yet 'ware false pride, Lord Wizard."

One of these days, Matt decided, Alisande was going to give him a real, full, unqualified compliment—and when she realized she'd done so, she'd probably have a heart attack.

"So," the princess went on, "if he cannot prevent her arrival at the Cynestrians' gate..."

"He can eliminate the gate." Matt's lips tightened. "And the convent with it. Sure. But wouldn't that indicate that Sayeesa, herself, isn't vital? Instead, it's her joining with the convent that's a key event."

"That, I can more readily accept," Sayeesa said. "Yet not fully; for I cannot believe I'd add much power to those iron, holy women!"

"Some change may overcome you there," Alisande said offhandedly, "transforming you to a greater force than we can think."

"I'll not hear more," Sayeesa said flatly, and nudged her pony on ahead.

"But I kinda think she wants to." Matt frowned at the ex-witch's retreating back.

"There may be truth in it," Alisande mused. "Yet it could be no more than their joining; the two could form a most potent combination. For, look you, Lord Wizard—the Cynestrians accept as novices only women who have sinned, and deeply. All within their walls are therefore penitent, laden with remorse—and, as a consequence, staggering in the intensity of their devotion. They fast and pray both night and day with greatest fervor, seeking to atone. 'Tis said they pray with vengeance—on themselves."

"Hmm." Matt pursed closed lips. "They could put out a lot of spiritual power, couldn't they? Come to think of it, they'd have to—what else could have held Malingo's army off all night?"

"If they did succeed in that," Alisande reminded him. "For which, let us pray... Yet their power is not prayer alone; for there are former bandits in their midst."

"Women?" Matt's eyebrows shot up. "Female bandits? In *this* kind of society?"

"'Tis our ways and customs formed them," Alisande demurred. "They are women who could not, would not, be subjected to a man's command; and in such a land as ours, there is scant space for such unfeminine women."

Sir Guy nodded. "These Ladies of the Waste could best most men. Nay, I've heard of them. Such a band did gather one short year agone—a small army, they were indeed—bandit-maids and scourers, who did loot and burn throughout these marches. They were, for several months, scourges of the West, lording it over all the borderland."

"This did begin when Astaulf came to power?" Alisande demanded, thin-lipped.

Sir Guy nodded. "As the king does, so do the subjects; and Astaulf is a bandit king. Yet when these bandit-maids had grown intolerable, the Mother Superior of the Cynestrians swore they gainsaid Nature, in that God made women to protect and care for others, not to sack and slay them. She vowed that she would bring them to repentance, or die in the attempt. Many of her order sought to join with her, but she'd not have them; the hazard was for her, and her alone. Thus she rode singly out to face the outlaw band. She found them, endured their torments and their insults, then began to speak to them of Christ and Blessed Mary. Thus she showed them the estate that they were born to and had spurned; and by Heaven! not a one of them who heard her could stand against remorse!"

"She brought them out repentant, as she'd said?" Alisande's tone was hushed.

Sir Guy smiled. "Each and every one. They rode back with her to the convent, turning postulant. If the walls of Saint Cynestria yet stand, your Highness, they are why; they are the ones who bore the brunt of fighting."

Somehow, Matt wasn't exactly eager to meet the good sisters— at least, not unless they were sure he was on their side. In the afternoon, he had a chance to mention this to Sir Guy.

"You never shall convince them of it," Sir Guy declared. "They're sure, these bandit-maids, that all that's male conspires against them—save Christ, which is why they're so devoted to Him. Still, if you can bring their Reverend Mother to believe you, her warriors will side with you; for they'll be ruled by her."

"Hmm." Matt chewed that one over. "Well, I'd better be my most persuasive—but I don't think that means charming."

"Indeed not," the Black Knight agreed. "She will see through whatever face you wear to your true one; so, best that be the face you wear."

"Yeah." Matt nodded. "Just my ordinary self."

"Nay. Your *true* self."

Matt turned slowly. "Whaddaya mean? I *am* my true self!"

"Then you know that you do hold feelings for our princess that are somewhat more than those of a liegeman for his lady?"

"Now, hold on! I don't know anything of the sort!"

"Then the face you wear lacks truth. Nay, do not speak—I've seen it in you. Admit these feelings, Wizard—at least unto yourself. This game you play must cease."

"Game?" Matt felt anger kindle. "What are you talking about? I'm not playing any game!"

"Are you not? 'Tis even as I've said—you will not acknowledge it, even to yourself. I pray you, do; yearnings hidden may weaken you—and through you, all of us."

Matt felt his emotions still and settle into an icy block. "If you're talking about lust, don't sweat it—I'm not exactly hot for her Highness's body . . . Well, not usually." He remembered her dance in the Stone Ring; but that had been an aberration.

Sir Guy turned away, sighing and shaking his head. "Well, I spoke my piece, and hard enough it came. Yet I bid you hearken to my words." He clucked to his horse and rode ahead.

Matt glowered at his back, coals of resentment smoldering in his belly.

The sun was low in the sky, silhouetting a low, sprawling building with a steeple rising up from its midst, perched on a low hill in the middle of a valley—the convent of Saint Cynestria. It looked much like the Moncairean monastery.

Matt wondered about the army that surrounded it. The levies didn't seem to be any more numerous than the host hemming in the Moncaireans; but there were some big holes in the gathering, empty patches of ground with a look of waiting to them, scrupulously avoided by the soldiers. He wondered who—or what—would be dropping in.

"How shall we attain these walls, Lord Wizard?" the princess demanded.

"How indeed?" Sir Guy seconded. "Be wary of your magic, for I see many more midnight robes and a host of gray."

"Yeah, they *do* look heavier in the magic arm. Well, sometimes there's nothing like good, old-fashioned violence. Stegoman, can you breathe out fire without letting it flame?"

"How mean you?" The dragon turned his head back to look at his rider. "I only know 'tis anger that sets flame."

"Okay, then, imagine you're angry—just pretending. And breathe out through your mouth . . . Yeah, that's right."

The dragon's jaw lolled open; a steady hissing sounded. The horses shied off, and Matt wasn't surprised; he could scent the odor himself. It was faint, but it was also redolent of decay. Methane, probably.

"Good." Matt nodded. "Just keep it up, now—pump out as much dragon-breath as you can."

Stegoman sucked in air and exhaled again. Matt recited:

> "The foeman now has little care;
> Let him have some moving air,
> Wafting from the eastern trees,
> With dragon's breath upon its breeze."

The air stirred about them, then settled into a steady breeze blowing against their backs. Stegoman kept hissing; the wind carried his fumes out toward the enemy. The dragon took time between breaths to demand, "How is this, that I grow not giddy?"

"It's the flame that does it," Matt explained, not quite accurately; it would take too long to explain what combustion products were.

"Wizard," Alisande said nervously, "will you do nothing?"

"Not for a while, your Highness." Matt wished for a wrist watch. "Stegoman's gotta pump out enough breath to cover most of the army between us and the gate." He leaned back, drumming his fingers on Stegoman's fin and whistling through his teeth.

About ten minutes later, he said, "Max?"

"Aye, Wizard?" asked the dot of light.

"Max, by this time, most of the army directly ahead of us ought to be blanketed with a kind of air that burns. Touch off a spark in the middle of it, will you?"

"Gladly," the arc spark murmured and winked out.

Matt leaned forward, keying himself up. "Ready, now. As soon as we see the flash, we ride."

The others looked up, surprised. Then they turned, bracing themselves in the saddles, but not without some trepidation.

A gout of flame exploded in the middle of the army, enveloping the whole march between the convent and the valley edge in flame.

"A triumph!" Stegoman roared with a six-foot flame. "Oh, wondroush wizhard!"

Matt bellowed, "Ride!"

Stegoman rumbled downhill like a beer wagon. The rest of the party followed out of faith.

The fire in the air damped and died in seconds, the methane spent; but everywhere it had touched, organics burned—grass, leaves, clothing, and hair. The army was in chaos, men running toward the nearest vat of water or wine, swatting out flames on each others' clothing, and bawling at the sorcerers to do something.

Into this mêlée charged a wall of drunken dragon, blasting fire all about him with a grand lack of discrimination. Howls doubled in front of him, and soldiers scrambled back out of his way. Stegoman scarcely had to slow as he cut his way through to the gates. A sorcerer did pop out to try a quick spell, but he seemed to have sudden difficulty moving his arms, and a second later, Stegoman converted him into a torch.

"Hoy!" Alisande stood in her stirrups, waving at the top of the wall. "Open! Travelers seeking sanctuary! Ho! I cry the hospitality of the house!"

A black-robed figure leaned out from the battlements, long veil flowing down across coif and shoulders, white band across the forehead. Then it disappeared; a moment later, the gates swung open. "Enter!" a voice commanded; but Stegoman was already in, and the others halfway through. The gates swung shut behind them, and the company found themselves in a narrow tunnel, with slit-windows in the walls. Barbed steel points bristled from the slits, and another gate walled them off ahead.

"Who called for sanctuary?" demanded a harsh, stern voice; it sounded like an old-maid schoolteacher.

Alisande tossed back her long blond hair. "I am Alisande, Princess of Merovence. My companions are Sir Guy Losobal; Matthew, Lord Wizard; and the penitent Sayeesa, who wishes to try her vocation in this House of Cynestria!"

"The vile witch of the moor?" The unseen speaker had nothing of censure in her voice; she sounded excited.

Sayeesa nodded. "So I was, till these good folks broke the enchantment that enslaved me and brought me to a priest. I repent my former ways; I reject Satan and all his works. Knowing my own poor, weak nature, I wish to shelter within your walls for the strengthening of my resolution."

"Attend a moment," the voice commanded. "We must speak to one another's faces."

Sayeesa sat waiting as if she were about to enter a throne room, seeming to strain toward the inner gate as if her saddle were holding her back from flying.

The gates swung open, and huge chains clanked as a portcullis rose. Three nuns waited, the tallest a step in front.

Sayeesa touched her heels to her horse's flanks, rode up to the portcullis, and swung down to kneel before the tall old lady.

"What seek you here?" the abbess demanded severely; but delight underlay her gorgon mask. She was tall and slender, with a long face that tapered to a pointed chin, a thin blade of a nose, and large, black, snapping eyes. Her mouth was a thin line amidst a net of wrinkles. Matt could find the traces of great beauty still lingering; but the beauty itself was dust, and any tenderness that might once have accompanied it seemed to have been burned out of the gaunt old frame.

"What seek you here?" she demanded again; and Sayeesa answered, "To try my vocation among you, Mother."

It was a repetition, but necessary; before, it had been for information; now, it was spiritual.

"Hold up your head!" the crone commanded, and Sayeesa's head snapped back as if a string had been pulled. Her face was humbled, filled with remorse—and a loneliness of a kind Matt had never seen before.

The abbess scanned Sayeesa's face intently; but if she found anything there, her own face gave no sign of it. "Why should you think you have a vocation?"

"I have sinned," Sayeesa answered in low and quavering tones, "so deeply that all folk of any conscience shun the sight of me. I have repented and been shriven. I've wandered, lost, alone, and near despair, though tended by these three good people. Yet when I saw these walls rise up before me, my heart turned glad; I began to feel that all my life led to your gates."

The abbess seemed halfway satisfied with that answer. "So you found your vocation when you saw our walls. And how came you here?"

Sayeesa's voice was scarcely audible. "I was sent here."

The old woman stiffened. "By whom? Tell me the manner of it!"

Sayeesa hesitated.

The abbess's voice softened amazingly. "Nay, child, speak— and fear not to say the whole of it. None will blame or sneer, for there's not a one of us within these walls that could not tell a tale to sicken your heart with loathing."

Sayeesa looked up, her eyes filling with tears. The abbess waved the other nuns away; they slipped back into the shadows beyond the portcullis. Then the abbess knelt before Sayeesa, caught her hands, and looked deeply into her eyes. "Now, speak!"

Sayeesa began to tell it in a low and trembling voice, a phrase at a time at first, then more freely, till she was pouring her heart out. The abbess knelt like a stone, hands clasped tightly around Sayeesa's, her face grave. Matt couldn't hear what passed; but finally Sayeesa sank back on her heels, head bowed low, hair fallen forward to hide her face, a sob shuddering through her frame.

"Nay, come, come!" The old nun's voice was gentle. "There is no shame in that; many sisters here would say the same. All new penitents think their sin the greatest ever done and therefore feel ashamed to look upon a sister's face." She hooked a finger under Sayeesa's chin, prying the face up; and she almost smiled as she said, "Come, child! You must know the silliness of that; 'tis foul pride's hidden side! There, you knew it ere I said it— now, did you not?"

Sayeesa gulped and nodded, a smile beginning to glimmer through her tears.

"Oh, your tale was harrowing enough," the abbess admitted. "Yet I've heard worse. Take heart, child; embrace God's Grace. You, like all amongst us, can yet atone . . . So." Her face became stern again. "A priest confessed you; and, in company with these good people, you came unto our door. On that journey, you were sorely tried, yet still held free from sin."

"But I came so near . . ."

"Yet still held clear! How near you came, child, matters not; you resisted, thereby gaining grace and strength. Aye, the priest was right to send you to us. I doubt not you are sincere in penitence and surely need our sanctuary for a while."

"Only for a while?" Sayeesa cried, almost in panic. "Mother! May I not stay as novice?"

"I cannot say, child." The abbess's face softened. "Though, Heaven knows, I would you could; for I sense a great reserve of strength within you, power I would most dearly love to have amongst us here. Yet withal . . ." Her eyes drifted from Sayeesa's face, losing focus. "I sense a weakness, too, a weakness that could bring great danger . . ."

She stood, with difficulty, and hauled Sayeesa to her feet. "Stay amongst us, then, awhile, and we'll discover your true nature. There, then—go within."

The two junior nuns stepped forward out of the shadows to escort Sayeesa into the convent.

The abbess turned to Alisande.

The princess swung down from her horse and stepped up to the abbess, her face neutral, but with something in her bearing that spoke of readiness for conflict.

"You honor our house, Highness," the abbess said formally. "Indeed, I rejoice at your presence; having you within shall strengthen my daughters' hearts this night."

"I thank you, Reverend Mother." Alisande half relaxed. "And my companions?"

The abbess gave Matt and Sir Guy a brief glance, which had nothing of friendship in it. "If they are yours, they are welcome; but men may not enter in this House. We have a guest chamber in the gate tower."

Stegoman got to stay in the courtyard, with a haunch of beef; apparently the injunction against males applied only to humans. The men's chamber was at the top of a long, narrow set of winding stairs, with a very large lock, and the abbess kept the key.

Sir Guy looked definitely unhappy. "I mislike small, closed spaces, Lord Matthew—especially when the door is fast."

"Yeah, it'll be fast enough." Matt knelt to peek into the keyhole. "A Boy Scout could go through this one—and if I can't spell my way out of this bind, I don't deserve to pass grade school."

"Eh?" The knight turned in surprise; then he grinned. "Aye, I had not thought! Certes, you'll open this latch when we need it. My thanks, Lord Matthew; you've set me at ease."

"Well, glad I'm good for something." Matt strolled over to the window and looked down at the ramparts, seeing a black-robed sentry every fifty feet. There was something in the way they stood that resonated with his mental image of the abbess. "I could be wrong, Sir Guy, but I think what we've got here is one of the most concentrated doses of fanaticism I've ever seen."

"Remorse has that effect." The Black Knight sounded as if he spoke from experience. "Be mindful, Lord Matthew, that every woman within these walls has been hurt most shrewdly by men and has hurt them in return—and the Devil's picture is of a male."

Matt turned, slowly lifting his head. "I see. It's a sin to hate your fellow humans—but it's okay to hate the Devil and his agents. Nice bit of sublimation."

"There's little of the sublime about it," the Black Knight snorted. "I wondered that they did not exile your dragon for his maleness and his fiery breath."

"Fire being associated with Hell?" Matt smiled bleakly. "Well, this is the West. I assume they've had dealings with dragons before, since we must be near dragon country."

"Aye, you speak aright. And dragons are strong allies in war. Yet sometimes I misdoubt me of the worth of our good Stegoman."

"Yeah, a drunken dragon's not the world's most reliable. There's a chance of curing him, of course, but . . ."

"Indeed? How might that be done?"

"I've got a pretty good idea of what's wrong with him," Matt said slowly. "But I'm no expert. If I'm wrong, I could leave him worse off than he is now."

"So you'll not attempt it?"

"Not unless it's a serious emergency. Then I might use a spell or so I've thought of. They might work, since he's full grown now."

"Why, how is this?" Sir Guy frowned. "Think you his malady began in childhood?"

"Before that—in infancy. From the few things he's let drop, I gather dragon parents lay eggs, but leave them alone to hatch. When they do, the hatchlings are on their own till they find their parents."

Sir Guy nodded. "Aye. And I've heard 'tis then that cowardly men seek to slay them, for even infant dragon's blood is powerful in magic."

"And he has a thing about hatchling hunters. Let's suppose one chased him up onto some high place. When he tried to fly down, his wings were too weak, so he fell. When he landed, it hurt a lot. That left him scared of heights. Maybe, later when he'd learned to fly, something attacked him and made him fall painfully again. So deep down, he figures flying is dangerous. But with his background, he can't admit that to himself—so he gets high, which makes his fellow dragons ground him. Shameful, but nowhere nearly as bad as being thought a coward." Matt wandered over to the window again. "It's night, and they're lining up on the battlements. "There's the abbess. And—Good Lord! It's Sayeesa!"

The ex-witch came a pace behind as the abbess mounted the steps. She wore a plain gray gown with a small white bib. A short gray veil hid her hair, and the coif was only a strip of white across her forehead—the habit of a postulant.

The abbess spread her hands, and Matt could hear her voice clearly. "Hear me, daughters! Be mindful of what befell us last night! You will be attacked again with all the evils they have. You will be racked with fevers, cramps, and nausea. Your limbs will turn to water; your flesh may fester and erupt in boils. These things, though real, are like illusions—let your mind be filled with God, and all these plagues will lose their power over you and vanish. But if you cannot clear your mind and heart of all but Him and the deeds you must do in His name, then lay down your weapons and retire to the chapel to pray, that you may strengthen those who remain upon the wall. There is no shame in such retreat, my daughters—only in failure of your resolve through reluctance to retire; for thus would you weaken those who remain."

She paused, looking from face to face. The sisters watched her, faces grave. The abbess nodded, satisfied. "And be wary of your greatest hazard—the urge to hate the things that come in forms of men!"

A low, harsh mutter passed along the wall. It made Matt's hackles rise. He felt himself trying to shrink into the stonework.

"You have all suffered at the hands of men!" The abbess drowned out the mutter. "You came here hating, until you stilled that hatred through prayer. Yet that, of all your urges, can most easily be reawakened. Be mindful that the sins of hate and lust for vengeance are our worst temptations. The men who shamed you were but tools of Satan and his minions, and all the creatures you may see before this wall tonight are but minions of his minions. They are enemies, but undeserving of hate or anger. The arrows that you loose against them will lose all power, if they're released in hatred or anger. Strike to save our sisters and those without these walls; strike to save men from temptation to hurt women; but strike not in hatred or for vengeance. If you cannot forego those, lay down your weapons and turn away this moment to the chapel."

Sir Guy grunted in surprise as a handful of nuns began moving toward the stairs, their heads bowed in prayer. A chill crawled up Matt's spine. If they didn't feel capable of striking without hatred after a speech like that, how deeply did their hatred burn?

Another handful of nuns came up the stairs—reinforcements from the chapel. The abbess turned away and began talking earnestly with Sayeesa and Alisande. Then a cry went up from the far end of the wall. A nun was pointing out into the darkness. The sisters set arrows to bowstrings.

Sir Guy raced Matt to the front window. They jammed into it together, looking out over the valley. There the front rank of the enemy was charging in with scaling ladders to begin the battle.

The nuns seemed unworried. The bandit-maids had brought their armory with them when they took the cloth, so they had a plentiful supply of bolts and arrows. After all, they'd been under seige for only one night and day, not for three-quarters of a year.

Thirty nuns triggered their crossbows, then stepped back while thirty more stepped up in their places, to loose and retire, while a third rank in turn shot and stepped back. Then the first rank, cocked and reloaded, came forward.

"Whosoe'er trained those ladies knew more than a little of warfare," Sir Guy observed.

The enemy soldiers ran into a steel storm as soon as they were in range. They howled and either died or retreated. A doughty few pressed on another fifty feet before they went down.

The former bandit-maids shouted their triumph.

"They may not need our help," Matt said hopefully.

Sir Guy disagreed. "The battle is scarcely joined, Lord Wizard."

The enemy took time in getting the next act together. Then a ram-tunnel came worming its way out of the line, forty feet long, with many pairs of feet showing below.

A big bandit-maid called, "Maud! Let in some light for them!"

"Certes," a nun called from above the door across the way. "We cannot have a centipede near our house. Turn, sisters, and lower the front a mite."

They had a small catapult, mounted to swing both horizontally and vertically. "Gently," Sister Maud cautioned. "Aim not where 'tis, but where 'twill be . . . Now loose!"

With a deep thrum, a boulder the size of a basketball leaped out over the field. It arced high, then swung down. The ram-tunnel captain saw it and bawled a command to back pedal. But the wooden centipede barely got into reverse when the stone crashed into the middle of the roof. The tunnel broke into two halves and beat a hasty retreat. Hoots of laughter followed it from the battlements.

Sir Guy shook his head in admiration. "Thus may we see the strengths of amateurs."

"Amateurs?" Matt looked up, startled. "I'd say those girls were pretty good."

"Aye, but they've've had small training in defense. They know not that a catapult's only for attacking a castle. They've but heard of it as a siege engine; so they've mounted one on their wall for a siege—and it has succeeded!"

A cry went up along the wall. "Malvoisin! Malvoisin!"

A fifty-foot structure loomed darkly in the first rays of the moon, four hundred feet out.

"It's not moving," Matt noted.

Sir Guy grinned. "Our doughty ladies have proven the efficacy of their catapult. The enemy dares not bring his engine within range. How then will he deal with this?"

The answer came quickly as Matt noticed tendrils of fog beginning to curl around the battlements.

"They wish to shroud us!" the abbess cried, and her hands began to weave symbolic gestures, while she chanted in Latin. Whatever the spell or prayer, the fog lifted before it had fairly started.

Matt gave a low whistle. "This abbess knows some magic!"

But it was hardly enough. The enemy tried a dust storm next. It hid the battlements completely before the abbess managed to dispel it. When the air cleared, the malvoisin was well within catapult range. Sister Maud and her girls swung the catapult to bear—and got hit with a plague of gnats.

Shrieks of distress filled the battlements. Through the dense, buzzing cloud, Matt could just barely make out the abbess, clutching Sayeesa's arm. Dimly he could hear the words of chanting. Sayeesa was using magic again—white magic, this time.

While they chanted, Alisande ran among the ex-bandits, shouting and exhorting them. Heartened by the princess they were fighting for, the bandit-maids bent to their tasks and peppered the malvoisin with crossbow bolts. The ladies at the catapult drew aim, while the gnats sickened and fell to the ground all about them. Then Sister Maud shouted and the catapult arm lashed out. The stone ball arced high and fell, tearing off the top of the malvoisin. It retreated hastily out of range.

For a time, the enemy was quiet.

"They make me nervous when they're still," Matt complained. "What's the hour?"

Sir Guy looked up at the sickle moon. "Midnight, Lord Matthew. When the forces of Evil are strongest. Now the real battle shall begin."

It started with an auxiliary army scuttling from the enemy lines toward the walls—cockroaches, three feet long. The battlements filled with oaths of disgust. Bolts riddled the insects, but they kept coming. The first ones began climbing the walls in spite of the chants of the abbess and Sayeesa.

It was definitely time for some technological aid. Matt began reciting:

> "Out of the moat, let fog arise,
> One to insure insect demise;
> Poisonous gas to soak inside—
> Pure aerosol insecticide."

A mist sprang up where the wall met the earth of the moat. The upcoming cockroaches keeled over, kicking, then stilling. But some of the first ones had already climbed up onto the battlements.

Most of the nuns were backing away from the giant insects, shrieking. Some were lifting their skirts and seeking heights away from the horrors.

"You do not flee such creatures," Alisande shouted. "You slay them!" She whacked at a thorax for emphasis. A few of the bandit-maids with stronger stomachs leaped to help her.

"Down to the battle!" Sir Guy ordered. "We must aid!"

Matt spun to the door, chanting:

> "By the pricking of my thumbs,
> Something wicked this way comes.

Bolts release and open locks.
Making way for him who knocks."

He knocked. The lock groaned, and the door clanked open.
Matt barreled through with Sir Guy a foot behind.

They clanged out onto the battlements. The Black Knight gave
a joyful shout as he laid about him with his sword. Matt leaped
for a roach just before it sank its mandibles into the habit of a
nun, and performed a quick vivisection on it. "Slay them!" he
shouted. "They're only flesh!"

The matter was debatable. At that size, their armor was almost
as good as Sir Guy's. But a monofilament edge worked wonders,
and Matt knew where to probe for weak places. He and Sir Guy
sliced up cockroaches right and left.

"See how they fare!" Alisande cried. "Will you let mere males
outdo you, then?"

With a roar of expletive negatives, the nuns waded in. A
few were bitten; but in a few minutes, the roaches were dead.
Matt joined Sir Guy in the disgusting task of shoveling the
corpses over the wall. He finished and turned to confront a
basilisk-faced abbess.

"This was your work, was it not? The fog that banished most
of the monsters?"

Matt swallowed, feeling like a schoolboy caught writing on
the wall. "Yeah. It seemed like a good idea."

"It was, indeed," she said grimly. "Though I mind having
bidden you to the gate tower. Nay, then. Abide here amongst us
this night. We will be glad of your aid. Yet stay apart from my
daughters, insofar as you are able."

Matt nodded in relief at his dismissal and turned to where Sir
Guy and Alisande were trying to repulse men who had sneaked
up with scaling ladders while the roaches distracted those within.
For a time, it was hot work, but no more magical manifestations
appeared.

He stepped back at last, wiping sweat from his brow and catching his breath. Beyond the walls, a thick fog had appeared, but
now was clearing.

A shout went up. Matt turned to see the malvoisin again emerg-
ing from the thinning fog. A hundred pale, fish-belly-colored
bodies slogged ahead, pulling it along, plodding like machines
and looking at nothing.

Thirty crossbows hummed with a single voice. Leather-vaned bolts sprouted in the pallid chests, but the marchers kept coming.

"Zombies!" Matt shouted. "The walking dead! Max!"

"Aye, Wizard?" The spark hummed beside him.

"Fire," Matt directed. "Burn them. They're long overdue for a funeral pyre!"

"I go," the spark sang, and winked out. A moment later, a sheet of flame erupted around the zombies. The stink of charred flesh drifted to the battlements. Each zombie was a living candle, but they kept moving until they fell as burned skeletons and the bones broke apart. The malvoisin caught fire and began burning fiercely. The abbess began a prayer for the dead, and voices joined in, until the whole parapet was filled with Latin.

Matt blew out a long, shaky breath. "Reverend Mother, how many hours till dawn?"

"Two," the abbess called back.

Matt nodded. "And probably the worst still to come." He looked up at Sir Guy. "What will they try next?"

The knight shrugged. "They may attempt anything, Lord Matthew. If 'tis foul or fell, they'll essay it."

Fifteen minutes went by without any sign of action. Matt brooded. His foreboding must have been contagious, because the warrior maids began to stir and mutter restlessly.

Then it appeared, fifty yards out and glowing—a naked incubus in a somewhat locally exaggerated form of Father Brunel.

Total silence fell as the nuns stared, shocked. Then they erupted into clamor.

"Sorcerer, appear!" the biggest bandit-maid shouted. "You who summoned this vile form, show yourself that I may sally out to skewer you through your entrails!"

There were no takers. The sorcerer might have been vile, but he wasn't that stupid—though he'd been a fool to think the sight of such a naked male would weaken this garrison. All he'd done was to get the women fighting mad.

Wait a minute . . . Anger . . .

"Hold your tongues!" The abbess's voice cut through the uproar, and the clamor lessened. "Check your anger! Hold it in abeyance, or Evil will gain some measure of power o'er you and weaken the strength of your bolts!"

"But Reverend Mother," the big nun cried, "how can we suffer—"

"You need not. Fire at the enemy—but loose your bolts in self-defense, not wrath. And let each bolt sink home!"

The abbess had countered the sorcerer's plan neatly; as long as the nuns felt themselves to be defending themselves, all their curdled, pent-up feelings were cleared for use.

Here and there, one still raged, mouthing insults and loosing bolts as fast as she could. The abbess came up behind one of them and coldly put her hand on the nun's shoulder. The nun whirled, staring up at her, then fell silent.

"Get you to the chapel," the abbess said, sternly but kindly. "Pray there for us."

The nun laid down her bow and turned toward the stairway, hands clasped, head bent, while the abbess moved to the next berserker.

Altogether, a dozen or so retreated to the chapel—the biggest loss they had suffered that night.

"See the price of anger, child," the abbess said to Sayeesa. "Let not—" She broke off, staring at the ex-witch.

Sayeesa stood frozen, her hands clenched tightly until the knuckles showed white, and her lips trembled.

"It has the semblance of one she knows," Matt explained.

"Aye, I know him!" Sayeesa fell to her knees, burying her face in her hands. "To my shame! Brunel, can I never be free of you?"

The abbess's face was a dam against anguish. "This, then, was the weakness I sensed. Nay, child, be not shamed. Each of us has failings. Get you to the chapel, there to pray with all your heart and soul!"

As Sayeesa turned away, the abbess's head swung about. "We are not yet cleared! Someone here hides a weakness fully as grave! Daughters, search your souls! Whosoever harbors faults that sight of men can raise, get hence, ere you weaken us in time of crisis! Go now to the chapel!"

But each nun stood fast, glancing at her neighbor out of the corners of her eyes. None moved to the stairway.

Then the incubus was gone—but another walked in its place, its movements fluid, sensuous. Something glimmered near it and grew into a pulsing shape that coalesced to a succubus, dancing with the incubus, moving its body in a rhythm that left little to the imagination. As the figures turned, Matt stiffened in horror. The incubus wore his face! And the succubus's hair was long and blond!

"How dare they!" Alisande shrieked. "What arrogance is this?"

Her words whipped the nuns into action. Bolts leaped from the battlements, each nun firing with anger chilled to a sense of mission.

Alisande raved on. "This comes near blasphemy, to see my form in such a show! This pairing's past obscene. It is—"

"Enough!" The abbess touched her shoulder, and Alisande stilled, her eyes widening. The abbess spoke with full censure. "You knew this weakness lay within you, yet you remained here with us, imperiling all. Such overweening pride's unworthy of a peasant; how much more demeaning is it in a princess! What would you, Lady—that your people all succumb to Evil, through the braggart's pride you show in your sureness of your soul's power?"

Abruptly, the abbess swung to Matt, who was staring in disbelief. "Do you stare like the mouse that sees the snake? Then must I think her Highness is not alone in this. I should have chained you in the tower, Wizard." She turned back to Alisande. "Nay, methinks there's no sin, but there's occasion of it. You harbor desires that could lead to sinful action, but will not acknowledge them, even to yourselves. You and your wizard must pledge your love or end it; for until you do, 'twill weaken you and all about you. To the chapel, Lady, and pray for guidance, that God send you understanding of this hot surge within your blood, and the course of action you must take."

Alisande stood immobile for a moment more, then slowly turned away, head bowed, toward the stairway. Matt stared after her, a typhoon of emotions boiling within him.

"I would dispatch you also to the chapel," the abbess told him, "save that you would cause more trouble there than here."

"Yeah, either way I'm not exactly an asset." Decision crystallized in Matt. "Thanks for your hospitality, Reverend Mother, but I think I'd better be moving."

"You speak nonsense!" the abbess snapped. "Magic rules this battle, Wizard. We cannot do without you!"

"I think you can. Max!"

"Here, Wizard!" the Demon hummed beside him. The abbess stared at the dancing spark, paling.

"Skip around the battlefield," Matt directed. "Speed up the aging rate for every mortal out there. Let every man there be well into senility by morning."

"I hear and go!" The Demon winked out.

"Serves them right," Matt growled. "I got the idea from one on their side who threw an aging spell against me. I countered it—but only by using Max. They don't have him to call on, and this should take them days to undo, if they can. I think your ladies can clear the field before then. So you won't need a wizard to help . . . What's the matter?"

"What was that creature?" the abbess whispered.

Matt hesitated, rephrasing his answer carefully as he saw her face. "An elemental of sorts, dedicated to neither good nor evil, but serving my intentions for the moment."

"I still mistrust it," she whispered, making the Sign of the Cross, staring at the battlefield where a spark skipped about, glimmering first here, then there.

"No," Matt agreed. "Don't trust elementals—nor wizards!" He pivoted to the inner wall. "Stegoman!"

He ran down the rampart until he was right above the dragon, set a hand on the wall, and dropped. Stegoman's head swung up under him. Matt managed to miss a jagged fin tip and landed hard astride the dragon's shoulders. Stegoman flexed his legs, absorbing some of the impact. Matt gasped for breath and rasped out, "Head for the gate!"

"Hold!" Sir Guy called, running down the stairway. "You'll not desert me, surely!"

The Black Knight made a prodigious leap and somehow managed to land behind Matt, grunting as he struck. "I've no time for my horse, it seems. But the noble beast will surely be released to find me later. Nay, Lord Wizard, if you must flee to adventure, I'll guard your back."

"You will not!" the abbess shouted. "You'll not live past fifty paces! Daughters, guard the door!"

She was too late. Seeing the dragon heading for them, the nuns had yanked the gates open and ducked out of the way.

"Fools! You ride to your deaths!" the abbess shouted. "Cowards, fearing women's scorn more than lances!"

Then Stegoman was through the doors and thundering down the passage toward the outer portal. A nun yanked it aside at the last moment. They shot out and down the talus slope, while the gate boomed shut behind them.

"Ride, brave heroes!" the abbess was shouting. "For your lives, brave fools! And may God go with you!"

Matt grinned. "I always did like a woman who was on your side, no matter what."

The first rank of footmen saw them coming and planted their pike butts on the ground, points slanting outward. Stegoman crashed into the line like a steamroller. For the next few minutes, all Matt could hear was the roar of voices and the clash of steel.

He laid about him like a maniac, slicing through pike shafts, armor, and helmets with fine impartiality. An enemy loomed up with a huge battleaxe swinging down. Matt leaned to the side; the axe hissed by him, and the big soldier stumbled after it, off balance. Matt marked the joint of helmet and backplate and swung. He didn't look at the effect, but turned to check on Sir Guy. The Black Knight was busy slicing. They hewed away until the enemy drew back, daunted by an animated blowtorch, a monofilament edge, and a human slicing machine.

Stegoman spotted a reasonably clear lane through the foe and waited not upon the order of his going. His legs pumped furiously, and the distance widened.

Then a howl rent the air, and the army of sorcery disgorged a pride of monsters—winged serpents dripping poison, long lizard things with crowns on their heads, and a host of vampire bats. At their sides ran four-foot hounds with blazing eyes and steel teeth.

Stegoman leaped into a bone-jarring gallop. They rode pell-mell into the foothills, with the howls and chittering growing louder behind them. The Black Knight cast a glance backward. "They are closer, Wizard, and will catch us ere the sun can rise!"

"What are our chances against them?"

"Ill. We would wound them sorely, but, being spawn of Hell, they heal instantly. They'll drag us all down to death."

"Aye," Stegoman growled. "I know these winged snakes. One touch with those fangs and even I must die."

"We cannot stand against them," Sir Guy asserted. "Now, me-thinks, 'tis kill or cure, Lord Wizard. The time is past, for mere conjecture."

"That's what I was afraid of," Matt said. At least this time he had his verse already figured out.

> "Let torn skin grow back apace!
> Mend this dragon, strut and brace!
> Yield airfoils, to be extended!
> Let this dragon's wings be mended!"

Leather boomed as fifty-foot wings caught the breeze and the dragon soared aloft with a hawk-screech of joy.

"Free!" Stegoman cried out as he spiraled upward. "Oh, bless a wizard who is mindful of his promise!" He roared out fire in exultation.

Matt leaned forward as the dragon banked into a swooping upward turn. "Stegoman! Level off!"

"Wozzhat?" The dragon looked back over his shoulder, pie-eyed.

"Level off! And don't breathe fire for a while, huh?"

As Stegoman started to obey, Matt relaxed. Then the knight was clasping his shoulder and pointing. "Look—in front!"

Ahead of them, dropping down toward them, came a flock of harpies, flapping stubby wings furiously to support their bloated vulture bodies. Matt could just make out stringy blonde hair, wasted women's faces, long, pointed noses, and lips twisted in homicidal grins around pointed teeth. They giggled gleefully as they swooped toward Stegoman.

The dragon stiffened, staring up in horror, and Matt remembered his blasting an owl and shouting about harpies that attacked hatchlings. Once in battle, spouting flame through the skies, Stegoman's drunken mind would hold no thought for the two who rode him.

There was no time to weigh Freudian theories. Matt began reciting the second of his prepared dragon-curing spells:

> "Canst thou not minister to a mind diseased,
> Pluck from the memory a rooted sorrow,
> Raze out the written troubles of the brain
> And, with some sweet, oblivious antidote,
> Cleanse the stuff'd bosom of that perilous dread
> Which weighs upon the heart?
> Therein the patient
> Must minister to himself."

Stegoman came alive to roar out a ten-foot flame. He soared up in a widening spiral, bellowing his rage. The harpies began screeching in fury, trying to beat their way up the sky to their escaping quarry.

The quarry leveled off, drew a bead on them, and went into a power dive, roaring and flaming. He swept through the flock of harpies, turning his head from side to side, sweeping the whole flock with flame. They screamed and whirled, trying to escape. But Stegoman made a second pass, catching the stragglers. Then he was sweeping upward again, leaving a flaming mass behind. Wreckage began to fall apart into separate burning fragments, blazing toward the earth.

"*I have done it!*" the dragon cried. He reared his head back and began climbing, gouting out fire as he bellowed, "The hatchling killers are dead! I have purged them from the skies!" He reached the top of his climb, blasting and roaring. "Who thinks he can defeat me, let him come against me! He who thinks he can best my breath and claws, let him rise up to try me!"

He was wildly euphoric—but he didn't slur a syllable.

Then a match flared ahead. It swelled to a torch, became a bonfire—and a creature seemed to stir within the blaze. It was long and serpentine, with stubby legs. The flame seemed to draw back into its body, leaving its outline etched in fire, while flamelets danced around its grinning jaws. "Nay," a thunderous voice rolled forth, "what fool is this who thinks to defy the elements that give him life?"

Sir Guy's steel fingers bit into Matt's shoulder. "What fell beast is this?"

"A salamander." Matt felt his hair trying to rise. "An elemental of fire. Someone must have summoned it against us."

"Small and crawling lizard!" the salamander boomed. "Pit your braggart's might against the true master of that element which fills you!"

"Flee!" Matt urged the dragon. "Fly away! You can't fight that thing. Believe me!"

Stegoman's answer was to jab his head down, flick his tail up, and dive. Matt wrapped his arms around a fin and hung on.

Stegoman streaked toward the earth at a sixty-degree angle. Behind him, a huge laugh shook the sky, and a streak of fire followed him. The ground shot up, and Matt heard the Black Knight singing a dirge behind him. Then they were slamming to a braking halt over water. Stegoman slewed and rolled over on his side five feet above the surface, bellowing, "Leap!"

Matt leaped. Water slammed into him and shot up around him. He went under, kicked out in a breast stroke, and broke to the surface just in time to hear the splash as Sir Guy's armor went in. *Armor*! The knight could never swim in all that weight. Matt dived again as leather wings boomed above him and the dragon shot skyward. Then the water all around turned orange as the salamander dropped down into the space the dragon had just vacated. Matt kicked hard, diving deep, feeling the water grow warm behind him. His hand brushed a metal arm; he seized it, hung on, and began exerting all his efforts to drag the knight with him. Sir Guy helped some—his thrashing was at least directional. Slowly, agonizingly slowly, they moved back toward the surface.

Matt's feet struck ooze. He sank in up to his ankles—but it was a place to stand, something to push against. He waded through the stuff and realized, with a surge of relief, that he was toiling upward, hauling some three-hundred-odd pounds with him. His back creaked and his arms screamed pain at his shoulders—then his head broke through the water. He sucked in one long, rasping breath as he shoved hard, taking a giant step—and the weight suddenly went off his hands. A moment later, Sir Guy's helmet broke water with an exploding gasp like a whale blowing. Matt dropped the arm, caught at a shoulder, and hoisted the Black Knight upright. "Okay, now?"

Sir Guy nodded, blowing and sneezing. "I . . . let me die, but . . . never by water."

"Me, too . . . How's Stegoman doing?" Matt craned his neck back, peering up anxiously.

The salamander had shrunk to a flaring point of light again, bright against the night's last darkness. Stegoman had disappeared.

Then a pencil of fire licked out, as the dragon dove at the salamander. His flame hit the beast, and the salamander brightened a little as its huge laughter rumbled through the night. Stegoman's flame winked out; Matt could just barely see him by the salamander's light, shearing off. But the salamander lashed out with its fiery tail, and Stegoman bellowed in pain.

"Wizard, to your left!" Sir Guy shouted, and Matt turned to see a huge rubbery tentacle swinging down at him. He whipped out his sword and chopped through it in one quick swipe; but two more poised in the air above him.

"Lord Matthew!" choked a muffled voice, and Matt pivoted to see a tentacle wrapped around Sir Guy's helmet. He leaped forward with an overhand swing; the tip of his sword scored through the rubbery arm, and it fell loose from the knight; but Matt felt a horrible, slimy coldness wrap itself around his leg, sucking, while a rope slapped itself around his waist. He howled, chopping at

his foot, slicing through the tentacle. It loosened, green slime
pumping out of it into the river; but the one on his waist yanked
him off his feet, dragging him toward deep water. Matt shouted,
flailing about him; then the pulling stopped, dumping him uncer-
emoniously into the water as the tentacle fell off, dripping ichor.
He looked up at Sir Guy, who stood with his sword at the ready,
gasping. A thin green line of slime coated the edge of the blade.

"Thanks for keeping me around." Matt struggled to his feet
with an anxious glance at the sky, just in time to see the pencil
of flame dart down at the salamander again. It hit, and the salamander puffed out into a fireball, engulfing the dragon. Matt heard
a shriek of pain, then the salamander's booming laughter. "I've
gotta help him!"

"Help yourself!" Sir Guy snapped. "You're afire!"

Matt looked down, startled, and saw a coal glowing through
the fabric of the purse hung from his belt. Hope surged, and he
yanked the purse open.

"Wizard," said the dot of light inside, "your wish is filled: the
sorcerer's army ages apace. The youngest of them now is fifty,
and still they age."

"Max!" Matt almost crumbled with relief. "Thank Heaven!
Another job for you, quick! Get up there into the sky, and cool
that salamander's ardor!"

"Salamander?" the Demon sang with delight. "Eons has it been
since I have seen one. Well did I choose when I began my travels
with you!" Max sprang into the air like a skyrocket.

"'Ware!" cried Sir Guy, and Matt whirled to chop at a tentacle,
then another two, then a fourth. He heard a startled, choking oath
and whirled back just in time to see two more ropy arms dragging
Sir Guy under. He splashed over to the Black Knight and sliced
into the muck. A green stain rose, and Matt leaned down to flail
in the water till his hand met steel. He locked his grip around it
and leaned back, lugging hard; Sir Guy surged up and out like
Neptune, spouting bilge. He shook his head, gasping for breath.
"We've bested them . . . again . . ."

"Yeah, but how about our boy?" Matt looked up just as a startled
squawk shredded the night. The salamander had dimmed amazingly, to a pulsing glow. With a joyful roar, the fire-pencil swooped
down on it.

"Flame out!" Matt cried. "Idiot! You're aiding and abetting the
enemy!"

But Stegoman had some good sense; his torch winked out, and Matt could just barely make out his form by waning moonlight as he struck the salamander with teeth and claws.

He's sober, Matt realized, with a surge of relief. He had to be, for that much thinking.

Stegoman shot past the salamander, raking long furrows in its side with his natural sabers. The elemental filled the night with its steam-whistle screech, flailing at the dragon with a short, stubby leg, ripping scales loose; then Stegoman was turning, flipping over to gouge a bite of the salamander's hide as he passed. The fire-spirit screamed and darted upward; but Stegoman swooped upward faster and dove down at it again, jaws gaping wide. The elemental boomed its terror and fell like a stone. Stegoman roared triumph and followed, crowding the salamander closely, herding it as it tried to dart to one side, then the other. Too late, the fire-spirit saw the river shooting up at it. It slewed to the side, but Stegoman half folded his wings and plunged down like a hawk, landing with all four feet in the salamander's back, claws out. The beast screamed and twisted free—straight toward the river.

Then the salamander was poised ten feet overhead, bleeding fire from several gashes and a long rip along its side. It reared back, clawing at Stegoman, bellowing in agony and horror. The dragon hovered just out of range, taking his time, setting himself; then he shot downward and slammed into the salamander. The fire-beast bounced into the water with a shriek that seemed to fill the earth, a terrible scream that raked along Matt's spine and nerves, paralyzing him.

Water slammed up against his back. He splashed about, thrashing, trying to get back to the sand bar—especially when he realized the water was heating up. An explosion rocked the river, and the waters glowed lurid orange. Steam seethed and hissed, and the water got downright hot.

"Stegoman! Get us outa here! Before we're poached!"

The dragon came, huge wings slamming air down in a gale. "Seize my legs!" he bellowed.

Matt's foot found muck; he leaned his weight on it, sheathing his sword, then jumped to catch the dragon's ankle. He saw Sir Guy hanging onto another leg as the dragon lifted slowly, laboring against the uneven burden, as the water began to boil. It drifted away under their feet; then dry land was beneath them as Stegoman lowered them gently. Turf hit Matt's feet with a jarring shock; he bent his knees. Sir Guy fell, rolling, with a clank and clatter, and rolled up to his feet, gasping, "'Tis done!"

"Aye," Stegoman rumbled, settling to earth beside them, folding his wings with a minor thunderclap. "Aye, 'tis done." He turned his head toward Matt, eye still lit with battle-glow. "I have won! None can best me in the skies—or can they?"

He was definitely sober. He wouldn't doubt his own prowess if he were drunk.

"Nay, speak and tell me, Wizard!" Stegoman commanded. "How could I best the monster that is the master of my breath?"

"You had a little assistance," Matt admitted. "I decided it was an unequal battle—and Max happened by just then."

The Demon hummed by his ear. "The salamander's fire now has cooled, and it is dead. The river boils for a mile."

"Well, the peasants will eat well in the morning," Matt sighed. "I hate to think of all those dead fish, though."

"Better them than I," the dragon growled, "or the knight, or thine own self." He turned to the dancing spark. "Demon, I thank and praise thee for weakening mine enemy."

Matt looked up at Stegoman, studying the dragon intently. "You *do* think you'll be safe flying now, don't you?"

Stegoman stilled, his glowing eyes burning into Matt's. Slowly, he nodded. "Aye. I am safe in the skies. Wizard, may good fortune shower on thee for returning me my wings!"

"I'll settle for a lift. The enemy's behind, for the moment, but I don't think it'll take them long to catch up. Are you ready for another trip?"

The dragon's wings stirred, but stayed folded. "I am," he said judiciously, "though mayhap I should rest . . ."

"Yeah, you do have a few burns there." Matt frowned at the long streaks of crimson he saw on the dragon's flanks. "And that salamander had claws."

Stegoman nodded. "Though he was unskilled in their use."

Matt fumbled in the purse at his belt, singing under his breath:

> "Let a salve for healing all,
> Even burns of first degree,
> Be within my beck and call!
> Let this wondrous ointment be
> Of an instant-healing brand,
> Here, within my groping hand!"

Something weighty and solid suddenly swelled under his fingers. He lifted a three-inch jar out of his wallet, unscrewed the lid, and winced at the smell. "Whew! Well, I only asked that it work!" He began a long walk around Stegoman, smearing ointment everywhere he saw a burn or cut.

Half an hour later, rested and healed, Stegoman pounded his way into the sky, crooning a victory song, with Matt and Sir Guy on his back. He caught a thermal and soared up, higher and higher, till they could see the dawn's first faint light, far off to the east.

"Wizard," the dragon grunted, "where shall I wander?"

"To the West." Matt turned to Sir Guy. "Can you tell him anything more specific?"

"Aye." The Black Knight leaned forward, pointing over Matt's shoulder. "To the right of the highest peak—there! The second, smaller peak, to the north. Land us there, just above the last of the trees."

Matt frowned; that didn't quite sound like the Plain of Grellig, the way the princess had described it. But Sir Guy knew the territory; Matt shut up.

Stegoman arrowed toward the smaller peak.

Dawn filled the sky behind them, lighting the mountains a glowing rose. It was a considerable distance; Matt lapsed into silence, beginning to realize how tired he was.

At Sir Guy's direction, Stegoman glided down to a level patch on the mountainside, just above the timber line. He hovered over it, wings cupping thunder, then slowly settled to the ground. Matt swung down off his shoulders and almost fell. An iron hand caught his arm. "Steady," Sir Guy murmured.

"I—I'll be okay." Matt was amazed at the wave of exhaustion that had suddenly hit him.

"'Tis only the body, claiming its due, when the need for fighting is done," Sir Guy said gently. "Do not be concerned."

Matt looked up at him, blinking owlishly. "Uh . . . thanks for the tip." He looked around foolishly. "Where we . . . goin'?"

"There will be housen for us for the day and night, if we need; never fear. But our great companion may not enter in."

"Oh . . ." Matt turned to Stegoman, shaking his head, trying to clear enough of the fog to manage politeness. "Sorry we can't ask you in."

"Be not anxious for me." The dragon looked down at him. "I shall care for myself—now! When I met thee, I was a lame and a stumbling thing; but now I am what a dragon should be. Lasting fealty do I swear to thee! As long as I live, I shall serve thee and thine heirs."

"I . . . uh . . ." Matt untied a quick knot in his tongue. "I . . . accept. With great and humble thanks, I assure you."

"Now to your rest, Wizard," Sir Guy said. "And I to mine; for I think that most of the blows I will bear for your sake will fall on us in a very few days."

Stegoman turned away, spreading his wings, and rose into the sky. His call floated back: "When thou dost call, I will come. Sleep well."

Matt gazed after him, blinking, trying to remember what he was supposed to do now. Sir Guy took his arm again, turning him away toward the hillside. "Come, then. We must find haven."

CHAPTER 16

Sir Guy pulled a strip of cloth out of his wallet and bound it around Matt's eyes.

Why the charade? As far as Matt could tell, they were just headed back toward the hillside.

Then something brushed his face, all of his face—and all of his body, too. For a few seconds, he felt as if he were wading through molasses that went clear over his head. Then he stepped past it into damp, cool air and stumbled, nearly falling. Sir Guy held him up and whisked off the blindfold. Matt stood inside a small cave, the roof a few feet over his head. It was filled with early morning sunlight. Ten feet ahead, the rock wall made a sharp turn.

" 'Tis a hidden place," Sir Guy explained. "Come, now; I will show you your bed."

"Uhhh . . . just a second." Matt held up a hand, weaving with exhaustion. "I've gotten to be a bug on security lately . . . Max!"

"Aye, Wizard." The Demon hovered before him, lighting up the inside of the cave. Sir Guy took a half step away.

Matt looked around him, blinking out beyond the cave mouth to the sun-filled valley. Something was wrong there. He frowned, thinking it through, then turned to Sir Guy. "Hey! If this place is so secret I had to wear a blindfold, how come I can see the outside like a picture-window view?"

"Did you see it ere we came into it?"

"Well . . . no . . ."

"Nor will any." The Black Knight smiled faintly. "We need no guard for our portal, Lord Wizard. No sorcerer can find this cave. If any should stumble upon it, he would see only a hillside; and if, by great misfortune, he should stumble through what seems to be a grassy, boulder-strewn slope to the place where we stand, he would be blinded or dead."

Matt was suddenly fully awake again. "But how, then . . . Sir Guy, I'm still alive. And I can see."

The Black Knight nodded gravely. "You are my guest, Lord Matthew. No power in this cavern will harm you."

Matt knew he should be grateful; but he was only numb—and getting number as the reassurance lulled his body, letting the adrenaline ebb and the drowsiness return tenfold. There was another question somewhere there that Sir Guy's answer had raised, but he couldn't quite phrase it; and there was some huge, hidden significance to what the Black Knight had just told him about the cave being hidden, but Matt couldn't think what it was.

He turned back to the Demon. "Just to reassure me, Max. Guard the door."

"'Tis a function with which I've some experience," the Demon hummed. "To your rest, Wizard."

He winked out of visibility, but Matt knew he would stay by the cave mouth, and woe betide the citizen who tried to pass him. He turned back to Sir Guy. "Okay. Where's the bunkhouse?"

The Black Knight turned away, going into the turn at the end of the cave. Matt followed him—and found himself in what seemed impenetrable darkness, after the glare of daylight. But there was some faint glow from the front. They came out of the tunnel into light—and Matt stood still, staring about him in wonder.

It was a cavern, lit by a soft bluish light that seemed to come from everywhere and nowhere, filling a long, narrow, high-ceilinged vault. Along the walls stood pedestals four feet square and two feet high, each supporting a great, carven chair. Suits of antique armor sat in the chairs—haubergions, knee-length mail shirts.

And there were bodies inside the armor.

They sat upright, leaning against the wall, bullet-shaped helmets on their heads, with nose-guards but no visors. The faces they showed were those of old men, bearded, and very pale. They sat with their eyes closed, still as statues. Maybe they were; Matt had the eerie feeling that he'd stepped into a wax museum.

Opposite Matt and Sir Guy, at the far end of the hall, there was only one dais, larger than the others. It had to be; the chair it supported was a throne, and a throne for a giant, at that.

The giant in question was at least seven feet tall and proportionally broader than Sir Guy. His armor was gilded, and a crown circled his helmet. A huge red beard streaked with white spread over his chest.

Matt tried to shake off the eerie feeling that was stealing over him, prickling his scalp. Somehow, he didn't think it was a wax museum.

"Aye, they are real; but they are dead." Sir Guy might have read his mind. "Yet their spirits still dwell in those bodies, Lord Wizard, in a magic stillness."

Stasis, Matt thought.

"They live," Sir Guy explained, "but they are dead. Let us greet them." He stepped forward, and Matt had no choice but to follow him.

A great voice echoed from the far end of the hall, seeming to come from a vast distance. "Welcome, Sir Guy de Toutarien! It is long since you have passed here to speak with me!"

Sir Guy advanced halfway down the hall and knelt. "Forgive me, Imperial Majesty; but the world presses hard upon this land of Merovence, and my skills were needed."

"Then surely, duty must compel you far from me." There was a suppressed eagerness under the giant voice. "Speak and tell me! Is it time?"

An eager, rustling murmur passed through the hall, like dry leaves stirred by a late-rising wind—the dead knights, hoping for battle.

Sir Guy shook his head, almost sadly. "It is not, Imperial Majesty. The nation can save itself, even in so hard a time as this."

Matt felt the hair at the nape of his neck prickle. But at least, he knew now where he was—in the tomb of Hardishane, the ancient Emperor. And those of the armored contingent were his Knights of the Mountain.

He stepped forward, taking his courage in both hands. "With all due respect, Sir Guy—can you be so sure?"

"Quite sure." The Black Knight gave him a reassuring smile.

"He speaks aright." Hardishane's voice rumbled with infinite regret. "There is no need for us yet, brave companions."

The whispering murmur filled the cavern again, a sad, disappointed sigh. It was eerie enough to chill Matt's thoughts for a moment. When they thawed, he began to wonder how Sir Guy had known what an Emperor confirmed.

And when had Sir Guy Losobal become Sir Guy de Toutarien?

"And who is this man you have brought guesting among us?" Hardishane demanded.

"He is Matthew, rightful Lord Wizard of Merovence, Majesty," Sir Guy answered, "a scholar of words and their power. Yet he is also loyal, courageous in battle, and sometimes humble to a fault. He is stout of heart and hardier than he knows. There is none I would rather have for shield-mate."

Matt stared at him, amazed to the point of shock.

"He is, then, worthy," Hardishane pronounced. "And who should be a better judge than Sir Guy de Toutarien?"

"Your Majesty does me too much credit," Sir Guy murmured.

"I do not." It was almost a rebuke. "Yet worthy as this wizard may be, he must bide in the chapel the whiles he is among us here."

Quarantine? Matt wondered. Maybe just a wise precaution, in case the wizard turned out to be a sorcerer.

"Escort him to the chapel, then." The dead Emperor seemed almost amused. "And show him there a pallet, for methinks that he is like to topple with his weariness."

Or maybe, Matt decided, it was plain old discrimination—they were knights, and he wasn't. They couldn't have the hoi-polloi mixing with their betters. He should have resented it, but he just didn't have the energy.

Sir Guy bowed and turned away. Matt turned with him automatically.

"Worthy knight."

Sir Guy turned back, eyebrows raised. "Majesty?"

"Moncaire must have the measure of this man."

Sir Guy inclined his head respectfully. "Your pardon, Majesty—but I believe he has taken it already."

"Well enough, then. To the chapel."

Sir Guy turned away again, and Matt stumbled after him, wondering what that business about measurements was. And what would Saint Moncaire have to do with it?

The chapel was a side cave, a nice little intimate grotto nestling up against the great hall. There were no pews—that had been a relatively late addition in churches—but the altar was gilded and very elegant, gleaming richly in the light of the single candle next to it. It was the only light in the place; mostly, the chapel was shadow.

Sir Guy led him to the back of the cave and put out a hand to stop him. "Here is your bed."

Matt couldn't see anything. He stuck out a tentative foot and felt fur brush against his shin, nearly to the knee. He sighed and started to fold into it, when one last stabbing worry straightened him. "Sir Guy . . . Malingo . . . are you *sure* . . ."

"Entirely, Matthew. There is not room for the slightest beginning of a doubt. Puissant as Malingo is, his power's not sufficient to find this cave; and even if he could, he'd not dare come in. His entrance here would be just such a sign as Hardishane awaits. He and his knights would rise, to charge throughout the Northern Lands, subduing all to remake the Empire anew. They would, in passing, obliterate the sorcerer who waked them. Rest your heart from fear and all concern."

Matt nodded, sighed, and let himself fold, tumbling forward. An ocean of fur pressed up against his side and cheek; his eyes closed automatically, and the darkness pressed in. After all, it had been at least three days since he'd had a full night's sleep.

"Matthew." Fingers touched his shoulder, and Matt came awake, tensed for battle, but feeling as if he were filled with sand. He could just barely make out Sir Guy's face, hovering over him. The knight had taken off his armor and had found a maroon robe of very rich material, belted at the waist. So this was how the local other half looked in their off-hours.

"Rise," the Black Knight said gravely, almost sternly. "You've slept the candle down."

Candle? Oh, yes—the one they used for telling time here, with alternating bands of red and white; each took an hour to burn through.

"How big a candle?" Matt muttered.

"Twelve hours," Sir Guy replied. "Rise and take up vigil."

Matt had never seen Sir Guy look so serious. He rolled off the pile of furs and came to his feet, frowning. "What's happening?"

But the Black Knight only turned away, beckoning. Matt followed, with a scowl.

Sir Guy paced down the nave to the altar. Matt stopped beside him and looked down at a suit of plate armor, just like Sir Guy's, only newer—brand-new, in fact; bright, silvery, untarnished steel.

"Kneel," Sir Guy instructed. "Begin your vigil."

Matt looked up, frowning. "Shouldn't we be back on the road? There's a war on, you know."

"The war may yet be lost, if you keep not this vigil."

Matt stared at him, but Sir Guy gazed back, unperturbed, with such a thorough sureness that Matt found himself turning and kneeling by the suit of armor. He tried one last, feeble protest. "Are you sure this is necessary?"

"Absolutely. Good fortune to you—and 'ware temptations. Newly wakened though you are, your eyelids will grow heavy. Impatience, ennui, hidden night-fears—all will assail you. Let them not disturb your watch. Be sure, 'tis vital. If you fail in this, dire actions will follow."

"But nobody's gonna come in and try to steal this stuff! Odds are, they couldn't even lift it! It can't walk off by itself, you know!"

"I do not know that, nor do you." Sir Guy's fingers dug into Matt's shoulder, almost as hard as his gauntlets. "Have faith in *me*, Matthew. I've never asked it ere this time. Have faith."

He turned away and was gone.

Faith! Matt looked up at the altar, glowering at the tabernacle. That's what it all came down to here, wasn't it? But he didn't doubt what the knight had said about this vigil's importance—to Matt's own life. Face it, he was a lackey here. He had no more place in that company of heroes outside than a private had in the officers' mess. If he tried to go back in there uninvited, those dead knights would find some way to skewer him. They didn't *look* as if they could lift their swords—but they didn't look as if they could still talk, either. Magic ruled here.

Okay. It was necessary for him to stay out of the way, and this was really a very polite way of making sure he did—instead of telling him to keep out, they gave him a job to do and told him it was important. Nice piece of face-saving; he'd be a fool to reject it and force them to get ugly. They were really being very nice.

But it rankled.

The more he thought about it, the angrier he got at being shuttled out of the way, so he wouldn't clutter up the space for the big guys! He had half a mind to charge out there and . . .

You will be tempted. Sir Guy's voice seemed to ring through his head, and Matt sawed back on his emotions, suddenly alert to danger from inside himself. Even here, Evil could reach in to tempt him into a rash act that just might result in having his head handed to him. And, as he'd had pointed out to him far too often for comfort, if he failed, Alisande's bid for her throne failed with him.

He rolled back off his knees, folded his legs tailor-fashion, and settled himself for a long night, summoning the patience that had lasted him through long, dull undergraduate lectures. But patience wouldn't come.

Then *think*, he told himself. He was supposed to be a scholar with inner resources that should cope with any amount of unfilled time. This was a church, a place of religion, so he might as well pray, if he couldn't do anything else!

But he'd never had much use for prayer. Faith! It seemed such an empty word, yet it was the keystone of this culture. He rolled that around in his mind. Faith could be the core of magic, as it was the core of religion. This whole universe might be built on it, somehow. What would happen here if the people stopped believing God had created the universe? Would everything disappear? But that line of thought was getting him into the type of stuff the followers of supposed Eastern cults chewed on in their meditations.

Meditation, he thought. He'd never really tried it, but it might help to get him through the night. He settled himself again and began trying to regulate his breathing with the only mantra he remembered. *Om mane padme om. Om mane padme . . .*

Abruptly, he jerked his head up, realizing he'd almost put himself to sleep. *You will be tempted!* To a man who'd only just wakened after days without rest, it was an easy temptation to give in to.

He began to regulate his breathing again until he had a slow, deep rhythm that would continue while he busied his mind again with the matter of faith.

Did Malingo have faith? In this world, he must; but he turned away from God and put his faith in the Devil. And it paid off— for a while. For now, Malingo's perverted faith gave him an edge.

He'd certainly proved adept at harassing Matt. There'd been the old witch and then Sayeesa; Malingo had moved her fifty miles or more, castle and all, to put her in Matt's path. Then there had been the peasants who came hunting her, whipping themselves into a lynch mob. And Father Brunel, who turned were again suddenly.

Something flickered at the edge of Matt's vision. Without turning his head, he began concentrating on the shimmer at the corner of his eye.

It took shape gradually, becoming almost solid—a figure in ancient armor. But its head was scarcely human. The face was piggish, lacking eyelids, and with a low brow; the mouth yawned wide, filled with three-inch, pointed teeth.

It paced toward Matt, drooling. He watched it pensively, feeling no fear or tension, sure that the thing did not exist. It was only an illusion. What else could get into a chapel that was guarded by Hardishane's cave? Besides, he could still see through it faintly. He didn't know who had sent it or why—possibly his own subconscious.

Could it hurt him? Only if he believed in it. And he didn't.

He put out a hand, spreading the fingers. The monster loomed over him, lowering its head. The shark-jaws gaped, enveloping the hand—and paused, not closing. The lidless eyes glared into his. Then, slowly, the apparition faded.

Matt's neck muscles twitched in a faint, satisfied nod. He'd known it was illusion, so it hadn't been able to hurt him.

What did that mean for the people of this age and place? Did their magic and their monsters exist only because they believed in them? No, surely not! Stegoman had to have pragmatic reality on his own, didn't he?

His mind went cartwheeling off through the night, never following a train of thought, but moving from one concept to another in free association, revolving endlessly around and around the problem of faith and reality.

Then something flickered to the right of the altar.

It came toward him, gaining substance as it moved, dragging a hundred pounds of chain wrapped around its body and trailing on the floor behind. It wore the tatters of a nobleman's robe, a thatch of unwashed black hair, and a festoon of beard flecked with spittle. The face had a broad forehead, a high-bridged nose, and thin lips—an aristocratic face; but the eyes were wild, making the whole face obscene with madness. It came toward Matt, giggling and drooling, hands outstretched through the chains, fingers flexing, reaching for Matt's throat.

Matt watched it. He couldn't see through the madman, but it had to be illusion; it couldn't by anything else.

The madman stopped with fingers an inch from Matt's throat, staring at him. Then it pointed at him, giggling. The giggle grew and broadened. It threw its head back, cackling with insane, gleeful laughter.

Then the fingers shot out, seizing Matt's throat. The face swelled with homicidal rage, and the eyes lit with a strange, unholy glee. It cackled and gibbered as the fingers dug in. Dimly, far away, Matt seemed to feel a ghost of pressure. That was wrong; he knew this madman wasn't real. It couldn't really touch him, couldn't hurt him. It was only a phantom, sent to try and tempt him—to test whether he was sure of the basics, or didn't know what was real and what wasn't.

Matt knew. *Now is an end to all confusion*, he breathed, framing silent words with his lips. The figure stilled, staring into his eyes—and, staring, it slowly faded away, till there was nothing between Matt and the altar.

Matt sat immobile, filled with a satisfying sense of rightness. His sense of reality had corresponded with actuality; what he'd believed was illusion had actually been illusion; so he was still alive. Whatever faith had to do with existence couldn't really be known; but the faith in his own perceptions could be. The test was drastic, but simple; and Matt had passed it.

What if he'd believed it was real?

Then it might have been able to hurt him—which was to say, Matt would have been letting his own mind hurt him. Even in his own universe, men could be destroyed by their illusions. Here the process was more direct.

His mind went pinwheeling off again into a hundred assorted concepts, all dealing with matters of faith and existence—until the armor stirred.

It clanked. The pieces shifted about and rearranged themselves. The pile of spare parts sorted itself out and heaved. A steel man rose up over Matt, towering there, silent and menacing, wearing Matt's sword at its hip. Then the hollow knight drew the blade, grasped the hilt with both hands, and swung it up.

Every centimeter of Matt's skin crawled with horror. He knew what that blade could do. If it even touched him, he was dead. Whether by his own substantial death-wish or someone else's spell, that sword was threatening him.

He was aware, with sinking horror, that he had passed the border—he'd accepted the illusion's reality, at least partially. Now, illusion or not, if the sword hit him, he'd die.

The sword was swinging down.

Matt realized in near panic that magic could never work against his own mind. Faith, he thought—and prayer! He began hastily muttering words he was not sure of, words from earlier prayers, his eyes seeking the altar.

The sword started to swing down—and stopped. The armor fell into separate pieces, crashing down onto the stone. The sword struck and bounced, taking a piece out of the cave floor; then it lay still.

Matt sat motionless, hands still clasped, hearing the blood hammer through his head.

Faith! When all reasoning was stripped away, and a man had to confront himself, his gut response gave the truth of what he believed.

A hand touched his arm.

Matt started—and looked up to see a maroon robe, with Sir Guy's anxious face above it. The knight's voice seemed to come from a great distance. "Are you well, Matthew?"

With infinite reluctance, Matt pulled himself back to reality, letting himself feel the stone of the floor and hear the echoes of Sir Guy's voice, until he was again immersed in the moment and life was real once more.

He looked down at the armor. It lay as it had fallen, not in the neat bundle he had first seen. And the great sword lay to the side and a little behind him.

He looked up at Sir Guy, smiling slowly. "I'm very well."

Relief lighted Sir Guy's eyes, but his face didn't move. He nodded, a smile coming to his lips. "And your watch?"

Matt grinned and stretched luxuriously, rising to his feet. "Well. Now I know what I believe."

Sir Guy's face registered a flood of joy. "Then you have it, Lord Matthew. Come, bear the armor out."

Matt frowned, not quite understanding. But he shrugged, bent down, and scooped up the pile of plate. It weighed at least a hundred pounds, probably much more; it felt heavier than that.

But he didn't even stagger under the load. Something had changed his body during the night, he thought, giving him unexpected strength. Or was that also faith? He followed Sir Guy out into the great hall.

The light had brightened. Somehow, there was a sense of anticipation in the air; the ancient knights were waiting for something big to happen. What was up? He turned to Sir Guy. "How long was I in there, anyway?"

"Only the night," Sir Guy answered. "Ten hours."

"Ten?" Matt stared. "I could have sworn it wasn't more than two or three."

"Nay, it was ten." Sir Guy watched him, with a slight smile. "And do you feel wearied?"

"Well, a little, maybe—but refreshed, at least in my head."

"But the body was tired. Might I suggest a bath?"

"A *bath*?" Matt's eyes lighted. "Hell, yeah! I haven't had a bath in a week!"

"Remove your clothes, then."

Matt squatted, setting down the armor, then straightened and peeled off his tunic and hose. He was faintly surprised to see they still folded.

Then Sir Guy led the way to the "tub". It was halfway to Hardishane, under the noses of two of the dead knights. A section of floor had been removed, revealing a pool in the rock. Natural, probably—spring-fed. Just looking at it, Matt shivered.

"Enter," Sir Guy murmured.

Matt sensed that he was on trial again. He bit down on a surge of irritation and stepped into the water. Icy chills shot up his legs as his feet went in. He stifled a curse, took a deep breath, and ducked under.

He almost shouted with agony, under water or not. Liquid ice wrapped around every cell of him. Was this how the knights had been preserved—by cryogenics?

He surged back up, breaking water like a volcano, sucking in air that seemed very warm. A faint, approving murmur echoed through the hall; at least he'd done something right. He cupped a palmful of water and began scrubbing. Sir Guy had gone—for a towel, Matt hoped.

A voice in his left ear snapped, "What is the first duty of a knight?"

"To his lord," Matt said automatically, looking up in surprise.

A grim old knight sat there to his left; dead or not, Matt was sure he was the source of the voice. "Then to his lord's lady."

"And what of the king?" snapped a voice to his right.

Matt ladled water over his shoulder and shuddered. "A knight is loyal to the king, of course—but that loyalty goes up through the chain of vassal and suzerain to his lord, and his lord's lord, on up to the king."

"And if the king wars with the knight's lord?" demanded a third voice.

What was this, the oral exam for his doctorate? "Then the knight must side with the right. But if his lord is wrong, and the king is right, the knight must go to his lord and formally remove himself from the lord's service. After that, if there's anything left of him, he can go offer his services to the king."

"Well answered," a fourth voice approved. "What is the first rule of battle?"

Matt scowled. "Offensive or defensive?"

"Correctly asked," the voice applauded. "In offensive, what is the first concern?"

It went on like that for what seemed hours, while Matt shivered in the icy water. Sir Guy came back, bearing some cloth folded over his arm, and stood listening respectfully as the knights threw question after question at Matt. Sometimes his response was wrong, and the asking knight corrected him sternly. But his study of history gave him the right answers at least nine times out of ten. That should have been enough, but apparently wasn't for these dead knights. They must have been saving their questions for centuries.

At last, Hardishane spoke. "Enough! He knows the rules of chivalry as well as any knight. Withdraw him!"

Sir Guy bent down, holding out a hand. Matt caught his wrist and clambered gratefully out of the pool. The dark air of the hall felt almost hot by comparison. He bit down to keep his teeth from chattering, then began a vigorous toweling of his legs to keep his knees from knocking. When he got up to the waist, Sir Guy took the towel. Matt started to protest, but the Black Knight started drying his back, and Matt realized he was up against ceremony.

"All that you have spoken is truth."

Matt looked up toward the voice and saw a grizzled old figure with a bush of white beard. It didn't move, but its voice crackled around Matt. "Yet we have spoken here of chivalry only; we have not talked of magic. Now I shall do so. Beware Malingo, Lord

Wizard. He is worse than he seems, for he is more demon than man. Yet therein lies his weakness."

Matt looked up, startled; but he didn't have time to think about it, because Sir Guy was handing him a set of hose—*clean*! Matt pulled them on; they fitted perfectly. Next came a tunic, then a quilted surcoat that went down to the top of the thigh. He was just finishing belting it when Sir Guy picked up a piece of armor and began buckling it onto him.

"Hey, wait a minute! I'm not supposed to wear a knight's armor!"

"Wherefore not?" Sir Guy picked up another piece and kept buckling.

"Well—isn't it against union rules, or something?"

Sir Guy shrugged. "You cannot deny you shall have need of it. We go to battle, Lord Wizard."

Matt gave up and let Sir Guy finish encasing him. It did seem irregular—but who was he to argue?

The armor fitted perfectly. It was beautiful—and heavy! Matt took a step and almost fell down. This would take getting used to.

"Keep your back absolutely straight," the nearest knight advised. "You must bear the weight on your shoulders, till you're horsed."

"And move slowly at first," another put in. "Let your body have time; it must learn anew how to balance and shift."

They went on advising, and Matt walked experimentally at their direction. They were patient teachers, which was rather surprising, after that cross-examination. During the instructions, Sir Guy disappeared again.

When the knights finally let Matt pull out his sword and directed him in the fine points of chopping when his arm felt like lead, he guessed he'd passed another examination. Just about then, Sir Guy came back, wearing his own lobster shell. "Come, Lord Wizard."

"Time to hit the road again, huh?" Matt faced the nearest bunch of knights, managed a shallow bow, and, even more surprisingly, managed to straighten up. He turned to the other row of knights and bowed again. "I thank you, sirs and lords, for your instruction and counsel."

An approving murmur moved through the ranks, but the nearest knight said only, "Go with Toutarien."

Sir Guy caught his arm before he could answer and turned him toward the Emperor. Matt's eyes went wide, but Sir Guy was striding down the aisle toward Hardishane, and Matt had to follow suit.

He wished someone would tell him what was going on.

Sir Guy stopped about five feet from the Emperor and muttered, "Kneel."

Kneel? Matt had barely managed a *bow*!

But Sir Guy was the only one in the room who wasn't looking at him. How the dead knights could watch with their eyes shut, Matt didn't know, but he knew they did—and it made him feel very spooky indeed. *Put it out of your mind,* he told himself sternly and bent all his concentration on bending his knee. Slowly, very awkwardly, he knelt. Firmly established with one knee touching the floor, he tried looking up.

The dead Emperor towered over him, vast and golden.

"Will you now," the giant intoned, "swear fealty to me and all my line, to bear me service, answer my call, and be loyal to me and all I adhere to, defending me and mine with your body and life, if need be?"

Matt stared up at the golden giant, seized suddenly by the realization that this man was the embodiment of all that had ever been good in army or aristocracy, and that the centuries had left nothing evil or weak to purge from him. "I so swear, and gladly; I am deeply honored, Majesty. Without let or reservation, I am your man."

"Well spoken," the voice approved. "Bow your head."

As Matt inclined his head, he saw Sir Guy step up to Hardishane and lug out the giant's great broadsword, staggering under the load. Then all Matt could see was the floor; but he felt the great sword lowering down, to rest on his shoulder.

"With this sword," the Emperor rumbled, "I dub you knight."

Matt froze.

Then, slowly, he lifted wide, incredulous eyes to the great, golden Emperor—and he began to curse himself for a fool, not to have realized what was going on, not to have been willing to admit it to himself when he'd begun to suspect.

"Rise, Sir Matthew," the Emperor commanded.

Matt rose, feeling totally humbled and amazingly exalted at the same time.

"Now I counsel you," Hardishane boomed, "beware of fell illusions and glamours; above all else, beware the works of Evil that manifest themselves in complaints of purposelessness; for we have ever purpose, if 'tis only to abide, to wait, and to insure that one waits after us, against the day that Evil shall arise; for only by awaiting thus, in readiness, can we forestall it."

"I shall remember, Majesty," Matt mumbled, head bowed.

"And do not bow your head, not even to me," the Emperor rumbled. "Stand tall and proud, for you are a knight of Hardishane's."

Matt snapped to attention.

"Now go, with this command." The Emperor's voice hardened. "Destroy the sorcerer Malingo; hale down his pawn, corrupted Astaulf. Restore this land to cleanliness and to God!"

"I shall so endeavor, Majesty."

Sir Guy turned back from sheathing Hardishane's sword and stepped up to Matt, muttering, "Turn and leave."

Matt stood a moment, startled. Turn his back on an Emperor? Then he shrugged—or tried to, in his steel weskit. He bowed, straightened, and turned away with Sir Guy.

As he did, his gaze swept across an empty chair at the Emperor's right, one only slightly smaller than Hardishane's throne, with gilded carvings traced over the surface. For whom was that? A knight who'd died in some way that left no remains, or one who was missing at the moment? He shivered at the thought of one of the bodies walking about the land. Then he put the puzzle aside for later consideration.

He and Sir Guy marched between the files of dead knights, while Matt seemed to hear a faint, distant choir intoning a triumphant hymn. And as they passed each ancient warrior, a word of advice sounded in his ear—a one-sentence summary of the wisdom of a lifetime:

"Never fight until your right cannot be questioned; then delay not to strike." . . . "Never fear to claim a higher place, for when you've reached your proper height, you will know." . . . "Never be too far from arms, for all men have the blood of Cain." . . . "Never seek more power than God gives, for He will match it to your tasks." . . . "Know yourself and always question what manner of man you have become . . ."

It continued until Matt's mind seemed to ring with the tambour of iron men's experience. Then they were entering the low tunnel that led to the outside cave. They turned the corner, and the misty cavern was lost to sight. Matt felt a pang of regret.

They came into the outer cave, and a humming spark of light

dropped down from the ceiling. "I thought to warm the water for you, Wizard. But I forebore."

Matt nodded numbly. "You were right," he said. "Very."

Stegoman flew down from a nearby mountain peak at Matt's hail. Sir Guy was looking about as if searching for something. Then he put his fingers to his lips and gave a piercing whistle. A few minutes later, his horse came trotting up. Apparently the nuns had released the beast, and it had found its way here, as the knight had said it would.

They rode up further into the mountains in the golden light of early morning. Matt was silent, riding with his eyes on the sky, head filled with the glory of the pageant he'd just lived through, ears ringing with the distant echo of broadswords clashing in ancient, fabled battles.

Then the ground swung upward into his field of view, and he saw a great cut through the peaks in front of him. The sides were long, sloping mounds of loose rock, with a sheer basalt face here and there, and clean-cut cliffs towering up above them.

It brought him out of his daze. "Uh, Sir Guy—where are we?"

The Black Knight turned in his saddle to grin back at Matt. "Do you wake, then? Nay, we ride through the peaks, to the Plain of Grellig. 'Tis a high valley, a bowl amidst the peaks, a day's ride off."

"And this is the pass that leads to it." Matt looked around him at the sheer cliff faces and the long, clean angles of the talus slopes. There was a trail here, but a very faint one; apparently the route wasn't traveled too often. There were patches of grass, and low bushes here and there, but nothing more. Nonetheless, the place had a stark majesty to it—one of the most beautiful places he'd seen. "Sir Guy, something occurs to me."

"Aye?"

"This is an excellent passageway through these mountains. Why is it so poorly traveled?"

Suddenly a figure roared down on them like an avalanche, eight feet tall, pop-eyed, hairy as a bear, with huge eyeteeth jutting like tusks from its lower jaw. It wore breastplate, greaves, and a helmet that looked faintly Greek; it bore two great broadswords, which it whirled about like daggers.

Matt shrank back in his armor. "What the hell is *that*?"

"An ogre." Sir Guy's sword hissed out. "Defend yourself!"

A surge of courage came up from some unidentified place, and Matt whipped out his blade.

The ogre bounded down on them with a bellow. Stegoman answered with a blast that sent flame gouting out a dozen feet, but the ogre leaped aside, then jumped in with a savage sword cut at Matt's head.

He swung up his shield. Then a bomb seemed to explode against it, and he was somersaulting off Stegoman's back to crash into the talus slope. Through the ringing of his head, he heard Sir Guy shout and the ogre answer with a roar.

Matt staggered to his feet and turned toward the battle. He saw the ogre whacking at Sir Guy from both sides, while the knight tried to riposte and the war horse lashed out with its hooves. Stegoman hovered before them, neck weaving and head bobbing, trying to get a clear shot at the monster. But the monster pressed so closely on Sir Guy that the dragon couldn't burn the ogre without destroying the knight.

Matt gathered himself and charged in.

The ogre turned on him with a roar, swinging one sword toward him. Matt met it with the monofilament edge of his blade. His arm throbbed with the blow, but the ogre was left with only half a sword as the severed point struck the ground. Then the half blade swung back in a vicious swipe, and Matt rolled desperately with the blow. It rocked him, but he managed to stay on his feet, turning and slicing at the huge thigh nearest him. The ogre jerked back, but the blade sliced a sliver from the skin.

The monster howled, slammed a blow at Sir Guy's shield, then turned with a series of cuts at Matt, who retreated until his back was pressed against something hard. The cliff face was behind him, thrusting up twelve feet to a slope of loose talus.

Matt ducked his head and swung up his shield just in time to catch another clanging blow. He saw that Sir Guy's horse was also backed against the cliff face, a few feet to his left.

"Curses upon all cowards in shells!" the ogre roared. He bent down to scoop up a boulder the size of a basketball.

"'Ware!" Sir Guy shouted, snapping his shield up to guard his head as the monster swung the boulder in a long, overhand pitch that sent it hurtling at bullet speed. Matt flinched under his shield, but he heard the rock strike far above. A rumble began overhead.

He took one step forward, shouting, "Sir Guy! Out, fast!"

Then rubble and pebbles were raining down and glancing off

his armor. He managed to get his shield up. Pain shot through his shoulders, but he held it while the avalanche seemed to go on forever. Finally, a few last bits of rock struck; then all was quiet.

Matt looked about quickly. All around Sir Guy and himself, a long slope of rubble trailed down to the earth, spreading out on all sides. The talus slope had come down, burying them almost to their chins. Sir Guy's horse barely held his head above it.

The ogre brayed huge, harsh laughter. "Eh, may that serve ye! Fools, to enter my mountains!" He hefted a sword and stepped forward, an ugly gleam in his eye. "To let others know to fear for their lives and turn back, mayhap I should hang a sign at the mouth of this pass—your heads!" He leaped, swinging a sidehand chop that would have bisected a rhino quite neatly.

A sheet of flame filled the hillside, hiding the ogre; Matt heard him bawl in anger and pain. The firestorm snapped out as suddenly as it had come, showing the monster a good twenty feet further away, rubbing burns amid a flood of curses.

"Aye, you mistook," Stegoman rumbled, behind Matt and out of sight. "Be mindful of me, foul ogre; come not near my knights."

The ogre answered with another spate of curses, but he didn't step closer.

Matt heaved a huge sigh of relief. "Thanks, Stegoman."

"'Tis your due, Wizard. Would I could aid you more in this."

"You can't?" Matt looked down at the apron of rock before him and frowned. "I see what you mean. A lot of those rocks are going to have to be lifted out, aren't they?"

"Aye," Stegoman rumbled, "and my claws are suited to digging, but never to lifting."

"Definitely a problem." Matt chewed at his lower lip. "We *do* have to get out of here, somehow."

"Nay, ye do not." The ogre stepped forward, just outside of flame-range, and sat down with the air of a man who has come to stay. "I canna come near ye whilst the dragon is near; but ye canna come out. 'Twill take ye some while to die of hunger and thirst, but die ye shall. Then shall I have your heads."

"'Ware, foul parody of man!" Stegoman bellowed, and his head thrust forward into Matt's vision.

The ogre hiked himself back a few feet and leered up at the dragon. "Nay, ye dare come no further away from them—for if ye do, I'll dodge past ye, to strike off their heads."

Stegoman roared out angry flame, but it was just punctuation, and when his fire died, the ogre still sat there, laughing.

Matt frowned, trying to figure it out. "You're one hell of a fighter—and you seem to have a pretty good brain. Why are you hiding out here, waylaying travelers?"

"Do not make mock of me!" the ogre bellowed, surging to his feet. "Is it not enough to be cursed with this form? Must ye now sneer at me for it?"

"He does not sneer," Sir Guy said, thin-lipped.

The ogre swung around toward him, staring in surprise.

The knight softened his voice. "My companion is a strange man—he seems to see only the abilities underlying the form. His question was honestly meant."

"Do ye think ye talk to a child?" the ogre growled. "Nay, I'll not be cozened!"

"Think what you want," Matt said, "but Sir Guy's giving it to you straight. Sure, you're ugly as sin—but the way you fight, I'd think any baron would be glad to have you in his army. Have you tried to enlist?"

"What need to ask?" the ogre grated. "Since men cast me out, they'd not wish me back."

"'Cast you out?'" Matt raised an eyebrow. "For real? Or did they just make you feel unwanted?"

"'Twas a full outcasting." The ogre frowned, puzzled. "What manner o' man are ye, that ye ken not the rite?"

"Rite?" Matt frowned, turning toward Sir Guy. "This is an actual ritual?"

The knight nodded. "With bell, Book, and candle."

"The priest it was who led it." The ogre clamped his jaws shut, his face hardening. "I was a child like any other, though somewhat longer of leg and arm. Yet when I came thirteen, and hair began to grow all o'er my body and my eyeteeth to lengthen, they cried I was possessed. Aye, they swore I was a thing from Hell, and even my own dad did beg me to quit his house. Yet I did fear—what would his neighbors do to him, for fathering such a monster as I'd grown to be?

"So I stayed. Therefore did they all, goodfolk, beseech the priest to cast me out. He came, with armored soldiers at his back, with a reed of holy water and a candle lit, intoning verses from his Book. I knew that where one soldier's beaten, twenty more do come; soon or late, they'd bear me down. So I turned and walked out from that village.

"Then, two nights later, hiding in the wood, I heard some villagers speak of how they had burned my father's house and driven him to the Church for sanctuary. I came back then and burned their roofs about them. Thereafter I foreswore all folk and did come here."

"So." Matt pursed his lips.

> "I, that am rudely stamped, and want love's majesty
> To strut before a wanton ambling nymph;
> Cheated of feature by dissembling nature,
> Deform'd, unfinish'd, sent before my time
> Into this breathing world scarce half made up,
> And that so lamely and unfashionable
> That dogs bark at me as I halt by them—
> . . . Since I cannot prove a lover,
> I am determined to prove a villain,
> And hate the idle pleasures of these days!"

The ogre's eyes kindled. "Aye, that is the way of it! That is myself! What words are these?"

"Shakespeare's, from *Richard III*." Matt had thought the quote might go over.

"His name was Richard? Mine is Breaorgh, it matters not! We are the self-same person!"

It was useful to know the ogre's name—but more useful for him to identify himself with Richard, Shakespeare's most evil king.

Richard hadn't always been the epitome of evil, though, even in Shakespeare's plays—he'd come by it gradually. Reverse the trend of the Bard's verses, and Matt might reverse Breaorgh's temperament.

> "I cannot weep, for all my body's moisture
> Scarce serves to quench my furnace-burning heart;
> Nor can my tongue unload my heart's great burden;
> For self-same wind that I should speak withal
> Is kindling coals, that fire all my breast,
> And burn me up with flames, that tears would quench.
> To weep is to make less the depth of grief;
> Tears, then, for babes; blows and revenge for me!"

Breaorgh nodded vigorously. "Aye, aye, 'tis me! For grief
I've known, that should loose a flood of tears! Yet I'll withhold
them, so revenge may burn!" And he took his unharmed broadsword by the point and drew it back, like a dagger ready to
throw.

Matt put his next choice of verse in, fast.

> "Oft have I seen a hot, o'er-weaning cur
> Run back and bite, because he was withheld,
> Who, being suffered with the bear's full paw,
> Hath clapped his tail between his legs, and cried.
> And such a piece of service will they do,
> Who do oppose themselves to ogres grown."

Breaorgh's lip curled. "Aye. Thus are they all, the small men.
They term me monster; but when 'tis time to show their courage,
they show their backs instead."

"Do I mistake?" Sir Guy breathed, round-eyed. "Or have his
fangs grown shorter?"

"They have." Matt felt relief starting to weaken his knees.
"Look closely, there—he's shedding. And his eyes are receding.
See, once he identified himself with Richard, whatever I did to
Richard would be done to him—and I've been taking Richard
backward. He may have been a monster in *Richard III*, but he
was warm and human when he started off as a teenager in *Henry
VI, Part II*."

He turned back to Breaorgh, feeling a chill grow within him.
Now came the dangerous part—Prince Hal. Would the identity
with Richard hold? It should—Hal and Richard were just opposite
ends of one Shakespearean continuum. A case could be made that
they were almost the same character, at two extremes—the character called King.

Well, nothing ventured . . .

> "Yet herein will I imitate the sun,
> Who doth permit the base contagious clouds
> To smother up his beauty from the world,
> That, when he please again to be himself,
> Being wanted, he may be more wondered at
> By breaking through the foul and ugly mists
> Of vapours that did seem to strangle him."

"Nay, ye canna mean that I am such!" Breaorgh bleated. "How could there be some beauty under my fell carcass?"

But he wanted to believe it. His eyes were almost normal, his hair cascaded down, and his fangs were just two white dots above his lower lip.

Matt grinned and went on.

> "And, like bright metal on a sullen ground,
> My reformation, glittering o'er my fault,
> Shall show more goodly and attract more eyes
> Than that which hath no foil to set it off.
> I'll so offend, to make offence a skill,
> Redeeming time when men think least I will."

Breaorgh had a very thoughtful look when Matt finished. The only sound was the soft rustle of falling hair.

"'Tis a lie!" But Breaorgh didn't sound too sure. "There is nothing of the good or honorable that I do hide. I am what I have always been—an ugly monster, and of monstrous temper! Am I not?"

"Look at your feet," Matt suggested.

Breaorgh stared, startled. Then, in spite of himself, he looked down—and stared again. Slowly, he lifted his eyes to the rest of his body.

"I yet would not call him clean-limbed," Sir Guy said judiciously, "but I've seen more hair on a country squire. And his fangs have quite vanished."

Matt had been so busy staring at the hair, he'd missed the final transformation of the face. "Hey! He looks almost handsome!"

Breaorgh looked up, fear in his eyes—the kind that can turn to fury. "What fell sorcery is this?"

"Wizardry," Matt corrected. "Looked in a mirror lately?"

The ogre glared. "A what?"

That was right, peasants wouldn't know about mirrors in this culture. "A slowly moving river," Matt suggested. "A pond. A puddle, even! Go look—you'll be surprised."

Breaorgh started to turn away, then hesitated, glancing at them sidelong.

"Don't worry, we'll still be here when you get back—not because we want to, maybe; but we'll be here."

Slowly, Breaorgh turned and started walking toward the slope he'd come from. His stride lengthened, quickened; then he was running up the slope, round a cliff—and was gone.

Matt heaved a huge sigh of relief and let himself hang limp inside his armor. "Of course, I wouldn't say the operation was a total success."

"Wherefore not? He is now clean-favored, even comely—if he bathes."

"Well, maybe. But there's still a little matter of an extra two feet of height . . ."

"A small concern," Sir Guy said airily. "Must you demand perfection? I cannot think there's a baron living that would not welcome him with joy into his private army."

Rock growled in a minor avalance, and Breaorgh came skidding and sliding down the slope. He hit the floor of the pass, pounded toward them, and skidded to a stop ten feet away.

Stegoman took a quick breath.

"Swallow it," Matt said quickly; and the dragon gulped, then belched, looking extremely discomfited.

"'Tis a miracle!" Breaorgh was wild-eyed, mouth hovering on the verge of a smile. "I am clean! My face is as it was before the change came on me! Ye are a wizard sure!"

"Well, now that you mention it," Matt said, "yes."

The ogre gave a cry of joy and dove at them, plunging his hands into the rock-pile. Matt shrank back inside his armor, then realized that Breaorgh wasn't reaching for him—he was heaving up boulders and pitching them away like softballs, plowing and digging his way into the talus slope like some monstrous puppy. Rock chips flew, and somewhere in the cloud of granite, Breaorgh cried, "I must see your foot!" He heaved away a last bushel of gravel and fell to his knees, seizing Matt's iron shoe. It was, amazingly, free.

So was the rest of him, for that matter. He glanced over at Sir Guy; the knight and his horse both stood clear of the rock-slide, too.

"I swear unending loyalty to ye!" Breaorgh bowed his forehead to the bedrock and jammed Matt's foot down on his neck. "This is the sign of it, your foot upon my head! I am your man, as long as I may live!"

"Uh, well . . ."

"Wizard!" Sir Guy said severely. Matt met his eyes and swallowed. Customs!

"I accept your service," he said to Breaorgh, "and gladly. I'll have great need of men; we're expecting a major battle any day now."

"Truly?" Breaorgh dropped Matt's foot and looked up, his face lit with glee. "May I, then, fight for ye?"

"Indeed you may!"

"You shall see the way of it," Sir Guy explained, "when you know to whom you have sworn fealty."

Breaorgh glanced at Matt's blank shield and frowned. "I see no arms."

"He has not yet been granted them; for he's the first in knighthood of his line. But as you've guessed, he's more than knight— he is a wizard. This is Matthew, rightful Lord Wizard of Merovence."

Breaorgh froze, bug-eyed again.

Matt nodded sympathetically. "You see how it goes. I'm told that, once having accepted the title, I can be sure Malingo will try and do something about it."

"Be assured he will!" Breaorgh scrambled to his feet. "But ye have no hope of besting him! The royal line to which ye've sworn lies in dungeon at far Bordestang!"

"No longer." Sir Guy moved in a little closer. "The wizard hath freed her."

Breaorgh squeezed his eyes shut and gave his head a quick shake. "Do I hear aright?" He turned to Sir Guy. "And the princess wanders free?"

"Free and toward these mountains." Sir Guy nodded.

Breaorgh's throat worked; he licked his lips. "Then I have sworn to aid her?"

"Well, in effect, yes," Matt answered, "if you meant what you said about being my vassal."

"Aye!" the giant roared. "I rejoice far more now in my oath! For the queen I'll fight!" He whirled away, tossing his sword up, catching the hilt, and slamming it back into the scabbard. "Nay, Lord Wizard! Lead me on! Set tasks before me—I'll do them all, and more! I'll hew and chop as none has, since Colmain was turned to stone!" He jarred to a halt, a sudden, thoughtful look coming into his eyes. "If I brought ye more ogres, say a round score, and they did aid ye in this fight—would ye, then, serve them as ye've served me?"

Matt took a deep breath, thinking fast. For all he knew, Breaorgh's colleagues might not even be of human blood. He had a vision of a twelve-armed, ten-foot tree trunk, with a mantis-head . . . "If I can," he said slowly. "I can't promise anything more than that, Breaorgh. If I can figure out ways to change them back to normal, I will—but I can't be sure. I can only promise that I'll give it my best shot."

"More than that, no creature could ask of ye!" Breaorgh cried. "That the greatest wizard in the land will try his best—'tis hope, at least! Nay, ye'll have a score of ogres battling for ye, Wizard!" He leaped away, sprinting across the pass, up the slope on the other side, and disappeared into a cleft between two cliffs.

Matt tried to mop his brow, but all he got was a clang that resounded through his head. "Ouch! I keep forgetting!"

"And have you, then, forgot me also?" A bright spark of light danced out of his armor to hover in front of his face. "I could have felled him and moved the rocks that bound you in an instant, Wizard!"

It was Matt's turn to be dumbfounded. In the heat of battle, he'd forgotten all about the Demon.

CHAPTER 17

They had almost come to the end of the pass when Stegoman stopped suddenly, lifting his head and craning it around, looking toward the backtrail. "I hear horses. Two . . . nay, three, approaching the lip of the pass."

Matt turned a questioning eye to Sir Guy. "Should we hide now and decide whether or not they're enemies later?"

The knight considered it briefly, then shook his head. "Nay, Lord Wizard. If there be only three horses, we are a match for them. Let us see their faces."

The heads of horses showed above the lip of the pass, then the bald spot of a tonsure.

"I think . . ." Matt said.

A steel helmet with a wealth of blonde hair cascading out of it poked up on the left, and long black hair came into view on the right.

"That *is* who I think it is—isn't it?"

Sir Guy nodded. "They have made good time."

Matt frowned. "We did have a twenty-four-hour layover. Even so . . ."

"They must have ended the broil at the convent quickly," Sir Guy said.

Father Brunel looked up and saw them. Relief and joy flooded his face. He waved frantically.

Then Alisande saw them and stiffened in the saddle. Sayeesa lifted her head, but her posture didn't change.

Father Brunel kicked his horse into a canter and slewed up beside them in a few minutes, breathing heavily. "Praise Heaven we have found you!"

"Oh?" Matt raised an eyebrow. "Someone on your trail?"

"Nay, nay! But 'tis sorely tried I've been, accompanying these two ladies!"

"This is good fortune, Sir Knight, Lord Wizard." Alisande pulled up beside the priest. "I had not thought to meet you till Grellig." Then she looked directly at Matt and stared. "How now, sir! What is this armor! Have you no respect for—"

"Highness, your Lord Wizard is now Sir Matthew, a full knight created," Sir Guy informed her quietly.

Alisande turned back to Matt with a frowning stare. "How can this be? Who has knighted him? Yourself, Sir Guy? You had ought—"

"Not I; and I may not tell who 'twas. Yet be assured, 'twas a lord of high station."

Alisande gazed at the Black Knight while it sank in; then, somehow, she began to look a little frightened. Matt wondered why she should be so upset at the news.

The princess nodded, turning away. "He is a knight, then." She glanced at Matt's shield. "No arms . . . but of course. You have not been granted them; and you are the first of your family to gain this estate, are you not?"

It rankled; Matt couldn't help feeling that his father, as a business executive, should rank with a knight; but, by the book, his family were definitely commoners. "True."

Without the slightest hesitation, she said, "Your arms are those of the Lords Wizard, which are quartered with those of your family, if you wish it. We shall award them to you with due ceremony, once I am crowned queen."

Nice kid! She went by the rulebook, even when it galled her— as Matt's knighthood seemed to. She'd probably be all for his painting the heraldic symbols on right there—if he could find a painter.

"Yet I think," Alisande went on, "we must add to the Lord

Wizard's arms some new device, which will cleanse them; for they have been sullied of late."

"Sullied? Who has been?"

They all turned to Sayeesa, who had just come up. She saw Matt, and her eyes widened. "Ah, then, the silvery gleam was more than a mail-shirt! Is he a knight, then?"

Alisande nodded.

"My congratulations, sir." Her voice was low, softly modulated; but her lips quirked with humor. "So the title I first accorded you, knowing it to be false, is now yours by right!"

Matt smiled. "Are you a seer, Sayeesa?"

Her face darkened. Her gaze strayed away, brooding. "If I am, I know it not. Still..."

Sir Guy cleared his throat. "We had not looked to see you so quickly, ladies. How has this come, that the siege of the convent was broken? And how is't you journey in Father Brunel's holy company?"

"'Twas your doing." Alisande gave him a wry smile. "When you had fought through the host of the enemy, the Reverend Mother cried, 'See, then, what true men can do! Come, will you do less?' Then out we came to the ramparts, to hurl at the enemy arrows and bolts and great balls of fire from the catapult, while this good postulant—" She nodded toward Sayeesa, and Matt realized, with a shock, that the ex-witch still wore a postulant's habit. "—did link hands with the abbess, who turned her power to ward off the enemy's spells. At dawn's light, Sister Victrix, who led the erstwhile bandits, sallied out with her sisters to sweep the field clear."

"Come on!" Matt scowled. "A mere hundred nuns, against that whole army?" Of course, by then the enemy must have been well aged...

Alisande nodded. "'Twas dawn; the power of the sorcerous army was waning, while ours waxed. And in that fortunate hour came knights of Moncaire, with this good priest leading. They rode into the rear of the baron's force and dealt blows about them recklessly—and our good Father Brunel strove as mightily as any of them."

"'Tis true, to my shame." The priest nodded heavily, and Matt realized, with a start, that he had a broadsword slung across his back. "Yet what must needs be done, must be done. Still, I'll carry the screams of the dying to my grave."

"So." Matt pursed his lips. "The enemy fled or got chopped

up, according to their taste; and you rode out after us. No chance the army would come back that night?"

Alisande shook her head, but Sayeesa said, "Some chance, surely; but the Reverend Mother would not hear of our staying to aid them. She commanded us forth, saying her Highness's quest was more vital than the safety of the Cynestrians' house. If, as we all expected, the army did not return that night, the Reverend Mother with all her nuns would soon follow us. They may be even now behind us, on the trail. She bade me accompany her Highness; for I've learned some small enchantments of her and might be of use, if sorcerers attacked our rightful queen."

"I hate to agree with her, but it makes very good sense." Matt pursed his lips. "Any chance to test the theory?"

"None." Alisande looked puzzled. "We passed the night in the open, lighted by a campfire; and not a soul did challenge us. Father Brunel slept soundly; Sayeesa and I stood watch-and-watch; we did not wish to waken him. He had ridden long, and warred as heavily as we, and had seen less sleep. Too, the night was still."

"Never a whisper of danger." Sayeesa's brows knitted, perplexed.

Somehow, it all sounded ominous. "That I don't like."

"Nor I, Lord Wizard," Alisande said darkly. "What does the sorcerer while all is calm?"

"Brews one hell of a storm for us." Matt managed a faint smile. "What else would he be using the time for?"

"Then there is small room for talk." Sir Guy turned his horse's head to the west. "Come, let us ride! We must be nigh Grellig ere nightfall!"

They rode out of the pass in close order. Matt made it a little closer. "Stegoman—bump up against Sir Guy's horse, will you?"

The dragon grumbled, but moved ahead and to the left, almost colliding with the war horse. Matt leaned down to get his head near the knight's ear. "Sir Guy—did you notice the look on Brunel's face?"

The knight nodded. "Aye. He looks like a man on the rack."

"I don't blame him, having to ride twenty-four hours with his main source of temptation right beside him. And she doesn't seem to have gained any charity toward him . . . Look, don't you think this calls for a thorough rundown on the military situation? As well as the spiritual?"

The knight flashed a grin up at him. "Will I take the princess and priest aside, do you mean? To question them, purportedly to every last small detail of their day and night? How long do you wish this questioning to take?"

Matt glanced at Sayeesa, then back at Sir Guy. "Maybe half an hour. If that lady can't learn to be at least polite, our little company might disintegrate from internal tension before we come anywhere near seeing a battle."

"There's truth to that. Drop back, Lord Wizard."

Matt straightened, and Stegoman slackened his pace. Sir Guy turned back in his saddle, calling, "Ho! Good Father!"

Brunel looked up; then he nudged his horse up beside Sir Guy's. They chatted in an undertone for a few minutes; then the priest shrugged helplessly and nodded toward Alisande. Sir Guy looked up and called, "Highness?"

Alisande frowned and moved up beside them.

Matt dropped further back, hearing only a faint mumble from the trio ahead, until he was even with Sayeesa.

She rode straight in the saddle, eyes forward, not even glancing at him. The ice was thick this summer. "I'd, uh, like to have a word with you about the security of our little band," he began.

"Security?" Sayeesa looked up, startled. Then her face cleared. "Ah, you mean a way of blending our magics, should need arise, to ward our friends."

"No, I had internal security more in mind. Between you and Father Brunel, you've laid a constant tension on this crew, which just might tear it apart. Couldn't you bring yourself to be at least barely polite to him?"

Sayeesa stiffened, lifting her head and turning straight forward again. "You ask too much."

"Why? You obviously don't find him repulsive."

"What means have you of knowing?" she snapped.

Matt shrugged. "That male succubus in Brunel's form, outside the walls of the Cynestrians. When you saw it, you folded up. Was that because you don't care about him?"

"What I care of him matters not," Sayeesa grated.

"Oh, no! It's just tearing our happy little family apart! If you care about him, why be so insulting? Are you miffed because he escaped your clutches?"

"Be still!" Sayeesa turned on him angrily. "What affair is this of yours? Chide me for my actions toward yourself, if you must, but never any others! What passed between himself and me is my affair and his, but never yours! Do you not know that those who meddle in others' lives may well destroy them?"

"Your own two personal lives might destroy the rest of us," Matt countered. A slow grin spread over his face. "And why would you get so angry if he *hadn't* escaped you?"

Sayeesa's face slowly set.

"He did, didn't he?" Matt jibed.

Slowly, Sayeesa bowed her head.

"I should think you'd be proud of it," Matt said gently. "Even under an enchantment, you had the goodness to keep a priest from breaking one of his vows."

"I had not," she said, so low that Matt could scarcely hear it, "nor did I wish to." She lifted her face. "There was no way to bring him to it, look you. Scarcely could I witch him into caresses, when he'd turn away and tell me, in long and tedious detail, how foul he was, how weak, how base! And all the while I desired nothing half so much as one light touch of his sweet hand! Yet worse—after speaking to this vein in some length, he'd turn to the door, saying he'd not sully me with his foul presence. Then had I to leap after him, to catch him back, to cozen, coo, and calm him, pouring praise out till he'd ceased to pull away; then slowly, gently, pull him toward embrace again. But no sooner would I touch him than he would shrink back and curse himself anew!"

"And you'd have to start the whole thing all over again?"

"Aye, not that it bore me any fruit! For look you, when last comes to last, this man is holy and is good—far too good for me! Lust he had abundantly, but 'twas not enough!"

"With a girl like you," Matt mused, "lust shouldn't have been all that was operating. A certain degree of romantic love would have been almost unavoidable."

She looked up, startled, then nodded slowly. "I thank you, Wizard. Yet you speak from your own heart, not his. Nay, his interest was of the body only."

"No." Matt shook his head, frowning. "There's some interest in you as a person, strong interest, or I mistake completely."

"Mayhap," she said somberly, "but his soul's so filled with God and ghostly duties that there's no room left for any woman. Not even the most beautiful and most holy of females could claim more than a minor part of his affections; and how much less myself? Ah, if only he'd not been a priest! I might then have claimed him! But no; for at the last, the thirteenth time, he turned away, opened wide the door, and bade me stay, for he'd not defile my beauty with his swinishness. Ah, to be defiled so!" she breathed, closing her eyes, head back. Then the eyes squeezed shut; she trembled, tears welling forth. "Nay, I must not think on this! Yet he blessed me!"

"He *what*?"

"Blessed me," she said again, with a short, breathless, incredulous laugh. "As he turned away to shut a door between us, he gave me blessing!" Her eyes closed again; she turned her head from side to side, her shoulders shaking. "Ah, if he were not of the cloth! I might then have some chance to win his heart, even now!"

"If only," Matt murmured. "Kind of makes him a challenge, doesn't it?"

She pivoted to glare at him. "What do you say?"

"If he weren't a priest," Matt said softly, "would you have given him a second look?"

"Be still, foul tongue!" Sayeesa turned on him, rising in her stirrups. "Is there nothing of chivalry in you, nor of gallantry? What true knight would even speak so to a woman! Have I held a mirror to you, that showed only the darkest nooks within your soul! Nay! Then why must you do so to me?"

"You haven't answered my question," Matt reminded her.

Sayeesa glared at him, speechless. Then slowly her face darkened to brooding; she turned away. "I cannot tell," she said, so softly he could scarcely hear. "In truth, I cannot say." She looked up at him sharply. "Can you?"

Matt tried to lock eyes with her, but his conscience gnawed at him; it *had* been a low blow, true or not. He dropped his gaze and rode away.

Sir Guy looked up, caught Matt's glance, and turned back to his conference. After a few more words, Alisande dropped back, looked up, saw Sayeesa's face, and stared, appalled. She moved beside Sayeesa quickly, murmuring to her.

Sayeesa rode stone-faced, ignoring her. Alisande glanced up to give Matt a venomous glare, then lowered her eyes and rode beside the ex-witch, looking very grave.

Sir Guy spoke on with Father Brunel for a while, the discussion apparently growing heavier. The knight seemed to be pressing a question sharply and not getting much of an answer. Finally, Sir Guy shrugged, smiled, said a few parting words, and let the priest ride on, head bowed, shoulders slumped, brooding.

Matt rode up beside Sir Guy. "How's it feel to play father confessor to a priest?"

"Unusual, to say the least." Sir Guy's eyes still held on Brunel. "And to no point. Let me advise you, from this moment: Never seek to tell a priest that he should not blame himself too harshly, for he'll argue you out, verse and chapter, why he should."

"Yeah." Matt eyed Brunel's back thoughtfully. "But from my little chat with Sayeesa, I can't figure out any sins they might have committed together that could account for this much tension between them. In fact, they didn't, which is much better reason why."

"I believe you have the right of it. The best I could piece out from his circumlocutions is that, at the worst, he has kissed her and, mayhap, given her a passing caress; but no more. From all I did hear, and all I can read into his words, he has ne'er bedded her—no, nor any woman."

"*What?*" Matt whirled about, staring.

"Never." The Black Knight turned his head from side to side, marveling.

"Oh, come on! What was all this garbage he was feeding us, about his being a sinner? One of the all-time greats, the way he made it sound!"

"Ah, but he says that he is. For, though he did not, in actuality, bed any woman, he oft did decide to do so. And all that is needed for the committing of mortal sin is the deciding."

Matt sat still for a moment, then nodded slowly. "Yeah, I seem to remember something about that, from my childhood catechism—seriousness, knowledge, and will: the three components of a mortal sin. It has to be wrong enough to be mortal; you have to know it's that bad; then you have to decide to go do it."

Sir Guy nodded. "Thus said the priest. The act itself, it seems, is not necessary."

"But he reneged on the decision! He reversed it! He drew back! He didn't do it!"

"Nay; for there came another moment of decision. On the verge of committing the act, he became uncertain; and had he, at that moment, decided again to do the deed itself, he would have committed a second mortal sin."

"Come *on!*" Matt tossed his head in exasperation. "Two sins for the price of one? What is this, bargain week at the Devil's booth?"

"It would seem that it is."

"So even though he's never been anything but celibate, he considers himself a sink of depravity."

"He does, Lord Wizard, he does. And can you gainsay him?"

Matt started to answer, then remembered which universe he was in, and bit back on the response. Even in his own universe, the traditional theology agreed with Brunel. These days, of course, there was some talk about a sort of relative morality...

He shook his head. This was Aristotle's universe, not Einstein's. Nothing was relative, here; there were only absolutes.

Father Brunel was educated in local theology, which came perilously close to also being local science. No doubt he was right—in this universe. No doubt, at all—or he wouldn't have turned into a wolf.

The sun was out of sight behind the peaks, firing the Western sky, when they rode down into a small valley nestled among three mountain peaks. Alisande reined in her horse. "Here is our camp for the night."

Matt frowned and looked around. It was a pretty place, but not much by military values. "Have you been here before?"

"Nay; but I know of it, and Sir Guy has doubtless seen it."

"Oh?" Matt raised an eyebrow at the Black Knight. "What do *you* think?"

"That we must see the dawn here, Sir Matthew." The knight swung down from his horse. "Come, set a camp."

Matt clambered down from Stegoman, still dubious. "If you don't mind, Your Highness—why here?"

"Because," said Alisande, "one of two yonder peaks is Colmain."

Matt stared. "Which one?"

"That I cannot say. 'Twill take some time to ascertain it, more than there's light left."

"Oh?" Matt raised an eyebrow. "How are you going to go about it? Ask the natives?"

"None would live near here; 'tis said to be cursed. Yet I will know, wizard, just as I know now that we are near him."

"But how..." Matt cut off the rest of the sentence and turned away to hunt fuel. It made sense, of a sort; and he was sure

Alisande wouldn't be able to tell him how she knew, other than that she'd have a feeling. Which figured. When Saint Moncaire brought Colmain to life in the first place, he'd probably included Hardishane's genetic imprint, or its spiritual equivalent—a sort of psychic fingerprint. And being psychic and therefore of energy, it would resonate to its harmonic waveform—the "print" of Alisande's soul. Just as Matt could feel forces gathering about him when he worked a spell, so Alisande would be able to feel Colmain's presence.

Which meant the spirit still lived, in the rock . . .

Matt veered away from the idea and laid kindling on a flat stone. "Hey, Stegoman! Got a light?"

"Must I?" the dragon growled.

Matt looked up, frowning. "What makes *you* so surly all of a sudden? . . . Oh. Your tooth."

The dragon nodded miserably.

"I thought it had rotted away, since it hasn't bothered you in so long! Better have it out, or it will *really* get fierce."

"Must I?" But Stegoman already sounded resigned.

"No question about it." Matt stood up, wiping his hands on his metal pants. "We might be fighting a battle tomorrow—and it *would* kind of slow you down."

"Well, then, if it must be, it must!" The dragon sighed. "Only be quick about it, Wizard—and render vanished a part of my body!"

"Oh, don't worry, you won't feel a thing—while I'm doing it." Matt pulled up some grass and went over to the dragon. "Lie down and open your mouth."

Stegoman grunted, folding his legs, and laid his head on the ground, opening his great mouth. Matt eyed the huge fangs suspended over his hands and decided that anesthetics were a great idea.

It was easy to tell the bad tooth; it was much darker than the rest. Matt squeezed the grass over it, watching drops of juice strike the bad tooth as he chanted:

> "Like an ache by sleep o'ercome,
> Let this dragon's jaw grow numb.
> That there be no slightest pain;
> Let this juice be Novocaine!"

The last drop splattered onto the tooth. Matt drew his hand back. "Okay, close your mouth."

Stegoman let his upper jaw close and frowned, lips working. "Wha've 'oo duh? I ca' fee' my hung."

"Hung? Oh, tongue. It worked faster than I thought. Well, let it sit a bit longer." He got up and sent to Sir Guy. "Do you carry a kit for fixing flats—uh, for changing horseshoes?"

The Black Knight nodded. "Certes. What knight would not?"

"Got a pair of tongs for drawing nails?"

Sir Guy nodded again and went to rummage in his saddlebags. He came back with a huge pair of pincers.

Matt took them and returned to Stegoman. He found the operation had drawn everyone but Alisande to watch. She would probably come, too, when she was done shooting dinner.

Matt knelt, grumbling. "Now I know why they call it an operating *theater* . . . Open wide, Stegoman."

The dragon opened his mouth but kept his eyes closed. Matt tapped the tooth with his finger. "Feel anything?"

"Ngo."

Matt put on a little pressure. "Now? Now? . . . Okay, brace yourself." He took a deep breath, jammed the pincers tight as he shoved with his foot, and threw all his weight against the handles.

He stumbled backward, holding a huge, dripping tooth silhouetted against the evening sky.

"Ow," Stegoman said, but not loudly.

"The tooth-hole bleeds," Sayeesa observed. "Should it not be bound?"

"Bound? Oh, packed. Yes, but . . ."

"Here." She thrust a wad of lint into his hand. "Torn from my petticoat. I had thought you might forget."

Matt packed the lint into the bleeding socket. "Okay, Stegoman, you can close your jaw now."

The dragon lowered his upper jaw gingerly, letting the full weight onto his lower jaw gradually. Then he opened his eyes. "I feel no pain now." He seemed to have recovered control of his tongue.

"Well, some of the drug's still in you. When it wears off, there'll be some pain. But it will pass—and stay gone!"

"My thanks, Wizard. And fear not—if there's pain, I'll bear it. Guard my tooth."

"Like a diamond." Matt turned to Sir Guy. "You wouldn't have a scrap of leather, would you?"

"Such as would serve for mending a bridle? Aye."

The knight brought it from his saddlebag. He must have belonged to the Coast Guard; he was always prepared.

With a circle of the leather and a thong, Matt fashioned a bag just large enough to hold the tooth. He held it out to Stegoman. "I could tie it around your neck."

"Aye, do so. Then he who would pluck it from me must slay me to get it!"

Half an hour later, Matt finally decided to draw the packing out, muttering:

> "Now let all go as I have plotted;
> Let this blood be fully clotted."

The wound looked clean. Matt watched it for a time to be sure there was no seepage. He started to throw the lint onto the fire, then stopped, remembering his sympathetic magic and what burning the blood might do to Stegoman.

"I'll wash it carefully," Sayeesa said, appearing at his side. She took the wad and slipped away.

A moment later, Stegoman sighed softly. "Ah, that feels cool and soothing."

Matt turned away, his doubts about sympathetic magic answered. He was feeling exhausted and let down. Playing dentist to a dragon was hardly his idea of fun. Then the appearance of the valley caught his attention, now that he was not concentrating on the tooth. He looked up at the sky, still red and gold in the west. The single eastern peak glowed against gathering gloom. "Hey, this place is beautiful, isn't it?"

"It is," Stegoman rumbled. "'Tis much like my homeland, Wizard, which is not far distant—only a few leagues to westward. Welcome to my country. Welcome indeed, for thou hast given me the chance to come home to it. Now dost comprehend the depth of my thanks?"

"Yeah, I think I begin to." Matt suddenly stiffened. "Hey! What's a jet doing here?"

A spot of bright fire moved across the sky, golden against azure.

"I know not of a 'jet,' but I know well that sight!" Excitement quickened Stegoman's voice as he rose. "'Tis a dragon, a high-riding sentry, gilded by the last ray of sunset!" He set himself and thundered, *"Glogorogh!"*

The point of light swerved sharply, then swung around in a circle, dimming as it swelled, spiraling down, till Matt could make out the sinuous, bat-winged form. Its voice echoed down, tinny with distance; "Who summons Glogorogh?"

"'Tis I, 'tis Stegoman!" The dragon's wings exploded as he leaped into the sky, flapping heavily till he caught a thermal, then gliding upward. Glogorogh sank lower, crying, "Thou dost lie, for Stegoman is slit-winged and exiled!"

"Nay, I speak truth! For my wings are mended, and I ride the high air again!"

Glogorogh pulled up ten feet above Stegoman, his wings cupping air with a boom that shook the valley. "It cannot be! . . . But thou hast his semblance!" And the dragon sentry flapped aside, veering away from Stegoman.

"More than his semblance—himself! Why dost thou flee? Dost not know me?"

"Aye, I know thee! I do not hold thee ill, Stegoman—but hover far from me! I have no wish to risk thine antics!"

Stegoman banked to a halt, sitting on an updraft, hurt and baffled. "Thou dost shy from me as though I were some unnatural thing!"

"And art thou not?" Glogorogh countered. "How is it thy wings are mended? What foul sorcery is this?"

"Not sorcery, but wizardry! A wizard from another world hath healed me, Glogorogh! And nay, not my wings alone, but all of me—my heady blood and flights of fancy! I could burn a forest now and still be clear of head as any of the elders!"

"If that is so, then I rejoice to hear it." Glogorogh still sounded skeptical. "Yet pardon me, that I do doubt. Thou must needs understand, thou wert a thing of peril!"

"Aye, I know it well," Stegoman rumbled. "Yet if thou dost doubt, then see!"

He whirled away upward, blasting, tracing a great half circle of fire across the sky, then spiraled higher and higher, trailing a fiery gyre.

Matt took a deep breath and crossed his fingers. Showing off had away of canceling out virtues.

But this was evidence, not bragging. Stegoman's torch cut off, and he dropped like a stone through the fading fiery spiral, then slapped his wings open with a thunderclap as he bellowed out, "Now see me! I am clear as any dragon could be!" And he wheeled away in a graceful series of curves. Matt stared, transfixed by the beauty of the flight.

Glogorogh's breath rasped in. "Nay, 'tis the dance of victory! And sure, 'tis warranted—for thou dost fly it without the slightest fault of line or place!"

Stegoman streaked back, hovering near. "Dost still doubt?"

"I cannot; I can but ride amazed! How comes this, Stegoman? A lifelong failing, of more than a century's duration, cured in mere years!"

Stegoman's mouth lolled wide in a grin. "'Tis no work of mine, as I have told thee, but all the gracious doing of this wizard that I spoke of. He came upon me and never once did he speak pity; nay, he's far too chivalrous for that! A lord he is, in bearing and in title, and a maze of scholarship bewildering, a very font of wisdom! He but chanted one brief verse, and my wings boomed wide about me! Then together we did face monster after monster—and, oh, Glogorogh! My spirit quailed within me! For at the last, there came a salamander—"

"A salamander!" Glogorogh shied back twenty feet. "Nay, Stegoman, thou dost jest! How could a dragon meet the very father of our blood and live to speak of it?"

"By wizard's power," Stegoman caroled, "by the aid of a familiar that he lent me! I drove it down with tooth and claw; too late, it saw the waters there below and struck into their bosom with a booming hiss that filled the world! The flowing element overbore the fiery; it lay chilled, damped out, extinguished! And all through the wizard's power!"

"Indeed, he must be wondrous, if his strength through thee could best a salamander!" Glogorogh definitely sounded shaky. "Where does he lair?"

"He has no home now," Stegoman rumbled, "for he fights for the Princess Alisande, to free the land from vile Malingo and Astaulf! He stands below, silver in the gleaming, knight, lord, and wizard!"

Glogorogh looked down, startled, saw Matt, and quickly averted his eyes. "He doth appear so slight—no greater than any other of the Handed Folk. Yet I cannot doubt your words." Reluctantly, he lowered his eyes to Matt again, dropping down to hover, wings rolling like great drums, just twenty feet above. "Great Wizard, thanks, from all the deepest wells of dragons' hearts! If we may ever aid thee, be sure we shall; all Dragondom doth stand within thy debt, for thou hast returned one lost to us!"

"Uh . . ." Matt swallowed. "I was just helping out a friend."

"Nay, I'll speak then for him," Stegoman bellowed. "We ride against the sorcerer and his pawn, good Glogorogh—and we ride without an army! Any aid that we may have, we'll need—and do not hover overlong in waiting. Go to the elders and the Council. Ask that I be restored to fellowship and tell them of his deeds! Then if they acknowledge tribal debt, ask that they aid us now—myself and this great man to whom I have sworn fealty!"

"Indeed I shall!" Glogorogh sheered off, winging upward in a high, wide spiral. "I shall lay the matter before them ere the midnight and demand their aid! I mind some few who owe me debts of battle, and more who stand in blood debt to yourself!"

"Conjure them by debts," Stegoman agreed, wheeling up with him. "Conjure them by honor! Conjure them by every means and bring them to us on the morrow, if thou canst! The storm gathers, and any hour may bring the deluge!"

Glogorogh turned and hovered. "Aye, we have felt great forces about to brew and boil around us. Yet we are loathe to act, seeing no part within this quarrel, and fearing that one act may start that which will force us again to fight for every inch of our high mountains!"

"Fight now, while you've got a few allies," Matt shouted up at him.

Glogorogh looked down, startled, then nodded. "I'll trumpet loud the cry. If the elders will not send a force, I, at least, shall come to aid you—and, I doubt not, several score of good young dragons!"

"My thanks and blessing on you!" Stegoman trumpeted.

"And mine!" Matt shouted, waving.

Glogorogh wheeled away over the mountain and was gone.

Stegoman spiraled down, swung over the valley in a long, great arc, and landed in the meadow before Matt, his wings booming shut. "'Tis done; and my heart sings high within me! Aye, I'll fly in my home mountains once again!"

"He certainly didn't seem to have too many reservations about accepting you." Matt lifted his visor, yanked off a gauntlet, and wiped his brow. "Whew! Your folks don't stop to mull things over much, do they?"

"What need?" Stegoman demanded. "Act, and if thou dost later find thyself deceived, act again to counter it."

"Leave the worrying to the High Command, huh?" Matt nodded judiciously. "But you might have been a little deceptive yourself, the way you sang my praises."

The dragon fixed him with burning eyes. "I was not," he said. "When wilt thou learn?"

It might have been Matt's imagination, but he could have sworn that Alisande had been trying to avoid him all day. To test the theory, he sat down next to her at dinner time.

Her back stiffened. She seemed to pull in on herself and inch just the slightest bit away from him. "Good even, Lord Wizard."

Good even? They'd been riding in the same company all day! Matt clamped his jaws on a tough strand of partridge. "Good evening, your Highness."

Off to a great start, wasn't it? Where did he go from there? "Pardon my ignorance, but—is this the Plain of Grellig?"

She seemed to think it over before she answered. Then, unwillingly, she nodded her head toward the two peaks to the west. "Nay, 'tis beyond—a high plateau."

"Just over there, huh?" Matt raised his eyebrows, looking across her. Sure enough, what he'd thought was a long saddle between the peaks was actually a bit beyond them, and was the lip of a high tableland. "Why did you make that the rendezvous point?"

"'Twill likely be the scene of our final battle," Alisande said offhandedly. "Malingo must know why we are here and also that, once we wake Colmain, he must crush us ere we can begin to march back towards Bordestang; for then, with every mile we march, we'll gain a hundred men."

Matt sat there, letting the chill of her words sink in. As soon as the giant turned back into flesh, then, they'd be facing a set of stacked odds that would make Crecy and Agincourt look like an even match. "That soon, huh? Well, I hope we'll be tooled up."

"The abbess and her warrior nuns ride to meet us." Alisande's face was stone. "And the abbot of the Moncaireans comes with all his men."

"Shouldn't we wait a little for them to catch up with us?" Matt asked.

The princess shook her head. "Malingo may try to crush us ere we wake Colmain—if he can."

It wouldn't take much, Matt knew—and something just as dangerous was shaking his confidence. "Uh, your Highness..."

She seemed to steel herself. "Aye?"

"We may have a grave interior weakness at this last battle..."

"We will not." She said it with utter finality, like the crash of steel doors—but there was a hollowness behind them. That unquestionable conviction with which she spoke on public matters was lacking.

Therefore, it had to be a private matter.

"That's not what the Reverend Mother thought," Matt reminded her.

Alisande's chin tucked up another notch. "I am mindful of her admonition, Lord Wizard—and I mind me there were two courses of action for me."

For *her*? Did she really think she could make this a unilateral decision? Come to that, did she think she could resolve it by a simple decision? "There were two," Matt agreed carefully. "That we pledge, or finish."

"I choose the second." Alisande bit the words off. "Purge any feeling you have for me, Lord Wizard, as I have done regarding you."

"Oh, really? You've totally canceled any emotions you might have toward me?"

"Completely," she answered, her face like flint.

"Just by an act of will, eh? You just kicked out anything you felt for me, except possibly regarding my strategic value. Right?"

"Indeed." She seemed to be wilting inside the armor of her skin.

"Well, there's a word for that, where I come from..."

"I care not to hear it."

"Repression," Matt grated. "It's bad business, your Highness, very dangerous. Repressed emotions tend to leap out at you when you least expect them—and usually at the worst possible moment!"

"They are not repressed," Alisande ground out, "but banished."

"An interesting theory." Matt tossed away a pheasant bone and stood up. "But for myself, I don't like going into battle on the strength of an hypothesis. You're the solar plexus of this army, Princess; so if there's a weakness in you, there's a weakness in the whole body of us!"

"But there is no weakness in me." She glared up at him.

"Oh? In case it hasn't occurred to your Highness, this isn't a public concern—that's only the fringe of it, the side effect. This matter is personal—and your infallibility just failed!" He turned away into the night, stalking past Sir Guy's raised eyebrow with a snarl.

CHAPTER 18

It had been a low blow, he had to admit an hour later, when everyone was bedded down and only the embers of the campfire lighted the site. When would he learn to control his tongue—and his temper? If Alisande had ever had any notion of admitting any feeling for him, she certainly couldn't now. He'd spoken in anger born of hurt—and now, alone in the dark, looking for the roots of that hurt, he had to admit his care for her was a lot more than he'd wanted to feel about anyone. He'd never permitted himself to want anything beyond the physical level, and that not strongly or often—because he'd known, instinctively, that any physical act would pull emotion in with it. There were people, he knew, who could split themselves so that desires of the body didn't touch the heart—but he wasn't one of them.

He stared out into the darkness, unseeing, trying to blank his mind until he could sleep.

His eyes focused on a spark.

He went rigid, nearly jumping out of his skin. Max—the Demon! What was it doing, out of his pocket?

Then his eyes adjusted to the contrast between the brilliant dot and the face next to it. It was Sayeesa, sitting up with her blanket about her, watching the spark intently—almost, it would seem, happily. The faint humming stopped, and she nodded eagerly. Her lips moved, and he could hear the low murmur of her voice. It went on for awhile; then the spark hummed again. The Demon seemed to be striking up quite a rapport with her.

That worried Matt.

He was still worrying about it an hour later, when the spark finally winked out, and Sayeesa lay down, rolling over in her blanket and drawing the fabric up about her shoulders.

Matt lay still, feeling the tension prickle through him, feeling like a lightning rod just before the lightning struck. What was going on here? He could feel huge forces gathering around him, vast, grinding, groaning, welling up about this valley and the plain beyond, ready to smash in, twisting, rending, destroying anyone who got in their way.

Which force would win? Good? Or Evil? Both were probably really quite impersonal—but not from his viewpoint.

They rolled down over his soul, wrapping him in a thick, unseen, dark cloud. He felt as if he were lying at the bottom of a well of molasses—felt he could almost hear the gnashing and grinding of those great forces, louder and louder...

He sat bolt-upright, staring out into the darkness, heart hammering. He *was* hearing a huge, slow, grinding sound, like a glacier chewing its way through a quarry.

Then he began to detect a pattern to it, a dipping, swinging, modulation that slowly formed itself into a word:

MMMAAATHHHEEEWWW.

The hair on his head tried to jump at the stars. He sat very still, digging his fingers into the grass, trying to hold himself down.

MMMAAATHEWWW! the groaning voice ground out again. WWWIZZARRDD MMAATHEWW!

He looked around him wildly. The rest of the company was asleep—and he should know better than to go out alone at night. Something bad always happened when he did. But...

He shook his head and slowly climbed to his feet, knees trembling. Whatever it was that was calling him, he had to find out. He picked up his helmet, fastened it on, picked up his shield, and turned away toward the sound of the voice with one hand on the hilt of his sword.

He was walking toward the Plain of Grellig.

The call was not quite to the plain itself, he found, as he toiled up the slope that led to a ridge between the two peaks. The voice was coming from the southern peak. He turned, following it, his footsteps slow, though the sound of his name was coming faster now, in a low, rumbling voice that shivered through his bones. He forced himself onward, step after step, till he came to the bottom of a forty-foot rock outcrop.

He peered up into the starlight and saw that the top of the peak was rounded off into a very craggy dome. Maybe it was a trick of the light, but he thought he could make out pocks and crevices whose shadows gave the appearance, very roughly, of a brow ridge, nose, and a slash of mouth.

"You come," the mountain grated. "At last you come. Have waited, Wizard, waited years by hundreds."

Matt tried to speak—had to try again. "Who . . . who are you?"

"Am Colmain."

Matt couldn't move. He was rooted to the spot. This was the end of the long chase, then—this great slab of granite with the voice of the earthquake.

But it seemed wrong, somehow. He'd expected more from a giant with Colmain's reputation—illogically, of course; giants weren't even really human. "How do you know me?"

"*Know* ye? *Summoned* ye, Wizard!"

"*You? You're* the power that's been backing me all this time?"

"Aye, aye!" the great voice rumbled. "Hundreds of years, sought through worlds while body stood here, seeking sphere where wizards learned changing of substances."

"Transmutation? Lead into gold?"

"Aye. Only wizard from world where can change lead to gold could change stone back to flesh! So summoned ye!"

"Well, you called the wrong wizard. I'm from the right universe—but I don't know anything about transmutation. My study is words and the things men make of them."

"What else is wizard?" the giant bellowed. "Knowing ye, or not have called ye! Wizard, change to flesh!"

Reluctance crystallized, and Matt balked. "We're planning on it in the morning. At the moment I'm worn out from a long day in the saddle. If I tried to do it now, I might botch it."

"Try!" the granite thundered. "Must try! Must do—and

now! Sorcerer-force comes! Army of Evil nears! Ye feel their coming?"

So that was the sense of great powers gathering that Matt had felt. "Uh . . . yeah, I've felt it."

"Then why nay-say? Hurry! Do now! Ere sorcerer blasts stone to gravel, and not waken ever!"

Matt stood immobile, hung on a decision.

"Do!" the cliff face bellowed. "Now! Or Hell takes!"

He was right. Malingo was gathering his powers, both physical and magical; and the forces of Good were approaching in response. It had to be done—and done quickly.

"All right. But I've never done anything on this scale before. It may take me a few tries to get it right."

"Once only!" the giant thundered. "Or lose life!"

Matt looked up, irritated. The giant wasn't in much of a position to threaten—or was he? If he had pulled Matt to Merovence . . .

He turned back, knowing he was going to try; overbearing or not, the giant was necessary. But how the hell was Matt going to work this miracle? Sure, he'd managed to turn Stegoman back from stone to flesh. But that had been a small job compared to this, and the change to a statue had been too recent then to have had time to set. This had been resting for centuries.

Still, maybe the theory was the same. In changing the giant to rock, the carbon must have been converted to silicon. That would cause a complete change in chemical bonds, resulting in a whole new set of molecules. If the silicon could just be turned back to carbon, maybe the process would reverse and the whole structure would come alive again.

He gathered pebbles into a small mound, added a handful of sand, and mixed grass into it. He really needed flesh, but he'd eaten it all for dinner. Still, what counted was having carbon in organic compounds.

But how was he going to put enough power into his verse? Maybe he'd better avoid specifics and stick to generalities. He had to indicate a change, a reshuffling, a turning . . .

The yin-yang symbol slashed vividly before his mind's eye, turning, endlessly turning.

> "Now the Wheel forever turns,
> Yin for Yang, until it burns.

> Silicon, now yield your place
> Unto carbon's rings of grace."

He'd also better throw in some mythical references.

> "Turning still, however small,
> Cycling powers govern all.
> Thus Medusa's face, reflected
> From a mirror unexpected,
> Turned her body into stone,
> Letting Perseus gain a throne.

> "Make the cycle turn again;
> Perseus' loss, Medusa's gain.
> Let this granite turn to flesh,
> Caught within the Weavers' mesh,
> Where he webs both cord and twine,
> Human lives to Clotho's line."

Now there was one thing he knew could be transmuted—and fast. He'd better throw it in for luck and power. He needed a whopper of a heavyweight spell.

> "Now to fill the needed sum,
> I invoke Plutonium.
> Fickle metal, lend your might;
> Life and flesh from stone excite."

An explosion rocked the peak. Matt leaped back, arms wrapped around his head. The earth heaved once under him. He looked up to see huge shards of rock flying from the cliff and turned, running.

Someone else was running—toward him. Long blonde hair waved in the moonlight. "Wizard! Reverse the spell!"

Matt skidded to a halt, dread gripping his entrails.

"Change him back!" Alisande screamed. "'Tis not Colmain!"

There was an avalanche-roar as the giant shook free from the cliff, gloating and laughing. "Ballspear!" The creature broke away a ten-foot shaft of rock for a club. "Ballspear, poor believing man. Now pay for folly!" He turned, lumbering toward them in twenty-foot strides. The huge rock swung down.

Matt yanked Alisande aside, diving. The great club smashed

into the earth two feet away. They rolled back up and ran, with giant feet slamming the ground behind them.

> "Open earth, with hunger's wit;
> Let him fall into a pit!"

The ground roared away from Ballspear's foot. The giant bellowed as he sprawled full-length into the huge pit. A roar of fury shook the earth, and a huge hand shot up over the edge, pulling until thirty feet of giant emerged, freeing him to the kneecaps. The ten-foot club slammed down at the end of a fifteen-foot arm.

"Go!" Matt shouted, shoving Alisande away. She took off, outdistancing him in his armor. The great bludgeon slammed down a foot behind his heels. Ballspear climbed out of the pit.

> "Earth turn wet beneath his shoes!
> Suck him down in mud and ooze!"

Ballspear lurched off-balance as his right foot sank a fathom deep. He fell to his knees, roaring with fury, and the huge club slammed down. Matt leaped aside. The club gouged the ground beside him. He kept running.

Alisande turned to wait for him, and he howled, "No! If you die, we all do!"

Ballspear rumbled interest, pulled his feet out of the mire, and waddled toward Alisande, ignoring Matt.

"Go!" Matt shouted furiously, and Alisande went.

Ballspear pounded into a run, club on high.

"Max!" Matt shouted. "*Do* something!"

"What?" The arc dot hummed with interest, zipping out through a chink in his armor.

It *had* to have orders! "Break his club!"

"How?"

"Weaken the molecular bonds!" Matt shrieked, turning to follow the princess.

The dot of light streaked toward the giant. The huge club hurtled down at Alisande—and exploded like a grenade.

Grenade! Matt made a frantic dive, caught Alisande right in the back of the knees, and leaped up to crouch over her, shielding her with his armor. Something clanged against his back, then another *gong* crashed through him, knocking out his breath. His elbows slammed into the earth, and Alisande cried out beneath him. He struggled back to his knees and saw Ballspear coming towards him, face huge and hideous with anger, like a broken mountain.

Matt staggered to his feet, yanking Alisande up with him, and ran. Great hands clapped together just behind him; something struck him a glancing blow, wobbling his stride for a few leaps. Then they slammed into a cliff face.

They spun about, panting, plastering themselves back against the rock, and saw the great hands groping for them, with a leering, six-foot face behind.

Then thunder blasted the night in a bellow of rage. "Turn, foul monster, and face your doom! Colmain comes!"

Another giant strode from the northern mountain, forty feet tall, bearing a thirty-foot spear of rock in his hand., He had dark hair over a broad forehead, deep-set eyes, a curly beard, and was dressed in bearskins. His footsteps thundered as he advanced on Ballspear.

"Something—I know not what—roused me from slumber. I see 'twas timely, for now you die, vile Ballspear!"

"Praise Heaven!" Alisande gasped. "But . . . how?"

"My spell!" Matt cried, insight electrifying him. "I didn't say *which* giant!" He'd thrown all his power into it and gotten overkill— or overwake. But, weakened by distance, it had taken longer to act.

Ballspear snarled and reached up to rip loose another club of rock. Whirling the bludgeon above his head, he charged Colmain, who ran to meet him. The club lashed out, but Colmain leaped aside, catching Ballspear's arm as it came down and pulling sharply. Ballspear stumbled, thrusting his club down at the ground for support, and whirled about to see Colmain's spear stabbing at his eyes. He swung the club up fast to knock the spear aside, whirled it around, and lashed out to smash into Colmain's breastbone. Colmain staggered, tripped, and fell. Ballspear brayed savage laughter, swinging the club above his head two-handed. Colmain stabbed upward with the spear.

Ballspear saw it coming and leaped back, but the spearpoint laid open his side with a sound like a monstrous rasp against boilerplate. He shrieked and stepped back to press one hand against his ribs. Colmain scrambled to his feet, holding the spear across his body like a quarterstaff.

Alisande yanked on Matt's arm, pointing. "Yonder!"

Matt looked up and saw, atop an eastern cliff, a gaunt, robed figure silhouetted against the rising crescent moon.

"Malingo!" Alisande cried. "He seeks to strengthen Ballspear and weaken Colmain. Quickly, Wizard, stop him!"

Easier said than done! But Matt had to try.

> "The giant's club is newly forged;
>   With forge's heat let shaft be gorged."

Ballspear crowed vindictively as his club smashed forward. Then his voice became a shriek, and the club went flying over Colmain's head to slam into the ground and sizzle, sending up smoke from burning vegetation. Ballspear licked his hands and moaned.

Matt looked up to see Malingo's hands snap tight as the sorcerer ended a spell. Colmain bellowed in agony, falling to his knees, dropping his spear to clutch at his ankles.

"Hamstrung!" Alisande gasped. "Heal him, Wizard!"

Matt tried:

> "Evil words their source descend on;
>   Heal Colmain's Achilles tendon!
>   Still all spells born out of hate!
>   Let his legs bear up his weight!"

Ballspear ran to his club and yanked it from the earth with a howl of triumph. He whirled—to find Colmain rising to his feet, grinning, his spear darting forward. Ballspear swore, and his club began whirling between them to form a flickering shield. Colmain snapped the spear down and drove it up at Ballspear's belly.

Malingo's hands wove a continuous serpentine symbol.

Even as the spear darted forward, it began to twist and writhe—and Colmain clutched a threshing python. He roared with disgust and threw the snake into Ballspear's face. The granite giant howled and leaped back, dropping his club to tear the looping python from his head.

Colmain leaped forward to seize the club and hurl it a thousand feet away from them. Then he bellowed with joy and strode for Ballspear. The granite giant turned to run, and Colmain sprang after him.

A mound of earth heaved up before him, extruding two huge, grasping hands that seized his ankles. Colmain's whole body jerked; he slammed into the ground like a liner striking a reef. Ballspear whirled with a savage roar, aiming a kick at Colmain's head.

Matt yelled:

> "He's going for the extra point!
> Throw his kneecap out of joint!"

Ballspear screamed in pain as his knee folded under him. Colmain shoved himself upright, kicking the earthy hands away with a snarl, and strode toward Ballspear.

Malingo, of course, was obligingly mending Matt's damage—but that gave Matt a slight edge in time. As Ballspear began to get his feet under him, Matt improvised a quick adaptation from Act V of *Macbeth*:

> "Let him begin to weary of the sun;
> Let all his spate of evils be undone!
> Make end to evil words. Blow wind, come wrack!
> Let titans fight *sans* magic at their back!"

Ballspear rolled to his feet and ran to the southern cliff. There he wrenched loose a boulder the size of a truck and whirled about, slinging it straight at Colmain and following it at a lumbering run. Colmain caught the boulder like a medicine ball and whirled it around in a great circle, to drive it into Ballspear's belly. The granite giant folded over the rock. Colmain dropped the boulder and caught Ballspear before he could fall, slamming a haymaker to his jaw.

On his cliff top, Malingo sawed the air frantically—to no effect. But he might regain his magic at any moment. Matt needed a way to make him cave in permanently.

Cave in . . . "Max!"

"Aye, Wizard." The Demon danced before him.

"Concentrate gravity under the cliff!" Matt stabbed a finger at Malingo. "Bring him down!"

"I go!" The Demon streaked off toward the sorcerer.

Again Colmain's fist slammed into Ballspear's jaw, and the huge head snapped up with a crack like a cannon shot. Then Colmain lifted the other giant over his head and threw him hard against the cliff. The whole area heaved. Ballspear bounced once and lay still. Colmain bent over the figure, then stood up slowly, rubbing his hand on his fur-clad hip and nodding. "It is dead."

Thunder cracked as a huge crevice split the cliff where Malingo stood. It shattered with a roar, crumbling and falling like solid rain. For a moment, a flailing silhouette poised in mid-air, before thinning, fading, and vanishing.

"'Tis done, Wizard," the singing dot informed Matt.

"Yeah—and well done, Max," he growled. "Confound the man! What reflexes! With absolutely no warning, he still projected himself away before he could hit bottom!"

"What was the thing which fell and did not strike?" a huge voice rumbled.

Matt turned to see the giant stalking toward them. "The sorcerer Malingo. The one who brought this all on us."

"He has returned to his armies," Alisande stated with total conviction. "He will approach us now only in the fullness of force."

Colmain peered down at her, his eyes widening. "I know that tone—in my bones, I feel it. The blood of Kaprin and now his heir!" Slowly, ponderously, he knelt, bowing his head. "You are the queen—and 'twas in your service I fought but now!"

Alisande drew herself up with regal presence. "I thank you for it, worthy Colmain. May all my enemies fall as did he!"

"They shall, do you but command it!" Colmain fixed her with burning eyes.

"Out upon them, then!" Alisande seemed to grow in stature. "But call me not queen. I stand here uncrowned."

"Yet still the rightful queen. My blood does clamor it!" the giant scowled. "Yet how is this? A queen uncrowned? Explain the way of it, for I cannot fight what I do not know."

"'Tis thus." Alisande took a deep breath and launched into a freewheeling account of all that had happened. Matt listened as names and events flashed by. They were up to his entrance on the scene in a few minutes; after that, his awe grew. Had they really done all that in so few days?

". . . and early this even, as I lay awake, I saw the wizard rise," Alisande continued. "Mistrusting his intent, yet loathe to wound him by my presence, I followed at a distance. I saw him work a spell to wake a mountain. But as I came closer, I could feel 'twas not aright and called to him—too late. Yet what he did, he did undo—" She turned to Colmain. "—by waking you."

"And aiding me against vile sorceries," the giant said. "Howbeit, much of this tale yet troubles me. The greater part of a year has passed, and the murder of a king is still unavenged? This must not be! Let us turn upon them and wipe them from the earth!"

"Aye, let us that!" a cheery voice called.

Sir Guy came riding up, with Sayeesa and Stegoman at either side, and Father Brunel behind.

"Why stare you so to see us?" He grinned. "You were scarcely overquiet." He looked up at Colmain, who was staring at him fixedly, and some quick sign seemed to pass between them.

The knight swung down from his horse, to kneel before Alisande. "Hail, Highness and commander! The smell of warring magics lies heavy o'er this field. The time, then, draws nigh?"

"It does," Alisande answered, staring at him.

"Then do I kneel for commands, my Princess! In war, knights must act under orders. Command me, then; for in *this* coil, you are my mistress!"

Matt saw Colmain nod with understanding. Of what? Something strange underlay all this . . .

A long-drawn hail echoed from the eastern slope. They looked up to see the gleam of early moonlight on polished armor, with huge horses bearing riders.

"What knights arc these?" the giant rumbled.

"The Order of Saint Moncaire," Alisande breathed, eyes glowing. "They have come to us in time!"

"And behold!" Sayeesa pointed to the southeast pass, where a line of white coifs and bibs floated above ponies' backs. "Yonder come my sisters!"

The nuns rode toward them in a long, straight line.

"Heaven be thanked that you have come!" Alisande cried as both groups drew near. "Yet what sent you by evenlight?"

The abbot swung down and knelt to her. "I cannot say, Highness—save that, as sunset neared, anxiety possessed me."

"And me." The abbess dismounted slowly. "I felt a sense of urgency and knew we must hurry." She glanced at Matt, her expression speculative. Then she looked at Colmain, and awe filled her eyes. "What is this mountain in manlike form?"

"The giant Colmain," the abbot answered, his face taking on a glow. "Nay, now we shall not die, but triumph!"

"Will we?" Matt asked the princess. "Does your infallibility tell you that much?"

"This battle cannot be avoided," she told him; but her gaze failed to meet his eyes. He felt prickles up his spine; she was sidestepping a full answer. Apparently, Divine Right wasn't working—or she was refusing to admit what it told her. And that could mean . . .

She turned and pointed. "But see—more come!"

A long file of men, some horsed, more on foot, came down the pass and across the valley. Pike heads glittered above them.

"Our loyal barons," the abbot said with pride, "and their stout-hearted men."

Sir Guy had been staring at the nuns. "How is this, Mother?" he asked. "Your ladies have no armor over their habits."

"Nay, they wear chain shirts beneath, and steel skullcaps." The abbess looked at Alisande and sighed. "But we have none for her, I fear."

"There is an answer to that," Sir Guy said. He turned away toward the northern mountain, pursing his lips, and whistled an eerie, warbling tune that slipped around definite pitches.

"What does the knight?" Sister Victrix asked. Alisande shook her head. Then her eyes widened, and she pointed.

Silently, a huge war horse, armored and caparisoned for battle, came down from the mountain. On its saddle was a glinting package, securely bound. When it reached the knight, he stroked the great head, then cut loose the bundle and held up a steel helmet and a knee-length mail shirt.

The princess took it and measured it against herself; its size matched hers. "A haubergion," she marveled. "How many years have gone since men wore such as this?"

"Centuries," Sir Guy answered. "Yet 'twill protect you, as this war steed will serve you."

Alisande wriggled into the haubergion with the delight of a teenager putting on her first formal.

Matt tore his gaze away and turned to Sir Guy, a question on his lips. Then he changed it for the one that had been bothering him for some time. "Who's writing the script for all this? Don't you find all the sudden coming together at just the right time too coincidental?"

"Nay." The knight shook his head firmly. "'Tis ever thus. When the time comes that matters must be settled beyond doubt, then all who fight do gather together, though they must come from the ends of the earth. When that time arrives, both Good and Evil muster their strengths to meet."

A neat arrangement, Matt decided. But he could wish his side had done a lot more recruiting and mustering.

"Ho! Wizard!" a great bear-voice roared from the southern ridge.

Matt whirled about to see a file of huge figures sliding and slipping down the slope. They came pounding up to him. They were hideous burlesques of humanity—pop-eyed, furry, barrel-muscled, and bandy-legged. There were a score of the ogres, led by Breaorgh.

They ground to a halt ten feet from Matt, armed with five-foot war clubs and war axes with six-foot blades. Breaorgh dropped to one knee. "Hail, Lord Wizard. I have come, in keeping of my word. Keep ye now yours."

"My thanks, Breaorgh." Matt swallowed heavily. "My thanks to all of you. Fight for us, and I'll do my best to change you back to normal. Understand, I'll try, but . . ."

"Aye. We know," a pig-faced ogre growled. "Yet had we known who companied ye, we'd have come without promises." He whirled to kneel before Colmain. "Hail, great one!"

The other ogres also turned to kneel. The giant nodded, a smile coming to his lips. "Hail, small ones. Welcome to our force. And know that at bottom you are human."

He turned to Sir Guy. "Four hundred knights, a hundred nuns, fifteen hundred of barons and their men, and twenty ogres, each worth ten normal men. Two thousand and some. How many are we like to face?"

"Five thousand, at least," the knight said promptly.

"Then we shall need more men." Colmain turned to face the southern mountain, smiling, and his voice lifted into a shout. "Come out, all you who live by stone! You must fight for me now, or Evil will enfold these mountains, and all your treasures— aye, even your lives—will be wrested from you."

In the moonlight, rocks heaved and rolled aside from secret cave mouths. Stunted three-foot men came out, pulling together into a ragged troop as they neared the army. Their legs were short, but their beards were long. They were thick-muscled and massive, dressed in leather tunics. They carried maces, axes, and great broadswords.

More emerged from the northern mountains and still more from the eastern peak. They straggled across the valley to mass before Colmain. One in the front rumbled, "Ye have summoned us, Lord of Rock. What coil brews, that ye hail us out by the power of the ancient compact?"

Colmain looked over the five hundred dwarves. "You are summoned to hoist your weapons against a sorcerous army that would enfold us all—and to fight for your true queen!"

The heads turned to study Alisande. Then the leader nodded gruffly. "Aye. We live by stone and earth, and you stand for the land, Majesty. We will do your bidding."

Colmain was doing his sums again. He sighed and shook his head. "Two thousand, five hundred. Doughty warriors who will make the enemy buy victory dearly—but victory will be his. We need more to face the teeth within the sorcerer's maw."

"Teeth!" Matt snapped his fingers.

Alisande glanced at him warily. "What mean you, Wizard?"

"I mean to get a thousand more," Matt cried. He whirled to Stegoman. "Hey, can I have your tooth?"

The dragon's head snapped back. "My body's part? Wizard, what—?" Then, reluctantly, his neck lowered. "Aye, or all my body. I have sworn."

"Thanks, Stegoman. You won't be sorry." Matt untied the leather bag, shook out the tooth, and knelt with it between his hands.

> "By the spirit fructifying,
> Let this tooth start multiplying!
> Let there be a thousand more,
> Equal to its length and bore.
> Let the valor of their donor
> Be to each a pledge of honor!"

There were two teeth, then four; then they spilled over and mounded up into a huge pile of dragon's teeth.

With all eyes on him, Matt whipped out his sword, gouged it into the ground, and ran, digging a long trench. He turned and ran backwards, repeating until he had six such channels. Then he scooped up an armload of teeth and began to cast them into the furrow, about eighteen inches apart. After a moment, Father Bru-

nel caught up a heap of teeth in his cassock and began sowing.
Then Sayeesa joined them, while Matt recited:

> "Unto Greece, whose name lives yet,
> Cadmus brought the alphabet.
> Men then learned the written word
> Bites far harder than the sword.
> Kingdoms grew and spawned empire;
> Written words then did inspire
> Warriors to the scribe's desire.
> On a green and fertile heath,
> Cadmus sowed the dragon's teeth,
> Reaping from them fighting men.
> Let it work this time as then!"

Seedling blades poked up from the earth behind him, surging
upward with leaf-shaped spear blades for eight feet before horse-
hair crests led Greek helmets into view. Grim Greek faces appeared,
then breastplates, armored kilts, and greave-covered shins. As the
three finished sowing, a long line of soldiers surged up behind
them. Within a few minutes, the last tooth had reached full growth.
The Greeks looked about, turning to stare at the first. He nodded
and stepped forward, snapping out a question.

Matt's two years of Greek studies had seemed useless—an
endless business of the *strategos* riding his *hippos* to the *potamos*
and archaic military maneuvers. But now, surprisingly, he understood that this *strategos* was asking what was going on.

Matt took a deep breath, remembering bits of Aeschylus, and
cried out, "Heroes, Hellenes, I call upon you to defend freedom,
as you've ever done and ever shall do!"

The leader looked startled to hear Greek—however mangled—
from the lips of this steel-plated alien, but he nodded. "What
enemy falls upon us now?"

"An evil magus," Matt replied, "with a horde of armies—"

"Persians!" they bellowed as one man, and the leader shouted,
"As did our sires at Thermopylae—form *hup!*"

When the dust settled, Matt found himself facing a phalanx,
bristling with fourteen-foot spears. The leader stepped out and
bawled, "Ready for battle, *sir!*"

Matt nodded, poker-faced, wondering if he were really doing

this. "Stand at rest, Strategos, but ready. The enemy may advance at any moment."

The spears sagged as the Greeks settled down in place, sitting on their heels, waiting patiently at ready.

Matt nodded and turned to the giant. "Three thousand and five hundred now, Colmain."

"And twenty ogres." The giant surveyed Matt with respect. "Can you summon more?"

Matt cursed silently. It could as well have been two thousand or more from the tooth. but he'd let his own unthinking prejudice trap him into the first round number that came to mind. Now it was too late. He shook his head bitterly. "No."

"Well, battles have been won against great odds before." Colmain sighed. "We can but hope. 'Tis not always the number of the men, but the skill and spirit that they hold."

Matt turned away, then remembered one other contribution he could make. He slapped his breastplate. "Hey, Max!"

"Aye, Wizard?" The Demon zipped to him from a knot of nuns. Matt eyed the cluster and saw Sayeesa among them. He frowned—but there was no time to worry about it.

"Look, we're expecting a battle any minute now. So do me a favor, will you?"

"If 'tis in my power."

"This is. Just flit around the field wherever the whim takes you, concentrating gravity—about four gees should be enough—under groups of enemy soldiers. Keep it random, so they can't figure out where you'll be next."

"Wisely planned," the Demon hummed judiciously. "If they knew where I might next be, their sorcerers might circumvent me."

Matt nodded. "Right. You're not to cause damage so much as to create confusion."

"Create? I? 'Tis near an insult!"

The moon came out from behind clouds. Now they could see a forest of pikes and spears rising up from a mass of men and horses across the valley. A figure in bright armor was at its head.

"Astaulf!" Alisande made the name an obscenity.

"He didn't strike me as intelligent," Matt said nervously.

"Mistake not, in battle he has few equals." her voice rose to command. "Master Colmain, command the right flanks with your dwarves and ogres. Sir Guy, take the left flank with the Moncaireans and their good barons and host of foot. Reverend Mother, let your ladies ride near me, for I'll command the center. And Lord Wizard, command your dragon-teeth men behind us in the center." She took a deep breath and bawled, "Commanders, to your commands!"

Sir Guy's blank shield snapped up far to the left, and the Moncaireans rode around the rear toward him. Sayeesa stood up in her stirrups, waving. The nuns homed on her and the abbess beside her.

Matt turned and called, "Spartans! Bring up your phalanx! March behind the black-clad ladies!"

The Greeks came to their feet and snapped into position.

It didn't make too much sense to Matt to put most of the cavalry on the left flank and the rest in the center. But maybe Alisande knew her troops better than he did. Anyhow, it gave him an excuse to stick near her; he had big worries about what Malingo might try to do to her.

He looked at the army of sorcery flowing across the valley; Sir Guy's estimate had been far too conservative. "Do we charge now?" he asked Alisande.

"No! If there is no battle, 'tis better for us. We'll march back eastward, gaining strength with each mile."

"They know that, of course?"

Alisande nodded. "And cannot permit it. There will be battle tonight. But let them begin it."

And win it? Matt noticed that she was still not claiming victory by infallibility. He studied the hosts of Astaulf again, worrying. And there were the spells of Malingo . . .

Maybe he could do something about them. He began shaping the verses in his mind. It would need power—more power than he had called on in waking the giants. He built the lines in his mind slowly and carefully.

Then something touched his thoughts—a feeling of dark evil intruding. Malingo! The sorcerer was already working to disable him! And there was no time now for his spell. Desperately, Matt cried out the only lines he could think of, sure they would not work, but forced to try.

> "Words were shaped within my head;
> Treat those words as being said."

A wind seemed to sweep across his mind, and the dark presence weakened, seeming to rise, struggling, to hover over him. Stalemate between himself and Malingo? If so, at least Astaulf's armies would not be able to invoke major magic.

And halfway across the valley, Astaulf kicked his horse into a gallop as he swung his sword overhead with a bellow. His whole army broke into a run with a vast shout.

Alisande sat her charger, waiting tranquilly, while the tail of Astaulf's army still flowed down over the ridge and until Matt could make out every detail of the usurper's armor.

"Now!" Alisande bawled. "Charge!"

Her army broke into a gallop with a shout of joy, thundering across the valley to meet the enemy.

As they charged, Sir Guy rose to stand in his stirrups, and his voice sounded above the battle, directed toward the foe with a pounding melody in archaic words. From his right, Colmain echoed it, hammering the meaning through:

> "Who was it fought for Hardishane?
>   Your fathers, lads, your sires!
> Who marched to war behind Colmain?
>   Your fathers' fathers' sires!
> They answered Deloman's first call;
> They fought with Conor, risking all;
> And now they feast in Heaven's hall!
>   Your fathers' fathers' sires!
>
> Who now shall stand against the foe?
>   Not you, my lads, not you!
> Who fights to gain the reign of Woe?
>   You do, my lads, you do!
> Who, out of fear of captains fell
> Now fights against the Book and Bell?
> And who shall taste the fires of Hell?
>   You shall, my lads, you shall!
>
> Yet even in this doom-lit hour
> Men may turn against the power
> That seeks to rule by fear and pain;
> And they Salvation still may gain!
> Or tell the sons they robbed of worth

That they helped bring them Hell on earth!
    Your children, lads, your sons!

Who now shall fight for Kaprin's bud?
    You can, my lads, you can!
Whose child will praise your siring blood?
    Yours shall, good men, yours shall!
If you turn now against your lords!
With pikes beat down their evil swords!
Then you shall live on Heaven's swards!
    Fight for your Queen, lads, fight!"

There was magic in the words, a weird magic that beat through Matt's head and drummed in his blood. And it was a magic for which Malingo was not prepared.

Pockets of Astaulf's army slowed, seeming suddenly reluctant. Their captains bellowed, lashing at them with the flats of their swords. The pockets swelled as they stopped, balking. The captains cursed and swung with the edges, lopping off heads.

With a roar of fury, whole battalions turned on their commanders, laying about them with their pikes and shouting: "Lord, forgive me!" . . . "Jesus, I do repent each blow I've struck for my foul master!" . . . "Die, devil! Heaven claim my soul!"

In a matter of minutes, almost a third of Astaulf's army had turned against him. That quickly, Sir Guy had changed the odds to a somewhat more even match.

"For God and Saint Moncaire!" Alisande cried, swinging her sword high as the two armies crashed together. She and Astaulf traded blows; then a horde of battling footmen surged between them, and they were lost to one another's sight.

On the left flank, Sir Guy mowed down soldiers, chanting war songs, with the Moncaireans following to bind the sheaves of dead. On the right, Colmain bent low, slapping knights from their horses and slinging them behind him for the dwarves to finish, while the ogres spread out to either side of him, crushing skulls.

Both flanks slowed as reinforcements surged toward them, stalling the advance by sheer weight of numbers. The battle settled down to personal combat and immediately degenerated into chaos, as repentant queen's men fought those whose greed outweighed their fear of Hell or of their sons' contempt. Knots of struggle formed all along the line.

Matt laid about him with his marvelous sword, catching blows on his shield and slashing in return. The air was filled with the roars of the berserkers and the shrieks of the dying. Pikes pressed in upon him from all sides. He had no time to try magic, even if the countering spells were gone. But they seemed to endure, since there was no sign of magic from Malingo, either.

An ancient Greek battle song roared in his right ear, and his left was filled with a battle hymn from Sister Victrix's band; he was caught between the classical and the medieval. He had lost sight of Alisande; he'd lost sight of everything but Colmain, Stegoman beneath him, and the swords and lances that stabbed at him from all directions. Here and there, above the clamor, he heard metal crashing together as Max pulled down pocket after pocket of enemy troops. Hoarse male screams filled the air.

Then a chorus of screeches came down from the sky. Matt looked up in alarm and saw a horde of harpies plummeting down toward the battle; in front of them came twelve-foot flying snakes, bat-winged and breathing fire.

"Firedrakes!" someone screamed nearby. "Lord defend us!"

Hell-spawn had joined the battle. Apparently the stasis on spells was wearing thin. The enemy roared with relief and waded in.

"To me!" Stegoman bellowed, lifting his head above the crowd.

Matt caught a blast of fire from a drake upon his shield and swore as the armor conducted heat to his skin. He rose in his stirrups to chop out full-length, slashing a firedrake in half. Liquid spattered as the two halves went flying, still writhing and snapping. A drop hit Matt's shield; in a few seconds he was staring through a hole the ichor had eaten.

"To me!" Stegoman bellowed again, and a chorus of roaring answered from the skies. Matt risked a quick glance up and saw a hundred dragons diving down from the heights, a shoal of fire before them—Glogorogh and the volunteers.

The harpies shrieked and flapped frantically upward, sheering off.

"Captains!" Alisande's voice came clearly above the lull in the battle the aerial combat had created. "Regroup your forces!"

They had time, because the dragons plowed into the firedrakes with bellows of fury and billows of flame. A score of younger dragons scoured the skies for harpies, sailing into a cluster of monsters and lashing fire about them, slashing out with claws and teeth. The harpies shrieked, ganging up on the dragons by dozens and scores; but the dragons were in full rage and in no mood to argue numbers. Charred harpies crashed down in the midst of the armies; manic women's heads went flying.

Lower, just above the soldiers' helmets, older dragons chewed up the fire-snakes.

The armies cowered under their shields as fire and acid rained about them. The allied commanders bawled commands at their troops, cajoling and bullying them into order again.

The rain of fire began to slacken. Matt risked a peek around the edge of his shield and saw only a few harpies, trying to flutter away toward the east, with the dragons in hot pursuit. There were no firedrakes, though snake bodies writhed upon the ground, splattering acid blood about them.

"Now," Alisande called, somewhere ahead, "hew a road for me to the usurper! Ladies, to me!"

The nuns howled, and the Greeks bellowed behind them, hammering into the churning enemy battle line.

Far away across the ranks, the moonlight revealed Astaulf, laying about him with the flat of his sword, knocking his own men aside to clear a path to the princess. Behind him rode a robed figure with a tall, pointed cap—Malingo, preoccupied with sword and shield.

The commanders surged toward each other, while dragons danced over the enemy, roaring blasts wherever they could make the most confusion.

Sister Victrix and her nuns formed up around Alisande—now only half their original number, but still laying about them with their swords, catching blows upon their shields, and chopping a way through the ranks for their princess, like a black arrowhead driving toward Astaulf.

Then a surge of the enemy broke through. A long knight's lance caught Alisande in the midriff, knocking her off her horse. She disappeared in the crush of fighting.

Matt screamed, "Forward, Stegoman! Torch them away! Plow through to the princess!"

The dragon roared, blasting fire straight ahead. His own men saw the dragon coming and leaped aside. A tiny spark sprang into Stegoman's flame, and it roared out an additional ten feet.

"Thanks, Max!" Matt laid about him like a maniac, chopping through any enemy in his way.

But the troops still loyal to Astaulf, greedy for goods and

careless of their souls, saw their chance to gain great kudoes by downing the enemy wizard and pressed in, howling for blood.

Matt chopped them away, noticing them only as obstacles. The monofilament-edged blade sheered through armor and bone. Soldiers died, yet more pressed in to delay him. But knight and dragon plowed through to the knot of nuns who were formed into a hollow circle, fighting valiantly against a crush of enemy. They battled bravely, but they were heavily outnumbered and went down, one by one, killing three men for each of them. They died, until only a score of them remained to guard their princess.

Matt, twenty-five feet away and high on Stegoman's shoulders, could see Alisande in their center, trying to struggle back to her feet with the aid of a spear, but with one leg badly twisted beneath her. Matt's heart seemed to lurch; he hewed about him frantically. He was fifteen feet from her, then ten. But now the nuns all lay dead or senseless, and only two black-clad figures stood between the princess and the enemy—Father Brunel, with a shield on his arm and a steel cap on his head, roaring like a wounded bull and laying about him with the strength of a gorilla; and Sayeesa, with two slender swords in her hands, stabbing at chinks in enemy armor.

Knights loomed up over them, with battle-axes raised high . . .

Stegoman bulldozed through the last few pikemen and leaped up to Alisande with a roaring blast of fire, white-hot to melt armor, turning his head in a long, slow arc to sweep the field clean. Max was still adding to the blast. Knights screamed and beat their way backward. Brunel and Sayeesa dropped to huddle low against the dragon's forelegs while white fire roared out over their heads.

Matt leaped down next to Alisande and fell to one knee, catching her up in his left arm, crushing her against his armor, his shield covering her back. She went rigid, staring up. He flipped up his visor. She recognized him and threw her arms around his neck in a hug that slammed the jaw of his helmet down onto her shoulder. "My wizard! You've come! I thought you had left me to perish!"

"No way, Lady." He braced himself and straightened, pulling her up with him. "Come on, now. Get your leg under you. Back on your feet!"

"I cannot. The leg is broken," she gasped, her eyes closing as the pain of the leg shot through her. "Do not leave me, Matthew!"

"Not until you're healed and back on your feet again. I'll make it fast—very fast!"

"Nay, do not leave me! Never leave me!" She hung on his neck, weighing him down. "Swear you'll not leave me—ever!"

"You're the princess—the heart and head of this battle." Matt pulled back against her weight, studying the leg. "I've got to try healing you—right now!"

"Swear!" she cried.

"Quickly, Wizard!" Stegoman rumbled. "They mass upon us, now—a hundred knights to encircle us. By their numbers, they'll wear me down." He loosed another blast, sending the knights back again—but not far enough.

By now, Matt hoped, the two counteracting spells should have mostly dispersed—enough for at least magic on a personal level. He risked a glance again at the threatening knights, then decided to make his verse short and direct:

> "By the love that is intended,
> Let this damsel's leg be mended."

Alisande gasped, her eyes startled. She leaned her weight on the leg tentatively, then stepped away, to stand straight and proud again. But her face was frozen, and she avoided looking at Matt.

"Aye, Lady! 'Tis even so!"

Matt turned to see Sayeesa toss her sword aside. There was a bitterness on her face that chilled him to the bone. She nodded grimly. "Aye, that did I seek, not knowing it—the fullness of love, not that of the body alone or the mere glamour of the forbidden. Thus I sought; thus was it denied." Her eyes sought Matt's for a moment; then she lifted her chin, her face resolute. "Yet even without it, I'll lend meaning to this life of mine. Spirit!"

"Aye, mistress!" A dot of light danced beside her.

"Come, then! Enter, and draw within me the power that is yours to sway!"

Her full lips parted, and the Demon darted into her mouth. She closed her lips and stood a moment, seeming to swell with power. Then she ripped off her postulant's habit and chain-mail shirt and cast them aside, revealing a sheer, short shift. Her body seemed to glow.

The knights froze, staring at her. So did Matt. She'd planned for this, somehow sensing it in her future!

Father Brunel shuddered, turning his eyes away. Sayeesa spared him a contemptuous glance, then moved toward the armored knights, her allure building with every step. Slowly, lazily, hips shifting in a magnetic rhythm, she strolled toward the wall of living steel, her eyes an open invitation to an army. She seemed to burn with desire. Matt felt an urge build in him and forced his eyes away.

A groan started somewhere in the ranks of the knights. One ripped off his helmet and tore at the fastenings of his armor, to be followed by another and another, until the air was filled with armor parts. They started toward her.

But her gaze strayed past them, seeking out a face toward the back of the press, pale and bearded, with a tall cap rising above the helmets. Malingo's eyes were riveted to her body; staring and sweating, he swallowed convulsively.

"Come!" she cried.

The sorcerer hung back a moment, torn between dread and desire. But he had kept himself from women too long to withstand Sayeesa, even in the midst of battle. He moaned and whipped out his sword, cutting at his own knights, slamming at them, roaring, "Fools! Churls! Garbage under my feet! Away! Let me to the woman!"

Startled, they pulled back, and Malingo surged toward Sayeesa.

She turned to Brunel. "Come, dog! We're alike enough for me to know. Your life, like mine, is fit only for atonement!"

The priest lifted his head, and Matt stared at him, shocked. The head that Brunel raised was only half human; ripples seemed to move through it as he fought the moonlight and the urge of his body. Then he saw Malingo hewing a way toward Sayeesa and understanding flooded his changing face.

With a howl, he flung off his cassock. His body shrank, and he fell to all fours, sprouting fur. Nose and mouth ran together, swelling out to a muzzle; his ears slid upward, growing points. A bush of a tail sprouted from his spine as his body contracted, writhing. Then it stilled, and a wolf leaped forward, snarling.

The enemy knights in the front rank gathered themselves suddenly, realizing it was a race between Malingo and them. They jumped toward Sayeesa, unarmored, hands reaching . . .

The werewolf smashed into them, snarling in fury, leaping, whirling, and slashing at throats, crazed and berserk. Hardened knights screamed and drew back, arms over their faces. The wolf churned through their ranks, a tornado with teeth, clearing a lane to Malingo.

Sayeesa ran down that channel to the sorcerer, arms wide. She passed the wolf. It leaped to keep up with her.

Malingo reached for her hungrily. She slammed into him, and his arms closed around her, hands tearing at her shift. Her lips locked on his for a very deep, long kiss. Then she thrust him away, stepping back with a wild, mocking laugh.

Malingo stared, dumfounded. Then he went for her again.

The wolf howled and leaped for his throat.

Malingo drew out a curved knife that seemed to writhe in his hand, its blade glinting silver. But his movements were curiously slowed.

The wolf shocked into his chest, bowling him over, snarling and reaching for his throat. With obvious effort, Malingo drove the flickering knife into its chest. It leaped back with a groan, falling huddled to the ground, blood welling from its side, struggling to rise.

Malingo snarled and fumbled in his sleeve, pulling out a flaming sphere. He heaved it toward Sayeesa, crying, "Die, traitoress! What enchantment have you flung on me?"

Sayeesa stood, laughing in mockery. The fireball struck and exploded. Flames leaped high about her writhing figure as she fell.

Malingo labored to heave himself to his feet, then tottered and collapsed again. The werewolf began crawling toward him, moaning deep in its throat with each labored effort.

Malingo hefted the knife as though it weighed a ton. "My death-curse upon him who stole my power! Yet I still have the power of hate, and I heap it upon him! May his flesh rot with pox, and his soul burn in Hell!"

Then the wolf struggled forward the last few inches and fell upon his chest. Malingo cried out, holding the knife so that the wolf landed upon its point. But the great jaws closed on his throat, tearing and ripping. The sorcerer's cry turned to a gurgle as his blood fountained out. Then the gurgle ceased, and the blood slackened to a trickle.

The wolf lay on his chest, slowly changing back into the figure of Father Brunel.

The field was quiet. Knights and footmen stared, horrified.

The Demon had done it, Matt realized. When Sayeesa had

passed it into the sorcerer with her kiss, it had drained Malingo's power—drained every bit of his energy. And the wolf had killed him.

Then far away, but swelling close in an instant, came a wild, exultant screaming. The sky was suddenly filled with leather wings, glinting red scales, and wild, manic laughter. A horde of demons plunged down toward the sorcerer's body, screaming: "He is ours!" . . . "He is carrion now for Hell!" . . . "Claim his soul!" . . . "Carry it to white fire, never dying . . ."

They churned down to engulf the body. But one scream of total despair rang louder than any of theirs, a human cry—the soul, realizing its doom.

The first demon touched the corpse, ripping it open.

Earth and sky boomed with titanic thunder. A vast, foul cloud boiled out of the body, stinking of sulfur and evil, to tower over the field, overshadowing all.

Matt felt his soul shrink gibbering into the middle of his being, trying to pull him in after it. Every human being on the field shrank down cowering, seeking to hide where there was no cover.

A voice boomed out of the cloud. "Bow, vermin, to a high lord of Hell!"

Above the armies, a huge devil began to form from the cloud. And its voice thundered about them.

"'Twas I made blood-contract with this puling sorcerer. My power was his in return for his soul and his willing acceptance that I dwell within him. Now I am loosed! Now I am master! Fall down and worship me, vermin, or die!"

A compelling impulse surged up in Matt, beyond his conscious control. He lifted his head and shouted,

> "Aid us now, preserving Power,
> Lest we die within the hour!
> Ancient patron, Kaprin's guard,
> Save us now, our only ward!"

"Who speaks?" the demon shrieked. "Cease those words!" A huge, shadowed tentacle extruded from the roiling cloud, arrowing down toward Matt.

A voice crashed through the valley. "Be still in your evil!"

All eyes snapped to the top of the northern cliff. There, glowing brightly, stood a stocky figure in a gilded chasuble, with an archbishop's cope and miter. He stood in a circle of light, but Matt made out the face.

"The priest who confessed me and Sayeesa!"

"Nay," Alisande gasped. "'Tis Saint Moncaire!"

"Who seeks to sully God's mead?" the saint thundered. "Go down whence you came! Vile demons, I have come to counter your power! Now I command you, by Him Whom I serve, to be gone!"

The cloud shuddered and quaked, then erupted in screaming imprecations in languages older than humanity's knowledge. The valley floor began to tremble.

Saint Moncaire held up his hand and began to chant in sonorous Latin. Flames pricked up all about the valley, rising, expanding, and dancing. Men shrank back, moaning in fear. The shrieking, ancient tongues rose to a piercing screech; but the Latin thundered over them, building and rising. The saint grasped his staff in both hands, lifting it above his head. Then he thundered, "*In Nomine Domine!*" and the staff snapped down to point at the demon. A ray of dazzling light lanced out into the depths of the Hell-cloud. It exploded with a roar that shook the valley.

Then, slowly, the light faded, and Matt's eyes adjusted until he could make out the field of huddled, trembling men. He looked out to see the tangled armies as they had been when the sorcerer died.

But in their midst was only a great, blackened ring with the crumpled, charred bodies of a man and a woman at its center.

With a despairing cry, Astaulf flung down his steel helmet and threw his sword into the charred ring. "Save my soul! Do what you will with my body, but grant me first a priest to shrive me!" He huddled on his knees, hands clasped, head bowed. "Never did I truly believe in Heaven or Hell until this moment! Now I know— and know the full foulness of my deeds! Draw and quarter me if you will; only allow me the Sacraments ere you deliver me up to the death I have earned!"

He buried his head in his hands, his shoulders shaking.

It was too abrupt, Matt thought—until he remembered that the influence of Evil was gone from the field and the presence of Good still lingered.

"Kill me, but save my soul from Hell!" a baron cried, casting down his sword and falling to his knees.

"Let me die in the Church!" another begged.

Matt stood watching as enemy after enemy surrendered, until the whole army of foemen was kneeling, heads bowed.

"Will you accept their surrenders, Lady?" Sir Guy asked gravely from beside Alisande.

She glanced at the Black Knight, then looked at the enemy, nodding. Her back straightened and her chin lifted. "Your surrenders are accepted," she called. "Dwarves, gather their swords!"

A single, joyful shout of triumph rose from the allied army. Then the dwarves scuttled over the field, gathering weapons.

"You must pronounce sentence upon them now, Highness." The abbess stepped up to Alisande, her gaze severe. "You have won the day. Prounounce their fates."

"Nay," Alisande answered, with equal firmness. "I have not the right. I am not yet crowned queen, and none here has the authority to serve me so."

"But one has," Colmain rumbled. He strode across the field toward Sir Guy.

"To be sure. One has." The knight skipped aside from the giant's path and lifted his head. A single name seemed to ring from his lips across the valley. "Moncaire!"

"Aye, Sir Guy de Toutarien." The voice spoke from above, and Matt turned to see the saint again standing atop the cliff, lambent in his halo. "'Tis meet that the princess should be crowned queen. Let the princess ascend to me. And do you, Sir Guy, attend and aid."

Alisande took the arm that Sir Guy offered, and together they began moving across the field. As Matt stared, he saw that a trail, steep but climbable, ascended to the top of the cliff. Had it been there before? He could not remember. But with the help of the knight, the princess began climbing, until she stood before the saint.

Moncaire's voice was deep and resonant, though he seemed to speak quietly. "You will serve as witness, Sir Guy. And who has the crown?"

For once, the knight's face registered total surprise. He stared about helplessly. Then his eyes turned to the Lord Wizard.

Matt saw that the saint was also looking at him, and he nodded, hastily shaping words into a spell:

> "For the ceremony here,
>   Let the royal crown appear

> From wherever it now lies.
> Make it just the proper size;
> Have it polished squeaky clean,
> Suitable to grace a queen."

Sir Guy grabbed at the object that appeared in the air. The crown shone brilliantly clean in the light of Moncaire's halo.

Saint Moncaire faced the forces on the field, and his voice lifted to reach the farthest man. "This night it is granted to me to give you a queen." Then he spoke to Alisande. "Kneel, daughter."

Poised now and certain, she knelt before the saint, while Sir Guy held up the crown for all to see. The soldiers were silent, eyes locked on the golden bauble. Then the knight gave the crown to Moncaire, who blessed it and turned to the princess.

"Do you, Alisande, swear to guard this land, to rule it for the welfare of all people within it? And do you swear to rule for Good and God, abhoring Evil all your days?"

"I so swear," she answered. "And may God strike me dead if I forget my vow!"

The saint set the crown gently on her head and stepped back. "Then rise and rule, Queen Alisande of Merovence!"

The soldiers shouted their acclamation as she rose, and the saint retreated farther.

A moment later, when Matt turned to look for him, there was no sign of the saint.

CHAPTER 19

The last few hours of night had been ones of fevered activity. The surviving Moncaireans had busied themselves in shriving the repentant enemy. Men had begun building a crude platform on the field and setting up the captured tent of Astaulf for the new queen. She had retired into it with Sir Guy and a few others, promising to give judgment in the morning.

Matt had not been among her councilors. She seemed to avoid him. But he had found work enough to fill his time, returning the Greeks to whatever time and place had been their origin and fulfilling his promise to the ogres.

Now the false dawn lighted an orderly field. The severely wounded, bandaged as well as they might be by the nuns, lay in rows at the side. Some still moaned, but most lay quiet in enchanted sleep that Matt had administered.

Beyond them, in every direction, were mounds of freshly turned earth, some marked with rough, improvised crosses, some not marked at all.

Those with lesser wounds or none knelt in ordered lanes, filling the center of the valley, their heads bowed over clasped hands. The defeated were in the middle, under the watchful eyes of soldiers. That was a mere precaution; their elbows were immobilized by loops of rope that passed behind their backs, and their wrists were bound before them. Their feet were hobbled.

Astaulf and his barons knelt in chains; they seemed to listen most devoutly of all to the abbot of the Moncaireans, who stood on the rude platform before a rough field altar, his stole about his neck. As he finished the cleansing and veiling of the chalice, the monks and nuns chanted the *Requiem*. The high funeral mass, begun by moonlight, was ending by early dawn.

Matt knelt behind the barons, ready with his sword and spells for the slightest misstep and glad he wasn't needed.

During Communion, the priests had distributed the Eucharist impartially to victor and vanquished alike. At peace with God, Astaulf and his barons knelt, seeming not to care what happened to their bodies. The depth of faith that could grant such tranquility had hit Matt more and more heavily as the Mass progressed, until he knelt now in awe of the meaning of the ancient ritual. He was realizing anew the significance and depth of the symbols, realizing that in this world, each symbolic movement and Scriptural reference was not an empty repetition of a memorized formula, but part of tho most powerful spell of all, affecting lives past and present, and changing the world about them at the same time that it held all constant.

The abbot turned to the armies, spreading his hands. "*Ite, Missa est.*" Go, you are sent forth; go, the Mass is ended.

With the rest of the impromptu congregation, Matt replied, "*Deo gratias.*"

The abbot bowed his head, folding his hands, and turned to take up the veiled chalice and the altar stone. He went down the steps slowly while the choir sang a dirge. Two soldiers mounted the platform and folded the camp altar, then took it down and away.

Suddenly the choir voices broke into the triumphant notes of the *Gloria*. As the hymn reached its peak, Alisande mounted the stairs, regal in a purple robe contrived from Astaulf's apparel, her golden hair graced with the crown. She stepped to the center of the platform. The choir soared into a fervent *Alleluia*. Their voices rang through the valley, then stilled.

The men below seemed frozen, motionless and silent.

From below came the prompting voice of Sir Guy. "Judgment!" he cried. "Let there be judgment upon the foul traitors—Astaulf and his barons!"

A dark, rumbling mutter filled the valley. Alisande held up her hands, and the rumbling died.

"We may not judge them here," she cried. "Justice must be calm and well considered, not merely of the moment's whim. We shall have these barons and their suzerain Astaulf to our capital in chains. There, in Bordestang, they will await the verdict of their peers and our sentence."

No one seemed to breathe. They stared in amazement. Matt nodded slowly. There was a lot to be said for due process as a check on tyranny. It looked as if Alisande's reign might be off to a good start.

"But the soldiers." Alisande's voice softened. "They who had no choice in service, who fought in fear of their commanders, or of vengeance being wreaked upon their wives and children—these can have small blame. Let them return to their families and their homes, to forswear the sword and spear and take the plow again."

This time the cheering nearly split the mountains. Loyal soldiers joined with the captured in the fervor of their applause. It seemed that Alisande would be not only a good ruler, Matt thought; she would also be a popular one.

When the chaos had quieted a little, Sir Guy called out, "And what of the sorcerers, your Majesty? The lesser sorcerers whom Malingo forged into an evil corps?"

"They are for burning, if any man can find them." Her voice crackled over the valley. She turned slowly, her face stony again as her eyes found Matt's. "Hunting them *should* be the task of our rightful Lord Wizard."

Then Alisande turned back as the nuns and two Moncaireans came up, bearing improvised stretchers, cloaked and shrouded, to lay before the Queen.

"What of these?" the abbot called. "What of Father Brunel, our fellow priest?"

"And this, my hopeful daughter?" the abbess stepped up beside Sayeesa's pallet.

"Take them home to the Houses of your Orders," Alisande commanded. "Let shrines be raised over their bodies, for they died as martyrs upon the field. Their souls, I doubt not, bask now in the bliss of Heaven."

There was silence as the abbot bowed in thanks, then led to a waiting horse, where the pallet bearing the remains of Father

Brunel was quickly tied. He mounted and turned to the knights remaining to him, swinging his arm overhead and bawling, "Ride!"

The Moncaireans moved out behind him, following the bier in solemn procession, chanting a dirge.

"Come, daughters!" the abbess cried, hoisting herself up side-saddle. "Let us bear her home. Our sorrow is our own!"

The small group of nuns mounted and turned their horses to follow her, raising their own lament as they bore Sayeesa's remains before them, slung between two horses with empty saddles.

They rode out of the valley in two solemn trains, side by side, bearing the repentant witch and the remorseful werewolf, who had fallen into the pits of desire and climbed back to glory. The procession disappeared around the eastern peak, and the soldiers turned to one another, murmuring.

Alisande called out, silencing them. "Go now to your lords! Set free your brothers who were forced to this fight, that they may return to their homes! Then follow your suzerains, with the blessing of the Queen upon you!"

A cheer bellowed out as she stepped from the platform. It slackened and turned into excited conversation as the whole field became milling chaos.

Matt elbowed his way through the press. Soldiers saw who he was and hastened out of the Lord Wizard's path. But even so, by the time he made it to the front, Alisande was almost to her tent, accompanied by some of the barons. She glanced back and saw him, but her face showed no welcome.

"Well, Sir Matthew, you are nearly home!" Sir Guy clapped him on his shoulder with a familiar, carefree grin. It reminded Matt of his former suspicion—and the new ones, which now seemed to have a better basis.

"Yeah." He put an arm around the Black Knight, leading him away toward Stegoman, who seemed to have found an isolated spot. The dragon was the biggest thing on the field, now that Colmain had gone off with the dwarves and the ogres. "All right," he said, determined to resolve the enigma of Sir Guy. "Just who are you, anyway, Sir All or Nothing?"

The knight smiled more broadly. "Why ask you that, and wherefore this epithet by which you call me?"

"It's what your name becomes in a language I know. Toutarien—*toute ou rien*. French, the language of chivalry—and I notice most nobles here have names not unlike that language. Don't give me the simple knight routine after I've seen Colmain recognize you and Saint Moncaire heed your call."

Sir Guy no longer smiled. "But who then should I be, Sir Matthew, other than the knight I seem?"

"I seem to recall a tale told by a certain Black Knight," Matt told him. "When Hardishane's line seemed to be ended, Colmain found a child of the Emperor's daughter's line to rule. But there were rumors of a child of the male line who was never found. True rumors, Sir Guy?"

Sir Guy studied Matt for a moment, then shrugged. "Aye, you would see what others never have and remember a thing I should never have mentioned. But swear to me, on your honor as a knight, never to speak of this matter to other ears!"

"On my honor as a knight, I swear," Matt promised.

Sir Guy nodded slowly. "There was such a child, hidden so well that Colmain never found him. He lived his whole life—and that line is longlived—in secret, as did his descendants. I am the latest of that line."

"But that would make you the rightful ruler, not Alisande," Matt said.

"Forbid such fate! I am rightful *Emperor*—but cannot claim my heritage till all these Western Lands be sunk again into Evil. Then will the only remedy be Empire, and mine heirs may again take up the scepter. Only then. While Good still reigns in Merovence, 'tis still the time of kings, not Emperors. And may that time not come whilest I still live!"

Matt was convinced he had heard the truth. "So you're not quite the carefree vagabond you seem to be. You've devoted your life to holding off the time when an Emperor will be needed again. You don't want power."

"Not at the cost of Evil gaining all these lands. I'll fight while breath is in my body to delay that day, as did my father and his father!"

"Yeah." Matt pondered it, trying to fit all the facts against this new knowledge. "Then I suppose it was you who drafted me?"

"Drafted? Ah—not so. I did but go to the Emperor's cave to wake Saint Moncaire and warn him that peril was come upon us. He knew, of course, but did need a mortal's asking to work upon it. 'Twas he who thought to seek a wizard from another sphere— one with knowledge unknown to this land, to give him power against Malingo. He wrote verse upon a scrap of parchment and cast it forth, saying the man who found it and labored enough to comprehend it must be, perforce, the wizard who could save this land."

It was neat, Matt had to admit— "a spell with an automatic filter to select only the right man."

"And now, rejoice!" Sir Guy gave him a ringing clap on the shoulder. "Your task is done! I am certain the good saint will send you home!"

Matt stared at him.

Sir Guy frowned. "Come, now! 'Tis what you've wished since first you came here, is it not?"

"Yeah," Matt said slowly. "Yeah, I said that, didn't I? Home." He could picture his run-down, disordered apartment with its student-cheap decor, his friends drinking beer from cans or sitting around the table at the coffee shop . . .

Somehow, it all seemed remote, unreal, like something he'd read about in a book. His eyes strayed to the tent where Alisande had gone. Then he sighed. At least, his leaving this world would relieve her of strain and remove the seemingly hopeless problem the Reverend Mother had spotted "Yeah, I guess I want to go home." He shook himself and looked back at Sir Guy. "So you had nothing to do with getting me here. But weren't you really managing the whole expedition?"

Sir Guy shook his head. "I sought to find the princess and wizard as soon as they were free, then saw that I became one of their party . . ."

"Conned me into drafting you," Matt interpreted. "I suppose you only did that out of curiosity?"

"Nay, 'twas to insure her safety and yours. But 'twas her kingdom, and she knew what needs must be, better than I."

Matt wasn't too sure about how much she knew, but he realized that Sir Guy had a nice respect for a jurisdictional claim. "You just came along for the ride, eh?"

"I lent a sword when needed," Sir Guy said judiciously. "And I had you knighted. I thought it best, for it gave you martial skills which were badly needed."

It made sense; in this world, conferring the title of knight would probably also confer martial skills.

"And now that the war's over and Alisande made queen, where are you going to wander—accidentally, of course?"

Sir Guy smiled. "Where situations seem amusing. Ibile, now—

I have heard a baron there seeks to gather knights to rebel against the sorcerer-king. A just and godly man, I hear. Mayhap I'll ride there. Though, in truth, I shall miss having a wizard at hand to make all easier."

"Yeah." Then a breath of inspiration touched Matt's mind. "Maybe I can give some help there. Max!"

"Aye, Wizard?" The humming dot was back with him.

"Max, how'd you like to go along and serve Sir Guy from now on?"

"To serve a ruler who fights not to rule?" The hum took on a note of amusement. "It has perversity. Yet 'tis not possible. He knows not the inner nature of things to give me proper orders."

And teaching modern physics to Sir Guy was more than Matt cared to think about. But there had to be another way. "You could tell him what orders to give, couldn't you?"

This time the hum had the quality of a delighted chuckle. "The very spirit of perversity! To give the orders which I then am bound to obey. Aye, Wizard, I'll do it!"

The dot of fire snapped to the knight and vanished into a chink in his armor.

"So you'll be on your way," Matt said to Sir Guy, "and Stegoman will be going back to his own people. I guess fate is busting up that old gang of ours."

"Nay," the dragon's voice rumbled down above his head. "'Tis not my plan, Wizard. For I've been away too long and have dealt too much with men. I've thought upon it, but I'd not take lightly again to the ways of my folk. Henceforth are my ways the ways of thy people."

"Then come with me!" Sir Guy cried. "In Ibile, you and I could prove ourselves formidable indeed together!"

"Aye." Stegoman nodded his great head. "But I must not."

"Must not?" Matt frowned up at the dragon. "Why?"

"Because I have sworn fealty to thee, Lord Wizard. Where thou goest, so go I; and where thou stayest, stay I."

"Ah, but you cannot go with him now," Sir Guy said. "For he will be going to his home, across a void which none but he may cross. He returns to that time and place from which he came. And you and I remain."

"Is this true, Wizard?" the dragon demanded.

Matt was saved from answering by the appearance of a young

soldier before him. "The queen would speak with you, Lord Wizard." His tone hinted at fear of addressing one so powerful.

So she had finished all other business and finally deigned to remember him! Matt nodded and strode across to the tent.

He found her alone, seated before a rough desk. Her head snapped up as he entered; then she rose wearily to her feet.

"You wanted me, your Majesty?" he asked.

Her head dipped in a slight nod. "To render our thanks to you, Lord Wizard. We are deeply grateful for your part in our inevitable victory." Her voice held all the gratitude of a man paying off a collection agent, and her face was a mask.

"Your victory didn't seem so blamed inevitable when I asked you about it," Matt reminded her. He was tired of the deep-freeze treatment. Maybe it was time he got out of this whole business. "Or does your infallibility work only by hindsight?"

Answering anger sprang into her eyes, but she held her voice level. "And would you have fought so well had you known we must win? Nay, I'd not weaken my forces by announcing victory before it was achieved."

She had a point, he had to admit reluctantly to himself. And this wasn't getting either of them anywhere. He'd made his decision. Now he might as well get it over with. "I'm leaving, your Majesty. I'm going to return to my own world."

She nodded, stone-faced. "Aye. As I knew you meant when you would not swear to remain, but did choose instead to attend only to my wound. Why, go then, sirrah! I'd not have a reluctant champion!"

She turned away. But now that he had been dismissed, Matt found himself unwilling to leave without some explanation.

"It's the obvious solution to the problem the abbess pointed out," he told her, "one she couldn't see. Emotions can't be banished—however much you may delude yourself—but I can be, even if I have to do it myself. Simple, isn't it?"

"There was another choice," she reminded him.

"To get married, or some such? Fat chance! You've made it plain enough that there's no hope of that."

"You did never ask me! Or do you also profess infallibility, to know the course of events before they come?"

He took a step toward her, then forced himself to relax. What did it matter if she had to have the last word? "All right," he said.

"If it will make you feel better to make it plain that you reject me, consider yourself asked."

She swung about to face him, and her smile would have curdled the milk of a unicorn. "Most nobly and courteously asked, Sir Knight!" Her short laugh was like a saw on thin metal. "But such asking, so I had believed, must come from the heart!"

He stared at her, anger and desire boiling together in him until they fused into one. He grabbed her by the shoulders and shook her. "All right, damn it! If you've got to draw every bit of satisfaction from seeing me make a fool of myself, have it your way! Contrary though you choose to be, I love you! Now will you marry me?"

Then she was in his arms, drawing him closer and turning her face up to meet his lips.

Stegoman found them a few minutes later, but he had sense enough not to interrupt. There was a broad smile on his face as he lumbered away to report to Sir Guy that Sir Matthew, Lord Wizard, would obviously not be leaving them.

ABOUT THE AUTHOR

"A wandering Catholic, aye,
A thing of texts and catches."

Early in life, Christopher Stasheff found a catch in almost every point of Catholic dogma except the main ones, and has been spiritually wandering ever since. He has a lot of doubts about the Church, but only questions about the Faith.

One day, he realized that most of the medieval fantasies he read seldom mentioned the Devil, and never God. He vehemently maintained that wasn't the way medieval Christians really saw the world—they saw God everywhere, in everything, and the Devil always lurking, looking for an opening—and that authors really ought to write their fantasies a little closer to reality. Then he realized that, being a fantasy author, he was stuck with writing his next story that way.

He spent his early childhood in Mount Vernon, New York, but spent the rest of his formative years in Ann Arbor, Michigan. He has always had difficulty distinguishing fantasy from reality and has tried to compromise by teaching college. He tends to pre-script his life, but can't understand why other people never get their lines right. This causes a fair amount of misunderstanding with his wife and four children. He seeks refuge in fantasy worlds of his own making and hopes you enjoy them as much as he does.

By the year 2000, 2 out of 3 Americans could be illiterate.

It's true.

Today, 75 million adults...about one American in three, can't read adequately. And by the year 2000, U.S. News & World Report envisions an America with a literacy rate of only 30%.

Before that America comes to be, you can stop it...by joining the fight against illiteracy today.

Call the Coalition for Literacy at toll-free **1-800-228-8813** and volunteer.

**Volunteer
Against Illiteracy.
The only degree you need
is a degree of caring.**

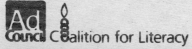

Ad Council   Coalition for Literacy

LV-2